NO LIMIT TO EVIL

(DS Pete Gayle Crime Thrillers Book 15)

By

Jack Slater

A burglary. A missing car. Two dead bodies and nothing else apparently touched. It seems like there's an obvious answer when DS Pete Gayle is called to the crime scene in an affluent area on the edge of the city. But is it too obvious? Then another death occurs. A connection is made that adds a whole new dimension to the case. Now he has to find the link between the victims before more people are attacked and possibly killed.

Copyright © 2024 by Jack Slater.

Jack Slater asserts the moral right to be identified as the author of this work.

This novel is entirely a work of fiction. The names, characters and incidents portrayed in it are the work of the author's imagination. Any resemblance to actual persons, living or dead, events or localities is entirely coincidental.

All rights reserved under International and Pan-American Copyright Conventions. By payment of the required fees, you have been granted the non-exclusive, non-transferable right to access and read the text of this e-book on-screen. No part of this text may be reproduced, transmitted, downloaded, decompiled, reverse engineered, or stored in or introduced into any information storage and retrieval system, in any form or by any means, whether electronic or mechanical, now known or hereinafter invented, without the express written permission of the author.

For Miriam with thanks for all your help and support.

May the doctors be very, very wrong – in the right direction.

Also by Jack Slater

DS Pete Gayle thrillers Book 1 Nowhere to Run

DS Pete Gayle thrillers Book 2 No Place to Hide

DS Pete Gayle thrillers Book 3 No Way Home

DS Pete Gayle thrillers Book 4 No Going Back

DS Pete Gayle thrillers Book 5 No Middle Ground

DS Pete Gayle thrillers Book 6 No Safe Place

DS Pete Gayle thrillers Book 7 No Compromise

DS Pete Gayle thrillers Book 8 No Compassion

DS Pete Gayle thrillers Book 9 No Stone Unturned

DS Pete Gayle thrillers Book 10 No Good Deed

DS Pete Gayle thrillers Book 11 No Fair Hearing

DS Pete Gayle thrillers Book 12 No Fear of Consequences

DS Pete Gayle thrillers Book 13 No More Than Bones

DS Pete Gayle thrillers Book 14 No Second Chance

Nowhere to Run: The Dark Side

The Venus Flaw

CHAPTER ONE

Pete's tyres crunched on the gravel in front of the big grey house in its wide, leafy gardens surrounded by mature trees that were mostly still bare at this time of year. He stopped beside the police car that was already parked in front of the black garage doors and switched off the engine as a uniformed officer stepped forward from beside the front door. 'Sarge.'

Pete nodded.

'This way.' The middle-aged stocky constable extended a hand towards the side of the house beyond the built-in garage.

'Forensics not here yet?' Pete asked, though the answer was obvious.

'They're on the way. So's the pathologist.'

Pete glanced around as they headed for the corner of the house. Daffodils provided a splash of colour along the base of the wall. More were clustered, along with crocus and the last of the snowdrops, beneath the evergreen shrubbery to either side of the wide gravel area in front of the house.

The first leaves were breaking out on some of the shrubs and smaller trees around them, bright fresh green against dark branches. It felt like the place was nestled in the woods, miles away from civilisation though it was only fifty yards from the nearest housing estate on the northern edge of the city.

A crow cawed from somewhere above and was answered by another. He looked up and saw dark shapes swooping above the branches, stark against the cloudless sky. Somehow, they felt much more fitting to the circumstances than the bright, cheery flowers.

The constable led the way around the side of the house, through a high wooden gate. Beyond it, a door led into the side of the garage which was backed by a conservatory that was tucked into an angle made by the garage and the rear section of the house. The lawn stretching away from the back of the house was smaller than Pete had expected and sheltered by a tall hedge extending all the way around it.

Another officer waited by the back door, beyond the conservatory. Taller and much younger than his companion, he looked barely old enough to wear the uniform, his expression matching the greenish hue of his complexion.

Pete gave him a nod. 'Your first?'

He swallowed, his Adam's apple plunging up and down, and nodded. 'Yes, sir.'

Pete gave him a brief hint of a smile. 'It gets easier,' he said as the young officer reached over to push open the back door.

'You can see where the glass was broken to allow the intruder to reach in and unlock it,' the older constable said.

Pete glanced down at the shards of glass glittering on the tiled floor inside the door.

'We've been careful not to touch anywhere he might have,' the man added.

Pete gave him a nod and let him lead the way inside. They entered a boot room-cum-utility. A washing machine stood to the left of the doorway, a dryer beside it, both under a worktop with a sink further along, under a small window. Opposite were coat hooks with a long bench beneath, a repurposed wardrobe at the far end, beside the door to the kitchen.

'The daughter called it in as a welfare check. She hadn't been round here. Just found the car missing and no response at the door or on the phone so requested we attend. I wasn't far away, so I swung by.'

'And where is she, now? The daughter,' Pete asked.

'She was pretty cut up about it all. Gavin's crewmate took her to the station to get her away from here. Said she'd see what she could tease out of her gently over a cuppa.'

Pete nodded. 'OK.' It sounded like a sensible approach. He would talk to her later.

By now they were in the large kitchen-diner which spread across most of the width of the house. Beyond, he could see a comfortable-looking sitting room through a pair of double doors that were mostly glass: square panels divided by thin wooden beading. The constable was heading that way. He stopped just inside the kitchen and stepped aside, nodding across to the left.

'You can see the first victim from here.'

Checking the floor before he moved, Pete stepped up to the doors and peered through.

At the far side of the room, a flight of stairs came down into it. A body lay at the bottom, crumpled awkwardly on the carpeted floor. It was a male. Grey-haired and dressed in a shirt and dark trousers, but that was about all he could see from here. Except that there was no blood-pool around the body. He glanced at the man beside him.

'Broken neck, by the look of it. Probably fell down the stairs in his rush to intercept the burglar, I expect,' the constable said.

Pete tipped his head. 'Possibly. The woman?'

'Upstairs.'

Pete took a step back and met the man's gaze. 'How did the daughter know the car's missing? The garage door's closed.'

He gave a quick shake of the head. 'They don't use it. Car's too big. They leave it on the drive.'

'Ah.' Pete knew the problem. His own Ford saloon didn't fit in his garage at home. His wife drove a tiny Fiat that was one of the few modern cars that would fit in a 1960's garage. 'So she thought the worst rather than they'd gone shopping and forgotten to take the mobile with them?'

Another shake of the head. 'It'd been three days. Normally, her mum phones her every morning like clockwork. One day, she could accept; two was worrying. Three was too much so she made the trip down from where she lives in South Molton.'

'OK. I won't go and see the mother until Forensics get here. Have you?'

He nodded. 'Not a pretty sight. She's on the bed. As opposed to in it. Stabbed. Several times. No obvious signs of sexual assault. At least we've got that to be thankful for, but...' He shrugged.

'It's precious little,' Pete finished for him. 'Yeah. We'd best go back outside and wait.'

He caught movement at the edge of his vision and glanced across at the wide doors in the back wall. 'On the other hand: no need.'

Three more people in white overalls passed the big glass doors and he heard the back door opening again. A white-clad figure filled the doorway into the utility – at least the bottom two-thirds of it. Round glasses, a blue mask, matching gloves and bootees completed the disguise that still allowed Pete to recognise the figure.

'Morning, Harold,' he said. 'Nice of you to join us.'

The crime scene supervisor stepped forward. 'I thought it'd be advisable, before you contaminate the crime scene too severely, Detective Sergeant.'

Pete glanced down at his own suit and bare shoes. 'I am wearing gloves.'

'Hmm.'

'Have you brought me some togs, then?'

'Do I have to think of everything?' Harold Pointer demanded. 'Don't answer that.' He turned away. 'Vicky,' he called. 'Fetch an overall and shoe covers for Detective Sergeant Gayle, please.' He turned back, his gaze shifting to the uniformed man beside Pete. 'I take it you'll be leaving?'

The constable nodded.

'I'll need the daughter's details,' Pete reminded him. 'And the names of the victims.'

He grunted. 'Yeah. Of course.' He held out a hand as Pete took his notebook and pen from his pocket. He handed them over and the constable scribbled quickly, speaking as he wrote. 'The victims are Heather and Sam Lockwood. Daughter's Danielle. Danni. Her address and phone number...' He took out his own notebook and copied them across. 'There.'

'Thanks.' Pete accepted his notebook back. 'I'll need you to stay on-scene while Forensics are here.'

'Right.' The man stepped outside.

'The second victim's in the bedroom, upstairs,' Pete told Harold.

Through the window over the crime scene manager's shoulder, he saw the technician who'd been sent back to the van returning with a folded white overall and a pair of blue plastic overshoes for him. She beckoned him outside and he stepped carefully over the broken glass inside the doorway.

'Thanks, Vicky,' he said, though he didn't know her.

He donned the overall, snapping it up to his collar, then slipped the covers over his shoes before following her back inside.

Harold had disappeared upstairs. Pete followed, careful where he was placing his feet as he went. On the wide landing at the top, he saw that all the doors stood open. Then the snap of the catches on a case drew his attention to one of them. He headed that way.

Harold was crouched over his open metal case just inside the door, his back to Pete. Beyond him, the head of the bed was against the wall to the left. Pete could see the body of a grey-haired female draped untidily across it, arms splayed wide, her skin already beginning to take on a faint greenish hue as decomposition took hold in the centrally-heated atmosphere. Her legs, half-off the bed, had fallen open, but her nightgown – medium length and flower-patterned – was covering her in a way that suggested this hadn't been a sexual assault. She was simply lying how she'd fallen or been pushed back across the bed.

What he could also plainly see was the cause of her death.

Red blossomed across the front of her nightgown and also spread thickly across the pale quilt around her head and shoulders, where it had spread from a deep gash across her neck. From this distance, he couldn't be sure of the cause, but he could also see some darkening on her cheeks, around her mouth and across the tip of her nose.

'Is that bruising coming out on her lower face?' he asked as Harold stood up.

The smaller man snapped around, shocked. 'I wish you wouldn't do that, Detective Sergeant.'

'What?' Pete asked innocently.

'Creep up and make me jump. It's not conducive to best working practice in these circumstances. Or any others, for that matter.'

'I didn't creep. Not my fault if they've got good carpets. Had good carpets,' he corrected himself. 'Anyway, the victim...' He nodded towards her.

Harold pursed his lips and turned to look, taking a step closer. 'Yes, it looks like it to me. A hand held over her mouth, perhaps. Though not for long, judging by the knife wounds. No knife in plain sight, though.'

'It might be downstairs or he could have taken it with him,' Pete suggested. 'Or maybe left it in the bathroom. I expect he'd have had to wash his hands, at least.'

'We'll see.'

'Any blood on the floor between here and the bed?' Pete asked.

'Not visibly, but we will check with luminol.'

Pete pursed his lips. The pale cream carpet would have shown any significant blood spray or droplets without the need for chemical enhancement. It wasn't as if the killer would have bothered to try to clean up. Still, it was in Harold's nature as well as part of his job-description to be fastidiously thorough. 'So, she was probably pushed backwards onto the bed, then stabbed. Or stabbed as part of the act of pushing her backwards. Then held down with a hand over her mouth while her throat was cut to make sure she wouldn't survive.'

'No doubt the pathologist will be able to give more certainty on that, either way. He can't be far away by now.'

'The place isn't ransacked as you'd expect from a burglar,' Pete observed, looking around. All the drawers and wardrobes were closed. Nothing looked out of place. 'What about downstairs? I came straight up here.'

'Downstairs appears the same, from what little I saw,' Harold said. 'I didn't see that much of it, either. I came up here as soon as I'd deployed my team.'

'I'd best have a quick check of the rest of the place, then. Carefully,' he added, grinning at the rotund little man with his round wire-framed glasses.

Voices came from downstairs. Pete thought he recognised one of them. Then the stairs creaked as someone started to climb them. He turned to see Doctor Tony Chambers reach the landing, clad much as he and Harold were, the hood of his white overall pulled up over his short-cropped silver hair.

'Talk of the devil,' Pete said. 'Afternoon, Doc.'

'Peter,' Chambers replied with a nod. 'Is the second victim in there?'

Pete nodded. 'What did you think about the male downstairs?'

'He's definitely dead,' Chambers quipped. 'More than that, I can't say yet. I thought I'd start up here and work down.'

'Right.' Pete hid his disappointment. 'You're in a good mood.'

'I thought that was usual.'

Pete tipped his head. 'More than some I could mention, but still…'

'Well, yes, all right. I'm off on holiday in six days. I knew nothing about it, but apparently Stephanie booked it and arranged it all with the hospital. I just found out.'

Stephanie, Pete knew, was his wife. They'd met several times over the years since he took the job of detective sergeant here in Exeter. Always friendly and pleasant, she was small and blonde; one of those women who could wear absolutely anything and make it look stylish. 'Somewhere nice?' he asked.

'The Blue Train.'

'That's South Africa, isn't it?'

'Yes. Something I've wanted to do for years, but work and other circumstances have always got in the way.' He stopped at the doorway to the bedroom. 'May I come in, Mr Pointer?'

Harold looked up from what he was doing. 'One moment, Doctor.' He turned to the corner of the room beside the doorway and lifted a stack of shallow metal boxes, about a foot square by three inches deep, with one of the larger sides left open, which served as stepping-stones across crime scenes that had yet to be thoroughly examined. Carefully, he laid them out from the doorway towards the bed where the victim lay. 'There you are.'

'Thank you.' The pathologist stepped forward, staying on the metal treads. It was just seconds before he turned back to Pete, in the doorway. 'Well, cause of death is pretty obvious here, Peter. I'll be able to give you more detail once she's back at the mortuary and cleaned up, but you've no doubt seen the two stab wounds. Why both were deemed necessary is beyond me. Either would have been sufficient. But that's your department more than mine.'

'Any idea of how long ago?' Pete asked.

'I'll check the temperatures and other factors, but the level of decomposition suggests three or four days, as does that of the victim downstairs, at least as a ball-park.'

'Which fits with the daughter's report.'

'She found them?' Chambers asked, his brows drawing into a frown.

'She reported them missing. Asked for a welfare check. An officer found them.'

Chambers nodded. 'Thank goodness for that, at least.'

'Yes. I'll have to talk to her. I suppose the sooner, the better, in the circumstances.'

'I can phone you with the findings from downstairs, if you want to get off and do that,' Chambers offered.

'All right,' Pete agreed. 'Thanks, Doc.'

*

By the time Pete got back to the police station near the far side of the city, Tony Chambers had called him and confirmed that the male victim had died of a broken neck, though he was reluctant to comment on whether that was as a result of the fall or by other means.

Pete found the female constable in one of the visitor rooms off the large reception area on the ground floor of the station, which had been opened during Covid so was still thought of as new by both staff and, from what he could gather, the public. She was seated opposite a tall sandy-haired woman who looked to be a few years older than Pete's own forty years. She was wearing a camel coat despite the heating in the station, which was set at a comfortable level for shirt-sleeves and, as Pete stepped into the room with its central coffee table and dark comfy chairs ranged around three sides, she was dabbing her eyes with a tissue that looked like it was already too wet to be effective.

He nodded at the constable.

'Hello. I'm DS Gayle. Most people call me Pete. I'm sorry for your loss, Ms Lockwood. I can assure you that my team and I are on the case and we will find out who did this.'

She looked up at him, her makeup practically gone – just faint smears remaining on her upper eyelids and on her cheeks where it had run – and her eyes swollen and reddened from crying. 'Thank you.'

Pete took a seat next to the constable, across the angle from Danielle Lockwood. 'Do you think you'd be able to answer a question or two for me? Nothing traumatic.'

She nodded weakly.

'I didn't know your parents so the more I can get a feel for their lifestyle, the easier it might make it to find out why or how this happened. Which isn't suggesting it was their fault in any sense, but we need to start somewhere. To build a picture of the possibilities.'

She gave another nod.

'So, they were both retired, were they?'

'Yes.'

'And no conflicts hanging over from work or with neighbours?'

'No. They're… Were both friendly, helpful. Got on well with people. Dad worked at the Met Office and mum was a primary school teacher, so they didn't come into conflict with anyone and they got on well with the neighbours.'

'How long had they lived there?'

'I was brought up there, so… We moved there when I was eight, I think. Thirty-eight years ago.' Her voice broke, her face crumpling again.

Pete leaned forward to pull a fresh tissue from the box on the coffee table and hand it to her. She took it gratefully and dabbed at her eyes again.

He let her settle herself for a few moments. 'They've said nothing about any problems they've had recently? Road-rage incidents, maybe, or anything like that?'

'Road-rage?' she demanded, meeting his gaze. 'How would that translate into something like this?'

'I don't know,' he said with a shrug. 'It certainly shouldn't. As I said, I'm just eliminating possibilities. I've already checked for other burglaries in the area, for example, and found none. What else was going on in their lives?'

'Nothing remarkable. They were staying at home, mostly. Getting their windows and doors replaced.' She crumpled into tearful sobs again. 'To make the place more... secure,' she gulped between sobs. Pulling herself together again after a few moments, she added. 'The back door and the garage door were all that was left to do. Dad said they were coming back next week. Had to wait for something or other for the garage.'

'Do you know which firm was doing it?'

She shook her head. 'No, sorry.'

'There's bound to be some paperwork at the house. We can find out through that. Are you an only child?'

Another shake of the head. 'My brother lives in Exmouth. He's older than me. Three years.'

'And how does he get on with your parents?'

'Well, he's... OK. Fine,' she said with a frown. 'Why? You're not suggesting...?'

Pete shook his head. 'I'm not suggesting anything. Just trying to gauge the family dynamic, who might know what and so on, that's all. What does he do for a living?'

'He's an architect.'

'Should we contact him for you, or do you want to? We'll need to speak to him anyway, of course.'

'I can do it. I should. But...'

Pete took out his notebook and opened it to a clean page. 'If you could jot down his details for me, that'd be helpful.' He passed it across with his pen.

She wrote swiftly and handed the items back. 'What about Mum and Dad? Their…?'

'The pathologist is with them now. He'll do what he needs to. I don't know how quickly, but it won't be too long. A few days, at most. It's not as if there's much doubt as to what happened. Then he'll be in touch to make the arrangements for their release.'

She nodded. Drew a slow breath. 'I can't believe this has happened. Why?' she met his gaze with haunted eyes.

Pete shook his head. 'I don't know. Yet. But we will do everything we can to find out and catch whoever did it.'

'Thank you. You're very kind.' Her gaze shifted across to the female officer.

'I've never worked directly with DS Gayle,' she said. 'But he has got a reputation for getting his man.'

CHAPTER TWO

'What can you tell us, Ben?' Pete asked as he took his seat at his team's workstation in the squad room on the first floor of the station.

The spiky-haired constable stopped typing and looked past the grey-haired and grey-suited detective between them. 'There's about a hundred and fifty burglaries a year in Exeter,' he said. 'But only twelve aggravated ones in the last year, and none of them were fatal.'

'What about two-in-one burglaries?' Pete asked, meaning the type that were aimed at stealing the car keys and thereby the cars belonging to the property owners.

'What, you're thinking we've got another gang like the one we had a few years ago?' DC Dave Miles asked from the far side of the cluster of six desks.

Pete recalled the case he was talking about. It had started with both he and Ben being almost run down as they attempted an arrest and ended with the involvement of the Armed Response unit. 'I don't know,' he said. 'But the car's not on the drive where they keep it. You could look into that. Check garages and so on, see if it's in for service or repair.'

'Ha! Dropped yourself into that one, didn't you?' The little uniformed PC Jill Evans, seated at Dave's far side, nudged him sharply in the ribs.

'Jill, you're with me,' Pete said. 'We're going to Exmouth, to talk to the victims' son. The rest of you, get out to the address and start knocking on doors, see what the neighbours can tell us. Except for you, Jane.' He looked at the red-haired detective constable seated directly across from him. 'I need you in the house itself, searching for anything to back up Dave's phone work on the car as well as the details of the window company that's been working on the house. Apparently, they're due back next week to finish the job. Including the back door the killer appears to have got in through. We'll need details of all the employees who've been to the house or dealt with the owners. And anything you can find in the way of a motive anyone else in the victims' lives might have had. Disputes of any sort. Paperwork and on-line. Get onto their phone providers. We'll need up-to-date call records; mobile and landline. Email addresses. Social media. All the usual stuff. Right, let's go. The sooner we get this killer off the streets, the better.'

*

Jill dialled using the car's in-built comms system as Pete drove down the grass-banked driveway out of the police station. It rang twice and was picked up with a brusque, 'Yes?'

'Aidan Lockwood?' Pete asked.

'Yes.'

'I'm DS Gayle with Exeter police. Has your sister spoken to you about your parents?' She'd said she was going to, but he'd left her alone so couldn't be certain.

'Yes.'

'Good. I'm sorry for your loss. I need to talk to you about them. Where are you?'

'In my office.'

Pete's eyebrow rose as he shared a glance with Jill. 'Which is where, exactly?'

'Exeter Road.'

Pete's lips pursed as he reached the end of the long drive and stopped to check for passing traffic. People handled grief in different ways, of course, but this didn't seem like grief so much as impatience. 'And the name of the company?' he asked.

'Barnes and Lockwood.'

He pulled out, turning left, towards the motorway junction and the Exmouth Road, beyond. 'OK, I'll be with you shortly. Again, I'm sorry for your loss, Mr Lockwood.' He reached for the screen and broke the connection.

'Not exactly distraught, is he?' Jill observed.

'He certainly didn't sound like it.'

'Should I talk to the other staff there – secretary, receptionist or whatever – while you interview him?' she suggested.

Pete nodded. 'Yes. See what they say about his reaction and how he got on with his parents, his business partner and anyone else he dealt with. He didn't come across as the friendliest character we've ever met. And look up the address of Barnes and Lockwood, will you?'

'Uh-huh.' She took out her phone and tapped in the company name on an Internet search page. A few taps and swipes later, she had it. 'Here it is. Just before the turn into Lawn Road.'

'Where's that?' he asked as they drove under the motorway on the big multi-lane roundabout.

She concentrated again on the little screen of her smart phone. Then chuckled.

'What?' he demanded.

'It's a good job you're not taking Dave down there,' she replied. 'It's right opposite a massage parlour.'

'Really?' His eyes went wide in surprise.

'Yep. I'd show you, but you're driving. More importantly for the rest of us, it's a little way past a big old pub on the left as we go down there. Looks like a short set of old three-floor houses. As opposed to the littler ones across the road, where the shops are.'

'Littler?' he said, glancing across with a smile.

'Like smaller, only with added sweetness,' she explained.

Pete raised an eyebrow again, unwilling to follow where she seemed to be leading: *'What, like you, you mean?'* 'I know some people who'd like to be thought of that way,' he said instead. 'But the reality can be a bit different.'

Her eyes widened. 'What's that mean?' she demanded.

'People are complex creatures,' he said. 'No-one's all sweetness and light.'

'Well, I'm deeply hurt and disappointed,' she said with a glum expression.

'Not,' he retorted.

'So, should I see what else I can find about Barnes and Lockwood?'

'Anybody would think you were treating him like a suspect, PC Evans.'

'I am. Until he isn't.'

He tipped his head. 'Go for it.'

*

A discrete sign, gold on black, stood on two wooden posts immediately behind the front wall of the long lawned garden that led up towards the left-hand one of three attached three-storey town houses. Having walked back down from where Pete had parked, up the side-road at the far end of the block, they headed up the concrete garden path to a half-glazed front door with a sign behind the glass that read, 'Open. Please come in.'

Pete pushed the door open, holding it for Jill to precede him. Letting the door close behind him, he took out his warrant card and they approached the reception desk to their left, behind a high frosted glass screen with a gap in it about eighteen inches wide and extending up from the counter to almost Pete's head height.

A woman in her fifties, smartly dressed with well-coiffed blonde hair and beauty-shop makeup, sat at a desk in the space beyond the screen. She was just getting up to approach the counter.

'Can I help?' she asked, then noted Jill's uniform.

Pete held up his warrant card. 'DS Gayle,' he said. 'This is PC Evans. I'm here to see Aidan Lockwood.'

'Is...?' She stopped. 'I'll let him know you're here.' Returning to her desk, she picked up a phone and tapped in three digits. 'Mr Lockwood, there's a police detective here to see you.' She nodded and put the phone down. 'He's on the first floor. First on the left.'

'Thanks.' Pete stepped across towards the stairs that led up from beyond the receptionist's space.

'Did Mr Lockwood tell you what's happened?' he heard Jill asking as he started up the dark red carpeted stairs.

At the first floor a fire door gave into a short corridor that ran right-to-left across the house. Standing at the left-hand outer wall, he could only go one way along it so he guessed the receptionist had meant the first – and only – door on the far side, towards the rear of the property. He knocked and opened it.

What he found beyond was not what he'd expected. There was no big light-box or easel. Instead, a small office with a workstation facing the side wall of the house, a tall window beyond the chair which was pulled up in front of a large computer screen. Another desk stood out from the workstation at right angles into the centre of the room.

The man seated in the angle of the two desks hit a couple of keys and the image on the screen switched to a mountain scene. He spun his chair to face Pete but didn't get up.

'Aidan Lockwood?' Pete asked.

He looked slim to the point of skinny in his navy suit and open-necked shirt with dark hair falling onto his collar. He pushed rimless glasses up on his nose. It was difficult to tell his height, but Pete reckoned he was around five-foot-nine or ten.

'That's right,' he said. 'And you're DS Gayle. Is that detective sergeant?'

'That's right,' Pete returned. 'Again, I'm sorry for your loss.'

'Yes, you've said. Why are you here?' His expression remained neutral, closed off.

'I'm handling your parents' case. I need to ask you a few questions.'

'You've spoken to my sister.'

'Yes.'

'So, why do you need to speak to me?'

Again, Pete had to suppress his instinctive dislike of the man and his response to the situation. 'Different people have different perspectives, different knowledge sets, experiences. For instance, your parents' car.'

'What about it?'

'It wasn't at the house when your sister arrived there this morning. Would you happen to know why or where it is?'

He gave a quick shake of the head. 'No idea. Are you suggesting it was stolen? That that's what they were killed for?'

'I'm not suggesting anything at this stage. We're simply exploring possibilities with a view to eliminate or confirm them. When did you last see your parents?'

He grimaced. 'Not for a while. January, I suppose.'

It was now late March. 'And speak to them?' Pete pursued.

'The same.' He said forward, leaning his elbows on the desk between them. 'Look, we're not – we weren't – close, all right? They had their lives, I have mine.'

'And yet you're their son.'

He grunted. 'Biologically.'

'What does that mean?'

'We had our differences,' he said. 'Look, why aren't you out there doing what you do to catch whoever killed them instead of wasting your time here, with me?'

'Because I need to know if I am wasting my time here,' Pete told him. 'Frankly, Mr Lockwood, the vast majority of murders are committed by close friends or family members of the victims, so those are the first people we need to eliminate from our enquiries. So, getting down to brass tacks, I need a detailed itinerary of your movements over the past three days, along with any evidence you might have to back it up, like receipts, phone data or corroborating witnesses.'

Anger flashed across the man's narrow features, his thin lips drawing tight, but when he spoke, his voice was stiff and controlled, his words slow and clear. 'I did not kill my parents so I suggest you get out there and find out who did. Detective.'

'I intend to,' Pete told him. 'But no-one's word is good enough without evidence, Mr Lockwood. So again, where were you?'

He sucked in a long, slow breath through his nose. 'The last two days, I've been here. Saturday, I was here all day, too. Sunday, I was at home.'

'Can anyone verify that about Sunday?' Pete asked.

Lockwood paused, staring at him. 'No. I was on my own.'

'You're not married?'

'No.'

'And where is home, exactly?'

'Henley Road.'

'And the evenings? You say you were here in the daytime, but…' He shrugged.

'In the evenings, I go home. At night, I sleep.'

'What car do you drive, Mr Lockwood?'

'A Honda Civic.'

'Colour?'

'Black.'

'Where is it now?'

'Parked up Lawn Road, why?'

'And how's business? Are you busy?'

He frowned. 'What's that got to do with anything?'

Pete waited.

'All right, yes, we're busy. That's why I was here all day, Saturday. We've got a big contract that's due out soon.'

'And yet your turnover's still well down on what it was five years ago, Mr Lockwood. Seems barely enough to pay the wages, from what I've seen.'

From what Jill had found on the Internet as they drove down here, at least.

'And the contract I mentioned will help correct that. Anyway, why ask if you already know the answer?'

'What was the problem between you and your parents?'

'What, I'm still a suspect, am I?'

'Everyone's a suspect until we can prove they're not, Mr Lockwood.'

'What the hell do you want from me? I've just been told my parents were murdered and here you are, treating me like I'm the murderer. I've got a good mind to lodge a complaint.'

'I'm just trying to get to the truth, Mr Lockwood.'

'Well, the truth is, I didn't kill them.' He sat back, folding his arms across his chest.

'So, what was the problem between you?'

'Irrelevant to this situation. Now, if you don't mind...'

Pete pursed his lips. 'If it's irrelevant, then it'll be discounted and it won't come up again but, at this stage, everything's relevant until we can prove it isn't. The smallest thing can lead to something bigger – something big enough in someone's mind to cause an outburst of violence like the one that led to your parents' deaths.'

Something shifted in Lockwood's expression. It was barely discernible, but Pete noticed it.

'My father was not my biological father,' he said. 'I was conceived before they married, with the help of another man. I don't know who. Mother never said. But things were not as wonderful in their marriage as everyone outside of it thought. My father resented me from as far back as I can remember. I suppose I reminded him of

Mother's *indiscretion*. So I got out of there as soon as I could and I seldom go back. Went back.'

'Your sister never hinted at any of this.'

'I don't think she was ever aware. He was very clever that way. Everything was about appearances, for him. She might have sensed some tension between them now and then, but the reason for it would never have been discussed. Not the real reason, anyway. And he was always careful not to have a go at me when anyone else was around.'

'So, why did they stay together?'

He shrugged. 'As I said, it was all about appearances with my father. A divorce would have been out of the question, even after Danni and I left home. It wasn't for us that they stayed together, like some couples do. And yes, I know all that gives me a motive. But I didn't kill them. I just stayed away from them.'

Pete nodded. 'All right. As I said, we will find out who did. Whoever that is. Thank you for your time. I'll be in touch.'

CHAPTER THREE

'Did you learn anything useful?' Pete asked as they walked down the long garden path.

'They're struggling to stay afloat,' Jill said. 'It's even worse than the latest Company's House figures suggest, according to the receptionist. Between Covid and the economic downturn since then… Nothing wrong with their work, she said, but they're barely getting enough of it to cover the bills and pay the wages. And she's actively looking for another job – not for the continuity of income; just because of the way they've been treating her.'

'Both of them?'

'Yes. Lockwood's got very short-tempered and angry over the past few months, she said. And Barnes is an outright bully, except to Lockwood.'

'Hmm.' They reached the end of the path and stepped out onto the pavement, turning left towards where Pete had parked. 'Strange that Lockwood would work with someone like that. He said his dad was pretty abusive in a sneaky sort of way.'

'Really? I thought the daughter said they got on all right.'

'He said she was probably unaware of what was going on. Said he wasn't senior's biological son and the old man resented him for it.'

'Two motives, then, with the money, if he thought he'd inherit.'

Pete glanced sideways at her. 'Did you find out which bank they use?'

'Of course.'

'Good.' He took out his phone as they rounded the corner into the side-street. 'Well, that's handy: we parked right across the road from Lockwood.' Walking the few yards up the hill to his own car, he took a photo of Lockwood's, then crossed the road to take one of the registration plate on the front of it. 'He hasn't got an alibi, as such,' he said as they climbed into the Ford. 'So we'll check traffic cameras and so on around the time of death. It's no good talking to his neighbours until we've done that so we'll head back. But, having said that, what we can do is stop off and collect any CCTV sources we pass on the way back. It could save time later and make sure we get hold of evidence that might get overwritten, otherwise.'

Jill looked across at him as he started the engine. 'You really don't like him much, do you?'

'It's not about liking him or not.' Pete swung the car into a three-point turn. 'It's about finding facts and collecting evidence. And like I said – he hasn't got an alibi. So if we can either give him one or prove he's a strong suspect, that's got to be a step forward, hasn't it?'

'OK. First stop, that filling station we passed on the way into Exmouth, then?'

'Yep.'

Turning right onto the main road, he used the car's comms system to make a call.

'DC Miles.'

'Dave, it's Pete. How're you getting on?'

'I've been onto the dealership for the Lockwoods' car. It's two and a half years old. They bought it as an ex-demo. He's kept it serviced since. Due for its next in late June. No recorded problems with it.'

'So, it's unlikely to have been put into another garage.'

'Yes. So I've put out an alert on it. If Traffic or ANPR detect it, it'll be flagged up.'

'If the plates haven't been changed already.'

'At least it gives us a chance. How've you got on?'

'Their son's got an attitude problem, a financial motive and no alibi.' Pete saw the distinctive red and yellow stripes around the roof of a filling station up ahead. 'We're going to make a stop or two on the way back, see if we can find any CCTV from around the time of death. In fact, the first stop's coming up now. See you later.'

He pulled in and they went inside.

Waiting for the three customers to make their purchases and leave, Pete approached the desk with his warrant card in hand, as if Jill's uniform wasn't enough to identify them.

'Hi,' he said to the tall south Asian behind the counter. 'DS Gayle, Exeter CID. I need to see your CCTV from the weekend, if you've got a minute.'

He glanced outside to check there was no-one at the pumps and nodded. 'OK, no problem.'

Leading them through to the back, he showed them into a small office off the storeroom where a desk held an old-looking desktop computer. Leaning over it, he tapped the keyboard, brought up the CCTV feed and looked up. 'You know how to use it?'

Pete nodded.

'I must get back to the counter.'

'OK, thanks.'

Pete took his place behind the desk and found that there was footage from both inside the shop and out, looking over the pumps with the road clearly visible in the background. He selected the outside footage and found the stored files. They were in twelve-hour chunks so, taking a thumb-drive from his jacket, he inserted it and downloaded everything from Saturday afternoon through Tuesday morning. Extracting the thumb-drive, he returned the feed to real-time, switched off the screen and they headed out.

'Thank you,' he called, raising a hand to the assistant, who was dealing with another customer as they passed through the shop towards the exit.

Back on the road, he used his phone through the hands-free system again.

'Chambers.'

'Hello, Doc. It's Pete Gayle. Have you got the PMs scheduled on our two victims from this morning?'

'I'm busy for the rest of today. I'll be working late as it is. I'll get to them first thing in the morning.'

'OK. I'll be there.'

He hung up and concentrated on driving.

Taking the most direct route to the victims' address, they passed two more filling stations, stopping at both to collect CCTV footage. They could have passed others by taking different routes but at this stage there was little point and plenty else to do.

Turning into the wide driveway, he parked behind Ben Myers' electric-blue Skoda and Dick Feeney's black Mondeo. The forensics team had clearly already left the scene but the same uniformed constable was still standing beside the front door.

'Hey, Bob,' Jill said. 'How's it going?'

The constable nodded. 'Haven't caught anyone yet.'

'You know him?' Pete asked as they stepped inside.

'Yeah. Did my beat training with him. A long time ago.'

Pete gave her a sideways glance. He still thought of her as a young officer, the junior of his team, but she'd been working with him for… Eight years, he realised with a shock. 'Huh. Time flies when you're having fun, eh?'

'That's the rumour,' she agreed as he led the way through to the big space at the back of the house. They found Jane seated at the dining table, going through a stack of papers.

'How's it going?' Pete asked.

She looked up, her ginger hair gleaming in the sun from the wide windows behind her. 'They've got a laptop each, a mobile phone each plus the landline. I've got requests in for the records for the phones. Haven't got into the laptops yet, but I have found an old address book that he was repurposing to keep all his passwords in. We haven't found one for hers. Haven't found any indication of where he might have taken the car, apart from the dealership, either.'

Pete nodded. 'We spoke to Dave about that, too. Seems like the killer may well have taken the car. Dave's put an alert out on it. Anything on the victims' financials?'

'Yes, I've got it all here.' She indicated a stack of papers on the table near her left elbow. 'They were pretty comfortable in that respect.'

Pete shared a glance with Jill. 'And yet their son was struggling. And not exactly close with them.'

Jane raised a sculpted eyebrow. 'You didn't manage to eliminate him, then?'

'No. What about the window company?'

'I've got their details here,' she confirmed. 'A local firm, based on the Sowton Industrial Estate.'

'OK, give me the paperwork, we'll go and see what we can find out from there. Anybody else they were dealing with recently that might throw up a suspect?'

'Not that I've found yet.'

'OK, we'll start with this.' He raised the three or four folded pages she'd handed him. 'And we'll give Dave a ring, tell him to start looking at the two-in-one burglary angle, see if we have got a car theft ring operating in the city again.'

Jane grimaced. 'They're unlikely to want to bring the pressure of a murder enquiry down on themselves.'

'Yes, but they don't exactly do hospital-grade checks on prospective gang-members, do they? Might have one that's gone off the rails.'

Jane shrugged. 'You never know, I suppose.'

He pursed his lips. 'Ben and Dick have had no luck, I suppose?'

She shook her head. 'They're upstairs if you want to talk to them. Not many neighbours around here, and they're pretty isolated from one another.'

'It'll wait. See you later.' He turned back the way he'd come.

As they stepped back out into the sunshine, Bob nodded. 'Quick visit.'

'Places to go, people to see,' Pete returned. 'Can't stand about here all day.'

'Someone's got to,' Bob retorted.

'Only until my lot are finished inside. Then we can lock it up and tape off the doors and the driveway entrance.'

'How's the daughter doing?' Bob asked.

'She was still pretty cut up about it when I last saw her,' Pete admitted. 'As you'd expect. There's an FLO assigned from her local nick.'

An FLO was a family liaison officer – a uniformed constable trained in how to handle victims and their families, whose job it would be to spend as much time with the family as they needed, to be a friend and someone to talk to, to keep them updated on the progress of the investigation and to report back to the investigation team with anything pertinent that they might learn while they were doing that.

Bob nodded. 'Seemed like a nice woman. And genuine.'

'Yes.'

And yet Pete knew how deceptive appearances could be – as would Bob after all his years on the force. And in this case, as much as her brother might have thought of her as spoiled and ignorant of what was going on around her, that too could easily have been an illusion born of his own experience-based prejudice.

*

Sowton industrial estate was the one that Chief Inspector Christine Naylor's office looked out over from the top floor of the police station on Sidmouth Road – a view that Pete was all too familiar with. But the address on the paperwork from Storm Windows and Doors meant that, rather than going past the station to access the estate, Pete went in from the north end, off the Honiton Road, and worked his way along increasingly narrow, cracked and potholed roads towards an area of smaller businesses.

He found the window fitters' tucked between a roofing company and a steel fabricators'. Parking opposite the blue metal-clad stretch of buildings between a pickup truck and a van, they headed across to the small door beside the open service entrance through which they could see stacks of empty window frames and doors.

There was no-one behind the counter when they went in but there was a bell-push attached to it with a small sign: Press for attention.

Pete pressed it. The door to their right opened after a few moments to admit a man in his forties, Pete guessed; tall and lean, dressed in dark blue overalls, he had dark hair that was turning grey and a hint of stubble darkening his cheeks and chin.

'Can I help?' he asked.

Pete raised his warrant card. 'Exeter CID. We need to speak to the boss.'

He responded with a grimace of surprise. 'I am the boss. What's up?'

Pete set the unfolded sheets of paper from the Lockwood home on the counter between them. 'You've been working at this address, off Stoke Hill,' he said. 'Or at least a team of your guys have.'

'That's our...' He reached for the papers and took a closer look at the top one. 'Yes, we're due back there next week to fit a couple of doors. Why? Has something happened?'

'Why would you ask that?'

'Because the police are here, asking about it.'

Pete tipped his head. 'Well, yes, something has happened. We need a list of all your people who've attended the address and, in fact, a full list of your employees, including any casual labourers. With contact details.'

'Why?' he asked with a frown.

'For elimination purposes,' Pete told him. 'There's been a break-in. Through one of the doors you'd yet to replace.'

'And they were out, were they? Didn't see who did it?'

Pete shook his head. 'They were in. I can't say too much at the minute. We're still investigating. But your clients are no longer with us.'

'No longer… What, they're dead?' His eyes widened in shock.

Pete nodded. 'I'm afraid so. So if we could have those lists… I'll need to speak to everyone who attended the property.'

He blinked. 'Yes. Of course. You think…?'

'Any possible witnesses are being spoken to.'

'Right. Yes. OK.' He turned away. 'Give me two minutes.'

He went through a door at the back of the small room. An automatic closer pushed it back into place behind him and Pete and Jill were left waiting.

It took longer than two minutes. Pete was beginning to wonder where he'd got to – if the impression he'd given of genuine shock had been real – when the door finally opened again and he returned with a sheet of paper in hand.

'A full list of our employees. We don't use casuals. Phone numbers and addresses are all there. The ones with stars by have been to that house.' He handed the sheet over to Pete.

'Thank you. Are any of them here, now?'

'Only me. The rest are out on other jobs.'

'You went to the address?' Pete checked.

'Yes. For the measure-up and the delivery. I suppose those doors are going to be wasted now – that we were going to fit next week.' He shook his head sadly.

'That's between you and the Lockwoods' family, Mr…?'

'Henderson. Sorry, I…'

Pete glanced at the list in his hand. Henderson was at the top. First name, Ian, his address only a couple of streets away from Pete's own in the Whipton area of the city. 'We understand. It's a bit of a shock to everyone. You didn't see anything or anyone out of place when you were there? Or they didn't mention any problems? Any reasons for suddenly changing all the windows and doors in the property?'

He shook his head. 'They just said it was time. The windows were old, inefficient. With the rising heating costs and so on, they thought it was time. And while they were at it, they'd get the doors done, too. Finish the job, you know?'

Pete nodded. 'And nothing out of the ordinary happened while you were there? No random callers? Lost dogs? Door-to-door salesmen?'

Another shake of the head. 'No. It's a nice, quiet neighbourhood up there. Out of the way. I can't believe this could have happened. So, you reckon it was a burglary, and…?'

Pete shook his head. 'It's too early to say for sure,' he said. 'But that's what it looks like. If I can just ask…' He glanced down at the list in his hand. There were eight names on it, only one of them female – Pamela Henderson, listed under Ian with dittos under the address and phone number. His wife or daughter, Pete guessed. 'Are any of these relatively recent employees?'

Henderson blinked. 'You think… No way. None of my guys would do something like this.'

Pete shrugged. 'We have to eliminate all possibilities, Mr Henderson.'

'I dare say, but you can eliminate that one. I'd vouch for all of my guys, a hundred percent.'

'But your most recent hires…?'

'Last year. April-time we took on Brian and another guy. Mark. He's not on there. Was only with us for the summer. Then, September, we took Andy on to replace him.'

'And this other guy, Mark – who was he?'

'Mark Collins. He was a buddy of Brian's but he had a problem with reliability. We had to let him go in the end.'

'I'll need his details as well,' Pete said. 'And anyone else who's left the company recently.'

'He's the only one. We don't have much of a staff turnover.'

Pete set the page down on the counter between them.

'I'll have to go and check the records.'

'OK.'

He took the paper with him and was back in moments. 'There. But I can't imagine he'd do anything like that. He was just… Well, he wasn't lazy or anything. Worked well, once he turned up. Just…' He shrugged. 'Like I said, not reliable. Family problems. I don't remember the details. We gave him what leeway we could, but at the end of the day, we've got a business to run and reliability's a big part of that.'

Pete nodded. 'So, when were you last at the Lockwoods'?'

'Like I said, when the windows were delivered. Last Tuesday.'

Pete's eyebrows rose. 'Doesn't take long to change them, then.'

'The bay took a while, and the patio doors, but otherwise, no. Couple of hours each, with two men doing it. There were four on that job because of the size of the patio doors and to speed it up. This time of year, you don't want things open to the elements any longer than you can help.'

'True,' Pete agreed. 'They made a nice, tidy job of it, then. The place looked pretty much undisturbed.'

'We do our best.'

Pete nodded. 'Worth knowing.' He paused. 'We have to ask this – standard procedure. Where were you over the weekend?'

'Where was I? That's when…? When it happened?'

Pete nodded.

'Well, I was here Saturday 'til mid-afternoon. Had lunch at the café up the road. Then we went home. Daughter came round for tea, spent the evening. Sunday, we went out for the day. Knightshayes. Been wanting to go there for ages and finally got around to it. Got home about half-five. Had some tea, watched Antiques Roadshow and a couple of things we'd recorded.'

'Knightshayes… That's National Trust, right?' Pete checked.

'Yes. Up by Tiverton. Not too far, but it's the local ones you tend to overlook, isn't it? Anyway, the weather was perfect so we decided to tick it off the list, you know?'

'*We* being…?'

'The wife and I. Pam. She'd be here normally, but she's got an appointment this afternoon. Dentist's.'

Well, that answers one question, Pete thought. *Pamela, on the list, is clearly the wife, not a daughter.* 'One last thing, then: we'll need you to come into the station on Sidmouth Road sometime – preferably today or tomorrow – to provide a set of finger-prints for elimination, if that's OK.'

'Really?' He sounded and looked suddenly dubious.

'You were in the house,' Pete explained. 'We're going to find all sorts of prints there. If we can tick off all those who were supposed to be there, hopefully that'll leave us with a set from someone who wasn't. Help us identify the offender. They won't go on file. Once the case is over with, they'll be destroyed.'

He pursed his lips. 'OK.'

'The same applies to your crew, of course,' Pete added.

Henderson nodded. 'I'll let them know.'

'Thanks. We'll be in touch if we need to follow up on anything. Thanks for your time.' He picked up the sheet of employee details from the counter.

'I'm sorry about Mr and Mrs Lockwood,' Henderson said.

*

Pete waited only for the door to close behind them before saying to Jill, 'Get back onto Companies House. See how they're doing. And text the Hendersons' address to Jane.'

He led the way across towards the car, climbing in, he started the engine and immediately made a call. Was still in the process of reversing out of his parking space when it was answered.

'DC Bennett speaking.'

'Jane, it's Pete. How are you getting on there?'

'About to wrap it up, why?'

'Jill's going to send you an address for the owners of the window company. I need you and Ben to go round there, sooner the better, and talk to the wife. See what she has to say about where they were over the weekend and about any employees that she wasn't so keen on.'

'Done,' Jill said from beside him as he drove past the little café that Henderson had mentioned.

'Right. Got it,' Jane said. 'You want us there before the husband gets home, I take it?'

'That's the idea.'

Heading south out of the industrial estate instead of back the way they'd come, he took them straight back to the station.

'About time somebody turned up here,' Dave said when they walked into the squad room a few minutes later. 'I was starting to feel abandoned.'

'Ah,' Jill teased, nudging him. 'Were you getting lonely?'

'More to the point, have you been keeping busy?' Pete added.

'No and yes,' the dark-haired DC replied. 'I've been busy enough not to miss you,' he added to Jill as she pulled her chair in beside him. 'There've been a few car thefts in the city in the past few weeks, but nothing to indicate a link between them. And they're all over the place. No specific area and no consistent make or even type of vehicle.'

'So, was it just a handy means of getaway?' Jill suggested.

'If so, how did the killer get there?' Pete countered. 'They didn't walk – it's too far out of town.'

She shrugged. 'Just a thought.'

'It hasn't come up on ANPR yet,' Dave said. 'Which suggests it's either been dumped somewhere or tucked away for future use or stripping down for parts.'

'The latter would suggest organisation, though, which you just said there's no sign of, lately,' Pete pointed out. 'We'll see what comes of it in the next day or two. There's plenty else to be getting on with. We'll need PNC checks on the Hendersons and their employees and the ex-employee. You can share that job between you while I get into the Lockwoods' finances, with an emphasis on the son's. Dick will be back here soon. He can start on the CCTV we collected on the way back from Exmouth.'

'You haven't eliminated Junior, then?' Dave asked.

Jill gave a dry chuckle as she smoothed the paper from Storm Windows out on the desk between her and Dave. 'Not by a long shot.'

CHAPTER FOUR

'He wasn't lying about the state of his finances,' Pete declared a few minutes later.

'Who's that?' Jill asked.

'Aidan Lockwood. His personal bank account's got all of a hundred and seventy-eight quid in it. And he's got no other accounts that I can find.'

'That confirms his motive,' Dave said. 'But I just found another fun fact. Former Storm Windows employee Mark Collins has got a record. Been inside, in fact, albeit only once, for ten months.'

'For what?'

'Burglary.'

Pete's eyebrow rose. 'Well, isn't that interesting? What about his buddy who's still with the company? Brian White.'

'Three arrests. No convictions. He got away with it once: not guilty. The other two, the CPS refused to charge him.'

'Doesn't that bloke do CRB checks before he hires people?' Jill demanded.

Pete tipped his head. 'You'd think he ought to, considering he's sending his employees into people's homes. Maybe he's a believer in second chances.'

'But to not even mention that they'd got records after we told him what had happened…' she retorted. 'Makes him look complicit, at a minimum, doesn't it?'

'Only to your suspicious mind, Titch,' Dave said with a grin.

'He claimed that nothing had happened to any of their other clients, but it might be worth checking on that,' Pete said. 'First, though, we'll find out if Collins and White have got alibis. Assuming they're the only ones on that list with records?'

'So far,' she confirmed.

As Dave nodded agreement the door opened behind Pete. 'Nice of you to join us,' he said.

'We can't all spend all day sitting behind a desk,' Dick said as he stepped across behind Pete to his chair.

'But now you're here, you can join the club,' Pete told him. 'We've got some CCTV footage for you to go through.'

'Oh, lovely. Looking for what?'

'A black Civic. The registration's on that Post-it.' Pete tapped the little yellow sticky note he'd put on Dick's desk in preparation.

'So, I'm looking for a black car at night?'

'We don't have a firm time of death yet, but possibly.'

'He should have his lights on,' Dave laughed.

Dick flipped him the bird.

'No, two,' Dave returned with a V-sign.

'Six, if we're lucky,' Pete said. 'Two front, two back and two on the number plates. We'll leave talking to witnesses and checking on alibis until we've got a time of death – hopefully in the morning. But there's three sets of footage to go through so, if you've finished what you were doing, Dave…'

'It would be worth getting requests in for mobile phone records, ready for the morning,' Jill said.

'True. The Hendersons, the Lockwoods – all four of them. We need to check on their financials too. And Collins and White.'

'I'll get onto it,' she said.

'You do the phones; I'll carry on with the banks. Oh, and we'll need an address for Danielle. I've got a phone number.'

'I'll look her up,' Jill said. And moments later: 'Did we know Danielle Lockwood doesn't live alone?'

Pete looked up over his screen. 'No.'

'Giles Bell is on the electoral register as second occupant. Two years older than she is, so a boyfriend, maybe?'

'Hmm. Worth finding out about him, too, then. She didn't mention him.'

'Makes you wonder why, doesn't it?'

'Your suspicious mind again?' Dave said.

'I prefer to call it a copper's nose.'

'Just be careful where you stick it,' Dick told her.

'I thought you were supposed to be concentrating?' she retorted.

'Doesn't make me deaf.'

Pete's phone rang on his desk as he tapped the new name into the search engine he was using. He picked it up. 'DS Gayle.'

'It's Jane. She's not at home.'

'Hmm. Shame. She's not expected back at work, so must have gone shopping or something. OK. Give it a few minutes and, if she doesn't turn up, come back to the nick. What you could do while you're there, though, is have a chat with the neighbours. See if they noticed any unusual comings and goings over the weekend. Keep it general. You're not targeting anyone. You know the drill.'

'Yes, OK. Will do.'

He glanced up as he set the phone back on its cradle and found the others all looking at him expectantly. 'Pam Henderson's not at home,' he said.

'Shame. Gives her and her husband more chance to confer before we talk to her,' Jill said. 'If they haven't already, by mobile.'

He shrugged. 'It was always a risk. And…' He stopped as the screen in front of him changed. 'Ooh. Giles Bell?'

'Yes,' said Jill.'

'He's interesting.'

'How come?' Dave asked.

'No current employment record – or police record, to be fair – and yet he's got four grand in his bank account. We're definitely going to need another word with Danielle and probably with him, too.'

CHAPTER FIVE

'Well, the delay has helped us in some ways,' Doctor Tony Chambers said as he folded back the sheet from the first of the two bodies laid out on the steel autopsy tables.

'How's that?' Pete asked. 'If they'd been there three or four days already…?'

'It meant that, starting this morning, we've already got the X-rays and scans done. So, in the case of Mrs Lockwood, here, we can see from those that, as I mentioned at the scene, either of the knife wounds could have been fatal on its own. The neck wound you can see severed both the internal and external jugular veins as well as the external carotid artery on the right side of her neck while the thoracic injury you noted at the scene penetrated upward through the diaphragm and into the heart.'

Pete's eyes widened as the second wound Chambers described – which, with the sheet folded down, he could now see as a narrow slit just an inch or so long, surrounded by a small area of bruising – reminded him of a recent case in which a man had been silently and efficiently killed in exactly that way, almost under Pete's and Jane's noses. But they'd got the man who'd committed that crime. He was languishing in prison now and would be there for a very long time. 'Another skilled and deliberate killer,' he said as Chambers reached for a blue-handled post-mortem knife.

'Indeed.' The silver-haired pathologist placed a bracing hand on the dead woman's shoulder and began the Y-incision. 'Which is borne out by the superficial and scan findings on our other victim, over there, Mrs Lockwood's husband.'

'Oh, yes?'

Chambers nodded and made the second cut, from the other shoulder, meeting the first over her sternum. 'His neck was broken, but not necessarily by falling down the stairs. When his collar was lowered, I discovered a distinctive bruise on the side of his neck.' He continued the cut down the centre of her chest and abdomen, carefully avoiding the entry-point of the possibly fatal wound.

Pete's lips pulled down in a grimace. 'So, was that done just to make sure, where we found him, or was it done at the top and then the body pushed down the stairs to make it look like an accident?'

'The other bruises on the body would suggest the former. Which is where the advantage of time lapsing before doing the post-mortem examination comes in. Peri-mortem bruising can take two or three days to become evident.' He set the knife aside and began to peel back the skin on either side of the incision he'd made.

'On the other hand, doesn't it make it harder to determine the time of death?' Pete asked as, despite the Vick's he customarily slathered his nose with for these occasions, the smell of decomposition assailed his senses.

'It can,' Chambers agreed. 'But if the victim has had a meal within four or five hours of death, the stomach contents can help. What they are and the stage of digestion.'

'And…?'

'We haven't got there yet, Peter. That's to be discovered this morning.'

'Oh, lovely.'

By now, Heather Lockwood's body looked like a carcass in a butcher's shop.

'You don't have to attend these activities if you'd prefer not to. Pass the croppers, please, Barry.'

'I know. But sometimes it can help, as you know. And it certainly helps focus the mind on why we do what we do.'

Chambers tipped his head. 'Very well.' He inserted the tips of what looked like a pair of garden loppers and bore down on the handles. The crack of the lower right rib snapping sounded like a branch being cut, only sharper. He moved the cutters up to the next one. *Snap.*

*

'OK, so what have we learned?' Pete asked as he sat down at his desk.

'Nothing useful from the garage forecourts yet,' Dick told him.

'I've got the phone records for Mark Collins, Brian White and Danielle and Aidan Lockwood,' Jill added. 'None of them were in the vicinity over the weekend.'

'I went through the bank records you requested yesterday,' Dave said. 'They don't show anything untoward, either.'

'Well, we can narrow down the time of death to Saturday night,' Pete told them. 'Between midnight and three a.m. And it was murder. The weapon used on Heather Lockwood was designed for the purpose, as opposed to being a normal kitchen knife. And we didn't find anything like that at the scene, which suggests it may have belonged to the killer.'

'Or he found it there and liked it, so kept it,' Dave suggested.

'Possible. But why would an average retired couple own a stiletto knife with a six-inch blade, sharpened on both sides? It's not what you'd normally have as a letter-opener.'

Dave shrugged. 'We don't know their history, do we?'

Pete drew a breath. 'Not sufficiently, as yet. All right. Let's concentrate on narrowing down our suspect list. Finish going through that CCTV, then check ANPR, mobile phone and bank records to try and confirm the rest of our suspects' whereabouts around the relevant timeframe. Jane, you're with me.'

'Where are we going?' she asked.

'To learn more about our victims. And Danielle Lockwood and her boyfriend.'

She blinked and closed down her computer. 'Does she know we're coming?'

'Yes. I called her on the way back here.'

'OK, then. Sooner we get there, the sooner we're back,' she said as they stood up together.

*

Having found Danielle Lockwood's address on the eastern edge of the small market town of South Molton, on the edge of Exmoor with her car filling the short driveway, Pete parked on the street outside. The low-lying bungalow overlooked fields behind. The front door was between the wide bay window and the built-in garage, the small front lawn neatly mown.

Pete led the way down the red tarmac slope between drive and lawn. Pressing the doorbell, he was surprised when it was opened by a male.

This would be Giles Bell, he guessed, taking his warrant card from inside his jacket. 'Hi. DS Gayle, Devon and Cornwall Police,' he said. 'This is DC Bennett.'

The male nodded and took a step back. 'Danni said you were coming. Come in.'

'Thank you.' Pete shared a glance with Jane. This was not what he'd planned or hoped for. He'd have much preferred to speak to them separately. But they were simply witnesses at this stage – and not even to the crime itself – so what could he do? He couldn't dictate the circumstances under which he interviewed them. He stepped forward and followed the man, who was three inches shorter than Pete's own six feet, three or four years younger than his forty years and lean with long dark hair and a day's stubble on his chin and cheeks, into the sitting room where Danielle Lockwood was in the act of getting up off the sofa.

'Miss Lockwood,' he said. 'You haven't met my colleague, DC Bennett.'

'Jane,' she said.

'Hello.' Danielle reached out to shake her hand briefly. 'Please.' She indicated the sofa she'd just vacated. 'Can we get you a drink or anything?'

'No, thanks,' Pete said, taking a seat. 'I'm fine.'

Jane declined too and they sat, Danielle and Bell taking the two armchairs which sat beside each other at ninety degrees to the sofa, their backs to the picture window at the rear of the long room.

'So, have you got some news or...?' Danielle asked, her voice trailing off.

'Not yet,' Pete replied. 'How are you coping?'

She shrugged. 'OK, I suppose. It hits me now and then. That I'll...' She stopped. 'It's good that Giles is here with me. I'd be a mess, otherwise.' She reached across to stroke his arm.

'You said you last spoke to your parents on Friday?'

'That's right. I normally speak to Mum, at least briefly, every evening. But they were out Saturday and I couldn't get hold of them Sunday. Or Monday. I knew they weren't going away, so I thought I'd best go down there and check on them yesterday and, when the car was missing and there was no response at the door...'

'But you didn't go around the back?'

She shook her head. 'The side gate's normally bolted. I can't reach over to open it like the officer did.' She reached for Bell's hand and grasped it. 'I'm… Glad, in a way. Or I'd have…'

'Yes,' Pete said. 'What made you suspect the worst when you saw the car wasn't there? I mean, they could have nipped down to the supermarket or something.'

She shook her head quickly. 'It was Tuesday morning. They're always in. Dustbin day. Dad likes to fetch them in as soon as they're emptied. I don't know why,' she added with a shrug.

'You said they were out Saturday evening. Where did they go?'

'Into the city, to meet up with some friends. It was a regular thing, once a month.'

Pete nodded and reached for his notebook. 'Have you got the details of any of those friends? It would be useful to talk to them.'

'Not as such,' she said. 'I know first names. A couple of the surnames, but that's all. They'll be in their address book, though.'

'Whatever you can tell me…' He readied his pen.

'Well… So, it happened Saturday night, did it? Is that what you're…?'

Pete's lips pressed together. 'Yes,' he said. 'A little after midnight.'

Her face began to crumple as emotion threatened to overwhelm her. Pete noticed Bell's hand squeeze hers. She blinked, tears breaking loose from her lashes to run unchecked down her cheeks. 'How?'

'First appearances are that it may have been a burglary that went wrong. It's too early to say for sure yet. Those friends you were going to tell me about…?'

She drew a breath. 'Yes. There were John and Marjory Taylor from two doors along. Derek Mooney. Susan Nelson. The others, I don't know. Only what Mum's mentioned in passing. Bob, Lisa, Anne and Ron. I don't know their surnames, though, or which of them were there on Saturday.'

'OK. And you were both here Saturday night, were you?'

'Yes,' she nodded and glanced at the man beside her again. 'I don't drink at the moment.' Her free hand went to her stomach and stroked it briefly.

'How far along are you?' Jane asked.

She went to speak, then paused. Her eyes widened. 'Halfway. Four and a half months.'

'It doesn't show yet,' Pete commented.

'No, but...' She grimaced. 'It was why Dad and I hadn't spoken in a couple of months, although I still talked to Mum.'

'He didn't approve?' Pete asked.

'No. He was a bit old-fashioned in some ways. Thought we should... Well, to be honest, he didn't think that: he didn't approve of Giles, either. Thought I could do better. It didn't seem to matter that we're happy.'

Pete tipped his head. 'Maybe it's just a father and daughter thing. They always want what they think is best for you. So, what do you do, Giles? It's good that you can take time off to be with Danielle at a time like this.'

He grimaced. 'I'm not... I'm between jobs, as they say. Finished just before Christmas.'

'Harsh,' Pete said with a grimace. 'What happened?'

'I had a difference of outlook with my boss. He was a bully, basically. So, I quit.'

'That's going to make it awkward to get a reference when you want to go for another job.'

He shrugged. 'Not really. I got on OK with *his* boss. And I've got another job lined up. Start week after next.'

'Doing what?'

'I'm a gardener. Worked at Castle Hill. I'm moving on to a place near Barnstaple. It's a bit further, and a bit smaller, but it's family-run so it should be good and it gives me a better chance at promotion.'

'Good. Good luck with it.'

Danielle shared a smile with him. 'We've just got to get another car and we'll be all set. We were going to go looking today, if… This hadn't happened.'

'How will you afford that?' Pete asked, thinking of the four grand in the man's bank account but not wanting to reveal that he knew about it. 'I don't imagine gardening pays a fortune.'

'I sold mine just after Christmas,' Bell said. 'Needed the money more than the motor.'

'So, you've got a bit set aside still?'

'Not as much as I had at the start, but enough, if we're careful.'

Pete turned back to Danielle. 'So, you work in town, do you?'

'No. I started here in town, but I'm at a spa resort a few miles south-west of here now. It's further to go, of course, but there's a better clientele and more scope for progression, career-wise.'

He smiled. 'I can't imagine there's much market for a beauty therapist in a little market town like South Molton.'

Her expression tightened briefly. 'People need to feel good about themselves, wherever they live.'

'I meant the number of people who can afford to spend that bit extra, as opposed to in a place like Exeter or even Barnstaple.'

She shrugged, mollified. 'I suppose. But I wanted to be in a smaller community, coming away from the city.'

'Really?'

She sighed. 'I was… A bit of an awkward kid. Didn't fit in with the in-crowd. And Aidan didn't help. He had a certain reputation. You know what kids can be like.'

'I do,' he admitted. His own son had been something of a problem child. And yet his daughter was exactly the opposite: pleasant, helpful, well adjusted, mature for her age. 'So, what was Aidan's issue?'

'He… I blame his diabetes. He's always had mood and self-control issues. An angry boy became an angry young man – only now he was big enough for it to be a problem. And the fact that he's… Well, he's not "out,"' she said, waving her fingers in the air like quotation marks. 'But I'm sure he's that way inclined, rather than hetero.'

Pete raised an eyebrow. 'I can't say I picked up on that when I met him.'

Another tiny flash of annoyance crossed her brow. 'They're not all camp and effeminate, Detective.'

'No. I did pick up on his anger issues, though. That can't help in a business environment.'

'I don't suppose it does, but he's very good at what he does.'

Still, it could explain why his business is struggling, Pete thought.

He asked a few more questions then drew a breath and released it. 'OK, well, I think that's all we need for now. We'll be on our way.' He leaned forward, elbows on his knees. 'But don't hesitate to contact Victim Support if you need them. They're there to help. You've got the number?'

'Yes.'

He fixed her with an intense gaze. 'And you can call me anytime you want to with any questions or any information that comes to mind, that might help with the case. Either of you,' he added, flicking his gaze across to her partner.

'Thank you.'

Bell got up to see them out and stood in the open doorway as they went up the short drive.

Pete waited until they were in the car before saying, 'Get your phone out and take a snap of the back of that car as we drive past.'

She raised an eyebrow. 'And here I thought you were going soft on me.'

He started the engine. 'That's what *they* were meant to think.'

She took out her phone and readied it as he swung the car into a three-point turn. 'Hence the "call me anytime with any questions."'

'Exactly. The questions they ask can be as telling as the information they offer,' he said.

'Ah, so, Master,' she said in an exaggerated Chinese accent.

'Shut up and take the picture, Grasshopper. Then you can get a search going for it on ANPR, see if it went anywhere over the weekend.'

CHAPTER SIX

Pete picked up his ringing desk phone. He'd been back in the squad room less than five minutes – only just long enough to grab a coffee for himself and for Jane and get back to his seat. He could tell by the ring-tone it was an internal call. 'DS Gayle,' he said into the receiver.

'Get yourself in here.' He recognised DI Colin Underhill's gruff voice.

'Your office?'

'Yes.' It was more of a grunt than an agreement and the line was cut before he could question further.

'The guvnor calls,' he said and stood up to head out of the squad room and along the corridor. He knocked and entered. Was surprised to find that Colin was not alone. There was a uniformed constable in the cramped space, too.

'Mike,' he nodded as he closed the door behind him. Then turned to his boss. 'What's up?'

'Another case that might be related to yours.'

'Really?' Pete frowned.

Colin nodded to the uniformed man, who said, 'There was a hit-and-run last Wednesday. A middle-aged male. Car knocked him over as it was leaving the location. He died last night. There's only four houses down there, but you know what it's like canvassing an area. There's always a few not in. In this case, just one, and they weren't in the next day, either. Or the next. Been on holiday, as it turns out. Got back last night and found that they'd been burgled and their car stolen with the keys that they'd left in a bedroom drawer. So, what's the odds that it was their car that knocked our victim over?'

Pete raised his eyebrows and turned to Colin. 'Pretty good, you'd think. And a break-in for car keys...' He nodded. 'Whereabouts was it?'

'Dunrich Close, off Magdalen Road.'

'What time?'

'Half past two-ish. Ambulance was called at Fourteen-thirty-three.'

Pete's eyes widened. 'In broad daylight. And the victim? Who was he?'

'His name was Mark Radbourne. Lived in the Close. He was on his way home from the pub, according to his wife. He'd been meeting up with some old work colleagues for a bit of a lunchtime get-together. The neighbour heard the impact, went out to see what was going on and found him. Called the ambulance and us and fetched his Mrs out.'

Pete let out a pent-up breath. 'It could fit with our case. What are the chances of forensics at the address the car was nicked from by now? Did they report the theft right away?'

'Yes, but who knows what they'd done before we got there? I mean, they made the right noises, but...' He shrugged.

'Who attended?'

'I did.'

'How soon after the report?' Pete knew how busy the uniformed branch could get. They sometimes might not be able to get to a location for a few hours, by which time the owners could have done anything to rectify the situation, as they saw it.

He grimaced. 'A couple of hours.'

Pete nodded. 'Have Forensics been sent?'

'Not yet.'

'Best get that done, then, ASAP. You've got the details of the car and so on?'

Mike nodded and handed him a folded sheet of paper. 'Car, owners' names, address and phone number. And the same for the victim.'

'Thanks.' Pete didn't bother to open the sheet now. He knew Mike of old. He was a good officer. Would have done everything there was to be done. 'No witnesses, then?'

Mike shook his head. 'People were all out to work or indoors, either having their lunch or a nap after it. We got Traffic to put a sign up asking for witnesses outside Zenith House, right by where the Close comes out, but we've had no response yet.'

'It's a busy road,' Pete said.

Magdalen Road was one of the main routes in and out of the city centre from the east. He knew where the close was – at least, he was familiar with the building Mike had mentioned beside its entrance. It was a distinctive white 1930s art-deco construction, known throughout the city and beyond, that for years had been a garage and car salesroom. And it was only a few hundred yards from a location where he and some of his team had spent a lot of time on a recent case, observing the address of a witness' grandmother.

'People must have seen a car haring out of there like a maniac,' he said. 'But who's going to take that much notice? Plus, it depends how often a person drives past there, doesn't it? There's no guarantee that your witnesses have seen the sign yet.'

'Or that they want to be bothered getting involved, if they have,' Mike retorted.

Pete pursed his lips. The uniformed man wasn't wrong. 'OK, we'll follow it up. Thanks.'

Mike nodded. 'I'll leave you to it, then. You know where to find me.'

'Yes.'

As he stepped out, Pete turned to Colin, seated behind his desk. 'If we've got two now, we're going to need one of the incident rooms. It makes the Lockwood case a lot less likely to be an inside job. Although we'll go and interview the car owner, see if we can find a connection to the Lockwoods, to start with.'

'Right. And get Forensics out there. And to check the victim's clothes. Might be some paint transfer to confirm or deny the car's make and colour.'

Pete gave a quick nod. 'We're on it.'

*

'So, what did the guvnor want?' Dave asked as Pete settled back into his chair in the squad room.

'To tell me about another car that was stolen last week, with somebody getting injured in the process. Fatally, as it turned out.'

Dave grimaced. 'Where was this?'

'That little cul-de-sac down the side of the old Volvo garage on Magdalen Road.'

'And what car was it?' Ben asked.

Dick chuckled. 'That's it, get your priorities right, Spike.'

Pete opened the sheet of paper Mick had handed him and flattened it on his desk. 'A Jag,' he said. 'S-Type.'

'What, like the old Morse-mobile?' Ben asked. 'That'll be off abroad by now, or stripped for parts.'

'I don't know one model from another,' Pete admitted. 'But you're probably right about what's happened to it.'

'And what about the victim?' Jane asked.

Pete related what he knew. 'So, if you can send Forensics to the address and to the hospital, to collect the victim's clothes – he'll be with Doc Chambers by now – Ben can come down there with me to find out what we can from the car owners, the victim's wife and any neighbours. Mike Sutton's already interviewed them, but it won't hurt to do it again. Dick, can you phone Mrs Anderson? Tell her not to clean the place up yet, if she hasn't already, so Forensics have at least got a chance of finding something useful. And while we're out, someone needs to get traffic camera and CCTV footage organised from Magdalen Road at the time of the attack.'

'A job for you, Titch,' Dave said with a grin, nudging Jill. 'A nice dark room with your best buddy.'

'Well-volunteered, Dave,' Pete said, drawing a triumphant laugh from Jill. 'Come on, Ben.'

*

Dunrich Close was a short and narrow dead-end road that went down the side of the art-deco former car salesroom, between it and a large, white-rendered house with extensive gardens stretching up to Magdalen Road. Beyond the big house, the road widened out into a turning area with a short row of garages on the left which Pete guessed belonged to the flats in the old showroom and three bungalows with attached garages of their own facing back up towards the main road.

He parked beside the white house on the right and they stepped out. The car had been stolen from the largest of the three bungalows, set over to the right, partially hidden by shrubbery, while the hit-and-run victim, Mark Radbourne, had lived in the bungalow on the left in front of them as they walked up. Pete headed there first.

The front door was on the left, in the porch that attached the garage to the side of the home. Pete reached for the bell-push but hadn't touched it when the inner door opened and a woman not much older than he was stepped through, reaching for the door. He took a half-step back and took out his warrant card.

Her dark hair was lank, her face dull and blotchy, with no makeup. 'Yes?' she asked.

'Hello, Mrs Radbourne?'

She nodded.

'I'm DS Pete Gayle with Exeter CID,' he told her. 'This is my colleague, PC Myers.'

'Come in,' she said without waiting to ask what they were doing there.

Pete stepped in, leaving Ben to shut the door behind them, and followed her through to a sitting room at the front of the house. When she offered them a seat and settled into an armchair that faced the net-curtained window, he realised that was why she'd known they were approaching.

'Thank you.' He settled himself on the sofa. 'How are you coping?'

She shrugged.

'I'm sorry for your loss,' he said. 'It must have been a shock. You didn't see what happened?'

She shook her head. 'I was in the kitchen, out the back. Heard an engine roar, but that was all until Trevor came knocking on the door and...' She stopped, shaking her head slowly. 'I still can't believe he's gone.'

'I was told your husband had been out with some former colleagues, is that right?'

'Yeah, just up to the Mount Radford.' Another shake of the head as Pete's mind conjured an image of the old Victorian-looking pub on a corner of Magdalen Road. 'A couple of hundred yards, that's all. And even then, he was nearly home. Right outside them garages over there, he was.' She nodded towards the short row that stood between them and the former showroom, facing out across the end of the close. 'Thoughtless bastard.' She blinked. 'The one that mowed him down, I mean, not Mark.'

'Of course,' Pete agreed. 'And that's why we're here. To find out who did it and catch him.'

'Don't know how I can help.'

'To begin with, can you tell us who your husband had been out with, specifically? Talking to them might help.'

'Don't see how. They weren't with him.'

'No, but they might have seen the car when it came out on Magdalen Road.'

She grunted. 'Yeah, I suppose. Hadn't thought of that.'

'You haven't been in touch with them since it happened?'

She shook her head. 'They were his mates, not mine. And I was kind of busy with Mark in the RDE until...' She shrugged again. 'Haven't felt like talking to anyone much since then.'

'It could help, if you've got someone you can talk to,' Pete said. 'Or, if not, there's Victim Support. They're trained to listen.'

She grimaced. 'Yeah, but... Not the same, is it? Not like they knew him, cared about him.'

'You've got no children?'

'No.'

'And he was meeting up with former colleagues, so was he retired or...'

'No! He weren't that old – or well-off. He took redundancy when the firm closed down last year. Hadn't got… Well, he had got another job. Hadn't started yet, that's all. Was due to next week. I'll have to let them know, won't I?'

Pete nodded. 'What did he do?'

'Car sales. He worked up the road, there, until they moved out to Marsh Barton.' She nodded again towards the front of the house. 'Then he swapped to Reynolds' in Heavitree. Easier to get to. But they hadn't got the space for the turnover they needed in the end. And things haven't been good with the economy since Covid, have they? So, in the end, they had to call it a day. He was about to start over the river. Cowick Street.'

Pete nodded. 'I see. So, who were these guys he was meeting?'

'Like I said – former colleagues from Reynolds.' She began to list names which Ben quickly wrote down, two of them complete, three others just first names.

'OK, thank you. We'll track them down and talk to them, one way or another. You're sure there's no-one we can call to come round and visit for you?'

She shook her head and sighed heavily. 'No, I'll be OK.'

'All right. One last thing: have you or anyone else in the Close had any work done recently? Garden work, new kitchen or windows or home car maintenance – anything like that?'

She frowned. 'Not that I know of. Why?'

'It's just a theory we have to explore. Thank you for your time.' Pete stood up and shook her hand.

Back outside, they found that the bright blue sky of earlier had dulled and was now pregnant with dark clouds, heavy with the prospect of rain.

'Seems like she's still taking it in,' Ben said as they walked down her drive. 'Still in shock a bit.'

Pete nodded. 'It takes some people that way, especially when it's sudden and unexpected like that. I'll be glad to find an excuse to get down here again in the next day or two and look in on her, make sure she's all right.'

He turned left out of her driveway and crossed towards the slightly larger-looking bungalow tucked away in the far corner where the car had been stolen from. Stepping around the shrubbery of its front garden, he approached the front door – again on the side – and rang the bell.

Again, a woman answered the door, this one older, perhaps in her sixties, her grey hair carefully styled in a bob, makeup immaculate. 'Yes?'

Pete noted that her accent was Welsh, her voice soft and musical.

'DS Gayle, Exeter CID. We're here about the burglary you suffered and the car that was stolen. Your neighbour, Mr Radbourne, who was knocked over in the process has sadly died as a result of his injuries…'

Her face fell. 'Oh, my God! That's awful!' she cut across what he was saying.

'It is,' Pete agreed. 'And it's why we're taking over the case. Is your husband at home, Mrs Jackson?'

'No, he's at work.'

'No problem. We just need a quick chat and to tell you that the forensics team are on their way.'

'Oh. Yes, I got a call a little while ago about that.' She looked slightly crestfallen. 'He said something about forensics.'

'That's right. They'll need to check where the burglar gained access, where he took the car keys from and anywhere else he might have left fingerprints or DNA.'

'Yes, I see that now… Sorry. I never thought. We've had a glazier come in already and board up the window he broke in through.'

Pete grimaced. 'That's why we came down here as soon as we took over the case – to try and make sure that at least some evidence was maintained. But in the meantime, you might be able to answer a few questions for us.'

'I'll try, of course. Come in.'

Pete followed her inside, passing the open kitchen door on his left. 'So, where does your husband work?' he asked as she headed for the room next to the kitchen, which he could see was the sitting room, in this case overlooking the back garden rather than the front.

'Risingbrook. He's a teacher.'

Pete stopped moving, barely aware of Ben stumbling behind him and almost walking into him, as memories flooded his mind of another case, several years before: a young girl abducted from the street outside Risingbrook School, his own son eventually implicated as being an accomplice.

CHAPTER SEVEN

'Are you all right, Detective?'

He blinked, her voice pulling him back to the present. 'Yes, I was just… Your husband teaches at Risingbrook School?'

'He's head of English. You looked like that was something of a shock.'

'It brought some memories back. My team and I spent a bit of time there, a few years ago. Do you recall the Rosie Whitlock abduction?'

She carried on through to the sitting room, which had French doors leading out to the garden and a false fireplace on the far wall, an electric flame-effect fire within it. She waved them to the sofa and took one of the armchairs that faced the back garden. 'I do. Terrible. Poor girl. You were involved in that, were you?'

He nodded. 'You're not at work today?' he asked, changing the subject.

'Retired,' she said. 'I'm four years older than Alan and, when he got the department head, we decided it was time. We don't need a lot of money, really.'

'I see. How did you meet?'

'At school. Not this one. In Monmouth. I was school secretary. Alan came there as a bright young teacher.' She smiled. 'We married three years later. Had… Had a son.'

Pete had noticed the photograph on the mantlepiece and intended to ask.

'He died. Eight years old, he was. Sixteen years ago now. Not long after we came down here. Leukaemia.'

'I'm sorry,' Pete said. 'I know how hard it is to lose a child.'

She blinked. 'Thank you.'

'So, what brought you to Exeter?' Ben asked.

'A promotion. A bigger, better school with better prospects. Alan got a job, teaching English. A big step up from Monmouth. Much more prestigious. And the hospital had a good reputation and would be a lot closer for Eric's treatment. He was already ill by then. Had been for a bit over a year.'

'And the car,' Pete said. 'How did that come about? It's not a regular run-about, is it?'

She smiled. 'It was an indulgence, I know, but why not? Alan's always been into older cars and I'm a huge fan of John Thaw. It's not exactly the same model as Morse had, but the differences are tiny and it's a hell of a lot cheaper than the genuine Mark 2. They're like hen's teeth, and priced to match!'

'So, when did you get it?'

'To celebrate Alan's promotion.'

'A while ago, then?'

'Yes.'

'And you've just come back from holiday.'

'That's right. We decided to take advantage of the Easter break, for a change. Ten days in the sun. The Azores.'

'Lovely,' said Ben.

'Hmm. But then, to come back to this…'

The doorbell chimed and her expression soured even further. 'Who's that now?'

'It could be our forensic team,' Pete suggested and rose with her.

He hung back, letting her answer the door, stepping forward only when he saw that he'd been right. The short, stout man in white overall and shiny round glasses was instantly recognisable. 'Hello, Mr Pointer,' he said from behind her.

'Detective Sergeant Gayle,' Harold said with a nod and was instantly back to business. 'If you could show me the point of entry, madam?'

She led them into the kitchen, where Pete saw for the first time that the half-glazed back door had its glass section boarded over both inside and, he presumed, out.

'Was the glass cut or smashed?' Harold asked.

'Cut,' she said. 'There's six panels of glass in it. The one nearest the lock was cut out and laid outside on the patio.'

Pete saw Harold grimace. 'Are the pieces still there? I presume it was double-glazed.'

'Yes. And yes.'

'And once inside, where did the offender search?'

She gave a shudder. 'All over, pretty much.'

'But you've cleaned up?'

'Some, obviously. Put stuff away that he left lying around, things like that. But...' She grimaced. 'I don't know. I don't feel... It doesn't feel like home anymore, you know?' She lifted her gaze to Pete, who was behind Harold and a head taller. 'It's been... Violated.'

'You'll get over that,' he assured her. 'It'll take time and effort. And maybe some redecoration or new furniture.' He offered her a quick smile as Harold stepped around him, heading for the kitchen door. 'An excuse to change things up a bit, maybe. Do some of the things you may have been wanting to and haven't got round to, if there are any. And some security features might make you feel better. A doorbell camera. Alarm system. Things like that.'

'Hmm. We talked about that last night, but where do you go that won't just be wanting to rip you off?'

'There's plenty of advice on-line. Police-UK, Which and so on.'

The crime scene supervisor returned with his metal case in hand. 'If you don't mind, Mrs Jackson, we'll make a start.'

'Oh. Yes, of course.'

'What about the garage?' Pete asked. 'You've obviously gone in and out from this end, but the outer door. Was it down when you got home?'

'Yes. It looked perfectly normal.'

'And you and your husband haven't touched it since?'

'Only to re-lock it with the key from the outside.'

Harold exchanged a glance with Pete, understanding his point, then started directing his team to other parts of the home.

'PC Myers and I will get out of the way,' Pete said to her. 'It might be best if you leave them a key and go out for a bit. Let them get on with it.'

She looked dismayed.

'I don't know how well you know Mrs Radbourne, but I'm pretty sure she could use a friendly face. And I'm sure Harold will make sure everything's ship-shape before he leaves, won't you, Harold?'

'Of course,' he said, tipping his head.

'I just need to check with you,' Pete said to the woman. 'Have you had any work done here in the past few weeks?'

'What sort of work?'

'Anything,' he said as, behind him, Harold started undoing the temporary repair the glazier had made to the back door. 'Garden maintenance, windscreen repair on the car, new kitchen or windows…'

She shook her head with a grimace. 'No, nothing.'

'All right. One last thing: do you know Sam or Heather Lockwood from Whitehorn Lane, off Pennsylvania?'

Her lips pulled down as she thought. 'No, not that I can think of. Why?'

'It's another case we're working. There might have been a connection, but clearly not. Thank you for your time.' He turned to Harold. 'I'll talk to you later.' Then he shook the woman's hand and left, taking Ben with him.

'No point going to the big house, is there?' Ben said as they headed out towards Pete's car. 'Mike's already covered it, according to his report. But Zenith House might give us something, and you'd have thought there'd be a security camera or two along Magdalen Road. Or do you want to go up to the school first and see Mr Jackson?'

'I don't see a need to go to the school. Mike already interviewed Alan Jackson. And as for Zenith House, whoever took that Jag either struck too damn lucky for words or knew it was there. Which makes the residents there as much suspects as they are potential witnesses. So, to start with, we'll track down the victim's buddies who he was out with before he was killed and find out if they saw anything. We'll have to arrange for Ops Support to do a CCTV trawl of Magdalen Road for us if Dave hasn't done that already.'

*

'Well, we've got no good news,' Dave said in response to Pete's request for an update as he settled into his chair, back in the squad room. 'Except for the fact that we've got Incident Room One as of tomorrow morning.'

'OK, so what bad news have you got?' Pete asked.

'We've finished going through the CCTV we collected and got bugger all of any use. And nothing from what Graham could give us, either. Or ANPR. We also checked on Aidan Lockwood's business partner and their receptionist, secretary or whatever she likes to think of herself as. Not their alibis, as such, but their movements.'

Pete nodded, hiding the disappointment he couldn't help feeling in spite of the reduced chance suggested by the new case of the Lockwood killings being an inside job. 'Did you arrange for Ops Support to do a trawl of Magdalen Road for us, for CCTV from last Wednesday?'

'Jane did.'

'When are they getting onto it?'

'Later this afternoon,' she said.

'By which time we'll hopefully have heard something from Harold, as well,' he said. 'Although I'm not holding out too much hope that it'll be positive. OK, we need to talk to White and Collins at the window company. See what they've got to offer in the way of alibis for either or both of the attacks. Jane, take Dave with you and talk to one of them, Dick and Jill take the other one. Ben and I have got some friends of Mark Radbourne's to track down.'

He took out his notebook and opened it on his desk. 'What were they, Ben?'

With chairs scraping and screens being switched off around them as the others prepared to leave, Ben took out his notebook and read out the five names, three of them just first names, and Pete wrote them down.

'Right, you take the top one, I'll take the second. The others, we can check with those two when we find them and, worst case, we can get onto whoever owned the showroom they used to work for. They have to keep all their records for seven years, to comply with the tax man.'

'Right. Of course, there is one link between these two cases.'

'What's that?'

'Teaching. Heather Lockwood was a teacher and so was Alan Jackson, until a few years ago. And he still works at a school.'

'True, but she was retired and she was a primary school teacher. Risingbrook is for secondary and beyond.'

'Yeah, but kids go from one to the other. I can see one going from whichever school she taught in on to Risingbrook and, especially if others took the same route, having a traumatic time extended through both.'

'But, what's that got to do with the teachers?'

Ben shrugged. 'Who knows? The kid might have seen them as not helpful or even adding to the problem for some reason. They might even be on some sort of list.'

'Then maybe I'll take both the names at the top of this list while you find out which school Heather Lockwood taught at and whether any of their pupils went on to Risingbrook.'

'OK.'

Leaving Ben to do as he'd asked, Pete reached for the phone book from among the books and files lined and stacked in the overcrowded, haphazard-looking open-fronted filing boxes along the backs of the desks, behind their computer screens.

Referring to the list, he opened the book around the mid-point and flipped through to the Ns. Quickly, he found what he wanted and gave a soft grunt. There were three listings for T. Naylor. One of them was in Clyst Honiton, another in the Polsloe district of Exter, and the third address, he recognised but couldn't quite place. He looked it up and found it was across the river, just south of Cowick Barton playing fields.

His lips tightened as he remembered having to visit the mother of a young girl about the same age as his own daughter who had been snatched off the street and murdered a couple of years before. They'd found her body, with others, in an old mine shaft in the woods outside the city.

He blinked away the memory and laid his pen across the flimsy page beneath the entry in Polsloe while he picked up his phone to dial.

'Hello?' A female voice answered after several rings.

'Ah. I was hoping to speak to Terry.'

'Who's speaking?'

'DS Gayle with Exeter CID. It's about his friend, Mark Radbourne.'

'Oh, is there…? Hold on.'

He heard brief muttering then a male voice. 'Hello?'

'Hello, is that Terence Nelson?'

'Yes.'

'You used to work at Reynolds' in Heavitree with Mark Radbourne?'

'That's right. I saw him last week. Why? What's happened?'

'There's been an incident. I'm afraid Mr Radbourne's dead, Mr Nelson. He was…'

'Dead? Are you for real? He was bright as a button, the other day.'

'He was involved in a hit-and-run incident, Mr Nelson. On the way home from seeing you and your friends, in fact.'

'How the hell…? It's only a couple of hundred yards! How can he have been…?'

'You didn't see anything? Or hear anything?'

'No, I… I can't believe this.'

'I'm sorry, Mr Nelson, but it's true.'

'And you said… But I thought… CID do murders and that, don't they? What's a hit-and-run got to do with that?'

'It happened in the course of another crime being committed, Mr Nelson. What time did you leave the pub?'

'About ten minutes after he did.'

'And you didn't see anything? A speeding car, for instance?'

'No.'

'How did you get to the pub?'

'I walked. It's not that far. We're only just up between Belvedere Park and the cemetery.'

'I see. I've got a list of names in front of me from Mrs Radbourne of the people she expected were probably at that get-together last Wednesday. I wonder if you can help me with it. Three of them, she only knew first names for and she hadn't got any actual contact details. There's only four on the list apart from yourself.'

'That'll be right.'

'OK, the first one is Derek Parsons.'

'He's in Birchy Barton. I've got his number. Hold on.' He set the phone down for a moment before picking it up again. 'Here it is.' He read it out and Pete wrote it down. Birchy Barton, he knew, was another suburb on the east side of Exeter, between the Devon and Cornwall Police headquarters and the hospital where his wife worked.

'Then I've got Andy.'

'He wasn't there. Was supposed to be, but he didn't turn up.'

'Ed?'

'Yeah, Ed Gulliver.' Again, he quoted a phone number and Pete noted it down.

'Dan?'

'Yep, he was there. Miller.' Another number was forthcoming, this one a mobile rather than a land-line.

'So, who else was there with you?' Pete asked. 'The more potential witnesses we can talk to, the more likely we are to come across someone who actually saw something.'

'Just one other chap, used to be in the workshop. George Masters. Actually, he left at the same time as Mark. I was next. The others stayed on 'til the place closed down.'

'Have you got a number for George?'

'No. Ed will have, though. He organised it.'

'OK, thank you for your help. And I'm sorry for your loss.'

'How's his Mrs coping?'

Pete grimaced. 'She's still in shock, but she's determined to get through it.'

He grunted. 'I can't say I know her, really. Met her a couple of times, but that's all.'

'She seems like a very private person,' Pete said.

'Yeah. Chalk and cheese, but they seem... Seemed to be happy together.'

Pete said his goodbyes, hung up and dialled the number he'd been given for Ed Gulliver.

'Yep,' the male voice answered briskly.

'Edmund Gulliver?' Pete checked.

'That's right.'

'I'm DS Peter Gayle with Exeter CID. I got your name from Mrs Radbourne. Mark's wife.'

'Oh, yes?'

Clearly, Ed Gulliver was not a man used to giving anything away in conversations. 'There's been an incident that we're investigating, Mr Gulliver. Following your get-together with Mr Radbourne and the others, there was an accident. A hit-and-run. Mr Radbourne was struck by a car in the process of fleeing a crime-scene. He died.'

'Shit. He's dead?'

'He died of his injuries last night, in the Royal Devon and Exeter hospital,' Pete confirmed. 'So, as you'll understand, we're seeking possible witnesses.'

'Shit,' he said again. 'Well, I can't help you there. Sorry.'

'No, I gather you stayed on in the pub after Mr Radbourne left. But there was a George Masters, also there, who might have seen something useful. I was told you might have his number.'

'Well, yes, I expect I have, but...'

Pete pursed his lips. Gulliver's hesitation was a problem he was coming across more and more often, these days: people not trusting an unfamiliar voice on the phone. He could understand it. Just because he said he was police, they didn't know that he was telling the truth. 'Have you got a mobile phone, Mr Gulliver?'

'Yes.'

'Well then, if we hang up and you call 101 from that, tell them you've got a message for me and they'll put you through.'

He grunted. 'OK,' he said and hung up.

'It's a sad reflection when you've got to do that,' Ben observed.

'True, but that's the way things are, these days,' Pete said. 'Better safe than sorry. How are you getting on?'

'According to her government listing, she was at Maizefield for fifteen years.'

The one Pete's own kids had attended. He could ask his daughter about her. But... 'It's not that likely that any of the kids from there would go on to Risingbrook,' he said. 'It's not exactly a posh area that it caters for. We'll have to check, though.'

His phone rang and he picked it up. 'DS Gayle.'

'Ed Gulliver. I've got George Masters' number for you.'

'Ah, thanks for getting back to me. OK, I'm ready when you are.'

Gulliver quoted the number and Pete wrote it down against Masters' name. 'Got it. Thanks again.'

Gulliver hesitated. 'I can't believe Mark's dead. Just wrong place, wrong time?'

'That about sums it up,' Pete agreed. 'Thirty seconds earlier or later and he'd have been as safe as houses.'

'Shit.'

His favourite word, Pete thought. 'Yeah. But whoever it was, we'll catch them.'

'I wouldn't mind the chance to deliver some natural justice when you do,' Gulliver said. 'The courts don't seem to be effective anymore.'

'Hmm. Sadly, Mr Gulliver, that would put you in the same position as the offender we're looking for.'

'Huh. At least you said, "sadly."'

'I couldn't possibly comment further. Again, thanks for your help.'

Pete hung up and dialled again.

The voice that answered this time sounded a lot older and a lot more cheerful. 'Hello.'

'George Masters?'

'That's me.'

'I'm DS Gayle with Exeter CID. I need to ask you a couple of questions, if that's OK.'

'CID? As in police?'

'That's right, Mr Masters. It won't take two minutes.'

'OK. What's it about?'

'You were at the Mount Radford with some friends last Wednesday.'

'Yeah, that's right. How do you know that?'

'I've just been speaking to one of them. Can I ask, did you notice anything out of the ordinary when you left? Anything that stood out?'

'I don't know. Why? What did you have in mind? Must have been something or you wouldn't be asking.'

'Perhaps a car speeding past or away? The sound of a racing engine?'

'I don't... Yeah, thinking back, I did hear something like that. Tyres squealing first. I remember thinking that was going to cost him a bit, to replace them. Then something roared away. But it was behind me. I was a few yards up College Road. I looked round because it sounded like a big engine. Meaty, you know? But I never seen nothing.'

Pete suppressed a sigh of disappointment. 'All right. Thank you for your time, Mr Masters. Have a good evening.' He slumped back in his chair and hung up.

CHAPTER EIGHT

'So, it looks like we'll have to visit Risingbrook, after all,' Pete said.

'We'd best get a wiggle on, then, if…' Ben stopped with a grunt. 'Forget that. It's not like a comprehensive, is it? It doesn't shut down and get locked up and deserted by four o'clock.'

'True. Still, the sooner we get the information, the sooner we can act on it. Come on.' Pete switched off his computer and stood up to lead the way out of the squad room once more.

By the time they got to the school it was after 4:00pm. All the parents picking up their non-resident children had dispersed and the big iron-work drive gates between their solid red and white brick pillars were closed. Pete parked on the street and they went in on foot through a smaller gate beside the main ones, walking up the wide, hard-packed gravel drive between expansive mown lawns towards the ornate brick façade. Big wooden doors at the top of wide stone steps gave into a hallway with checkerboard marble floor tiles and dark wood panelling, the contrastingly modern reception desk sitting over to the left, staffed by a woman in her fifties, iron-grey hair coiffed and sprayed into a neatly curled helmet above arched eyebrows, an aquiline nose and thin lips. She looked up from the computer she was typing rapidly into as Pete stepped in, followed by Ben, and one eyebrow rose.

Approaching the desk, he took his warrant card from inside his jacket. 'DS Gayle, Exeter CID.'

'Yes, I remember you.'

It was Pete's turn to raise an eyebrow. 'Really? That was a long time ago.'

'But a memorable occasion. How can I help you, Detective Sergeant?'

'I presume you keep a computerised record of the students here. Names, addresses, emergency contacts, when they came here and so on?'

'Yes.'

'Does it include which school they came from?'

'It does.'

'And is it searchable by those schools?'

'No.'

He grimaced. 'That's a shame. We need to find out which male students would have come here, if any, from Maizefield Primary over the past… Let's say ten years.'

'May one ask why?'

'There's a link between two recent deaths that involves the two schools.'

'I see. Well, I'm afraid you've got your work cut out for you then. Assuming the head grants you access to the records. We have twelve hundred pupils a year through Risingbrook.'

'Are they divisible by male and female, at least?' Ben asked.

She tipped her head in a nod.

'Well, that's something. It's still twelve thousand records to scan through, though.'

'We'd better see the head and get his permission as soon as possible, then,' Pete said, looking to the receptionist.

She picked up the phone at her elbow and dialled. 'I have Detective Sergeant Gayle and a constable here for you,' she said without preamble when it was answered. 'Very well.' She hung up.

'Mr Fergusson will see you now. His office is…'

'I remember it,' Pete broke in. 'Thank you.'

He led the way past the central stairs and along the corridor to the right, passing formal photographic portraits, most of them black-and-white, of previous school principals. He hadn't reached his destination, marked by a black sign with gold lettering that stuck out from the wall above one of the several doors, when the door opened and the man Pete remembered stepped out.

'Detective. I hope you're not bearing more bad news for us?'

'That depends if you've had the latest,' Pete said.

The now greying fiftyish man's face fell.

'Have you heard about Mr Jackson's car?' Pete asked.

Fergusson's expression lifted. 'I have. He told me earlier. Is that what you're here about?' He raised a hand. 'Come in.'

'In a way,' Pete admitted, stepping into the high-ceilinged office with its book-lined walls and large mahogany desk in front of the tall window.

'Please, take a seat,' Fergusson offered, stepping around to the far side of the desk. There were two hard-backed chairs on the near side of the desk. Pete and Ben sat down.

'Someone was knocked over in the process of the theft,' Pete expanded. 'He later died in hospital, which brought the case to us, and we're exploring the possibility that it might be linked to another case – in which a teacher from Maizefield Primary school in Whipton was killed.'

His eyes widened in horror. 'That's awful. But how can we help?'

'We wondered if the perpetrator might have attended both schools,' Pete explained. 'So, we were hoping that your computer records might provide us with a list – albeit probably a short one – of male pupils who've come here from there over the past ten years or so. I gather from the receptionist that won't be the case – at least, not easily. But we still need to try. To either confirm or discount the link.'

'I see. No, Catherine's right: our system won't make that an easy search. But of course, you can have whatever access you need, in the circumstances. We're eternally grateful to you for bringing Rosie Whitlock back to us, Detective Sergeant.'

Pete nodded, accepting the comment. 'Thank you. How are the records filed? By name, date, or what?'

'By year and then by name.'

'But they're divisible by gender?'

'Yes. It was only in 1982 that we first accepted girls so…' He shrugged.

'When does the system go back to?'

'1983. Before that, it's all on paper and we haven't transferred any of it.'

'Right.' Pete nodded. 'We won't need to go nearly that far back. At least, I hope not.'

'The only issue is data-protection. I'm afraid the governors would have kittens if I were to allow the records off the premises. We have some rather prominent people's children here, as you're aware. We do have a computer room that you could make use of, however, if that helps?'

Pete grimaced. 'How many terminals?'

'Twenty-eight.'

He tipped his head. 'More than enough for the six of us, then.' That would still leave them up to two thousand records each to scan through, but it had to be done. 'All right. I'll call the rest of my team in.'

*

Pete waited until he was standing outside the big doors of the school, gazing across the expanse of grass towards the road before calling Jane's mobile number.

It was picked up almost immediately. 'DC Bennett speaking.'

'How did you get on?' he asked.

'Just checking his alibi now, but it looks like Brian White's in the clear. He was playing in a darts tournament Saturday night. Plenty of witnesses.'

'So, you're back at the nick?'

'Yes, why?'

'Are you all there?'

'Yes.'

'Good. Get yourselves down here to Risingbrook. We've got two or three hours' work here, between us, ploughing through old school records.'

'Oh, joy. OK, we'll see you in a bit.'

He'd barely hung up when his phone rang in his hand. He checked the screen. The number was withheld, which suggested a work call. He tapped the green icon. 'DS Gayle.'

'The Dunrich Close case is going to be on the news tonight,' Colin Underhill's gruff voice said.

'Why?' Pete demanded, frowning. 'We've got nothing worthwhile to tell them yet.'

'The press got hold of it somehow so the Chief's going to do an announcement. Reluctantly.'

'It might be useful to do one at some point, but not now. We're not ready. We're still waiting for the results of a CCTV and witness search on Magdalen Road and the forensic search of the address where the Jag was stolen from.'

'I'm just giving you the heads-up.'

Pete sighed. 'I suppose I'd better ring her and give her a quick briefing, then.'

'Yep.'

Before Pete could say more, his boss had hung up.

'Problem, boss?' Ben asked from a step behind him and to the side.

'The Chief's planning to do a press release tonight on the Dunrich Close case,' Pete told him.

'What for?' Ben demanded with a frown.

'To fend them off. They've got hold of it from somewhere.'

Ben shook his head. 'It makes you wonder how, doesn't it? Who told them?'

Pete shrugged. 'It's premature but, depending on what Ops Support come back with, it could be useful. We said so ourselves, earlier.'

'Yeah, but in a managed way, not going off half-cocked, making us look like idiots.'

'*We're* not going on there, the Chief is.'

'Huh. And if she feels like an idiot, guess who she'll blame. It won't be the press, I bet.'

Pete sighed. 'No. Nor the guvnor. I'd best give her a ring and get it over with.'

He lifted his phone and dialled.

*

There was no-one in the high-ceilinged classroom when they went in so they clustered at the far side from the door, switched on the machines and settled in, dividing the records, which were stored on CDs, between them.

They'd been working solidly for almost an hour and a half when Jill's voice came from behind Pete.

'Hello, hello, hello. There's a familiar name.'

He turned to face her. 'Who's that?'

'Richie Young. Remember him from the Rosie Whitlock case? The goth boy – or as close to it as he could get away with in a place like this.'

'I remember.' Richie Young had been an awkward lad, the same age as Rosie Whitlock. He'd had a crush on her, and Pete recalled that he'd had several illicit photos of her on his phone. They'd cleared him of any involvement in her abduction, but he still remained vaguely on the radar because of those pictures. 'Is he relevant?'

'He went to Maizefield. Came here on a scholarship.'

'So, yes. Well spotted.'

Young was the first male pupil they'd found who had attended both schools.

'How old would he be now?' Dave asked.

'Twenty,' Ben responded. 'Old enough to drive. And to buy what he needed to break into the Lockwoods' and the Jacksons' without attracting attention.'

'Right,' Pete said. 'Make a note. We'll check him out when we've finished here.'

Silence descended on the room again until Dick said, 'Here's another.'

'You're awake then, Grey Man?' Jill said.

'I've got more stamina than you, Titch.'

'What have you found?' Pete asked.

'Gavin Prescott. Came here in 2014 so he'll be... Twenty-two now. Address back then was on Pinhoe Road. No note of any scholarship,' he added, looking at Jill.

'Ooooh!' she retorted. 'One up for yours, then. His parents could afford to send him here.'

'Which begs the question of why they sent him to the local primary school to mix with the plebs first,' Dave said.

'Well, maybe you've just answered your own question,' Jane suggested. 'To let him mix with the plebs for a bit, let him get used to dealing with ordinary folk before they stuck him in here with the upper echelons. Teach him how to interact at all levels.'

'Or they came into some money,' Ben put in.

Jane tipped her head. 'Yeah, or that.'

'Either way, another one for the shortlist,' Pete said. 'Let's finish what we're doing, then we can look them up on the PNC and go from there.'

Ten minutes later they had finished trawling the school records and the two names they'd found had been checked and both come up negative.

'All right,' Pete said. 'Let's find out their current addresses and any vehicles associated with them.'

'Richy's still living at home,' Jill said. 'Or he was at the last council voter check.'

Dave looked up from his mobile phone. 'Gavin Prescott comes up with an address on Thackeray Road.'

'He hasn't moved far, then,' Dick said.

'No. And he's got no car.'

'Richy has,' Jill said. 'A Seat Ibiza in black.'

'Surprise, surprise,' Pete said. 'I seem to remember everything he owned was black when we last dealt with him.' He turned back to Dave. 'Prescott might not have a car of his own, but has he got access to one? Does he live alone?'

'Yes, according to the electoral register. He might borrow his dad's or his girlfriend's car, though.'

'Has he got a licence?'

Dave grimaced. 'Since when did that make a difference in certain circles? But no, he hasn't.'

'Less likely, then.'

'Yeah, but you don't drive to somewhere you're going to nick a car from, do you? You get a lift.'

'True, but you've got to be able to drive away from there. We'll check their socials and see what more we can find out in the morning. See if they've got alibis. But it's turned six now and some of us have got homes to go to and reasons to get there. How's Marjory, Dick?' he asked, Marjory being the older man's wife.

He grimaced. 'Not so good. But the carer's pretty flexible.'

Pete nodded, knowing that Feeney didn't like discussing his home life, though they all knew his wife's multiple sclerosis was getting worse. 'OK, let's get out of here. I've just got a couple of messages to check.'

His phone had pinged with a couple of incoming messages while they were working, but he'd ignored them as he concentrated on what he was doing. Now, he opened the app and saw the one on the top of the list was from Harold Pointer.

'Forensics must have finished,' he said and opened the message.

Dry as ever, Harold had typed: *Dunrich Close search complete. No non-resident fingerprints found. DNA samples taken. Results 36hours.*

'No help there, then,' he muttered. And it wasn't worth forwarding the message to Chief Inspector Naylor. She'd have already given the press briefing. He scrolled down to the next message. This was from Andy Sumner of Ops Support. 'Magdalen Road canvas complete. No CCTV covering Close entrance. More distant examples obtained. On your desk. No witnesses found.'

The more distant CCTV could prove useful when it came to building a case against whoever the offender turned out to be but it was unlikely to help in identifying them. Pete pursed his lips.

'We haven't cracked the case yet, then?' Dave asked.

Pete put his phone away and closed down the computer in front of him. 'No.'

CHAPTER NINE

Pete closed the Internet on his computer and looked up at the rest of his team, all of them working diligently despite the early hour – it was not yet 8:00am.

'Nothing on either of their Facebook pages,' he announced.

'Nor their Instagram or X,' Jane replied.

'Emails look clear and innocent,' Ben reported.

'You got into their emails?' Pete demanded.

Ben shrugged. 'Speeds things up, doesn't it? If there's nothing there, it doesn't come up and if there is, we get a warrant and go back and find it legally.'

'I don't think that's the attitude our politically correct brethren would encourage,' Dick said.

'So what is? Letting someone else get injured or killed while we faff about waiting on stuff there's no need for?'

'In a word – yes,' Dick said. 'By the strictest letter of the book or not at all and never mind the consequences, that's their mantra. You know that as well as I do.'

'End of the day, we've got nothing on either of them,' Jill said. 'Nowt on the PNC, socials, emails… The only place we haven't checked – and that would need a warrant – is WhatsApp.'

'And the games forums,' Dave added. 'I've heard of them being used for criminal communications before.'

'But there's no indication that Prescott's into gaming. Nothing in his socials, anyway.'

'Nor his emails,' Ben added.

'Doesn't mean he doesn't use the forums,' Dave pointed out. 'You can delete things out of your email.'

'Yeah, but they're recoverable from source,' Ben pointed out.

'Really?'

Ben nodded confidently.

'So,' Pete concluded. 'Either they're not linked – and to be fair, Young was a geeky kid a couple of years younger than Prescott so it's unlikely they'd have struck up any kind of friendship at school, though you never know – or they are, and they're very aware of the dangers of having that link exposed to outsiders. Like us, for example. I think the best course is for me and you, Jill, to go and speak to Richie Young while Dave and Ben track Prescott down and have a word with him so that they can't confer in between us speaking to one then the other. Dick and Jane, you can move us down to Incident Room One and get everything set up for both cases. Something links them. We've just got to figure out what. Or who. And when you've done that, see if any other teachers have been targeted. Particularly at the two schools where our victims worked, but more broadly as well.'

'If you're going down that road, why just teachers?' Dave asked, shutting down his own computer. 'Why not other staff or even pupils or their parents?'

Pete tipped his head. 'Fair point. But let's talk to the two lads first, before we get too excited.'

*

Richie Young had a job in a small record shop on South Street in the city centre of Exeter. An old-fashioned bell tinkled from above the door as Pete stepped inside, followed by Jill. He looked around. Racks of twelve-inch albums lined three walls and filled a space in the centre, leaving just enough room for two people to pass down either side to and from the counter across the back.

Richie – his hair now several inches longer than Pete remembered it and dyed jet black to match his T-shirt and jeans – was serving a customer. He glanced up at the sound of the bell but didn't show any recognition. Pete waited for him to finish what he was doing and for the customer to leave before stepping up to the counter. With one other customer still in the shop, he was thankful that the music was no more than a background hum so he could keep his voice down to a conversational level.

'Hello, Richie. DS Gayle. This is PC Evans.'

'I remember you.'

'Have you got a minute? We need a word.'

He glanced at the customer, a female of around Pete's own age, who was rifling through the racks at the far end of the shop. 'What about?'

'Do you remember a Mrs Lockwood? Primary school teacher.'

His eyes widened. 'That's going back a bit. Yes, vaguely. Why?'

'And at Risingbrook, a Mr Jackson.'

'Taught English. Yes. What about them?'

'That's my question. What have they got in common?'

He shrugged. 'They're both teachers.'

'And they both taught you.'

He shook his head. 'Jackson did, Mrs Lockwood didn't. I was in Miss Smith's class. You still haven't told me why you're asking about them.'

Pete pursed his lips. 'One more connection between them – and you: Gavin Prescott.'

'Who's he?'

'You don't remember him?'

'Gavin Prescott? No.' He thought for a second. 'Hmm. There was a Prescott at school. Two or three years above me. He might have been Gavin or Gary or something like that. Is that him?'

Pete nodded. 'That's him. You're not in touch with him in any way?'

His lips pushed up. 'No. Why would I be?'

Pete shrugged. 'I don't know. Shared interests, maybe. Gaming. Records.' He raised a hand to indicate their surroundings. 'I didn't know places like this still existed.'

'There aren't many. We get trade from all over.'

'What is this, all new stock or second-hand, or what?'

'A mix. Vinyl's made a comeback, the last few years. People seem to like the imperfection of it.'

Pete nodded. 'I like an LP myself. Got quite a few.' Jill nudged him from behind. He turned and found the customer waiting with a couple of LPs in hand. He stepped aside. 'You go ahead.'

He stood back while Young served the woman, then stepped forward again. 'So, to answer your question: something's happened to both Mrs Lockwood and Mr Jackson.' He continued to watch carefully for a reaction. 'Mr Jackson's car was stolen last week. A man – a neighbour – was run over and killed in the process. And in a separate incident, Mrs Lockwood was killed too. In her case, there's no bones to be made about it: she was murdered.'

Young's eyes widened again in shock. 'My God! Like I said, she didn't teach me, but now I think of her, she always seemed like a nice woman.'

'And what about Mr Jackson?'

He shrugged again. 'He could be a bit of a prick at times but he was mostly OK to me.'

Pete's eyebrows rose at that. 'A bit of a prick how?'

'If he was in a bad mood, the whole class suffered. And he was never generous with his marks. Gave people a C when they deserved a B, a B when they should have got an A. Things like that.'

'Maybe he was trying to push you to do better by the time you got to exams.'

He grimaced. 'Nobody saw it that way. His pass-rate was good, though.'

'But he made enemies along the way?'

'I don't know about enemies, but not many friends. You said his car got nicked?'

Pete nodded.

'That old Jag?'

'That's right.'

He sucked air through pursed lips. 'That'll have pissed him off, I bet! He worshipped that car.'

'I wouldn't think he was too chuffed at his neighbour getting killed, either,' Jill pointed out.

He turned to face her for the first time. 'No, but… You know what I mean.'

'Actually, I don't,' she said. 'I've never met Mr Jackson.'

'If you had, you'd know. He treated that car better than he did us kids. Constantly cleaning it, polishing it.'

'So, he got it looked after properly?' Pete asked.

'Hell, yeah. Serviced twice a year, needed or not. And it probably wasn't. But regular as clockwork. You could tell because it wasn't in the car park. First week of the autumn term and first week of March.'

Pete nodded. 'So, having come from a school like that, how did you end up here?'

Young looked around. 'This place? It's mine.'

Pete's eyes widened in shock. 'Yours? What, outright?'

'The business, yeah.'

'When did you start it?'

'Two and a half years ago.'

Pete tipped his head. 'Must have taken a bit of setting up. And financing, post-Covid.'

'I got a business start-up loan. They were pushing them at the time. Trying to get things moving after the pandemic, I suppose. And I'd always been interested in records, so I knew the market.'

'Going well, is it?'

He shrugged. 'The rates and the loan repayments make it tight some months, but I'm surviving.'

Hence still living at home with your parents, Pete thought. 'Good for you. Long may places like this prosper.'

*

'No other school staff in or around the city have been attacked or burgled recently,' Jane said as Pete hung his jacket on the back of his chair in Incident Room One.

As usual, the Incident Room was arranged with the front section laid out to match their workspace upstairs in the squad room. The end wall adjacent to this was almost filled with a huge whiteboard while the back section of the room was occupied by small individual desks laid out classroom-style for auxiliary staff who would help with grunt work like answering phones after a press release and helping with CCTV viewing or research. As yet, those desks were unoccupied, but Colin Underhill had said that they would be in place by the afternoon, in view of the Chief Inspector's press release last night, which Pete had yet to view.

'We're both convinced that Richie Young's got nothing to do with what's happened to our victims,' Pete replied. 'Have you heard from Dave and Ben?'

Jane shook her head. 'Prescott works for his dad's firm. He's out on a job, so they went off after him, but that's all we know as yet.'

'And his dad's a plumber?'

She nodded.

'So, he's got a fair degree of flexibility on his comings and goings. No-one keeping an eye on him from one minute to the next.'

'Which would make it easier for him to hold down a job and do a bit of extra-curricular on the side,' Dick said.

'Yeah, but it would still have to be coordinated with whoever was going to take him to the locations,' Jane countered. 'The two we know of weren't just a quick stroll away.'

'Depends where he was working at the time,' Dick countered.

'But, if you're right, it could be useful for us,' Pete said. 'An accomplice might be the weak link we need, depending how involved they are.'

'Yeah, once we find them,' Dick said.

'Has there been much response from the press release?'

Jane shook her head. 'Eight, so far. We were about to get started looking at them.' Her desk phone rang and she picked it up. 'DC Bennett... OK... Hello, DC Bennett speaking.... Yes... I see...' Her pause was longer this time. 'OK, thanks for letting us know. We'll look into that.' She hung up. 'Nine,' she said, looking up at Pete. 'That was a woman who saw the Jag – or a similar one – speeding away from Dunrich Close on Magdalen Road, heading east.'

'Well, that's more than we could say for sure before. What about the others? What do they say?'

'Don't know yet. I've got the file here.' She lifted a slim beige folder from her desk.

*

'Oh, nice of you to join us,' Jill declared as Ben followed Dave into the incident room. 'Another ten minutes, we were going to go to the front desk and report you missing.'

'There you go, Spike,' Dave said with a laugh. 'She does care, after all.'

'I care about the amount of work the rest of us would have to pick up,' she retorted. 'More from Spike than you, of course, seeing as we do most of yours already.'

'Cheeky mare. What have you been doing while we were out, then? Solved the case, have you?'

'No, but...'

'Thought not,' he said over her unfinished reply. 'Seeing as we've found another suspect.'

'What, you've been out all morning and only found one suspect?' Dick demanded. 'Who's that, then?'

'Well, who did we go out to talk to?' Dave shot back.

'Prescott? How long does it take to interview one person?'

'And check his alibis, which turned out to be false.'

'OK,' Pete said. 'But what have you got other than suspicion to suggest he was actually involved in what we're looking into?'

'Yeah, well, we haven't finished the job yet, have we? Had to come in eventually and do some office work to tie things up.'

'Come on, then. Give us the full story.'

'We started off by asking him about Alan Jackson,' Dave said, pushing up his sleeves and leaning forward onto his desk. 'Straight away, he got evasive. We mentioned the car, and he denied even knowing it existed. Thing is, before we spoke to him, young Spike suggested we talk to one or two of the others on those lists of pupils – ones he might have known. And with three of them, we hit paydirt. They were buddies of his. So that way, we knew a bit before we got to him. Knew he was lying when he denied knowledge of the Jag, for instance. And that he didn't exactly get on with Mr Jackson. So then we went further back in time – asked him about Mrs Lockwood. Well, he had to admit to knowing her: he was in her class, wasn't he? He claimed to have got on with her OK but couldn't really say much more. Again, as if he was telling us stories to shut us up and get rid of us. Which he might have been. The lad he was with was definitely nervous about something. So we asked what he was up to last Wednesday and Saturday night. He said he was working on Wednesday. With the same lad, who backed him up on it. But when we asked for verification of where and when, he suddenly got forgetful. "One job runs into another," he said. "Job to remember which was when."'

'Probably true if you're doing several different ones a day,' Pete said.

'Yeah, but they denied having a diary of any sort with them and, when we checked back with his dad's office – i.e., his mum – without telling her why we needed to know, she told us that, in fact, he was between jobs, middle of Wednesday afternoon. He finished one at lunchtime, didn't start the next until 3:00. And they don't work Saturdays, except for emergency jobs – which he doesn't do.'

'So, he's got no alibi, knowledge of both victims, and maybe the accomplice he'd need to take him to the locations,' Ben added.

'We need to look more thoroughly at him, then, for sure,' Pete acknowledged. 'Did you get his phone details? That might confirm – or at least suggest – where he was.'

'I asked him about that. He declined,' Ben replied.

'Now, why would he do that?' Dick said. 'Presuming you put it to him in the right way, of course.'

'Exactly,' Dave agreed, pointing across the desks at him.

'And yes, we did,' Ben added.

'So, who's his buddy, where did he go to school and has he got a police record?' Pete asked.

'His name is Jimmy – or James – Bissett,' Ben replied. 'Aged eighteen. Lives with his mother in Polsloe. And yes, he has got a record. He's been in trouble since he was twelve, one way and another.'

'Which ways, specifically?'

'Theft. Resisting. Possession of a bladed article twice. And of class-B drugs on three occasions.'

'Not a quick learner, then,' Dick said. 'How did he manage to get a job with the Prescotts?'

'He's a cousin. His mum's Mrs Prescott's sister.'

'She's single?' Dick asked. 'You said he lived with her, not with his parents.'

Ben nodded. 'Father not listed and she's never lived with a male other than Jimmy since she left home.'

'Is he her only child?' Jill asked.

'Yep. But she is currently pregnant.'

Jane raised an eyebrow. 'How'd you know that?'

'We haven't just been talking to Gavin Prescott all this time,' Dave said. 'We've been all over. Including Polsloe, to check on Jimmy's alibis.'

'And?' Pete asked.

'He was at home on Wednesday at the time of interest, but not Saturday night.'

'So, where was he?'

'That, we don't know yet. Just like Gavin Prescott.'

'Then we'd best find out,' Pete said. 'Let's get the two of them ruled in or out, one way or another.'

'We thought we'd start with Jimmy's known associates,' Dave said. 'Given he's got a record, there'll be a list on file.'

'Good idea,' Pete agreed. 'What about Prescott Senior and his wife? They're business owners. Are they the upstanding citizens they ought to be?'

'As far as we know,' Dave said. 'Neither of them have got records, at least.'

'And they haven't worked at either victim's address or in the vicinities recently?'

'Certainly not for the Lockwoods,' Jane said.

'Mrs Jackson didn't mention a plumber, either, but it'd be worth checking,' Pete said. 'And going back to the Prescotts, telling them that, given Gavin's link to both victims, we need to eliminate him so we could do with making sure of where he was on both occasions. Which means talking to his friends. Could they provide us with any names or contact details, as Gavin's reluctant for some reason? Emphasising that, whatever reason that is, as long as it's not what we're investigating, we're not interested. We just need to eliminate him. They know you, Dave…'

He nodded. 'All right. I can do that.'

'Good. The rest of us will hit the phones and see if we can find young Mr Bissett an alibi for Saturday night, then I'll go and see Mrs Radbourne again and, now we know which way the Jag went on Magdalen Road, we can start on the more distant CCTV and see if we can figure out where it might have gone.'

'We know it didn't get as far as the traffic cameras on Heavitree Road,' Jane pointed out as Dave left the room. 'We already checked that with Graham.'

'So, it turned off somewhere short of there,' Pete agreed. 'The question is, where?'

'Ops Support collected CCTV from the old folks' home and the solicitor's up there,' Jane said. 'Plus a couple of doorbell cameras: one just past the Barrack Road crossroads on the right, one on the left just past Manston Terrace and another CCTV camera at the new flats across from there.'

'That should narrow things down a bit.' Pete called up James Bissett's police record on his computer and scrolled down to the known associates listing. He copied the list and emailed it to the others. 'There we go. Let's divide and conquer.'

CHAPTER TEN

Pete was in the act of hanging his jacket on the back of his chair in the Incident Room, where he'd returned after visiting the recently widowed Mrs Radbourne when there was a knock at the door behind him and it opened to admit a line of eight uniformed officers, six of them female. The woman leading them was almost as tall as Pete's own six feet, and almost as broad at the shoulders, he noted, her blonde hair scraped back into a regulation bun while her lips were painted dark red, emphasising the almost colourless paleness of her blue eyes.

'DS Gayle?' she asked.

He nodded. 'That's me.'

'PC Bernie Douglas, Ops Support. We're here to help.'

'Good. OK, gather round. I've just got back myself so we can all get up-to-date together.' He stepped across to the big whiteboard and turned to the rest of the team. 'Dave, how did you get on at the Prescotts' place?'

'She gave me a few names. I've been back long enough to expand on that, given that two of them have got criminal records. Drug possession and, in one case, theft. So I've been able to place Gavin Prescott in a house in St Thomas in the early hours of Sunday morning.'

'How firmly, given what you've just said about drugs?'

'Three people put him there from around 10:30 Saturday night until 2:00am at least, and he was still there at 7:00.'

Pete nodded. 'OK. He's off the list, then.' He picked up a marker from beneath the board and wrote beneath Gavin Prescott's picture. *Alibi. Sat 22:00 onwards, St Thomas with friends.* 'OK. Was Jimmy Bissett there, too?'

'No,' Jane said. 'We've exhausted pretty much every possibility with him, but we can't find him an alibi for Saturday night into Sunday morning.'

'And there's no CCTV of any kind around his home address? Doorbell cameras, anything like that?'

She shook her head. 'Not the wealthiest neighbourhood.'

'True.' He wrote under Bissett's picture, which they'd added to the board while he was out, *No alibi Sat/Sun.* 'Mrs Radbourne isn't aware of anyone in the Close having had a plumber recently. And no mobile car-wash or garage services of any sort, either – for the Jag or any other vehicle down there.'

'A good thing the CCTV up Magdalen Road was helpful, then,' Jill said.

'In what way?' Pete demanded, focussing on her.

'He turned off up Polsloe Road.'

'OK, good. We know he didn't go out along Heavitree. And there's a corner shop up Polsloe.'

'Yeah, no external cameras, though,' PC Douglas put in.

'But there are on the flats across the road from it,' one of her colleagues countered.

Pete gave her a nod. 'Thank you…?' He raised an eyebrow, leaving the comment open.

'PC Collins, Sarge. Diane.'

'Thank you, PC Collins.'

'There's more than plenty of places he could have gone after there, though,' Dick said.

'If he kept going in a straight line, he'd end up at the bottom of Stoke Hill,' Ben pointed out. 'And it's easy to get from there across towards the Lockwoods' home.'

'How's that relevant to anything?' Dave demanded.

Ben shrugged. 'Just saying.'

'The Lockwoods had their car nicked, right?' Douglas checked.

'That's right,' Pete agreed.

'We had another case, the other day, where a couple were attacked in their home by a burglar. There was no car stolen, but that's because it wasn't there. The husband had taken it in for an MOT and it failed, so was being re-done the next day.'

'What, and the perp didn't notice it was missing before he broke in?' Dave demanded.

'They keep it in the garage,' she told him.

'So, he wouldn't have known until he was in,' said Jill.

Pete nodded. 'But he knew they had a car. They woke up, did they?'

She shook her head. 'They weren't in bed. It was a clear night. There was a good view of both Mars and Saturn, apparently. They'd got a telescope out and the patio doors open, looking through it. He came in and…' She shrugged. 'Ambulance was needed for both.'

'Where was this, and when?' Pete asked.

'Last Tuesday, on Armstrong Avenue.'

'That's… Again, not far from the Lockwoods,' Ben said.

'So, do we think he's local to that part of the city?' Dave suggested.

'He certainly knows it well,' Pete said. 'We'll need to check for any connection between the victims in that case and the Lockwoods and/or the Jacksons. Were the victims able to provide a description of the offender?'

'Smaller than average. Five-foot-five or six, lean and wiry. Strong. And vicious. Seemed like he enjoyed hurting them for the sake of it. Description's limited because he was wearing a stocking, but he's IC-1 with dark hair.'

'There won't be an e-fit, then,' Dick said.

'What about his voice?' Jane asked. 'Did they say there was anything distinctive about that? An accent, maybe?'

The tall woman shook her head. 'Local was all she could say.'

'He's a busy bugger all of a sudden, though,' Dick said. 'So, why now? Or where's he been until now?'

'How did he get access to the address on Armstrong?' Pete asked before anyone could respond.

'Over the side gate, presumably aiming for the back door but, as I said, they'd got the patio doors open so he just charged in, full-on aggression from the outset. Shut the doors behind him and blitzed them.'

'If he's such a little-un, how did he control two people who were both awake and aware from the outset?' Dave asked.

'He floored them both immediately with punches to the nose, tied the husband with some sort of reinforced tape – ankles first, while he was down, then stood on his head while he bound his hands and, before she could recover, he was onto the wife. Taped her hands behind her, all the while demanding the keys for the car. They told him it wasn't there, but he didn't believe them. Not at first, at least. And by the time he did… Well, he was enjoying himself too much to care, by the sounds of it.'

'He raped her,' Jill said.

Douglas nodded.

'Presumably, he'd brought the tape with him?' Dave asked.

'Yep.'

'So, was he planning something of the sort, or was it just in case?'

She shrugged. 'We won't know until we catch him.'

'*If* we do,' Dick added. 'What was the car he was after?'

'A mini.'

'What – proper job or the new type?'

'From 1983.'

'So, between that and the Jag, this is sounding targeted,' Ben said. 'Like organised.'

'Yeah, but with that level of violence?' Dave countered. 'Those gangs don't normally go in for that type of thing. In and out as fast and unobtrusive as possible is their thing. It's all about the profits. And drawing attention doesn't help that.'

'Not always,' Ben countered. 'Look at that gang over London way, a couple of years ago. They went after cars, jewellery, whatever they could get their hands on at the time, and they seemed well into the violence. There was even a TV program about them, end of last year.'

Dave nodded. 'Gypos, weren't they?'

'Travellers,' Jane corrected him. 'But yes, they lived on some big caravan site in the outskirts. Massive operation, in the end, wasn't it?'

'Yeah, they were so forensically aware, the Met had to find out what they were driving and track them that way, although that wasn't easy, either. They spotted them and took evasive action more than once.'

'All of which we could do without,' Pete said. 'But we need to follow it up. Who's he going to be working with to dispose of vehicles like that? We weren't aware of an on-going operation of the sort.' His gaze focussed on the newcomers clustered at the far end of the workstation. 'We already checked when the Jag came up.'

'So, we need to look for likely suspects,' Douglas suggested.

He nodded. 'And check the CCTV from Polsloe Road. The flats you mentioned. And there's some shops at the far end, on Blackboy Road. There might be something there for us. What about this couple on Armstrong Avenue? Who are they and are they OK now – out of hospital, at least?'

'I don't know,' Douglas admitted. 'I haven't been following it up. But their names are Rachel and Tom Danscombe. They're in their sixties. No kids, as far as I know.'

Pete nodded. 'You met them, though?'

'Yes. I was on the follow-up team.'

'So, who's case was it?'

'Sergeant Fairweather's'

'I'll have a word with him, then.' With jobs allocated, he sat down, picked up his phone and dialled as the Ops Support team filed out to go about the tasks he'd assigned them.

'Fairweather.'

'Andy, it's Pete Gayle. How you doing?'

'OK. Busy. Why, what's up?'

'The Danscombes.'

'What about them?'

'Their case might tie into one I'm working.'

'What, the Lockwood one?'

'Yes. And the Dunrich Close killing.'

'They're connected?'

'We're exploring the possibility.'

'So, where's the link to the Danscombes?'

'Didn't it start out as a car-theft burglary gone wrong?'

'Yes.'

'So, how are they? Are they home?'

'She is, although not much. He's still unconscious, so she's in the RDE with him most of the time. After the offender finished with her, he set about her husband with the leg of a chair that he'd smashed over the poor guy's head. The purpose appears to have been to cause brain damage at least: or at worst, to kill him and traumatise the female into not being able to testify.'

'How is she?'

'Traumatised. Can't remember much of what happened. Brain probably choosing not to as a defence mechanism, I expect, but what may or may not come back in time, who knows?'

Not much help as a witness, then, Pete thought. 'What about the neighbours? Did they see or hear anything useful?'

'No. It was the wrong side of midnight.'

'Who called the ambulance?'

'She did. Dialled with her nose as her hands were still bound.'

'So, you've got nowhere as far as a possible offender?'

'We've got DNA, but no matches in the system. And no fingerprints. He wore gloves.'

'Right. So, on one level, he's aware and organised while, on another, he's out of control and frenzied.'

'That's about the size of it, yeah.'

'OK, thanks, Andy. I'll have a word with my guvnor about merging the cases. Takes at least that one off your hands, eh?'

'Hmm.'

'Have you heard of any others that might be related? Similar MO's or car-related?'

'No. There's always car thefts here and there, but nothing to link any others to this that I know of.'

'OK. Well, that's something, at least. Go steady.' He hung up and returned his attention to the team around him, his gaze sweeping from one to the next. 'So, what do we know for sure? One thing is that the offender knew in advance about the Mini and the Jag. The question is how? What have they got in common? Do they use the same garage? The same tyre fitters? The same supermarket, even? He's got the exact addresses so either he's followed them, he knows them or he's got access to some form of records about the cars that can give him at least partial owner-details.'

'Following them seems unlikely,' Dave said. 'I mean, you're not going to be exactly unobtrusive, mooching about down Dunrich Close, are you? And how's he getting around? You don't expect to stick a push-bike in the back of a Mini, do you?'

'No, but you need two feet to drive most cars,' Jill pointed out. 'And if you've got them, you can walk.'

'Yeah, but how many thieves have got the inclination to walk anywhere?' Dick countered. 'By definition, almost, they're lazy sods, aren't they? Want the easy way to everything.'

'He could use a skateboard,' Ben suggested. 'They're small and portable.'

'Or a scooter,' Jane added. 'Electric or otherwise. A thief or burglar's not going to worry about the legality of riding one on the streets, is he?'

Dave pointed a finger at Jane. 'You don't see many of them, but a lot more than you do skateboards, these days. And they do fold up. At least, some of them do.'

'OK,' Pete said. 'He could have used any of those methods to scout the locations as well as to get to them to commit the offences, so let's get back onto the CCTV at the times in question. See if we can pick up a common thread.'

CHAPTER ELEVEN

The Danscombes lived in a 1970s detached house of pale brick and greenish tiles near the southern end of Armstrong Avenue, where it joined Rosebarn Lane. The garage was attached to one side of it while the main door was in the far side, facing the side wall of next-door's garage. About six feet from Pete's shoulder as he stood facing the door was a thin wooden gate that gave access to the rear garden. At his other shoulder stood Jill Evans, her uniform as immaculate as ever.

He checked his watch and rang the bell, taking out his warrant card in readiness.

There was no response. All was quiet in the house, though he'd heard the bell through the double-glazed door. He waited a few moments, then rang it again. After another wait, movement showed through the rippled glass panel. A lock snicked and the door opened a few inches.

She wore a pale pink dressing gown, one hand grasping it closed below the neck while the other held the door. Her silver hair was shoulder-length and neatly styled, though her face, along with the hand at her neck, was heavily bruised.

'Yes?'

Pete raised his ID. 'Mrs Danscombe? I'm DS Gayle with Exeter CID. This is PC Evans. Sorry for the early call, but I didn't want to get in the way of you visiting your husband. We've taken over the case from the uniform branch so could we ask you a few questions? It won't take long.'

'But…' The relief was evident on her face, though tempered with confusion. 'I'm not dressed yet.'

Pete smiled. 'We can give you a couple of minutes if you'd prefer, but the sooner we get the information we need, the sooner we can catch the individual who put you in this situation.'

'Hmm.' Her lips began to purse but she stopped the movement almost immediately, discomfort showing in her eyes. 'OK, you'd better come in.' She stood back, allowing the door to open. 'Go through.' She indicated an open door that gave onto a sitting room.

Stepping through with a nod of thanks, Pete found himself in a through lounge/diner that reminded him of the house Dave Miles had moved into a few months ago, in another part of the city.

'Sit down, I'll just be a minute,' she told them and headed for the stairs.

While Jill complied, taking a seat on the sofa that faced the front window, Pete remained standing for a few moments, taking in the room. As PC Douglas had described, French doors opened onto the rear garden, which faced another in the next street over a six-foot panel fence and was neatly maintained with a mix of shrubs and flowers in borders surrounding a lawn. Inside the patio doors stood an oval dining table with four chairs pushed in around it, a sideboard to one side and a display cabinet on the other, filled with a mix of old-fashioned ornaments, mostly on a wildlife theme. All were in teak wood that matched, in style, the age of the house.

The telescope Douglas had mentioned was leaning awkwardly against the junction of the rear and side walls, next to the sideboard, its small siting scope lying on the otherwise unoccupied top of the sideboard. It looked like the instrument had been knocked over during the attack and the secondary scope broken off in the process.

Pete took a seat next to Jill as he heard a creak at the top of the stairs.

When she came into the room, Mrs Danscombe had dressed in a soft pink sweater and dark slacks, her hair combed out loose onto her shoulders. 'Can I get you anything?' she asked. 'Tea? Coffee?'

Pete shook his head. 'We're fine, thank you. We don't want to hold you up any more than necessary.'

She dipped her head and stepped in, taking the seat in the corner behind the door, across from them. 'You say you've taken over our case? Why's that?' she asked, sitting forward.

'We think it may be related to some others that we've been working on,' Pete told her.

'There's others?' Her eyes widened in shock. 'How many people has he attacked already?'

'Things are moving rapidly,' Pete said. 'We're working two other incidents at the moment, both in the last few days. How's your husband? Has there been any improvement?'

Her lips tightened but were, again, too painful to complete the expression she'd been about to show. 'Nothing to speak of as yet,' she admitted. 'They say it could take a while, though. You never really know with these things. It's just a matter of patience.'

Pete nodded. 'You have our sympathy. And our promise that everything that can be done to catch the perpetrator will be done.'

'Thank you.'

'Now, I'm not going to waste time asking questions that you've already given answers to. We've got the case file. But the fact that yours is one of three cases that we believe may be related suggests that there's some kind of connection. Some common ground between you and the other victims. So that's what we're here to try and find. It may be something completely ordinary, routine, something that you wouldn't think twice about. So, often, the best way to find it is by going through paperwork, comparing receipts, bank records, phone records, Internet searches – things like that. So, with your permission, while you're spending time with your husband, we'd like to do that. We just need you to collect together the paperwork and devices for us and we can take it from there.'

Her bruised eyes had widened again as he spoke. 'That's an awful lot of work, Detective. Are you…?'

He smiled. 'A lot of police work is drudgery rather than chasing down criminals, Mrs Danscombe, and we've got a dedicated team that are used to that sort of thing. It's not a problem. The more, the better, in some senses. We're more likely to find what we're looking for. And my name's Pete.'

She tipped her head. 'OK. Pete. On your head be it. As long as you find the vicious bast…' She stopped, shaking her head. 'There was no need for it. For any of it. The bloody car wasn't even here. And what's it worth, anyway? Old thing like that, it's more sentimental than monetary value, I'd have thought.'

'You'd be surprised,' Pete said. 'Classic cars are quite a thing. Some of them can be worth a serious amount of money.'

'Yes, but a Mini…?'

'A proper one,' Jill put in. 'They're collectible, these days, if that's the right word. There's owners' clubs and all sorts.'

She sighed. 'Well, I'd better get you that paperwork, then, hadn't I? And phone… Do you mean landline or mobile?'

'Both,' Pete said. 'Although, with a mobile, if you don't need it for a day or so, it's easier if we have the device itself. We can bring it back as soon as we've finished with it. And you use a laptop or a desk computer?'

'We had an old desk computer until last year. Our son-in-law got us a tablet and got rid of the old thing for us.'

Pete glanced at Jill. 'We weren't aware that you had children, Mrs Danscombe.'

'Not locally. And just one – a daughter. Tiff. She lives in Towcester, up near Northampton. Works for the council up there.'

He nodded. 'You've told her what happened, have you?'

'Yes. She's coming down next week. Soonest she could get away. They've got problems up there. Financial, you know? And a lack of staff to deal with them. Anyway, let me get this stuff together for you.' She stood up and opened the door.

'Do you want a hand?' Jill offered.

She glanced back, looking momentarily reluctant, but then nodded. 'OK. Thanks.'

Jill followed her out and back up the stairs. While they were gone, Pete stood up and stepped over to the telescope. He picked up the smaller scope from the sideboard and turned it in his hand. It wasn't going to be a simple fix, if it was fixable at all, he saw. The screws attaching it to the main barrel had been torn out by an impact, the metal around the holes bent and ripped. Also, it was a reflector-type telescope, so much more delicate than the alternative, though it made for a more powerful magnification in a given size of instrument. The mirror would have been knocked completely out of alignment, he guessed. It would be a matter of replacement rather than repair.

He returned to the sofa to wait. Got up to open the door when he heard the two women on the stairs again. His eyes widened when he saw what they were carrying. A visit to the Andersons last evening for the same purpose had produced a fraction of what he saw now.

Jill was leading the way, her arms filled with a large bundle of papers. 'They're not in order, so we've got the lot,' she said when she saw him gazing up at her. 'Mrs Danscombe's got the tablet and iPhone.'

Pete nodded. 'I'll go and get an evidence bag from the car.'

Minutes later, with everything tucked into a sack-sized paper bag, he paused on the doorstep. 'If there's anything you remember that you might not have mentioned before – it doesn't matter how small a detail or whatever – don't hesitate to call and let us know,' he said. 'You've got my number. Use it anytime, to pass on anything rather than put it off and forget it again.' He gave her a brief smile. 'I know what it can be like. Or if you've got any questions, OK?'

Standing once again in the doorway, looking out at them, she nodded. 'Thank you, Detective.'

'Pete,' he reminded her. 'And say hello to your husband for us when he wakes up.'

She gave him a wan smile. 'I will.'

*

He was still sorting the paperwork into categories and sources, prior to sorting it into date order while Jill had transferred the Internet history from the tablet computer and was downloading the iPhone when Ben suddenly announced into the quiet of the big room, 'I've got something.'

'I've told you before – don't tell us; tell your doctor and get it treated,' Dave retorted.

'Unless it's relevant to the case,' Pete qualified.

'It is.'

'So, put us out of our misery,' Jill said, looking up over her screen at him. 'Where are you looking, for a start?'

They all knew he was going through some of the CCTV that PC Douglas and her team had collected the previous afternoon.

'Blackboy Road: the crossroads with Polsloe Road. The caff on the corner's got a camera and so's the offy across from it.'

'And what have you got from them?' Pete asked. Sometimes, getting information out of Ben was like pulling teeth. And some of those times, it was deliberate, he knew: Ben could be a wind-up artist when he chose to be.

'I reckon our suspect walking up Polsloe, past the caff, towards the crossroads.'

'Well, put it up, let's all have a see,' Dave said.

'Hang on, hang on,' Ben protested and tapped at his keyboard. 'Pull the screen down, if you're that impatient.'

Dave got up and complied while Pete hit the remote for the blinds over the windows and Dick crossed to the door and flicked off the room lights. The screen in front of the whiteboard glared white for a moment, then was filled with an image – a paused video of a male walking along a street. A grey hatchback car was passing him towards the junction, just a few feet away. Across the road was a large Victorian brick house with a bright red door. The camera was looking past the house, down a street that Pete recognised as Blackboy Road, more houses beyond the one in the foreground, shops on the other side.

'There,' Ben said. 'Bring up the image on your laptops of scooter-man that PC Nelson, over there, found last night from Magdalen Road and compare the two. I reckon it's the same bloke.'

'Except that one was on a scooter,' Jill reminded him. 'And heading away from Polsloe Road.'

'And didn't come back, that we're aware of,' Ben countered. 'Unless, of course, he came back in a vehicle. Such as, for instance, a nice old Jag. And what's that he's carrying? It looks to me like it could be a folded-down scooter in a bag made for the purpose.'

They all saw what he meant. Held low, down the side of his leg, on his left side – the side away from the camera viewpoint – was a long, narrow black bag about the width of the male's thigh.

Pete brought up the other image on his computer as Ben had suggested and looked from one to the other. In both, the subject looked smaller than average, lean, and was dressed in dark jeans and a black jacket with a dark red baseball cap. The one on Magdalen Road that had been found yesterday evening, while he was out speaking to the Andersons, was a rear-view only, but the similarity was close enough. Unfortunately, the cap was pulled low over his face on the new shot, so you couldn't make out his features for any hope of identifying him, but it certainly looked like the same person.

'OK,' he said. 'It looks like the same person to me, though his brief might question it when it comes to court. So, you're suggesting he took the Jag and left it somewhere on Polsloe Road between Magdalen and Blackboy, or one of the side-streets off there. We know it's common practice with car thieves: park it up somewhere for a day or two, to make sure it's safe before they take the next step with it. But that's a bit close, isn't it?'

'Handy, though,' Dick countered. 'And with all the cameras around – like that one,' he added, pointing at the screen hanging from the ceiling. 'They can leave it as long as they want on a residential street and pick it up some night when it's harder to see.'

'So we need to search those streets and, if it's not there, the camera footage from all around them from then until now,' Pete concluded.

'There's a bloody lot of possibilities round there,' Dick pointed out sourly.

'And we've got quite a few pairs of boots to do the job,' Pete countered. 'Look over there.' He jerked a thumb over his shoulder at the Ops Support team occupying the desks in the back half of the room.

Dick grunted.

'First, though, let's see if we can see where he goes from there,' Pete suggested. 'Like you said, Ben, there's another camera across the road if this one doesn't show us. Let it play.'

Ben tapped his keyboard and the image burst into motion, cars, pedestrians and even a bicycle suddenly in motion, this way and that. The figure they were concentrating on stepped forward abruptly towards the right of the screen and out of the static camera's angle of view.

'Let it play,' Pete said in case the man decided to head down Blackboy Road towards the city centre.

Ben complied, but the figure didn't reappear.

'OK,' Pete said after a full minute. 'Let's try that other camera. The one on the off-license.'

The image disappeared from the screen. More tapping at Ben's keyboard and, after a few moments of glaring white screen, it was replaced with another image. This one was looking at the same junction, from a different angle – looking across towards the end of Polsloe Road from above and to the left of one of the traffic lights that governed the junction. Ben tapped his keyboard again and the frozen image started into motion then sped up, rapid movements reminding Pete of an old black-and-white movie, though this was in startling, modern colour.

'There,' Jill said abruptly.

Pete had seen it too. 'Slow it down.'

Ben reduced the footage to normal speed and then reversed it a few frames before letting it play again.

The male they were looking for stepped into view, moving towards them across the front of the shop they'd been viewing from before. He paused at the roadside, looking right and left, waited for a car and the bicycle they'd seen before to clear his path, then stepped out across the road, towards the camera.

'He's keeping his bloody head down,' Dick said. 'No way we're going to ID him from this.'

'Let's see where he goes,' Pete said.

They watched as the figure reached the pavement at the near side of the road, turned to his right, towards the junction that formed the northern part of the crossroads, and stepped out of shot.

'So, he carried on up Mount Pleasant Road or went up towards Pinhoe,' Jill said. 'What have we got from there, in either of those directions?'

'Nothing on Mount Pleasant,' Jane said. 'It's residential, so why would there be? Apart from maybe a doorbell camera here or there, that we haven't found. There's one at the health centre, but it doesn't give a view of the street. So the first chance up that way is St James', but that's only if he turns right onto Prince of Wales Road.'

'There's one at the shop on the corner of Thurlow.' Pete recognised Bernie Douglas's voice from behind him.

'The next junction up towards Pinhoe, right?' Pete recalled. 'Who's got the footage from that?'

'I have,' said Bernie. 'It was next on my list to check. I'll do it now.'

She scribbled a note on the pad at her elbow then selected a thumb drive from amongst those on her desk and pushed it into the port on her computer. In less than a minute, she had the footage loaded. 'OK, here we go. Hold on.'

Everyone in the room paused, waiting.

She hit a key harder than necessary. Then again. Another pregnant pause.

She sat back. 'Nothing. He didn't get that far.'

'So, he either lives in the flats on the corner or he's gone up Mount Pleasant,' Dave said. 'And into a black hole, effectively.'

'Unless he got picked up by someone else in a car,' Ben said.

'Oi! I thought I was the one supposed to throw that kind of spanner around,' Dick said.

'Must be your age,' Ben shot back. 'You're getting slow. You know what they say – you snooze, you lose.'

'So, we start with the car,' Pete said before an argument could ensue. 'Find the Jag, if it's still there, and we can put a tracker on it, see when it moves and where to, and attack the situation from that end. Come on, everyone – tighten your laces and get your coats on. It's time for walkies.'

CHAPTER TWELVE

Rather than flood the streets with uniforms that, if spotted, would put the offenders off from returning to the stolen car if it was still there, they went in their cars – a mix of personal and unmarked ones. It still took over an hour, but at the end of it, there was only one conclusion to be made.

The Jaguar had already been collected.

Which meant a lot more time spent in front of computer screens, checking CCTV footage for the past ten days.

Pete divided them up once more into two teams – one to collect the footage they would need while the other moved north to start knocking on doors, searching for anyone in the area of Mount Pleasant Road or the four-storey block of flats on the junction with Blackboy Road who might recognise the male they were looking for from the images they'd captured of him so far. He led the second team while Bernie Douglas led the first.

They were faced with a maze of Victorian and Edwardian terraced houses – streets that provided back-street routes in several directions towards other parts of the city without passing any commercial premises. And, with an electric scooter in the bag he was carrying when he was last seen, it would have required little effort to follow any of them. But they had to start somewhere, so the most sensible course of action was to work outward from where he was last seen.

They were an hour and a half in and starting along the first of the side roads off Mount Pleasant, working the left side first, just on the principle of "left and right," when they got their first hint of a bite.

Jill stepped away from the second house in a short row between two side-streets and hurried along towards where Pete was stepping up to the door of the fifth and last in the block.

'Boss,' she called.

Hand raised towards the knocker because there was no bell-push, he paused and glanced across.

'I've got something.' She raised a hand to beckon.

Pete stepped away and met her on the narrow pavement half-way between the two homes, opposite an ugly grey block building with a large sign on the side that faced them, declaring it the premises of the local Conservative Club.

'What have you got?' he asked.

'Lady there says she recognises our suspect. She's seen him coming and going past here. No specific times or dates, but she's certain she's seen him. Sometimes on his scooter, sometimes on foot.'

'Excellent.' Pete's gaze drifted across to the club premises. 'Is that…? Hmm. Good find. Do my one, would you, while I make a quick call?'

'OK.' She stepped around him and up to the door he'd been about to knock on while he took out his radio.

'DS Gayle for PC Douglas.'

'Douglas.'

'Have you been to the Con Club on Elmside yet?'

'Not yet, no.'

'OK. I'm across the road from it, so I'll do it now.'

'Received. Thanks.'

He clipped the radio back onto his belt and crossed the road. It was approaching noon, so there was bound to be someone in there, he guessed. He tried the door but it was locked so he knocked. Waited. After a few moments, it was opened by a middle-aged male in shirt and tie.

'We're not open yet,' he said.

Pete raised his warrant card. 'I'm not here for a drink. I'm on duty,' he said. 'Pete Gayle, Exeter CID. I saw your CCTV camera out here and wondered if I could have a look at the footage from it.

'Oh. Well. Yes, I suppose. If you can operate the system. I'm opening in a few minutes and I've still got a bit to do.'

'That's OK. Just point me towards it and I'll manage, thanks.'

The man let him inside. It was dark, but there were lights on. Pete had noticed security mesh over the outside of the windows. Now, he saw there were wooden shutters on the inside. The man led him across the main bar area, where chairs were still upended on top of circular tables, and towards another door, to one side of the bar that occupied the central portion of the rear wall. Through into a corridor, he opened a door on the right and stepped inside. Sitting himself behind the desk that faced across towards a set of shelves full of box files and catalogues, he waggled the mouse to wake up the computer and clicked into a program then looked up at Pete.

'It's stored on a separate hard drive, up there on the shelf, but the access to it is here.'

'Thanks.'

The man stood up. 'I'll leave you to it. I'll be in the bar.'

The program was one Pete had used several times before, in various locations. He quickly found the list of files, took a thumb drive from his jacket and downloaded the ones that might be relevant, according to the timeline he'd got from the theft of the

Jaguar as well as the CCTV they'd already found, then opened the likeliest and let it load as he withdrew the drive and tucked it back in his pocket.

Keying it up to as close as he could get to the relevant time, he pressed play and fast-forward and began to watch. Sure enough, after a couple of minutes, a figure crossed the frame rapidly, standing upright, balanced, on an adult-sized scooter. He paused the replay, wound it back and hit play again.

The figure re-entered the frame, gliding right to left across the end of the alleyway that gave access to the club premises. He pressed pause and zoomed in. The body-shape, size, the jeans, black jacket, maroon cap – all fitted.

'Gotcha,' he murmured. 'Now, where were you off to, eh? Not far away, I bet.'

He took out his phone and took a photo of the screen, then closed down the program and left the room.

The first few customers were already in the bar by the time he emerged. Three middle-aged males stood at the bar while two older men occupied one of the tables near a window – all of which were open now, the shutters folded back. Pete raised a hand to the man behind the bar. 'Thanks for that,' he said.

'Got what you wanted?'

'Yep.'

Back outside, he quickly found the others. They'd moved on past the next side-turn and were now on this side of the road. As they left the properties they were at, he collected them all together on the pavement.

'Confirmation,' he said, patting his pocket. 'CCTV from the Conservative Club there. Our man came sailing past on his scooter just a couple of minutes after he crossed Blackboy Road.'

'Which side of the road was he on?' Dave asked.

'The far side,' Pete said with a jerk of his thumb.

'So, he's either on this street or he's gone up one of those going off it over there,' Jane said. 'Salisbury and… What's that other one, further along?'

'Rosebery,' Ben said.

She nodded. 'So, how do you want to play it?' she asked, turning back to Pete.

'Keep on keeping on,' he said. 'Finish going along here first. Then, if no-one recognises him, work our way up Salisbury, then Rosebery and on from there if necessary. The street they join up with at the far end.'

'Iddesleigh Road,' Ben said.

'Bless you,' said Dick.

'Which comes out onto Old Tiverton Road, right?' Pete checked.

'So does this one, if you carry on round the bend.'

'I don't see the point in doing that, just now, if no-one else recognises him by the time we get to the bend,' Pete said. 'Let's get to it. Sooner we find him, the sooner we can knock the job on the head.'

*

Pete's stomach was growling and his head was starting to ache when he knocked on yet another door just short of halfway up the left side of Salisbury Road. The rows of Edwardian terraces on either side of the street were enhanced with strips of white brick running horizontally through their faces, bay windows on both floors with decorative hanging tiles between the windows. The front doors were two steps up from the pavement that they opened directly onto.

This one was different from those around it only because it was painted in a pale greyish green, a modern colour amongst the majority of those around it which were either white UPVC or painted in bright, primary red, blue or black. It was opened by a diminutive female, her grey hair tightly curled as if she was attempting an Afro style with European hair. She wore a beige cardigan over a blouse with a pleated woollen skirt, their dull colours not matching either the modernity of the door's colour or the bright blue of her eyes as she looked up at him despite the advantage of the two steps between them.

'Yes?'

Pete held up his warrant card and introduced himself. 'We're conducting enquiries in the area in the hope of trying to find and identify this man,' he said, holding up his phone with a picture of their suspect. 'Do you recognise him at all?'

'Of course,' she said. 'He lives over there.' She nodded towards the far side of the road, just a few doors up from where they stood. 'Ewan. I talk to his mother every now and then in the corner shop. She sometimes fetches the odd thing for me if she's going and I can't.'

'Ewan,' Pete said, feeling the familiar tingle of success run through his body. 'And he lives with his mum, does he?'

'Yes, that's right,' she nodded.

'Do you know their surname?'

'Oh.' She looked disappointed. 'No, I don't. It's never come up. Sorry. Why? Has something happened? He's all right, is he?'

'He's fine as far as we know,' Pete said. 'We just need to speak to him, that's all. He may be a witness in a case we're investigating. Which door is theirs?'

'The blue one.' She pointed and he turned to see. It was three doors further up the sloping street. Not surprisingly at this time of day and in common with many of the houses up here, there was no car parked in front of it. He'd noted signs as he worked his way up here declaring that parking was with resident's permits only. He turned back to her. 'Well, thanks for your help, Mrs…?'

'Gilbert.'

He nodded. 'Thank you, Mrs Gilbert. Have a good afternoon.'

Stepping away from her door, he looked for Jill on the street and spotted her a few doors down on the far side. Checking for traffic, he crossed towards her, waiting until she'd finished with the male she was talking to before approaching.

'I've got a first name and a house,' he told her. 'You and I can give it a knock. Where's Ben? He seems to know this area.'

'Next-door. He got invited in.'

Pete raised an eyebrow.

'Old dear liked the look of him. Thought he needed feeding up or something,' she said with a grin.

'Don't we all,' Pete grunted. 'I could eat a bloody horse.' He took his radio from his belt and keyed the mike. 'DS Gayle for PC Myers. We need you up the street, Ben.'

'On the way, boss,' came the response and moments later the door opened and he emerged, nodding and thanking someone inside as he stepped out.

He turned to face them, licking his fingers. 'What's up?'

'You know this area,' Pete said. Are there alleyways down the backs of these properties?'

'Yes, they go in off Iddesleigh Road.'

'Right, get yourself round there and tucked in behind the one six doors up from here.'

'You found him?'

'I've found where he lives.'

'Right. I'll radio when I'm in position.'

He set off at a brisk walk up the street and soon disappeared from view around the corner at the top.

'So, you said you'd got a name for him?' Jill asked.

'Ewan,' Pete said. 'No surname yet.'

'Should we knock on next-door first and ask them?' she suggested.

'No, he'd probably hear. These places aren't exactly Fort Knox and we don't want to spook him if we don't have to, even if Ben is out the back by then. He could garden-hop instead of going out to the alley, cause all sorts of hassle that we don't need.'

Jill shrugged and it wasn't long until Pete's radio hissed and Ben's voice came over it. 'PC Myers. In position.'

'Roger,' Pete responded, then hooked the radio back onto his belt and they started up the street towards the target house.

Reaching it, his lips pulled down as he glanced at Jill. 'How's that for ironic? The first doorbell cam I've seen today.'

Jill chuckled as Pete reached for the button. 'He's going to be more aware than most of the need for security, isn't he?'

'Yeah.'

He heard the chime from inside and in moments, the door was opened by a female in her fifties, he guessed, the expression on her broad face sour as she took in their appearance and who they were.

'Yeah?'

Pete held up his warrant card. 'I'm DS Gayle with Exeter CID,' he told her. 'This is PC Evans. Do you recognise this individual?' He held up his phone with the picture from the CCTV at the corner of Polsloe Road.'

She frowned, her wide forehead creasing beneath swept-back curly brown hair. 'Maybe. Why?'

'We need to speak to him. He may be a witness to an incident we're investigating.'

She grunted. 'He hasn't said nothing to me.'

'He being…?'

She pursed her lips. 'My lad. Not that I'm saying that's him. Looks a bit like him, but…' She shrugged. 'Hard to tell, isn't it?'

'The angle's not perfect,' Pete admitted. 'But does your Ewan have a maroon cap like that, and a black jacket?'

'Yeah, but that don't make him unique, does it?'

'And a scooter?'

Her faced pinched. 'He's got one, yeah. What he does with it, though – where he rides it – I can't say.'

Pete smiled. 'We're not interested in that, Mrs…?'

'Miss. Price,' she added reluctantly.

'And your lad is…?'

'Ewan. But you can't talk to him. He's not here.'

'Really? That's a shame. We could really use his input. Do you know where we might find him?'

She grimaced. 'No idea. He's out, that's all I know.'

'Do you know when he'll be back?' Pete persisted.

'No. He comes and goes as he pleases.'

'What, and doesn't eat here, for instance?'

She shrugged. 'Sometimes. But that's up to him. He's old enough to manage for himself.'

He nodded and took a card from his pocket. 'Well, when he does come back, could you ask him to contact me?'

She grunted. 'I'll tell him. Don't know if he'll do it.'

Pete pressed his lips together briefly, tiring of her attitude. 'I could really do without having to keep coming back here until I speak to him, Miss Price, but I'll do it, if necessary. The incident we're investigating was extremely serious and, as I said, we really do need to talk to him as soon as possible.'

'Well, like I said, I'll tell him when he turns up. But when that'll be…' She shrugged.

'Does he not carry a phone with him?'

'It's off. I've tried it already, this morning.'

Pete frowned. 'When did you last see him?'

'Yesterday morning.'

'And is that normal for him?'

She shrugged. 'Not normal, no, but it happens now and then. He'll be gone overnight, turn up the next day. Spending the night with some girl, somewhere, I expect.'

'And how often is "now and then?"' he asked.

'Look I ain't his keeper. He's over twenty-one. What he gets up to of a night's up to him.'

'Agreed, but for the sake of example, how often has he been gone overnight, this past month? Or fortnight, even? To put things in perspective.'

'The last few Saturday nights. One night, middle of last week, he didn't get home till sometime in the early hours. And middle of the week before last.'

'And today's Friday,' he said. 'Which doesn't fit that pattern, so would you like to report him missing, Miss Price?'

Her frown sharpened. 'No. He'll turn up. Always does.'

'Well, if he doesn't, we're here to help, OK?'

She grunted.

'We'll leave you to it, then. But do tell him to call me when you see him.'

Another grunt and she stepped back, closing the door.

Jill looked at him. 'What do you reckon?' she asked.

'Not the happiest person to see us today,' he said. 'But I believed her.'

'And he's off on his toes, do you think? Without telling her?'

He shook his head. 'He'd have told her something, even if only so she could pass it on if anyone came looking for him. Like us, for instance.'

She dropped her voice to a murmur. 'So, we need to keep an eye on the place?'

He nodded as they stepped away down the street. 'At least we can do it remotely, these days.' He took out his radio and keyed the mike. 'DS Gayle for PC Myers.'

'Boss?'

'He's not in. Check for somewhere we could place a remote camera to cover the back gate there, then come back around.'

'Will do.'

Looking up and down the street, he saw the rest of his team standing at open doors here and there. They'd all worked their way further up the hill by now. He saw Jane on this side of the road. As he watched, she turned away from the house she'd been dealing with and started to head further up the hill. He keyed his radio again.

'DS Gayle for DC Bennett. Turn around.'

She complied and waved. He beckoned and started towards her. They met a few doors up from the Price residence.

'How are we doing?' she asked.

He tipped his head to the left, towards the far side of the road. 'In a few minutes, I need you to knock on the black door over there and ask if we can place a remote camera in their upstairs window. Emphasise that its battery operated, just needs charging once a day and it'll only be for a couple of days. Three at the most. And we can come and go through their back gate, so no-one needs to know about it.'

'I take it our suspect's not at home.'

'Correct.'

'OK. And then back to base?'

'Yep. We'll gather up Dick and Dave while Ben finds a location behind the target address.'

CHAPTER THIRTEEN

'They may have parked it up for a day or two to make sure they weren't followed,' Bernie Douglas said with the whole joint team congregated back in the incident room after a late lunch. 'It's a common trick. But there's no way out of that area without passing a camera. It's just a question of which one and when. There's not that many of them, to be fair, but it's still a lot of hours of footage to scroll through.'

'Then we split it up and take a portion each,' Pete said. 'It's Friday today. The Jag was taken Wednesday lunch-time, last week, so that's ten days. There's fourteen of us. How many cameras?'

'Six, but two of them are next-door-but-one to each other.'

'So, depending on the quality of each, we could narrow that down to five,' he concluded. 'Let's concentrate on the most likely timeframe first. We should be able, between us, to get through Thursday night this afternoon. If we don't find anything, then we pick it up in the morning, working outward from there until we spot it.'

'We've already started copying what we've got so everyone can have access to it all,' Bernie said. 'But it's a big job.'

Dave chuckled. 'Try emailing it to all of us: you'd crash the servers. That'd really get Chiefy's drawers in a tangle.'

'One of these days, you're going to call her that at the wrong time,' Jill told him. 'And she'll have your balls for dinner.'

Dave grinned. 'There's an answer to that, Titch, but I'm far too much of a gentleman to say it in female company.'

'Hah!' Jill barked. 'That would be a first, if it were true.'

'Let's start by all pitching in to make enough copies of the footage to go around,' Pete said, cutting off the banter. 'Then it'll be time to dim the lights, break out the Murray mints and knuckle down for a few hours of "find the Jaguar."'

*

'Well, let's hope we have better luck finding Ewan Price than we did this afternoon, spotting the Jag,' Pete said as he drew up three doors down from the Price residence on the narrow street of terraced houses, streetlights gleaming off the roofs and windows of the cars parked up both sides, and off the windows of the houses and the stripes of white glazed bricks that ran through the walls.

It was 8:45pm. He'd picked Ben and Jane up from their homes after spending an all-too-brief hour and a half in his own with Louise and Annie. They'd given up on the CCTV at just after 6:00, having searched through the footage from the previous Thursday night into Friday morning without finding any sightings of the missing Jaguar.

'If you head around the back again, just in case, Ben, we'll give the house a knock and see if he's in. If not, you can put the camera in place while we go around to the back of the house across the road and put one in there. I'll move the car up to Iddesleigh Road.'

'OK.' Ben stepped out of the car and headed up the street away from them. Pete and Jane sat still until Pete's radio hissed and Ben's voice came over it.

'In position.'

Pete keyed the mike. 'Received. Going in.'

They stepped out and he hooked the radio onto his belt as they approached the blue front door. He pressed the bell.

It was snatched open in just a couple of seconds. The woman's expression shifted from hope to disappointment in an instant as she recognised Pete.

'He's not back, then?' he asked.

'No.'

'So, do you feel like it's time to report him missing?'

She sighed. 'I feel like it, yes, but...' She stopped, pursing her lips.

'Then, do,' he said. 'It can't do any harm, can it? And if he's genuinely missing, then it's not wasting our time.'

'I know, but... What if he's up to something he hadn't ought to be? Then I'd just be dropping him in it, wouldn't I?'

'That depends on what he's up to,' he said. 'But if you think he might be in trouble, that takes priority, surely? As his mother, you've got to be more concerned with his safety than anything else. That's only natural.'

'Yes, of course, but...'

Pete raised his hands. 'I can't tell you what to do, Miss Price, but if it were my wife in your position, she'd have been onto the nick by now, for sure.'

Her nose crinkled. 'Yeah, but... OK. You're here. Can't you take a report or whatever?'

'Shall we come in? This is DC Bennett, by the way. She's a colleague of mine.'

She grunted and stepped back.

Inside, with the door closed, Pete took out his phone and dialled. When he got through, he identified himself and said, 'I'm with a Miss Price of Salisbury Road, Exeter. She wants to report her son, Ewan, missing.'

'When was he last seen?'

'Hang on, I'll pass you across.' Pete gave her the phone and they waited while she went through the standard list of questions then handed the phone back to him.

'Have you got a picture of him?' Pete asked. 'Maybe on your phone?'

She blinked. 'Um… I don't… We're not that sort of family, you know? We just get on with our lives. Do what we need to get by. It's not like we have family barbies or days out to the beach every Sunday.'

Pete pursed his lips. 'OK, what about something with his DNA on, just in case? A comb, a hat, a piece of clothing that he's worn and hasn't been washed yet?'

She grunted. 'There's a T-shirt and socks in the wash-bin upstairs. But…'

'That'll be perfect.'

A sigh heaved out of her. 'OK.'

Pete nodded for Jane to go with her. In moments, they were returning down the narrow stairs, an evidence bag in Jane's hand containing a pair of dark socks.

'We'll get that to Forensics,' Pete said. 'Then, if worst comes to the worst… I mean, I hope it doesn't, obviously, but if it does, or if he's been in an accident and he's lying unconscious in hospital without any ID on him, then we'll be able to identify him and let you know.'

'Hmm.'

'That'll be our first port of call,' he said. 'And I'll let you know as soon as there's any news, OK? And you let me know if he comes home, safe and sound, as we all hope he will.'

She nodded. 'Thanks.'

He stepped across to the front door and opened it. 'We'll talk again soon. Meantime, try not to worry, eh? It doesn't do any good, anyway.'

She grunted. 'That's easy to say. Not so easy to do.'

Pete tipped his head. 'I know, but like you said, he might just be shacked up with a girl somewhere. Dosed up on weed or whatever, without a care in the world. Wander in later like nothing's happened.'

'Huh. Then, what? You'd have him for possession or wasting police time or something?'

He shook his head. 'We can't do him for possession of something that's already gone. And nobody's wasting police time. We do still want to talk to him, but that's for another day now. Take care.'

He opened the door, held it for Jane and stepped out behind her, heading for his car.

Waiting until they were inside it with the doors closed, Jane said, 'That was a bit smooth.'

Pete gave her a quick grin as he started the engine. 'The opportunity was there. Shame to waste it.'

He saw the blue front door close as he pulled away up the street.

Parking once more on Iddesleigh Road, he radioed Ben as they headed for the alley that led down behind the houses opposite the Prices'.

'He's not at home,' he told the spiky-haired constable. 'We're going to place the second camera now. See you on Iddesleigh.'

'Received. First camera in position.'

*

With the small remote digital camera set up in the corner of the front bedroom window one house up from the Prices, angled across towards their door, Pete had dropped Ben off at home and was on the way to Jane's when his phone rang. He tapped the icon in the car's comms screen to answer.

'Pete Gayle.'

'It's Colin. Get yourself up to Woodbury Common.'

'What, now?'

'Take the Yettington road from the crossroads at the top and, a few yards down, there's a carpark on the right. You'll see us.'

He glanced at Jane, in the passenger seat beside him. 'What's going on?'

'Car fire. An old MG. With a body in it.'

'Oh. Shit. Related to our case?'

'It's an older car and the body was tied down.'

Pete frowned. An old MG, so it could be related, but... 'Why waste the motor, then? Makes it a bit pointless, all around.'

'You'll see why when you get here.'

Pete sucked air across his teeth as he signalled to make the turn into Jane's road. 'OK. I've got to stop off at Forensics briefly and I'll be on the way.'

'Right.' Colin ended the call.

'You don't want me to come with you?' Jane asked as the line buzzed dead and Pete reached for the screen to close it.

He shook his head. 'No need. There's plenty to do in the morning, whoever that is up there.'

'OK.'

He pulled up outside the house she shared with her husband. 'Say hello to Roger for me.'

She nodded. 'Night,' she said as she stepped out.

'Yeah. Doesn't sound like it'll be a good one.'

'Yeah, rather you than me.' She shut the door and stood at the kerbside as he pulled away.

*

Driving through the village of Woodbury, he headed up onto the moor beyond. A wide expanse of heather and bracken, dotted with small patches of woodland, Pete had been up here several times, bringing Louise and their two children up to Woodbury Castle, an iron-age hill-fort that was now no more than a raised ring of earth and stone covered in trees that kids loved to run up and down.

As he neared the crossroads at the top, where he'd turned left towards the Castle, the memories flooded back and he was forced to swallow a lump in his throat at the loss of those innocent times, and of his son. He could see nothing until he rounded the last bend in the narrow road, just a few yards short of the junction, his view blocked by the surrounding trees. But then he emerged at the crossroads and there were vehicles parked all around, blue lights flashing, head- and taillights glowing. Through an arch in the trees ahead, he could see the entrance to a small carpark, blocked off by a fire engine and an ambulance. Beyond them, pulled in at an angle towards the grass verge was the black estate car that belonged to the pathologist. To Pete's right, parked along the side of the road that crossed between him and the carpark entrance, were a police patrol car, DI Colin Underhill's old-style Range Rover and another car that he recognised: a dark blue Volvo saloon.

He grunted. What was he doing here?

He turned to the left and pulled up half onto the verge a few yards along so that anyone coming out of the junction behind him would be able to see to do so. Stepping out of the car, he crossed the road towards the centre of all the activity. Found Colin standing with a tall, lean figure at the entrance to the carpark, looking on as the fire crew wound up their hoses and a figure in a white overall leaned into the near side of the low, sleek-shaped but clearly burned-out form of a car at the far side of the small open space.

'Guv,' he said. 'Mark. What's going on?'

Colin and DS Mark Bridgman turned to face him.

'Why two of us?'

'If it's related, it's obviously yours,' Colin said. 'If not, with what you've got on the go already, Mark will take it on.'

So they both needed to attend the scene. Pete nodded. 'What do we know?'

'Doc Chambers is just getting started,' Mark told him. 'But so far, we know the fire was spotted by a passing delivery driver. He didn't stop – it was already too well established for him to expect to be able to do anything useful – but we've got his details. Comes from Buddleigh. He called 999. Fire crew got here, started putting it out. Were nearly done before they realised there was a body in there.'

'Have you had a closer look?' Pete asked.

Mark nodded. 'Not pretty.'

'I guessed.' Even at this distance and through the Vicks he'd slathered over his nose, Pete could smell the sickening combination of burned rubber and plastic, fuel and roasted flesh. 'I'd better do the same, I suppose.'

He stepped forward. Blue and white crime scene tape ringed most of the carpark, but the uniformed man standing at the side of the entrance still held the roll, waiting to close off the entrance as soon as everyone had vacated the scene. Pete nodded to him and stepped across towards the burned-out vehicle which was surrounded by a wide ring of dark mud and puddled water. Feet splashing softly in the after-effects of the fire-crew's work, he stopped well clear of the car itself. 'Evening, Doc. What do you know?'

The crouching overalled figure turned. 'Hello, Peter. I wasn't expecting you as well as DS Bridgman. What I know is, this was no accident. I'm afraid we have a murder on our hands.'

Pete had guessed that much from what Colin had said. 'How come?'

Chambers rose to his feet and took a step to one side. 'See for yourself,' he offered with an outstretched hand. 'But be careful. It's messy.'

Pete nodded and stepped forward. Immediately, he could see the figure in the driver's seat, head tipped back against what remained of the headrest. He took a step to the side, to get a better angle. The figure was completely blackened. The torso was almost burned through, bones sticking out white and charred from the ribcage. The face was also burned down to the bone in places. Pete frowned. Stepped closer and leaned down. 'What the hell is that?'

'Specifically?' Chambers asked.

'Around his neck.' Pete glanced up. 'I assume it is a he?'

Chambers nodded. 'It is. Hair length – what little remains at the back of the skull, against the headrest – foot size and hand size suggest it, along with the shape of the skull, although the overall size left a question at first. He's smaller than average. Or young. I can't tell yet. And what I believe you're referring to is not cheese-wire, but it's almost as thin. And steel, not copper. If you take a second look, you'll note it's around the wrists, as well.'

'So, he was tied down with it, then…?'

Chambers nodded. 'One hopes he was dead first, but again – I'll be able to tell more, back at the mortuary.'

Again, Pete was forced to swallow a lump in his throat, but this one was of horror and nausea. 'I hope you're right.' His mind was working, figuring, adding facts and… 'I'm not sure, obviously, but I've got an idea of who this might be,' he said. 'I just dropped off   a   DNA   sample   at   Middlemoor.'

CHAPTER FOURTEEN

'It's got to be linked,' Pete said, back at the carpark entrance with Colin and Mark. 'It's either Ewan Price in there or it's his work. I'd lay odds on it.'

'So, prove it,' Colin said.

'I was dropping off a DNA sample from him at Middlemoor on the way here. What do we know about the car?'

'It's an MGB GT,' Mark said. 'And it used to be green. There's traces left on the door post and the edges of the door where Doc Chambers opened it to get access to the body. The number plates are gone, but the VIN number should be safe. Depending on the year, it'll be on the other door post or behind the front bumper. We haven't checked yet. Couldn't get access. There haven't been any reported stolen locally in the past twelve months. Not of that colour.'

Pete nodded. 'So again, it's either the owner in there or it was taken recently. Like in the last twenty-four hours at most, unless they were lucky enough that the owners are away on holiday without it. Like they were with the Jag on Dunrich Close.'

'Whoever's in there, I wouldn't call him lucky,' Colin said.

Pete tipped his head in agreement and moved back towards the car as Doc Chambers beckoned the photographer in and stepped clear.

'Is it going to disturb anything if I open the other door?' Pete asked. 'To check for the VIN number.'

'No, go ahead,' Chambers said. 'David, hold off for a second. DS Gayle needs to check something.'

The photographer nodded.

Moving around to the far side of the car, careful where he was putting his feet in the darker space, shadowed by the car itself, he pulled on a pair of nitrile gloves and reached for the door handle, noting that the lock plunger was in the raised position. The handle was still warm to the touch, despite the cooling effect of all the water the fire crew had doused the car with. He pulled and the latch clicked and released, the door swinging open surprisingly smoothly.

To Pete's relief, he found the VIN plate immediately, the closed door having protected it from the intensity of the fire. Crouching, he took out his phone and photographed it. Checked the result and stood up, stepping back and closing the door.

'All yours,' he said to the photographer. 'Thanks.'

'You got what you wanted?' Doc Chambers asked.

'Yes. When will you do the PM?'

'It'll be first on the list in the morning. Your case?'

'It looks likely.' Stepping away, he opened the photo he'd taken, zoomed in so he could read it easily and used his radio to call Control. 'Can you do a VIN check for me?' he asked the operator.

'Yes, go ahead.'

He read out the number.

'Stand by.' She was back in moments. 'Control for DS Gayle. That VIN comes back to a green MGB GT, 1975 model, owned by a Michael Hardman of Bindon Road, Pinhoe. It's got no markers on it.' She read out the vehicle registration number.

'Do we know anything about Michael Hardman?'

Another brief pause. 'Nothing on PNC.'

'OK, thanks.' He put away the phone and the radio, made a note of the VRN and headed back towards Colin and Mark. 'The car's from Pinhoe,' he said. 'Not reported stolen, but if it's recent, it might not have been, yet.'

'Doesn't bode well for the owner,' Colin said as yellow lights flickered behind him, a vehicle recovery truck pulling up to the crossroads. 'Whether it's been nicked or not, with the key being in the ignition.'

'Hmm. I'll go and check on them. I'll let you know what I find.'

*

Pinhoe was an area in the north-east of the city, a former village that had been absorbed by urban sprawl. Pete could have called Dave to go and check on the Hardmans as he now lived in Pinhoe, but as he was already out and working and Dave had gone home several hours ago, he went himself.

He found the road just a few yards from the edge of the city. Turning in opposite a row of substantial semi-detached houses that backed onto fields, he entered a street of 1960s and '70s bungalows. It forked a few yards in and Pete took the left fork, heading downhill, and quickly found the number he was looking for on the right. In common with its neighbours, it was detached but close, only a couple of doors up from the turning circle at the end of the cul-de-sac. He pulled up onto the lowered kerb almost directly opposite a streetlight.

Unlike the lush planting of the one across the road from it, the open plan front garden was fully covered with block paving. The garage door at the right side was white, along with the window frames, which included a dormer in the high roof, while the front door was a green that matched the colour of the car the occupants had owned.

The house was in darkness and, as he approached the front door, he could hear no sounds from within until he pressed the doorbell and it chimed musically.

There was no response.

He waited for several seconds then tried it again, pressing three times in quick succession. He could always apologise later, if necessary. When there was still no response he took a couple of steps back and looked to either side but saw no way around to the back of the property. The garages were built tight against the neighbouring properties.

He sighed.

Checking his watch, he found it was approaching 11:00pm. Not an ideal time to be knocking up the neighbours, but better than 1:00 in the morning. He went up-hill. The front of their bungalow was paved like the Hardmans', divided from it by a wall that was low enough to step over. A white estate car sat outside the garage at its far side.

Their doorbell, when he pressed it, was a different tune to their neighbours', but just as musical. But here, after a few brief seconds, there was a response. A light came on somewhere inside. Movement showed beyond the rippled glass of the door. A brass chain stretched taught as the door opened, showing one eye and a portion of a male face, a hint of grey hair remaining above the ear, cut almost to stubble.

Pete raised his warrant card. 'Sorry to trouble you at this time of night. I'm DS Gayle with Exeter CID. I was trying to get hold of your neighbours, the Hardmans, but there's no response.'

'Won't be. They're not in, far as I know.'

'Not in?' Pete checked, frowning.

'Heard 'em go out s'afternoon, haven't heard 'em come back.'

'You heard them, you didn't see them?'

'Saw the car drive off.'

'What time was this?'

'About half-five, six. Somewhere there.'

'Is that usual for them? To be out this late?' Pete had looked them up before coming out here. Mr and Mrs Hardman were in their early sixties, just the two of them living here.'

'No, I suppose not, but…' He shrugged. 'I don't know. They might have gone out somewhere, for a change. Theatre, cinema… Why? What's CID after them for?'

'Can you describe Mr Hardman for me?' Pete asked instead of answering the question.

The older man's mouth pushed up. 'He's about five-nine, five-ten. Average build, I suppose. Grey hair. More of it than I've got. Craggy features, they'd call it, I suppose.'

He'd yet to get an official measurement, but the body in the car had looked smaller than that, to him as well as to Doc Chambers, who'd described him as smaller than average. So it was unlikely to have been Hardman out there on the moor. Which suggested… He blinked. 'OK, thank you, Mr…?'

'Norton. So, what's going on?'

'That's yet to be determined, Mr Norton. But it may not have been Mr Hardman driving his car away from here, earlier.'

'What, it was being nicked?' He shut the door abruptly, slid the chain off and opened it properly, revealing that he was clad in pale striped pyjamas.

'Possibly,' Pete said. 'Do you keep a spare key for their house? In case of deliveries or emergencies.'

'Nah.' He shook his head. 'T'other side might. The Coopers.' He nodded towards the Hardmans' property and beyond. 'They seem to get on pretty well.'

'OK, thank you. I'll give them a knock.'

'They keep that old motor in the garage and I never heard anything in the way of it being broke into, so…'

'The door looks intact,' Pete confirmed. 'I'd better get on and see if I can get hold of that key as they're not answering the door,' Pete said. 'Thanks again for your help.'

He stepped away, angling across the paved front of the bungalow towards the lower corner, where it joined the pavement. Heard the door close behind him as he reached the public footpath.

Two doors down, he pressed another doorbell, this one at the side of a white UPVC door behind a lawned front garden with a gravel drive leading up to the garage.

There was no response to his first press of the bell, so he tried again and knocked, to back up the demand for attention.

A light flicked on inside and he heard a voice faintly through the double-glazing. 'All right, all right. What's the bloody panic?'

He saw movement. This time, the door opened fully. The male standing before him was in a dark dressing gown and slippers, his lower legs bare.

'Yes? What's so…?' He stopped as he saw the warrant card that Pete was holding up.

'Police, Mr Cooper. I won't waste your time. Do you have a key for next-door, the Hardmans'?'

'Yes, why? What's wrong?'

'I tried raising them and can't get a response. I need to check they're OK.'

'Oh, right. Why? Has something happened?'

'Something has, yes. What, exactly, we're not sure of yet. If you could lend me the key, I'll hopefully be able to find out.'

'Hold on a tick, I'll come with you.'

'That's not necessary, Mr Cooper. I'll handle it.'

'Not with a key I've given you, you won't. Not that I don't trust the police, but I don't know you, do I? And you're not in uniform.'

Pete pursed his lips. 'The quicker, the better, then, eh? And once we're in, don't touch anything, OK?'

He grunted. 'Wait there.'

The door closed and Pete waited. It was no more than a minute before it opened again and the man – almost as tall as Pete's six feet, but ten years older, with a full head of greying hair that hadn't been smoothed much by the sweater he'd pulled on along with a pair of grey joggers and white-striped trainers.

'Right, let's go,' he said, raising a key on a dark leather fob.

Pete led the way, stopping at the green front door and putting a hand out for the key.

Reluctantly, it was handed over.

'Stay behind me and, as I said before, don't touch anything, OK?' Pete said and waited for the nod of response before turning to insert the key into the door and turn it.

Stepping inside, he used his pen to flick on the light switch. 'Where do they sleep?' he asked, his voice low.

'Upstairs, in the dormer.'

'We'll start there.'

The stairs were immediately to Pete's right as he stood in the entrance with a ninety-degree bend at a half-landing just three steps up. He listened for a moment, then, hearing nothing, began to climb. There was a small galleried landing at the top – three steps across to a closed doorway. Taking a glove from his jacket pocket, he pressed down on the very tip of the lever-style handle until it clicked and he could push the door gently open.

The vertical blinds covering the window let in enough light from the streetlight across the road to show him all he needed as he felt the other man begin to crowd him from behind. As the door swung to the left, he saw feet on the floor in front of him, a figure on the bed to his right. Opening wider, the door allowed him to see the trousers bundled around the ankles above the feet. The figure on the bed was female. A woman of mature years, slim, her hair still dark – or perhaps it was dyed. It was impossible to tell in this light. But more pertinent was the fact that she was naked and splayed out, limbs tied to the feet of the bed with some sort of cord.

The handle of a knife protruded from between her breasts. There was very little blood. Just a trickle, black in the artificial light, ran over her ribs and down onto the sheets at her far side.

The male facing her was of similar age and also bound – in his case to a wooden rocking chair. What was visible of his face was darkened by bruising. His jaw was pulled wide, something thrust into his mouth, then taped in place, the tape wound several times around his face and head, covering both his mouth and nose.

Pete took a step back, bumping into the man behind him, then turned to face him. 'You don't need to see that, Mr Cooper.'

Horror showed on his face. 'They're…?'

'Dead,' Pete confirmed and raised a hand towards the stairs. 'Let's step carefully out and I'll call it in.' To emphasise the point, he reached for his belt and unhooked the radio, lifting it into view. 'I'll keep the key for now.' He tucked it into his jacket pocket.

'Right. Of course. I'll…' He turned, moving hesitantly as if stunned by the news. Which, no doubt, he was, Pete reflected, following him to the stairs.

As they descended, he asked, 'Is there internal access to the garages in these places?'

Cooper looked back over his shoulder and reached for the banister.

'Hands,' Pete snapped. 'Don't use them.'

He blinked. 'Oh. Sorry.' He turned back to continue down. 'Yes, from the kitchen. Why?'

'Because their car was stolen.'

'So...' He reached the half-landing and turned again, keeping his hands to himself this time. 'They were... That was done for the sake of that old MG?'

'At least partly, yes, it seems that way.' Pete raised a hand towards the front door.

'Jesus,' the man breathed, shaking his head. 'What's the world coming to? It's a bloody rust-bucket anyway. Whoever has it's going to have to spend a fortune fixing it, same as Mike was about to.'

He stepped out to the paved frontage, Pete following him.

Something sparked in Pete's brain. 'About to?'

'Yeah, he'd got it booked in for next week, I think it was. Or the week after, maybe.'

'Do you know where?'

He shook his head. 'Why? How can that matter now?'

'It might,' Pete told him. 'It's something that we'll need to check on.' He raised the radio and keyed the mike. 'DS Gayle to Control.'

'Control.'

'I need uniforms and the pathologist, if he's finished up on Woodbury Common, to attend my location on Bindon Road, Pinhoe. Two bodies discovered.'

'Received, Sarge.'

'Thanks for your help, Mr Cooper,' Pete said, lowering the radio. 'I expect you'll want to let your wife know what's happened.'

He blinked and gave a soft grunt. 'Yeah. I'd best...' He glanced at his own front door, then back at Pete.

'They'll be here in a few minutes, I expect. There'll be comings and goings for a while tonight, I'm afraid. You'll need the curtains shut, if they aren't already.'

CHAPTER FIFTEEN

Alone again, Pete returned to his car so that he could speak without the chance of being overheard. His call was picked up on the second ring.

'Yup.'

'Guv, it's Pete. The body in the MG isn't its owner. He and his wife are here. Also dead. And not peacefully.'

Colin grunted. 'I'll tell Mark to stand down. Do you need anything?'

'No, I've got Forensics and the doc on the way.'

'OK.'

They hung up and Pete sat and waited. He wouldn't re-enter the bungalow until Forensics gave him permission but he had to remain on-scene, ready for when that happened. First to arrive was a patrol car. It went past him, down to the turning circle at the end of the road, swung around and came back up to park nose-to-nose with his silver Ford. The uniformed driver got out and approached as Pete buzzed his window down.

'Sarge. What's happening?'

Pete pointed across at the Hardmans' bungalow. 'Two bodies inside,' he said. 'Husband and wife. Their car was stolen this afternoon. Found burned out up on Woodbury Common a little while ago, with another body inside.'

'Nasty.' The constable's expression twisted into a combined frown and grimace. 'Is this related to the other car thefts I've been hearing about, then?'

'We think so. You're on your own?'

He shrugged. 'You know what it's like, Sarge. Not enough… Of us to go around at the best of times.'

Pete noted the hesitation, as if he'd been going to say something else and stopped himself. 'I'm aware. I don't know how long you'll be here. Depends on Forensics and how they get on in there. As you can see, you're the first to arrive apart from me, and I found them, along with the neighbour.' He nodded towards the property next-door. 'Given the time, we'll wait for morning to knock up the other neighbours, to find out if anyone saw or heard anything or if they've got doorbell cameras. Better disturbing their Cornflakes than their kip. Especially as we already know where the car ended up.'

'Which leaves us to find out how the perp got here,' the constable said. 'Who brought him, maybe. And if he left any prints or DNA inside,' he added with a nod towards the bungalow behind him.

'Among other things,' Pete agreed and took out his phone to text Dave Miles, giving him the details of what was happening and where and telling him to get here bright and early to speak to the neighbours. He then sent a similar text to Ben Myers, to come out here in the morning and help Dave with the task. As he was pressing Send, an engine sounded up the street behind him and the constable standing outside his car glanced up.

'Forensics is here.'

*

Pete used the Vaseline on his nose again when he attended the mortuary at the Royal Devon and Exeter hospital the next morning. It didn't block the smell completely, but it made it tolerable when he stepped into the chilled room.

All three of the post-mortem tables were occupied, each with a white plastic sheet over the body laid out on it.

'I thought we'd start with the two easily identifiable victims, rather than doing them in the order they were discovered,' Chambers declared when Pete arrived. 'Then we can take our time with the third victim.'

'Whatever you think's best, Doc.'

Chambers nodded. 'Then let's begin.' He stepped across to the furthest table from the door and folded the sheet back, carefully removing it.

It revealed a man in his fifties, of average build with little trace of excess fat on him. His hair had been dark but was fading to a steely grey. It was still dark, though, dense and curly on his torso and upper arms as well as his legs and pubic region.

'We have a male,' Chambers announced for the recorder on the light fitting over the table. 'Aged in his fifties, identified through photographs, driving licence and fingerprints discovered in the home where he was found as Michael James Hardman. He appears to have been in good health.' He quoted height and weight. 'He was found bound to a chair with masking tape and more of the same wrapped around his lower face, cutting off his airways. Initial examination reveals no sharp-force trauma, though there is extensive bruising on the face and there has been blood-loss from the nose. There are also traces of bruising on the hands and forearms, suggestive of defensive injuries.'

He manipulated the nose. 'The nose is not broken. There are pressure marks on the wrists consistent with the tape binding. Also, matching marks on the ankles. We appear to be looking at a blitz attack. Our victim was overpowered, bound to the chair and then the tape applied over his lower face with the intention of suffocating him. Again, this is supported by the petechial haemorrhages in the eyes. We'll check toxicology, of course, as well as the CO_2 level in the blood.' He turned to the stocky, dark-haired man in green scrubs who'd had little to do, so far, but watch. 'If you could take a blood sample, Barry, and cover him up... Thank you.'

Moving on to the next body, he once again carefully folded back the covering sheet. 'Next, we have a female, discovered in the same room as Mr Hardman and identified through similar means as his wife, Sheila, aged fifty-two. She appears to have been in good health, outwardly fit and well-nourished. There are marks from binding at wrists and ankles consistent with the cords found tied around them and binding her to the casters on the bed. These show some tearing of the skin, showing that the victim fought against her bindings either during or after their application.'

Pete looked from her face, which had been handsome, rather than pretty, and framed by brown hair cut in a wavy bob, to the wrist nearest to him. He saw the narrow, hard lines of redness around it and traces of blood and torn skin where she'd struggled. 'What was she bound with?' he asked.

Chambers looked up. 'I thought you saw her, Peter?'

'Only in semi-darkness. By the time I came back in, after the forensics team and you'd done your jobs there, she was already in the HRP.'

Colloquially known as a body-bag, especially in America, the official term in the UK was a human remains pouch or HRP.

Chambers nodded. 'It was a braided nylon cord, about 4mm thick.'

'So, something he'd brought with him for the purpose, like the masking tape.'

'It would appear so.'

'Was there a bag of any sort in the MG, up on Woodbury Common?'

'There was the remains of what appeared to have been a rucksack on the back seat, yes. The buckles, at least, with traces of the straps they'd been attached to.'

Pete nodded. That supported his theory. 'Thanks. Sorry. Carry on, Doc.'

Chambers turned back to the body in front of him. 'There are faint bruise marks on the chest, the breasts and the right cheek.' He pointed to her cheekbone, where the slightest discolouration was evident below the eye and in front of the ear, then her chest, where a fist-sized mark was evident, though only when Pete looked closely, between and above her breasts.

'Another, similar mark is evident lower on the torso,' Chambers continued, and pointed to her stomach, just below the sternum. 'Possibly from a punch. But in this case, there are no defensive injuries on the hands and arms. The subject is in full rigor now, but I did perform a sexual assault examination on-scene, given the circumstances, and I can confirm that there was bruising and some tearing of the vaginal tissue, consistent with rape. Certainly, there had been some form of sexual intercourse in the pre- or peri-mortem period. I took a sample for DNA comparison.'

Pete couldn't help but glance at the victim's sparsely-haired pubis as Chambers spoke. He looked away and met the pathologist's gaze. 'So, she was back-handed, thrown onto the bed, winded with a punch to the chest or the solar plexus or both, and tied down then raped,' he summarised.

'And then killed with a single stab-wound to the centre of the chest, the blade being left conveniently in-situ for us. It was a carving knife. Nine-inch blade that went in, in a single blow, between the fifth and sixth ribs on the subject's left side, up to the hilt. We performed an X-ray which confirmed that the blade transected the left cardiac ventricle and stopped when it impacted the junction of the fourth rib and the spine. She exsanguinated internally.'

Pete nodded. 'The blade being left in place stopped it coming out,' he guessed.

'Indeed. And so to Number Three.'

They moved on again. Barry covered the second body and Tony Chambers removed the sheet from the third. Now, the smell assaulted Pete's nostrils all the more powerfully, despite the menthol-infused petroleum jelly he'd smeared around his nostrils.

He grimaced at both the smell and the sight, though any sympathy he might have felt for the victim laid out in front of him was tempered by what he'd just seen and who he suspected this to be. Even so, this was a human being. He couldn't help but feel horror at the sight.

'Looks a hell of a sight worse in daylight than it did last night,' he said, looking at the charred and blackened remains.

'You can see the detail now,' Chambers agreed. 'We have a male victim, as evidenced by the shape of the skull, the jawbone and the sizes of the hands and feet,' he said for the recording. 'Heavily burned. There is extensive charring and even complete destruction of the epidermal layers and underlying tissue over the vast majority of the body. The smell of an accelerant is evident, namely petrol.' He glanced up at Pete. 'You'll have noticed at the scene that the side windows of the car had been lowered by two or three inches, which shows a degree of forethought and knowledge on the part of the perpetrator. Most don't think to do that, so a fire set inside a car will quickly burn out for lack of oxygen.'

Pete nodded. 'Yes, I've seen that more than once. It can help us out no end.'

Chambers tipped his head in agreement. 'There is a small amount of skin remaining on the sides of the neck and the top of the scalp that allows us, on cleaning, to confirm the victim's race as white European, though hair and eye colour are impossible to determine. We have already taken dental X-rays with a view to confirming identification.'

'If it's who I suspect, you might find it helpful to know he lived in St Sidwell's, when it comes to that,' Pete said.

'We'll start the search in that direction then. Thank you,' Chambers acknowledged. 'On the subject's anterior aspect, the centres of burning appear to have been at the feet and in the lap or groin area, spreading upward over the calves and the torso. The accelerant was poured into the car's footwell and into the subject's lap. As you saw at the scene, he was tied into place with wire around his neck and the headrest of the car seat and his wrists were tied with the same wire. It had suffered somewhat in the fire but, back here and cleaned up, it turns out to be garden wire with a diameter of 1mm.'

Pete frowned. 'That's thin for garden wire, isn't it?'

Chambers tipped his head. 'It comes in a variety of thicknesses from 1 to 3mm, I gather. As you say, I use something thicker myself – 2mm. But I dare say there are applications for the thinner variety. But back with our victim here… The tissue damage is extensive so a detailed examination is going to be needed and, even then, we may not determine actual cause of death.'

'Is it possible to rule the fire itself in or out in that respect?' Pete asked.

'Yes. When we open him up, we'll check his lungs and throat for burning and smoke. That's the easy part. And we should be able to check for strangulation, too, despite the wire holding him in place. Internal bruising and the condition of the hyoid bone. But if he was beaten, stabbed or shot and the bullet didn't remain within the body… As you can see, the condition of the body won't make that easy to spot. Not externally, anyway.'

'Unless on his back,' Pete suggested.

Chambers grimaced. 'Unfortunately, that doesn't apply in this case. The burning seems to have had three centres of intensity – the lap and groin area, the feet and the lower back.'

'The lower back?' Pete interrupted. 'How'd that come about? He was in a car seat.'

'He was,' Chambers agreed. 'But the first thing about that is that it was a pre-safety regulation seat and the second was the lithium battery in the footwell behind him.'

'Lithium battery?'

Chambers nodded deeply. 'The remains of an electric scooter. Some of them are notorious for catching spontaneously on fire due to connectivity issues, as you probably know. And lithium is highly volatile anyway. Burn away the plastic casing of a battery like that, exposing it to air, especially with flame involved, and you've got a recipe for an extremely hot and intense fire that's very difficult to extinguish.'

Pete grimaced. 'Don't tell that to the terrorists.'

'Quite. So, moving on...' He reached for a scalpel. 'It's time to begin the internal examination. We'll start with the throat, given the fire damage.'

He lifted the chin slightly and Pete grimaced again at the crackling sound of brittle burned flesh giving way under the pressure of his gloved fingers. He paused, looking up at Pete. 'And there we may have an answer to your question, Peter.'

Pete frowned, looking closer despite the smell and the sickening sight of charring over raw meat. Something else was embedded there. 'What is it?'

'A chain. With a tag suspended from it.' His blue-gloved fingers delved carefully, manipulating the chain delicately free of the roasted flesh. Now Pete could see it. A roughly inch-and-a-half by half-inch tag came free, dangling from the chain along Chamber's finger. Something was cut into it: a small cross at the top and some writing descending from it along the length.

'What does it say?' he asked.

The pathologist used the finger and thumb of his free hand to wipe it, then raised it to a better angle.

'Ewan.'

CHAPTER SIXTEEN

'It's Pete Gayle. Where are you?' he asked as soon as the connection was made as he walked back to his car from the post-mortem room at the Royal Devon and Exeter hospital.

'At work. Why? Have you found him?'

'Where's work?' he asked, ignoring her question for now.

'The Spar shop on Thurlow Road. What's going on?'

'I need to talk to you. In person. It won't take long. I've just got a couple of things to follow up on, that's all.' A harmless lie that would ease her mind until he could see her.

She let out a sigh. 'Christ, I thought…'

'Sorry, but… You've still heard nothing from him, then?'

'No.'

'I'll see you soon.' He hung up and continued to his car. Thurlow Road, he knew, was just a short walk from where she lived, off Blackboy Road. He made it in a few minutes through quiet mid-morning traffic. Turning into the side-street, he parked a few yards up from the little corner shop and walked back. He couldn't see her on the shop floor so took out his badge and interrupted the cashier.

'Sorry,' he said. 'I'm looking for Charlene Price.'

'If she's not stacking shelves, she'll be out the back.'

He nodded and turned away.

'You can't… Excuse me.'

Pete ignored the middle-aged woman's protests and headed for the door he'd noticed alongside the fresh fruit and veg racks at the rear of the shop. As expected, it was locked, accessed by a staff ID badge. He knocked heavily. In moments, she was there, on the far side of the little eye-level reinforced glass pane. She opened the door for him.

'Sergeant…?'

'Pete,' he corrected. 'Is there somewhere we can talk briefly?'

'Um… Yeah. The office, I suppose. She won't be using it while she's on the till.'

He nodded and stepped through, following her into a short corridor between a single door on the left and two on the right that led to a storeroom. She opened the door on the left and entered.

It wasn't the smallest office he'd ever been in, but it reminded him of several others in its basic functionality. A desk in the middle, a chair behind it and another, less comfortable one on the other side. Shelves. Filing cabinets. A computer and printer. Phone. A small window with reinforced glass covered with a venetian blind that should have been white but was dulled with dust.

Automatically, Charlene took the less comfy chair.

Pete took out his phone as he sat down across from her and brought up a picture. 'Do you recognise this?' he asked and leaned forward across the desk to show it to her.

She gasped, her gaze flicking up from the little screen to meet his, eyes wide with horror. 'Yes. It's Ewan's. Where'd you…?'

Pete had had Barry clean the necklace and pendant after Doc Chambers removed it from the victim and lay it out on a clean piece of waxy white bench-coat paper for him to photograph.

'Where'd you get it?' she asked, finishing the question this time.

Pete closed the image and put the phone away. 'I'm sorry, Charlene,' he said. 'I've got some bad news for you.'

He watched her face crumple as he spoke.

'No,' she gasped.

'There was a car fire last night, up on Woodbury Common. He was dead before it was lit, but…'

'No!' This time the denial was louder, more definite.

'Ewan's gone, Charlene. I'm sorry.'

Her eyes flashed as she met his gaze again. 'Are you? You were looking at him for some sort of crime, weren't you? A serious one, if you're CID. Oh, God.' She broke down and began to weep uncontrollably, head in her hands as she hunched over on the chair.

Pete waited until she'd begun to calm a little. He really wanted to get up and go around the desk to her, to comfort her with just a hand, a gentle word. But as a male officer alone with a female subject, in the present political and social climate, he couldn't without risking an accusation of inappropriate behaviour, as sad as that was.

When her sobs began to ease and she took out a tissue to wipe at her eyes, he spoke. 'We wanted to talk to him about something, yes. But whoever he was, whatever he'd done, we didn't want or expect anything like this. And we will do everything possible to find out who did it. You've got my word as a father on that.'

'Won't bring him back, though, will it?' Still, her tone was almost accusatory as she wiped her eyes again and looked up at him.

He tipped his head. 'No, it won't. But it will get some justice for him. And make sure whoever did that isn't free to do it again, to someone else. I'll need your help, though.'

'With what? I don't know most of what he gets… Got up to.'

Pete shook his head. 'Not that. Would he have any records at home? Bank, mobile phone bills, anything like that?'

She shook her head with something between a grimace and a sneer. 'He done all that sort of stuff online.'

'Did he have a computer?'

'Yeah, he liked his games. It's in his room.'

Pete nodded. 'Can I get access to that?'

She glanced around vaguely. 'I'm…'

'I'm sure, given the circumstances, they'll give you some time off. The rest of the day, at least.'

She frowned. 'We're short-staffed as it is.'

'Maybe, but given what's happened…'

She grimaced. 'I can…'

He stood up. 'I'll tell her. You grab your coat and I'll take you home.'

'I don't know…'

'Well, I do. You need some time to process what's happened. To grieve for your son.'

And he did know all about that. His throat clogged at the memories that came flooding back, unbidden, into his mind once more. He shook his head, dispelling the thoughts and images, and stood up abruptly. 'Grab your coat,' he said and stepped out, heading back to the main shop.

The woman at the till was no longer serving, though there were one or two customers moving among the shelves. He crossed straight to her, taking out his warrant card again.

'I'm DS Gayle,' he said. 'Exeter CID. I'm taking Charlene home.'

She looked horrified. 'But I can't...'

'She's just lost her son,' Pete said. 'That's what I came here to confirm.'

'Oh. Oh, my God. Sorry. I'll...' She stopped as the rear door opened and Charlene Price stepped through, shrugging into a denim jacket while somehow manhandling a handbag at the same time. She waited until Charlene was closer before saying, 'I'm really sorry, Charlene. Take as much time as you need, yeah? I'll manage.'

'I won't... Thanks. I'll see you soon.'

'No worries. I expect Nat'll appreciate a bit of overtime if she can arrange cover for Davey.'

Charlene's mouth pushed up as Pete held the door for her and raised a hand to indicate direction.

'She won't get cover,' she said as they crossed the narrow road towards his car. 'Never can.'

'Not your problem,' Pete said. 'Not today, of all days. It's not your shop. You just work there. And, given what's happened, they'll do without you for a bit. How they do it is up to them.' He unlocked the car and sat in, leaning across to open the door for her.

'Thanks,' she said as he switched on the ignition.

As soon as his phone connected to the comms system, he placed a call.

'PC Evans. How can I help?'

'Jill, it's me. I've got Miss Price with me. I'm taking her home. Can you come and meet us there?'

'Yeah, course. See you soon.'

'Thanks.' He ended the call and checked the side mirror before pulling out. It took just a few moments through the side-streets to reach Salisbury Road and there were few cars parked along there at this time of day, so he pulled up right outside her door.

She let them in and headed straight for the kitchen at the rear. 'Do you want a drink?'

'Actually, yes, I could do with something. But I can do it.'

'No, I… Want to keep my hands busy.'

He nodded. 'Understood.'

'What do you want? Tea? Coffee?'

'I don't mind either, as long as there's a couple of sugars in there,' he said. 'Tea, I take milk in, coffee I can do either way.'

'Coffee it is, then.'

'OK.' He let her make a start, bustling around the small space, darting here and there, switching on the kettle, fetching out cups, the coffee, the sugar, a spoon. Once she'd done, he leaned on the doorjamb and asked gently, 'Tell me about Ewan. What was he like as a youngster?'

Her face softened as she glanced up at him. 'He was a cheeky little mite, right from early on. Always smiling. Mischievous. In a good way, though. Fun.'

He nodded. 'No dad on the scene?' He'd seen it so often. Single mothers, struggling to bring up a child on their own. Or not struggling – relying on the state and anyone who'd step in to help – to take the responsibility that they denied.

'Was at first,' she said. 'Until he was four. Then he died. Got killed.'

'Oh, I'm sorry. What happened?'

'Lorry crash on the M5. He was in a car, on the way home. Didn't stand a chance.'

'God. That must have affected Ewan.'

'It did. He pulled back into himself. Then, starting school… Even then he was little. Got picked on. Drew back even more. It was like a vicious circle. The more he pulled back, the more he got picked on and the more he got picked on, the more he tried to avoid folks.'

'Hmm.' Again, Pete saw the parallels with his own son, Tommy. He'd also been small for his age, picked on because of that and, probably, he imagined, because of Pete's job in the police. After a while, Tommy had switched things around. He hadn't grown, but he'd turned vicious. Had Ewan done the same? But what was it about senior citizens? Or was that just chance? Was it the cars they owned rather than who they were?

Now was not the time to ask about that kind of thing.

The doorbell rang, breaking his thought process. He pushed himself upright. 'I'll get it.'

Turning, he went through to the front door and opened it. It was Jill.

'Good. Come on in.' He stepped back. 'You can stay with her while I go up to his room.'

He led the way back to the kitchen. 'It's my colleague, PC Evans,' he said.

'Jill,' she corrected. 'How are you doing? I was sorry to hear about Ewan.'

She grimaced and gave a soft grunt.

'Truly,' Jill said. 'No matter what the circumstances were.'

'Can I go and have a look at his room?' Pete asked.

'Yeah.'

'Do you know the password for his computer?'

'Huh! As if.'

'He wouldn't have written it down anywhere?'

'Doubt it. He wasn't much for writing.'

Pete nodded. 'Never mind. If we had his phone, it would be easier, but..'

'He didn't have it with him?'

He shook his head. 'Not when he was found, no.'

'I'd... I want to see him.' she asked abruptly.

He grimaced. 'We haven't formally identified him yet, Charlene. It wouldn't be right for you to see someone who isn't your son.'

'Well, I can identify him. I thought that's what you did: asked a family member to do that.'

He shook his head. 'Sometimes. But you wouldn't be able to identify him anyway.'

'Of course I would! I'm his mother. I've lived with him for the past twenty-two years. If I can't, who can, eh?'

Pete gently shook his head again, reaching out to place a hand on her arm. 'I said earlier, he was in a car fire. There's... Too much damage for a visual identification. There's no need for you to see him like that. Far better to remember him as you last saw him, alive and well. Which reminds me: which dentist did he go to?'

'He hasn't been to one for ages. But when he did, it was Spicer Road.'

Pete raised an eyebrow at the irony of that. Spicer Road was a side-turning off Heavitree, almost opposite the old police station. 'OK, thanks.'

'How did he die? You said it wasn't the fire.'

Pete released a breath, relieved that they were on safer ground now. 'Blunt-force trauma. A blow to the head.' There was no need to tell her about the pathologist's other findings: the pre-mortem injuries he'd found on the body. She didn't need to know about them. Not now, at least.

Her face crumpled and she began to weep once more. Pete shared a glance with Jill and stepped away, heading for the stairs.

*

Pete had never seen anything quite like what he found in Ewan Price's bedroom. To say it was a computer for games was like saying a Rolls Royce Silver Ghost was a means of getting from A to B: technically true but wholly inadequate in a descriptive sense. Three TV-sized screens stood together on a length of worktop that spanned one end of the room, angled in towards each other to give a more immersive view. In front of them were a keyboard and mouse, a joystick, a steering wheel, microphone, earphones and even a virtual reality headset.

This was not a lad who was into collecting fancy trainers.

The hardware that ran the system was an upright unit with a disk drive and four USB ports that Pete could see and, over to one side near the end of the big desk, was a combined printer and scanner, beside which was a phone charger, currently switched off and disconnected. At the opposite end of the desk, a router's several lights flickered at him as if it were alive and watching.

Then he noticed the little round ball clipped to the top of the central screen. A camera.

He dropped to his knees. Found the mains outlet that fed the whole setup and flicked the switch before unplugging everything from the base unit. Then he searched the rest of the room. He found a substantial-looking charger plugged in across the room but switched off and with nothing connected to it. For the scooter, perhaps, he thought.

He checked the wardrobe. Clothes were few and ordinary. One pair of black leather shoes sat in the bottom, a light coating of dust suggesting they got worn only rarely. A chest of drawers contained T-shirts, sweaters, socks and underwear. Pete went through everything, not expecting to find anything untoward, but needing to check anyway, for the sake of doing his job properly. He found no surprises.

Finished, he picked up the computer unit and took it with him down the stairs.

Charlene had calmed down, was in the sitting room now, seated on the sofa with Jill. Pete saw a faint smile on her face as they talked. She looked up as he entered the room, saw the computer under his arm and the smile faded.

He lifted it slightly. 'In the absence of his phone, this ought to be able to tell us what we need to know,' he said. 'His friends, contacts: all that sort of thing. We'll get it back to you as soon as we can.'

'No rush. It was his. I didn't use it. Just insisted he paid the lecky bill, seeing as it used so much.'

Pete smiled. 'It's a fair old rig he'd got up there. And I don't suppose the scooter helped, in that respect, either.'

'He weren't keen on bikes and we couldn't afford a car.'

'He learned to drive, though.'

'Yeah. Investment in his future, weren't it?' Her expression turned bitter. 'Got an hour off each week from his job, to do it.'

'What job did he do?'

'He worked at the garage in Polsloe.'

Pete felt a spark of interest flare. *Did he indeed?* 'When was this?' he asked.

'From when he left school until last November.'

'What happened?'

'He had a bit of a disagreement with the management. You know they were taken over?'

'No, I didn't.'

She nodded. 'Used to be a family firm. But then the old boy decided he wanted to retire. He was seventy-two, to be fair. Place was bought out by one of the multiples. New management put in. Ewan... Well, he had enough of the bullying. Decked the bloke and walked out.'

Pete nodded. 'Some people never grow out of the bullying attitude they took on as kids,' he said. 'I suppose they continue to get away with it, so see no need to change. What about after the garage? What did Ewan do then?'

She shrugged. 'It's hard to get a job without a reference, isn't it? And like I said, he'd been there since he left school.'

'What about the old man – the one who'd sold the business?'

'He had a stroke. He's still alive, I think, but...' She shrugged.

Pete grimaced. 'That's a shame.' But it reminded him of something else she'd said. 'You said he didn't have a father-figure in his life before that, as such. What about grandparents? Uncles and aunts?'

She shook her head. 'His dad was from Rugby in the Midlands. Moved down here as soon as he legally could, to get away from his family, and never went back. He didn't have a good time of it up there, from what he said. Not that that was much. Didn't like talking about it and I didn't push him to. I was brought up in care. Never knew my parents. Got fostered a few times, but none of them lasted long. And the last one…' She shuddered. 'Well, after that, I wasn't going to push Luke to mend bridges he didn't want to.'

'Not a good experience?'

'No.' The single word was said flatly, in a tone that brooked no continuation of the subject.

With no need to press it, Pete let it drop. 'I'm sorry to hear that. So Ewan was on jobseeker's allowance?'

She nodded. 'He'd started to pick up a few little jobs here and there, recently. Brought in a bit of cash. He didn't say much about it. Just that it was with cars again. Moving them around. I thought it must be like those blokes you used to see on the sides of the main roads, thumbing lifts with those weird number plates, back in the day. The hours were a bit odd sometimes, but…' She shrugged. 'Depends where you're going, I suppose, doesn't it? And it was a start, at least. A foot in the door.'

Pete shared a glance with Jill, whose eyebrow arched, but this wasn't the time to disillusion her.

'What did you want to talk to him about, anyway?' Charlene asked.

Pete blinked. 'Exactly that,' he said. 'His last source of income. Shifting cars. There's been some activity around the city, recently, that we're looking into.'

'What, nicking them or something?' Her eyes sparkled, challenging him to say yes. 'He wouldn't…'

Pete grimaced. 'Nicking them's only the first part of the process. After that, as you say, they need to be moved. And those moving them don't necessarily know where they've come from or how. But they can give us information on *who* they've come from, where they're going to and so on. He hasn't mentioned any new names in his life recently, has he?'

She shook her head. 'No. Like I said, he don't... Didn't talk about it much.'

'OK.' He tapped the computer on the carpet beside his knee. 'This should be able to help out.'

She grunted. 'How... How's knowing who his friends are going to help find out who killed him? Won't have been his best buddy, will it?'

'It wouldn't be the first time,' Pete said. 'But no. The point is, it'll give us more people to ask about what was going on in his life: who he was associating with, working with. Anyone might know anything. We don't know until we talk to them. And if anyone reaches out to you, you will let us know, won't you?'

'Hmm.'

'By the way, another thing you mentioned: he went to the garage straight from school. Which school was that?'

'How's that relevant?' she demanded with a frown. 'It's years ago.'

'Again, it might provide a link. Whoever he's been working with recently might have been an old schoolmate, for instance.'

Another grunt. 'Jimmy's. St James'.'

'I know it,' Pete nodded. 'My daughter's there now. Studying hard for her GCSE's this summer.' She was planning to stay on for another two years, for A levels, but that wasn't relevant here.

Charlene grimaced. 'Ewan preferred working with his hands. I reckon, these days, they'd call him dyslexic or something. Then, he was just behind, you know? Which didn't help. He got teased for that, too.'

Pete pursed his lips. 'Kids can be cruel.'

'Huh. Teachers, too, sometimes.'

He frowned. 'Teachers?'

'Yeah. His English teacher, especially. Nasty, self-satisfied sod, he was.'

Pete grimaced, wondering. 'What was his name?'

'Jackson.'

A frown snatched at Pete's brow and he exchanged a glance with Jill. ''Do you know his first name, by any chance?'

'No idea. Why?'

'Oh, nothing. Probably just a coincidence,' he said. But while he was in this part of town, he would drop down to Dunrich Close and check it out.

CHAPTER SEVENTEEN

Pete turned the Ford around in the end of the little cul-de-sac of Dunrich Close and pulled up alongside the white-rendered garden wall of the big white house opposite the former garage and car showroom. He'd sent Jill to retrieve the cameras they'd set up to overlook the Price residence as they were no longer needed. Then, with Ewan's computer strapped down in the boot of his car so it couldn't slide around, he'd set off to see what he could learn from Mrs Jackson. Now he locked the car and strode purposefully around to the bungalow in the corner behind the walled garden.

Ringing the bell, he waited only a moment before the door was opened.

'Detective,' Mrs Jackson said. 'I wasn't expecting you. Have you got some news for us? Have you found the car?'

'Not yet,' he said. 'We have found out who we think took it, though.'

'Well, then…'

'He can't tell us what happened to it. He's dead.'

'Ah,' she said with a grimace. 'Do you want to come in?'

Pete nodded. 'I do need a brief word.'

She led the way through to the sitting room, Pete closing the front door behind them.

'How can I help?' she asked when they were settled and he'd refused a drink.

'I just need to clear up a couple of points,' he said.

'Yes?'

'I've been led to believe your husband didn't come down to Exeter for the job at Risingbrook.'

She blinked. 'Well, no. Not directly. He went to a state school first. Had a couple of years there, then moved to Risingbrook. Why's that important?'

'Which school did he come to, to begin with?' Pete asked.

'St James'. Why?'

Pete nodded. 'That's what I was told. The relevance being that there has to be a connection of some kind between the incidents we're looking at. Between the victims, the cars...' He spread his hands. 'Something they all have in common. And that is a possible link. The other one we've come across today is a garage near Polsloe Bridge. Did your husband ever use it?'

'I wouldn't know. I don't get involved in that side of things.'

Pete pursed his lips. 'Does he keep all his paperwork, receipts and so on?'

'Yes.'

'Then, if he did use the place, there'd be a record of it in his files.'

'Well, I suppose, but... It'd take a while to rummage through and find it.'

'It could be important.'

'Well... OK.' She got up and headed for the spare room. In moments, she was back with a green hanging file in hand. 'It's all in here, but it's not in any order.'

'If we spread it out on the table, I can help sort it out, if you like,' he offered.

She gave a slight grimace. 'If you've got the time...'

'Not really, but anything to get the job done.'

'OK, then.' She headed for the dining table in the back part of the room and sat down, opened the folder and, as Pete joined her, took a handful of papers off the top of the pile. 'Here, you have those, I'll have the rest.'

They began spreading everything out, trying to put it into date order, to be refined later in the process.

'What's so important about this particular garage?' She asked as they worked. 'Have the others been there?'

'We're still checking on that,' he said though she was the first to be asked. 'But the possible offender used to work there.'

'So, he'll have seen the car come in and taken a shine to it, you think?'

'That's the working theory for now.'

'What's it called?'

'Back then, it was Nolan's. It's Tyre Pro now.'

'Right.' She slid another piece of paper off the pile in front of her and was reaching across to add it to another, smaller pile when she paused. 'Like this?'

Pete glanced across, took the sheet she'd exposed and said, 'Yes. Exactly like that.' He searched for the date and finally found it. 'Three years ago. Excellent. Thank you.' He took out his phone and photographed the sheet. 'Can I borrow this?'

*

Minutes later, he was back in his car and heading for the station. As he drew up to the junction at the head of Dunrich Close, he used the comms screen to make a call.

'DC Bennett speaking. How can I help?'

Spotting a break in the traffic, he pulled out, turning right, away from the city centre. 'Jane, it's me. Amongst all those papers you collected from the Lockwoods, do you remember seeing anything from Nolan's garage, by Polsloe Bridge?'

'Not off the top of my head, no, but I can check. Why? Have you got something?'

He explained what he'd found so far. 'I'm on the way back there now, via the tech department at Middlemoor. Thought you might be able to get a head-start looking for it, in case there's something that ties in.'

'OK. What about the mini? The Danscombes. And the MG.'

'We'll get to them if you find anything from the Lockwoods. At least we've got everything from the Danscombes. I don't suppose anyone's started going through it yet, have they?'

'Huh! Chance would be a fine thing.'

'Have we heard from Forensics yet about the Hardman property?'

'They finished there a few minutes ago.'

'Right, Dave can go out there and search for paperwork, then, if needs be, as it's on his doorstep, almost.'

'He'll like that.'

'We can't be wicked to him all the time.'

'Why?'

He laughed. 'He'll get a complex.'

'Nothing he doesn't deserve.'

He heard a male voice in the background.

'There you go, see,' she said. 'Not everything's about you, Dapper.'

'I'll see you soon,' Pete said and ended the call.

*

He shrugged off his jacket and hung it over the back of his chair in the incident room. With Jill having got back before him, his whole team were there although, being Saturday, Bernadette Douglas and her Ops Support crew were absent.

'Yes,' Jane said, looking up at him as he pulled the chair out to sit down.

'Steady on. We can't. We're both already married, remember?' Pete retorted.

'Not that. The Lockwoods. He usually took the car to the Volvo dealership, regular as clockwork. But on one occasion, a couple of years ago, he took it to Nolan's. Had an exhaust fitted.'

'Maybe the Volvo place couldn't fit him in,' Dave suggested.

'Which gives you an early knock-off,' Pete told him. 'Or not really.'

'What's that mean?'

'It means you get to go and have a rummage at the Hardman house, see if you can find anything showing they took that MG there at any point. I'll go through what we collected from Mrs Danscombe.'

'OK, but all that's going to show is a link to a dead man. How are we going to find the bugger who killed him from that?' Dave demanded.

'One step at a time,' Pete told him. 'I've just dropped off that particular dead man's computer with the technical team next-door, so they can get into it for us. Hopefully, we can find out who he was in touch with from it, seeing as whoever killed him appears to have nicked his phone. While they're doing that, though, another thing I got from his mother was the number of that phone. I don't know if it was the only one he had, of course, but we can at least get the data from it, from his provider – including call and tracking data.'

'What's the number, boss?' Ben asked. 'I know it's Saturday afternoon, but I'll see what I can do.'

Pete took out his notebook. Flipping it open, he passed it across to Ben. 'Apart from that, the next thing on the agenda is tracking where he took the cars. We've got dates and locations for the thefts. We need to fan out from the others like we have from the Jacksons' and collect any and all CCTV footage. Any joy on the Jag yet?'

'Nothing yet,' Dave reported.

'OK.' He tipped his head. 'You clear off. The rest of us will carry on here. We'll have a day off tomorrow, rest and recuperate, ready to plough on, on Monday.'

*

He'd finished going through the papers they'd collected from the Danscombe household without finding what he was looking for and started searching their tablet computer for anything useful when his phone rang and he picked up.

'DS Gayle.'

'It's Dave. Three for three. They took the MG to Nolan's several times. Tyres, an exhaust, even a set of brake pads.'

'Great,' Pete responded. 'Well done. You get off home, then. We won't be long getting out of here.'

'You found anything from the other couple with the Mini?'

'No,' Pete admitted. 'But it looks like they don't keep receipts that much. Just the essentials. I'm working on the computer now, trying to find anything in the way of a booking for it.'

'Still, three out of four can't be coincidence.'

'No, that's right.'

'And we've got a photo of him. Maybe Mrs D can ID him from that in a lineup.'

'Maybe.'

Pete didn't want to put her through that if he didn't absolutely have to. Seeing the face of the male who'd attacked her and her husband again, whether at home or in the hospital, at her husband's bedside, could only add to the trauma she'd already experienced and you never knew what the consequences of that might be. And it wasn't like they could charge Ewan with anything now. Her only connection to the case at this stage was the burned-out car. Whoever had burned it didn't need to have known who she was or where she lived.

'See you Monday,' he said and hung up. 'How are we doing?' he asked, looking around at the rest of his team.

'Nearly there,' Jane said. 'A few more minutes.'

'Same here,' Jill agreed.

'And me,' said Ben.

'Hmm,' Dick murmured in agreement.

'OK.' Pete bent back to his own task. He'd completed document and image searches as well as the Internet search history and was scrolling through emails when Dick let out a sigh and sat back in his chair, his computer returning to its home screen.

'Done?' Pete asked.

'Yes, thank God.'

'Anything?'

Dick shook his head, picked up his mug and drained it.

Pete returned to what he was doing. Over the next few minutes the others finished what they were doing too. Jane was the last to sit back with a heavy sigh. 'Sod all,' she declared. 'Anybody else?'

'Nope,' said Dick.

'Nothing,' Ben added.

'Nor me,' Jill put in, completing the set.

'Well, he didn't fly it out with a Chinook,' Jane declared. 'So where the hell did he go?' She got up and crossed to the big map on the wall at the back of the room. Stopping what he was doing again, Pete watched as she stared at it. They'd marked the locations of all the cameras they'd been checking. Making a quick note of the date and time he'd reached on the email list from the Danscombes' tablet computer, he stood up and went to join her.

'So, what other options are there?' he asked.

'Well, if they're breaking the cars up for parts, they can't be using a place like Nolan's, that's in the city,' she declared. 'People would notice.'

He nodded. 'Agreed. And they haven't used the main roads out of town or the motorway, or they'd have been picked up on ANPR and traffic cameras. So how can they have slipped past the cameras we've used?'

She reached up to trace the lines of the roads outward from the area they knew the Jaguar had been stashed in. Each one, in turn, ultimately led past one of the cameras until she came to the last possibility.

'If they went straight north,' she said. 'Up to St James'. Then where? Left, they pass cameras we know about, Stoke Hill takes them up towards Stoke Canon, Poltimore, Killerton or Rewe. We haven't been out that far yet. Pennsylvania Road only takes them to Stoke Canon or Cowley. Or...' She stepped closer. 'Turn right along

Prince Charles Road and you go past the supermarket and the pharmacy but if you knew about the one at the pharmacy – or even suspected it – you'd just use the service road. It wouldn't pick you up from that distance. And you can turn left up here and weave through the estate, and come out further along to avoid the supermarket.'

'Then where, though?' Pete asked, following her argument and the route she was tracing.

'Well, it takes you out towards Pinhoe. Or down Summer Lane, past the school and the arena.'

Pete blinked. 'Hmm. The school that Ewan Price went to,' he said.

'And what do we think of coincidences?' Dick asked from behind them, at the cluster of desks.

'Not a lot,' Jill answered as Pete turned to face them.

'Worth checking on Monday, when everything's open again,' he agreed. 'But for now, I reckon we ought to do like Dave and clear off home.'

CHAPTER EIGHTEEN

Pete pictured the map of Exeter in his mind, with pins marking the four locations of the attacks they knew were connected along with Ewan Price's address. The former Nolan's garage was smack in the middle of the area outlined by the pins – even more so if you discounted the Jacksons' address, which they knew was linked by a personal connection. But where were the cars going?

It wasn't Nolan's – he still thought of it by that name although he knew it had changed hands almost two years ago. Situated on a main road and surrounded by houses, someone would have remarked on that amount of out-of-hours activity there. Or at least, the people Ewan was stealing the cars for would expect it. No, as Jane had suggested before, it had to be somewhere unobtrusive. Either out of town or on an industrial estate. And the easiest of those to access from the area he was looking at was Sowton, out behind the police station and force HQ. Plenty of small units and dead-end roads, easy access to the motorway, once they'd done whatever they did to the vehicles – stripping them down or changing their identities. And even, he imagined, the extra bonus of thumbing their noses at the police who were almost overlooking them.

He sighed. Checked the clock on the nightstand. 6:45am. Sunday.

This was supposed to be his day off. Louise's, too, as it turned out.

Annie was back at school now and studying hard for her upcoming exams. But again, it was Sunday. She deserved a day off, too, surely? What could they do? Where could they go?

It was already getting light outside, a soft glow seeping through the tan curtains.

'I thought you weren't working today,' Louise said from beside him.

He blinked. 'Hello. I didn't know you were awake. And I'm not.'

'You're thinking about it, though. I can hear the cogs whirring in your brain.'

'Actually, I was just thinking about what the three of us might do today.'

'And?'

He sighed. 'It's a bit early in the year to get your cozzie on and go down the beach.'

'So?'

'What, you want to do it anyway?' he asked with a grin.

'No, idiot.' She rolled towards him and punched him lightly on the arm. 'I meant, so what else have you come up with?'

'I haven't got that far yet.'

'Hmm. So, what else were you thinking about?'

Pete squeezed his lips together. 'OK. I was thinking about the case. About where they might be taking the cars they're stealing because, if we can figure that out, it'll lead us to whoever killed Ewan Price.'

'Old ones like that: you've got two choices, haven't you? They're stripping them down for parts to sell or they're stolen to order and shipped out of the area. They're not going to drive them away because they'd be too distinctive. Get picked up by traffic cameras or patrol cars in no time. So they'd put them in containers.'

Pete reached for her hand under the covers. Some people – a lot of people – he knew would have said something like, "Well, he's no great loss to the world, so why fuss about it?" But not Louise.

And not just because of their son, whose reputation, by the time he died, was not much better than Ewan Price's, though in a different way. She also realised that, whoever Ewan was, whatever he was like, that wasn't the point. The point was that whoever killed him was just as bad or even worse, to have been able to do that to him.

Plus, Louise simply wasn't the judgemental type.

'That's what I was thinking,' he said. 'So, they'd need somewhere quiet and out-of-the-way. And with space to load them up into a container, if that's what they're doing. Or privacy to create that much noise without getting noticed if they're stripping them.'

'There's more than enough farms around here,' she said.

'True. And farming doesn't pay like it used to. But this is a specialised operation. It doesn't feel like a farmer diversifying to survive. It's more organised than that. And a container truck's going to cost a pretty penny, never mind a farm if you don't own one already.'

'Unless you get left it, like that bloke you arrested last year that was making guns.'

'True.'

'But you're not convinced.'

'You know how I feel about coincidences.'

'Doesn't mean they don't happen. And not every criminal lives in a council house or does it out of poverty or drug addiction.'

'I know that.'

'Well, they couldn't expect to get away with stripping them down in an industrial unit, down Marsh Barton, could they? The neighbours would notice after a while. Especially now they've been on the news and in the papers. People see nice old cars coming and going, they're going to pay attention, if only to appreciate them, and then they see something in the paper, they'll put two and two together in a flash. Anybody with half a brain would, anyway.'

'Hmm. So then it just becomes a question of where and when they're loading them up. And it's not like that would take long to do, if they're organised. A pair of steel ramps and a careful driver, it'd only take a few minutes. But they couldn't do that on the average residential street, which is where the Jag that Ewan stole from the Jacksons the other day was parked up until it was moved. Not that we've found out yet when that was done or where to.'

'And until you do, you're stuck. So there's no point worrying about it until you're back in the nick tomorrow. Meantime, you've got today to spend with us. Emphasis on the "With us" part.'

He smiled. 'I know. And I want to do exactly that. Which brings us back around to how to spend it and where.'

'And how to drag the young 'un away from her books, as she's just as work-obsessed as you are, lately.'

'One of us needs to persuade her to have a day off, then. It'll be good for her brain.'

'I rest my case, Your Honour.'

Pete chuckled. 'So, any suggestions?'

'Other than pneumonia from Exmouth, you mean? Well, she's still into her wildlife so I suppose there's the otter sanctuary at Buckfastleigh. Or that place at Ottery St Mary. Or the marine aquarium in Plymouth. The deer at Powderham.' Her lips pushed up. 'That's about as far as my list goes.'

'Well, any of those are close enough. Even the Eden Project's only a couple of hours away, if it comes to that. I suppose we'd best ask her.'

She gave a chuckle. 'Now, there's a thought!'

'How about I go and get the kettle on and you give her a knock, see if she wants a cuppa to start the day?'

'Chicken,' she accused. 'How come I'm the one to give her a knock?'

'You're female.'

'So?'

He shrugged. 'Just saying.'

She chuckled. 'OK, scaredy-cat. Off you go.'

He swung his legs out of bed, threw a dressing gown on over his pyjamas, slipped his feet into his slippers and headed for the kitchen. Minutes later, the three of them, all in dressing gowns and slippers, were grouped around the table in the kitchen that extended across most of the rear of the house with a back door at its end, facing the six-foot panel fence that divided their garden from next-door's.

'So, what have you got planned for today?' Pete asked Annie, whose dark hair was still mussed from the pillow as she took a sip from her steaming mug.

'Studying. Maths today.'

'Hmm. We've been talking about that. I know there's no right or wrong way to study and revise. There's probably as many methods as there are students. But there are things that you need to avoid in the process.'

She lowered her mug and stared at him, a frown beginning to nudge her brows closer together as she wondered where he was going with this conversation.

'The main one, as I found to my cost a long time ago, is overdoing it,' he said. 'You need to come up for air every now and then. Not just in terms of the expert-recommended twenty-minute blocks with a break in-between, but also the odd day off from it completely. And with your mum and me both free today, for a change, we were thinking you might like one of those. Do something together, the three of us, while we've got the chance.'

Her frown deepened, the two characteristic little vertical lines appearing between her brows. 'I can't just drop it all. It'd mess up my schedule completely.'

'I know you've got a plan. A schedule. The point is, it shouldn't be over-full. Your brain can only process so much at a time, whether you like it or not. Over-do it and you can get a form of burn-out that makes it impossible to take in anymore, however much you think you need to. Whereas, if you give it a rest, let something else in now and then… I don't know how it works, but it lets you absorb and retain more in the long-run. With the point being to retain it, rather than just read it. You follow me?'

'Yes, I follow, but…'

'What were you studying yesterday?' he asked, cutting her off before she could form an argument.

'English and history.'

He grimaced. 'I found history bloody awful at school. Boring as hell. Now, I find it fascinating, but I suppose it's all about the context; the relevance. I mean, a lot of what I've learned about since then didn't ever come up in the school curriculum. But that's designed to make it easy for the examiners, isn't it? If everyone was learning about different things, they'd need actual historians to run the exams and mark them instead of general teachers with tick-sheets to follow.'

'What's that got to do with anything?' she demanded.

He shrugged. 'I'm just saying. But I think the point is, if you step away and do something completely different now and then, it can give context to what you're studying, make it stick in your mind better.'

'I think what your dad's trying to get around to is, if you were banned from your books for the day, what else would you want to do?' Louise put in. 'Where would you like to go? What would you like to see?'

'But…' Her frown sharpened again. 'I don't know. I mean, what are the options?'

Here we go, Pete thought, expecting something outlandish – or outlandishly expensive.

'Anything,' Louise said.

'Anything?' Annie checked.

'Anything we can manage in a day.'

'Well, obviously. All right.' She paused, head tilting to one side as she thought about it. 'Talking about history, there's the King Tut exhibition. I'd like to see that.'

'Where is it?' Pete asked.

'Dorchester.'

'Really?'

'Yes, really.'

'That's what you want to do?'

'If you're going to drag me out somewhere, yes.'

His lips pushed up in a shrug. 'Not what I was expecting at all, but if that's what you want…'

'Well, I'd like to see the Staffordshire horde, but that's up in Birmingham. I think, even with your blue lights, that'd be pushing it a bit,' she said with an impish grin. 'And we can see stuff here in Exeter any old time, so… While I've got the chance…'

'OK, then. That's what we'll do. How fast can you get dressed?'

Her eyes flashed wide. 'You'd be amazed.'

He grinned and, in the hall, the phone rang, cutting off his response.

Annie's face fell as his own grin faded and Louise's lips pursed. Pete got up and headed for the hallway to take the call.

'Hello?'

'It's me.' He recognised Colin Underhill's deep, dry voice instantly.

'Guv. What's up?'

'There's been another classic car theft. A dark red Jensen Interceptor, taken from Matford Road.'

'Shit. What's one of them?'

'An old British fast-back – what they used to call a Touring car – from the sixties or seventies. Bit like a cross between an E-type Jag and a sofa in a greenhouse. Great big wrap-around back window.'

Pete grunted. 'You make it sound bloody awful. You want me there?'

'No, you're OK. I'm on-site. Uniform let me know because of what the car was, but there was no violence involved. Just a break-in for the keys.'

'It suggests Price wasn't working alone, though,' Pete said. 'It's a bigger set-up than that.'

'Always was. But who killed him and why?'

'What, you think he was attracting too much attention with the violence so they turned it on him? That's a bit counter-productive, isn't it?'

'Unless we were meant to think it was revenge for one of the attacks.'

'Or unless it was,' Pete countered.

'Something for you to find out, starting tomorrow. See you then.' He hung up, leaving Pete holding a dead phone.

He set it back on its cradle and headed back to the kitchen.

'Work,' Louise said.

'Yes. Colin.'

'You're going in.'

'No, actually. Colin's handling it. He was just letting me know, ready for tomorrow. So we're still good to go to Dorchester if we can all be ready in time to get there and back before dark.'

CHAPTER NINETEEN

'I've got him.'

The shout came from the back section of the room, occupied by the Ops Support team.

It was coming up to 2:00pm. Pete had been about to call another break to rest their eyes and reinvigorate their attentiveness. He glanced across. One of the two males in the predominantly female team was holding up his hand, reinforcing the impression in Pete's mind of the layout back there resembling a junior school classroom. He stood up and strode quickly across.

'What have you found?'

The uniformed officer, a fresh-faced youth Pete guessed was barely out of training college, leaned back in his chair. 'He went up past Risingbrook School. Was caught on the cameras at the gates there.'

Pete's mind went straight to Alan Jackson and his Jaguar. Then to former pupils Richie Young and Gavin Prescott. They still didn't have an alibi for Prescott.

But then, as a former pupil, surely, he'd know that the school had cameras on the gates, wouldn't he? He sighed and took a position behind the uniformed officer so he could watch over his shoulder.

A tap of the Return key and the footage on the screen in front of them came to life, a set of headlights moving steadily towards them.

'He's not rushing,' Pete observed.

'No, but there's two ways to play it in a nicked car, aren't there? You get the hell out of Dodge as fast as you can or you ease away, trying to blend into the background. And those lights are pretty distinctive.' He paused the footage and hit another key, the screen flipping to a set of still photographs of the type of car they were looking for.

He was right, Pete saw. Twin headlights on a wide body, a rectangular grille between them. It was clearly styled after the Jaguars and Aston Martins of the time.

'And then you see the back,' the younger man said and clicked another key.

Back to the footage. The car swept past the gated school entrance and eased away up towards the junction with Magdalen Road. Pete didn't even need to try to recognise the lozenge-shaped combination light units as the streetlights gleamed off the car's unique wrap-around back window.

'Nice one,' he said and leaned down to peer more closely at the screen. The timestamp read 10:54pm. 'Well done,' he said, standing back. 'That's definitely a clip for the evidence file. We know it was stolen between six and eleven-thirty, when the owners got back from the theatre. And they're not a common car, by any means. Plus, from what we can see, the colour fits.'

It was a shame you couldn't read the number plates, but he'd learned long ago not to expect miracles.

'There you go,' he said to Dick Feeney as he returned to his desk. 'We're not starting from scratch again. We've got the first stage. He went up past Risingbrook school at six minutes to eleven. Which puts him onto Magdalen Road at five-to. So we just need to track him from there.'

'Sounds like he might have the same plan as Ewan Price,' Jill said. 'Hide it in the streets around Ladysmith for a day or three, to make sure we're not onto him before he takes it on to wherever it gets picked up from.'

'Who's got the footage from the junction of Polsloe Road and Heavitree? And the top end at Blackboy Road? Let's see if he shows up on that, to start with.'

'I've got the crossroads on Heavitree,' Diane Collins said.

'I've got the two from the Blackboy Road junction,' Bernie Douglas said and turned to the female next to her. 'Here, you take one of them. It'll save time.'

'I've got footage from the solicitor's on Magdalen, if that helps,' the second male member of the Ops Support team added.

'It could,' Pete replied.

With a time to focus on, it took only a couple of minutes.

'I've got him,' said Diane.

'Me, too,' said the male.

'Here he is,' Bernie said. 'Looks like he's crossing.'

'He is,' the woman next to her confirmed. 'And going up Mount Pleasant.'

'OK, then,' Pete concluded. 'We've already got footage that would pick it up going east or west from the top of Mount Pleasant – passing the post office or the supermarket. Let's check that.'

'I've got them,' Ben said and rummaged on his desk. 'Here, Dick, you have the post office, I'll have the supermarket.'

Again, it didn't take long.

'He didn't go east,' Ben said. 'At least, not past the supermarket.'

Moments later, Dick tapped his keyboard and leaned back in his chair. 'Didn't go west either.'

'All right,' Pete said. 'Time to get some fresh air. Dave and Jane, you can take Rosebarn Lane, I'll do Stoke Hill, everyone else search the streets around Mount Pleasant.'

'That'd be a hell of an up-yours if they'd parked it up by where Price lived, wouldn't it?' Dave said.

'It's a lot of effort to go to, just as a wind-up,' Jill countered. 'I mean, they'd have to expect us to find it.'

'If they expected us to identify him,' Ben countered. 'He was a fair old mess up there, in a car that didn't belong to him.'

'Still…' she persisted.

'We don't know it's there yet,' Pete said. 'Let's go and find out. We can rub their nose in it later, if it is.'

*

Pete walked up Rosebarn Lane to look for Dave and Jane and met them coming down the hill past a short row of smart-looking pale rendered houses set back behind raised lawns fronted by a low stone wall.

'Got anything?' asked Dave.

Which suggested they hadn't. 'No,' Pete said. 'You?'

He had checked the CCTV at the school on Stoke Hill, but found no sign of the car they were looking for.

Dave shook his head. 'Found some footage, but no Jensen on any of it.'

'Same here.'

As he turned to walk with them, back down the hill towards the junction, he took his radio from the clip on his belt and keyed the mike.

'DS Gayle for PC Douglas.'

'Douglas.'

'Any joy from your end of things yet?'

'Not yet. It's not on Salisbury or Elmside or any of those streets around there. We're working the east side of Mount Pleasant now. You know Monks Road takes you right along to the railway station, don't you?'

And the pub and former Nolan's garage just beyond it, he thought. 'Yes, I'm aware. We'll leapfrog you and go directly there, see what we can find in the way of CCTV that'll tell us if our man went past there.'

'Sounds like a plan.'

He lowered the radio. 'Right, let's go. There's a few shops around the station as well as the pub and the garage. There's bound to be a camera or two somewhere there.'

*

In fact, there were three: one on the south side of the road, on the front of a funeral director's on the corner of a side-turn that led off directly across from the end of Monks Road, the other two on the north side, beyond the bridge that gave the little railway station, which was out of sight of the road, its name. The first was on the pub that stood snugly up against the embankment of the railway line, the second on the front of a Chinese takeaway, a couple of doors along in the middle of a short terrace of shops.

The Chinese was closed at this time of the afternoon, but Pete headed under the wide arched bridge and across to the funeral director's while Jane and Dave went into the grey-rendered pub that, with its black lintels, sills and guttering, looked as dour and funereal as the place he was heading for.

The camera, he saw as he approached across the side-road, was aimed tight across the shopfront. But that meant it would pick up any passing vehicle or pedestrian on the main road. It wouldn't give him a number plate, but it was as close to ideal as he was going to get, he thought as he stepped up to the door and entered.

A woman in her fifties, dressed in a black skirt-suit, dark hair carefully styled around a broad face with subtle make-up and carefully sombre grey eyes looked up from behind a desk as the bell tinkled above the door. She didn't smile, but she did stand up and extend a hand in greeting.

'Good afternoon. How can we be of service?'

Pete took out his warrant card and introduced himself. 'I'd like to see the footage from the camera you've got on the shopfront, if possible,' he said. 'From Saturday night.'

She grimaced. 'There'll be a fair bit of it, between the station and the pub, but you're welcome to look. What are you looking for, if you can tell me?'

'A stolen car that may be related to a more serious crime,' he said.

It didn't hurt to be as forthcoming as he could without jeopardising the case when someone was offering to help.

'I see. I can't bring it up on this computer, but I'll take you through to the one in the back office.'

'Thank you.'

Pete followed her through a door into a back room that was set up with a couple of desks, shelves of catalogues and four coffins of various designs on stands, their lids open to display their plush-lined interiors. Continuing past them, she opened another, heavier door and it was only now that Pete's nostrils caught the faint hint of the purpose of the building. The woman didn't comment as she opened the first door on the left off a short connecting corridor. It led into a small office space, a clone of dozens of others he'd been in for similar purposes over the years. A desk took up most of the room, shelves opposite holding files, catalogues and other books as well as a printer and the supplies for it. A tall filing cabinet stood in the far corner, made of dark wood rather than the much more usual painted metal. A sick-looking plant trailed from a pot on top of it, gaining light from the small window in the far wall that was covered with a half-open vertical blind. A computer took up at least half the desk surface and there was a chair behind and one in front of the desk.

The woman settled into the chair behind the desk, fired up the computer and went into the program that would provide the footage he was looking for. Then she looked up at him. 'Saturday night, you said?'

'That's right.'

'What time?'

'Probably sometime shortly after eleven.'

She nodded. 'It dictates which file I should open,' she explained and tapped a key. 'There we are. I'm afraid it starts at noon. They're twelve-hour files.'

'That's OK,' he said. 'My problem, not yours.'

She gave him her first hint of a smile and stood up to allow him access. 'I'll leave you to it, then.'

'Thanks.'

When he took her place in the chair, he found that she hadn't increased the temperature of the leather at all.

The road took up the top third of the screen, which was better than he'd imagined it might be, from his point of view. Streetlights lit the scene with a yellowish tinge that the software wasn't set up to correct.

With no obvious way of setting a start-time, he hit the Return key as the door closed behind her and followed it with fast-forward, speeding it up to thirty times real speed. As the timestamp approached 23:00, he slowed it to twice normal speed and watched people hurrying past, this way and that on the pavements on both sides of the road. Cars darted past, too, headlights gleaming, their shapes harder to pick out from this angle, though he was sure he'd see the distinctive rear window of the car he was looking for if it passed.

He sat for several minutes, eyes glued to the screen, but it didn't. Eventually, he stopped the footage, took a thumb drive from his pocket and plugged it into the computer. Coming out of the video file, he copied it onto the drive, removed it and shut everything down.

Either Bernie and her team would find the Jensen parked up in the streets they were trawling now or it had gone up into the residential streets off the far side of Prince Charles Road, either to park up for a day or two or simply to bypass the supermarket at the eastern end of that road and head out towards Pinhoe or beyond. Which meant more leg-work tomorrow.

CHAPTER TWENTY

'This one's interesting.'

Pete looked up and saw Jane looking at him over her computer screen.

'What have you got?'

They'd been going through Ewan Price's phone data since it came in that morning while Bernie Douglas and her team scoured the streets off the north side of Prince Charles Road for the missing Jensen Interceptor. The raw data had had to be sorted, the numbers attached to names, and now they were going through those names, checking who they were, where they lived and whether they had police records.

'Derek Tasker,' she said. 'Lives in Whipton. And he's got a record for ag assault – he came out from a four-year stretch last year – and a job as a recovery truck driver with a company based over the back here on Sowton industrial estate.'

Pete nodded, grimacing. 'Another for the short list.'

'And here's another,' Dick said. 'Vehicle theft, driving without a licence or insurance, drugged driving. Price might not have had a record himself, but he certainly mixed with people who had.'

'Sounds like another one who'll bear having a chat with.'

That was number five, as far as Pete was aware.

They went back to their search. This was the relatively quick part of the task. Slogging through the pages of raw data from the phone company, compiling the list they were working from now, had taken several hours but it had turned out to be a relatively short list in the end. Price had maintained regular contact with only a couple of dozen people among the many numbers he'd contacted just once or twice in the weeks the data covered, which turned out to be the usual doctor, dentist, barber and so forth.

To speed the process up, Jill had compiled a basic three-generation family tree for Ewan, listing his parents, grandparents, uncles, aunts and cousins. Pete now typed one of the outstanding numbers into the system and hit return. It came back to an Alan Turner. He checked the list Jill had compiled. A cousin on Ewan's father's side.

He typed in the next number. Another relative's name came up.

Reaching the end of his portion of the list, he entered the last name and hit return. Ian Reece came up in the result screen. Who was he? Pete entered the name in the electoral role and got an address in the Polsloe area of the city. He made a note, then put the name into the PNC.

'And another one,' he said when the screen changed. 'Last known address just a few hundred yards from Price's, with a record for handling stolen goods.'

'What sort?' Dave asked, looking up. 'Wouldn't be big metal ones with four wheels by any chance, would it?'

'That'd be nice, wouldn't it?' Pete said. 'But no. There's no specifics, which there would be if it was vehicles. Still might be worth a chat with him, though.' He stretched his neck and rolled his shoulders. 'I reckon a bit of a jaunt out's called for before we knock off for the night as we haven't heard from Bernie yet. How are you getting on?'

'One to go,' Dave replied and bent back to his keyboard.

'Two left,' said Jane.

'And me,' Ben agreed.

Dick hit his keyboard harder than necessary. 'Done,' he said.

'Last one going in,' Jill added.

Dave grunted. 'Well, that's his gran. Thought I didn't recognise the area code.'

'His mum told me they weren't in touch,' Pete said.

'Well, there's something to ask her again about then,' Dave said.

'Hmm.'

'Do we know if he'd got a girlfriend?' Jill asked.

'No,' Pete replied. 'We don't. His mum wasn't aware of one.'

'I've got Rebecca Campion with an address in Newtown, One of his main contacts. At least two or three times a week. And his locational data puts him at her address quite often, too.'

'Saving the best for last, were you?' Dick asked.

Jill tipped her head. 'Left me something to look forward to. And they'd all got to be checked, regardless of how often he contacted them.'

'OK, another one for the shortlist, then,' Pete said. 'Let's see where they all are and we'll split up, work in pairs and see who's at home. If they're not, we've got their numbers. We can call them and see if they're willing to meet up. At this stage, they're all potential witnesses – even those with records.'

It took just moments to compare notes, exchange names, addresses and numbers and head out with two names for each pair to try to contact except for Pete and Jill, who had three.

They started with Rebecca Campion.

Jill looked around as Pete pulled up on the narrow street opposite a white-rendered bay-fronted house with a detached garage, a small front garden separated from the road and pavement by a low brick wall.

'This would be an ideal spot for Price to have parked those nicked cars up for a couple of days, to make sure they were safe to move on,' she said. 'Quiet, out of the way and less than a hundred yards from Polsloe Road.'

'Very true,' Pete agreed. 'A shame his location data doesn't put him here on the nights in question.'

'Yes, but that's because he was bright enough to leave his phone at home on those nights, isn't it?' she said, opening her door.

'If he's really our man,' Pete cautioned. 'Let's see what Ms Campion has to say about him, shall we?'

'What do you mean, *if*?' Jill demanded as they crossed the road and entered the driveway of the property.

'We're still waiting for the DNA,' Pete reminded her, heading for the door, which was on the side of the house, between it and the detached garage. 'Until then, he's only a suspect. It could be his next-door neighbour, for all we know.'

'Yeah, right,' she snorted as he reached for the doorbell and pressed it.

'Just saying. You know what Dick says about assumption.'

The door opened and he blinked as one of his own assumptions was dashed.

The woman standing in front of him was not twenty-ish, but closer to his own age with grey starting to show in fine strands among the dark hair at her temples though her complexion was still smooth. No makeup decorated her fine-boned face with a small nose between brown eyes that were puffy and reddened.

'Yes?' she asked, then her expression changed as she saw Jill's uniform.

Pete raised his warrant card. 'I'm DS Gayle. This is PC Evans. We're looking for Rebecca Campion.'

'That's me.'

'You're a friend of Ewan Price's?' he checked.

She frowned. 'Yes. Why?'

'You're aware of what's happened?' Pete guessed from the state of her face.

She blinked. 'His mum told me.'

'We're trying to find out who did that to him,' he explained. 'And to do that, we need to know as much as we can about his life, so we're speaking to as many people as we can who knew him. Could we ask you a few questions?'

'Yes. Come in.'

She stood back, allowing them inside. The place was clean and tidy, but hadn't been updated in a long time, Pete saw as she showed him through to a lounge that took up the whole front of the house. The carpets were old-fashioned, dark and patterned in swirls though, by contrast, the furniture was modern and stylish – all white and chrome. Hardly practical for a family home, he thought.

'Have a seat,' she offered. 'Do you want a drink of anything?'

'No, thanks,' Pete declined, moving towards the sofa that faced the bay window and along it so that Jill could sit beside him.

Rebecca took a seat across from him. Perching primly forward, she took out a handkerchief and dabbed at her eyes. 'How can I help?' she asked. 'I don't know what to tell you.'

'How long have you known Ewan?' Pete asked.

'Since he was a tot. A couple of days old.' She smiled. 'Me and his mum, we go back to junior school. Been friends ever since.'

'According to his phone records, you had quite a lot to do with Ewan, too,' Pete said. 'You got on well?'

'Yes. I'm… I was… He didn't call me aunty, but I was like a surrogate aunt to him, I suppose. He… Well, technically, he had one. His dad had a sister. But after he died, his family didn't want anything more to do with Charlie and Ewan. Cut them off completely. I don't know why. I know Luke didn't get on with them but you'd think, Ewan being their grandson, they'd want to stay in contact with him, at least, wouldn't you? But…' She shrugged.

Pete grimaced. 'I see.' *And with Charlene coming from a care-home background, that left him to grow up without any other real relatives – particularly older ones.* 'I can see how that would make you important in his life.'

Her mouth pushed up. 'I suppose.' Her nose twitched. 'He had his issues, as they call it these days – he was troubled in some ways, you know? But he was always good to me. Helpful and that.'

He nodded. 'Do you know if he had a girlfriend?'

She shook her head. 'Not since school, as far as I know. He split up with a girl not long after he finished at Jimmy's. Didn't go well. Put him off a bit, I think. Not that he was the other way at all, but…'

He was nodding again. 'I understand. What about other friends that he had since then? Do you know any of them?'

Another shake of the head. 'He kept his life pretty well divided up. The different parts completely separate, you know?'

'So, you don't know even who any of them were?'

'Not really. But there was never any need to. There was us, and there was that other part of his life. I mean, I knew he worked at

Nolan's. I knew about when they got taken over, how he didn't get on with the new boss. But not really much about his social life, as such. He'd tell me that he'd been out to the pub occasionally or other odd bits, but...' She shrugged. 'He did tell me he was making a bit of money on the side recently. Might turn into a regular job. But I don't know where that was.'

'We've got people following up on that,' Pete said. 'Do you know how it came about?'

She shook her head. 'Through a mate, I think, but I don't know the details.'

'OK. Well, thanks for your time.' He stood up. 'We'll get on. We're sorry for your loss.'

She nodded and stood up to show them out.

Back in the sunshine on the far side of the street, Jill reached for the door of the unlocked Ford. 'Sorry for her loss? He was an 'orrible little shit.'

He pursed his lips. 'But she doesn't know that, does she?'

'Hmm.'

They sat into the car and Pete reached for the ignition. 'He might be no loss to the world at large, but he's a loss to her,' he said.

Jill pursed her lips. 'Yeah, I suppose.'

'Where next?'

'Ian Reece is closest. He's only a couple of streets away. Then we've got the male in the halfway house on Belmont.'

'Reece it is, then. And he's got a record for handling stolen goods, right?' Pete continued along the road to a junction just short of the dead-end and turned left then right, towards Polsloe Road.

'Yes. He was a small-time fence making a living off the products of burglaries and thefts – so mostly off the drug addicts of the city.'

'And now?' Reaching a T-junction, he stopped and checked for traffic. Waited for a silver hatchback and a bicycle to pass.

Jill shrugged. 'He's in a private address. Rented. And not on benefits, so he's turned things around somehow.'

Pete pulled out behind the cyclist, then overtook him, heading north. 'Good for him. We hope.'

A couple of minutes later, he was turning right into a street of Victorian terraces opposite Heavitree Hospital. 'What number?' he asked.

'Nineteen.'

Like so many streets in this city and across the country, the redbrick houses had been built as two-up two-downs opening directly onto the pavement, but most of these had been extended upwards with gabled dormers built into the roofs.

He found the one he was looking for near the far end of the street and pulled in directly across from it. The door was painted a muddy blue and there was a brass knocker in its centre with a spy-hole at eye level above it. Pete rapped it hard twice and took a half-step back to the edge of the pavement.

The door was opened by a woman in her early twenties. Another surprise. He raised his warrant card. 'Hi. I'm DS Gayle with Exeter CID. This is PC Evans. We're looking for Ian Reece.'

The frown that had been forming on her small, pretty face took full effect. 'What for now?'

Pete raised an eyebrow. 'Why? What's he been up to?'

'Nothing. Don't stop you lot coming round here after him, though, does it?'

'We just wanted to ask him about a friend of his, that's all.'

She gave a grunt. 'He ain't no grass, neither.'

'That wasn't the idea. The friend in question died. We're trying to find some background information about him, in hopes of finding out why.'

'Died? What do you mean, why?'

'I mean, he was killed. And Ian may be able to tell us something about his life that leads us towards who did it.'

Another grunt. 'Well, he ain't here, is he? He's at work.'

'Oh. We weren't aware he had a job. Where's that, then?'

'Yeah, right. I tell you that, you'll go round there and put the whole thing at risk, just when he's sorting himself out. No way.'

'He's not a suspect in anything,' Pete argued. 'We just need to ask him about his friend, that's all. If his boss asks anything, we're there to inform him that his friend died. Which is true.' *Unless he already knows,* he added in his mind. *But we'll judge that from his reaction to the news.*

Her lips were tight, her stance confrontive. 'Well, I'm not telling you where he works. I'll ring him, tell him you want to talk to him and why. That's it. What friend was it?'

Pete could see she was going to remain adamantly protective of her man. There was nothing to be gained by pursuing this any further. 'Ewan Price,' he said.

She paled instantly, eyes closing briefly as her mouth dropped open.

After a moment, she drew a breath, steadying herself. 'Ewan's dead? How? When?'

'You knew him?' Pete asked.

'Yeah. We was at school together. What happened?'

'He was killed. By someone he knew. Which doesn't mean we're looking at Ian for it,' he added quickly, hands rising in a placatory gesture. 'But he might know who we should talk to about what Ewan's been getting into lately.'

'Ian never hurt nobody. He hasn't got it in him,' she declared.

'No-one's said he has,' Pete reassured her. 'We just need to pick his brains, that's all. Get him to call us, yes?'

'Hmm. You never said…' She grimaced. 'How was Ewan killed?'

'He was in a car fire,' Pete said. 'We don't know the…' He stopped as her face contorted and she spun away from the door, slamming it in his face.

Jill looked up at him wide-eyed. 'Well, *they* were more than just old schoolmates.'

'Enough to give Ian Reece a motive, do you think?'

'It was a really personal and a really angry way to kill him.'

CHAPTER TWENY-ONE

Pete had just turned into Belmont Road and was driving along in front of a row of large pale-rendered Georgian-looking gable-roofed town houses opposite the mature trees and open lawns of Belmont Park when his phone rang.

He glanced down and, recognising the number, nodded for Jill to touch the comms screen to accept the call.

'Dick, what can we do for you?'

'Were you aware that Isca Recovery and Rescue had a fire on Thursday night? An arson attack, no less.'

'Isca Recovery? That's where Derek Tasker works, isn't it?'

'Yes.'

And there's the relevance, Pete thought. Derek Tasker being one of Ewan Price's primary phone contacts. 'Well, no, I wasn't. And what does Mr Tasker have to say about it?'

'He's not a happy chappy at all. Puts his credibility with his boss at risk, him being an ex-con. Not that he was ever involved with arson, that we know of.'

'No, but there was obviously a reason for it. Have they ever had problems like that before?'

'No.'

'Hmm. And then, the following day, his buddy Ewan Price is killed in a car fire. It'll bear some follow-up, that's for sure.' Pete rounded a bend in the road and came to a fork. Taking the right-hand option, he pulled over. 'What do the owners say about it?'

'I spoke to the boss. He knows nothing. Except that it's put two of their vehicles off the road – one of them permanently – and it'll push up their insurance costs. Which he's not happy about, obviously. He was hoping we'd got some news for him about it. Like that we'd caught the person responsible. Not that he called them a person, exactly.'

Pete chuckled. 'I can imagine. That'll be a uniform job, though, won't it?'

'Yes.'

'Worth a word in the right ear, see what they've found so far.'

'I'll get onto the duty sergeant, shall I?'

'Yes. A problem shared and all that. Might lead to something. OK, Dick. Thanks for that.' He ended the call and switched off the ignition.

He'd parked outside a balconied mews that sat behind hedged lawns opposite a small carpark. They got out of the car and approached the door they wanted. A black iron knocker was in the middle of the dark green door above a vertical letterbox. Pete rapped it twice. The door was opened by a male in his fifties, Pete guessed, his hair thinning and grey, complexion pallid. His prominent Adam's apple bobbed at the sight of Pete's warrant card and Jill's uniform.

'Come in.'

They stepped into an entrance hall with a reception desk behind a reinforced glass screen, the frame around it painted white to match the row of pigeonholes on the opposite wall.

'How can I help?' the man asked as Jill closed the door behind them.

'We're looking for Paul Jacobs,' Pete told him.

'Should I ask why?' He stopped short of the door beside the reception counter and turned to face them.

'You're the manager here, are you?' Pete checked.

He nodded. 'John Miller.'

Pete drew a breath. 'We need to speak with him regarding one of his friends. He died in suspicious circumstances on Friday night.'

'I see. Well, I'll add you to the list, then.'

'List?' Pete asked, one eyebrow raised.

'Of people who want to talk to him. Me being at the top, followed by his probation officer if he doesn't turn up to his meeting tomorrow.'

'He's absconded?'

'Yep.'

'As of when?'

'Friday, as it happens.'

Pete's mouth pushed up as he nodded sagely. 'Interesting. I think we'd best see what we can do about finding him, then, eh?'

'Hmm.'

*

Jill shook her head as they settled back into the car. 'I'll never understand why they don't report their residents missing as soon as they drop off the radar like that. I mean, all right, I understand what he said about how often it happens and not wanting to waste our time and all that, but still, for those few who genuinely are missing, it's vital time they're losing, waiting for them to miss a probation appointment. I mean, it can lose us anything up to six days. They could be anywhere by then. Or dead when we could have recovered them alive.'

'Which, bearing in mind who we're talking about, wouldn't be such a bad thing, in some minds,' Pete admitted, swinging the car out from the kerb into a three-point turn. 'But you're right. In this case it was going to be five days he'd been missing before it was reported if he didn't turn up tomorrow. That's too long to be useful. We need to get onto his phone company when we get back and get the data from it. At least having his account details, not just the number, will make it easier and hopefully quicker for them to process.'

She grunted. 'We hope. I'm not going to hold my breath.'

'All right. The other way to track him would be with CCTV.' He made the turn and headed back the way they'd come. 'Given where we are, he can't have got far without being picked up on a camera somewhere. Whichever way he went, something's got to have picked him up to at least give us a direction, especially as we know what time he left here.'

'Assuming he walked,' she cautioned as he turned into Clifton Road, heading back towards Heavitree. 'Didn't get a lift with someone. Like, perhaps, in a nicked car.'

'Well, I'll tell you what,' he said. 'We're here. Let's leave the car and do some walking ourselves. See what we can find.' He pulled into a space at the roadside and stopped the car. Picked up his phone and dialled.

'Ben,' he said when it was answered. 'I've got a little job for you when you get back to the nick. Get onto Paul Jacobs' mobile phone provider and get his records. He's missing.'

'Missing? I thought he was on probation.'

'He is. Due for his next meeting tomorrow, which is why it hasn't been reported yet.'

Ben grunted. 'Helpful. Missing as of when, out of curiosity?'

'Friday.'

'Interesting timing.'

'Exactly.'

'OK, I'll get on it. We're on the way back now.'

'Nothing of interest to report?'

'No.'

'OK.' Pete hung up and opened the car door. 'We'll split up, save time. I've got the off-licence down the road there. Where do you want to start?'

They quickly planned their respective routes and set off.

*

As Pete stepped up to the metal-framed glass door of the brutalist grey student accommodation block on Blackboy Road, he couldn't suppress a smile. A prominent sign beside the doorbell told him that CCTV was in operation here.

'Excellent,' he muttered and reached for the bell.

'Yes?' asked a tinny voice.

'DS Gayle, Exeter CID.'

The door buzzed and he reached for the handle to open it. Inside was dark and as coldly functional as the outside of the multi-floor block suggested. A reception desk stood over to the right, a woman who, at a good fifteen years older than Pete, was probably not a student, seated behind it. She looked up from what she was writing with one thin, manicured eyebrow raised.

He presented his warrant card.

She peered at it and then up at him. 'How can we help?' she asked, her tone distinctly unhelpful.

'The sign by the door says you've got CCTV. Plus, I noticed the camera on the wall out there. I could do with seeing the footage from it, from last Friday, if that's OK.'

She nodded. 'Can I ask you to sign in, please? We keep a comprehensive log of non-resident visitors.' She pointed to the wide book that sat open on the front of her desk, behind the computer screen on its slender stand.

'Sure.' Pete took out a pen and complied.

The woman nodded and reached for the keyboard of the computer. 'Friday,' she said. 'What time?'

'If we start from 10:00am…'

She tapped at the keyboard then wheeled her chair to one side and tipped her head, suggesting he should come around to her side of the desk.

'Thank you.'

He stepped around the desk and leaned down to look at the screen. It showed a paused image of the street outside, looking across the cobbled central reservation towards the row of old shops and the pub opposite. Quickly seeing how the program worked, he reached for the keyboard and set the footage in motion, then sped it up, scrolling through to 10:20, when the manager of the supported housing around the corner on Belmont had said that Paul Jacobs had left there. From that point, he slowed back to natural speed to observe each passer-by before speeding it up again until the next person passed.

A couple of minutes later, he hit pause and took a copy of Jacobs' mugshot from his jacket pocket. Nodded and stood upright. 'Can I get a copy of this?'

'Do you have something to put it on?'

He took a thumb drive from another pocket and held it up.

'Very well.' She pointed under the desk.

Leaning back, he saw the base unit of the computer tucked into the shadows under there. He leaned down and inserted the drive. It took moments to download the file. Then he downloaded the next one, which ran from midnight on Friday to noon on Saturday, just to be sure he'd got every possibility covered. 'Thank you,' he said as he pulled the drive from the port and stood up. 'That'll be very helpful.'

'May one ask what he's done?' she asked, showing interest for the first time.

'He's missing,' Pete said. 'Since Friday.'

Her thin eyebrow – which, from this distance, he thought looked like a pencil line rather than actual hairs – rose again. 'My mistake, then. I thought that was a mugshot you had of him.'

'It was. But he served his time and now he's gone missing. So we're looking for him.'

'I see. Well, the best of luck, then.'

Pete nodded, unsure of the reason behind the sentiment. 'Thanks again.'

He waited until he was outside and heading back towards his car before using his radio.

'DS Gayle for PC Evans.'

'Boss?' she responded almost immediately.

'I've got him on Blackboy Road at 10:24, outbound.'

'Nice one. I'll meet you back at the car.'

'Roger.'

*

Moments later, he was on a tarmac footpath that cut across a grassed corner towards a day nursery and a chapel on a narrow back-street that dead-ended a few yards short of reaching the roundabout to his right when his phone rang. He took it out and checked the screen, then hit the button to answer.

'DS Gayle.'

'You been telling my Mrs Ewan Price is dead?'

Pete pursed his lips. 'Who's this?'

'Ian Reece.'

'Ah. Good. I wasn't aware you were married, but yes, I did visit your address earlier.'

'What you on about Pricey for like that?'

'I wanted to ask you about him. And he *is* dead. He was found on Saturday night.'

'Yeah, well… She was bloody near throwing up, time you'd finished. There was no need for that.'

'I didn't tell her anything that wasn't true. Anyway, when can we meet?'

'I'm on my tea-break. I get lunch at one.'

'OK. Where?'

'You ain't coming here. Belmont Park.'

Pete pursed his lips. In another fifty yards, he would be walking past that exact spot. But he was looking for help from this man, not to arrest him – at least, for now. He checked his watch. It gave him an hour and a half to get back to the station, get some things under way and get back here. It was better than nothing. 'OK,' he agreed. 'Belmont Park at one. Which side?'

'South entrance.'

Pete's lip twitched. Exactly the one he was about to walk past. 'I'll be there.'

The line clicked dead as he walked past the side of a huge old house with a private gated entrance on his left, the road curving away to the right, down the side of the park which he imagined had started out as the grounds of the grand mansion he'd just walked past.

If you're not, I'll be coming after you at home this evening, for wasting police time, he thought.

*

'So, what do we know, that we didn't first thing?' Pete asked as he led Jill into the incident room.

The rest of his team were all there, though Bernie Douglas and her Ops Support team were still out on the streets, searching for the Jensen or any footage of its passing.

'The phone data you asked for from Paul Jacobs' number's on the way,' Ben said. 'Won't be today but should be in first thing tomorrow.'

'Well, he's missing, as of Friday. Last spotted heading east up Blackboy Road past the student digs. What else?' His gaze took in the three other faces looking up at him as he shed his jacket to hang it on the back of his chair.

'Andy Fairweather's lead on the arson case over on Sowton Industrial Estate,' Dave reported.

Good, Pete thought. That could make things easier. He'd always got on well with the big, burly uniformed sergeant with his shaggy black beard and down-to-earth attitude.

'He's got some CCTV from a few of the other businesses over there but hasn't identified anybody from it yet. Kind of short-handed, what with everything else that's been going on, he said,' Dave added.

'Aren't we all?' Pete retorted. 'All right. I'll give him a ring.'

'Derek Tasker's been keeping his nose clean according to his boss and his probation officer,' Dick said. 'Comes in, does his shifts, good reports from his clients, always on time at New North Road.'

New North Road being the location of the city's probation office, Pete knew, in a tall old redbrick house almost within sight of the old prison. 'OK. Still, he's well-placed to be involved in what Price has been getting up to recently. He'd stand an interview. And a look at his phone. Especially the locational data.'

'On what grounds?' Dick argued. 'Just that he knows a man who might have been committing offences? I can't see the Chief signing off on that.'

Pete pursed his lips. 'Me neither. So we need something more.'

'How are we going to conjure that up?'

'It's not a question of conjuring. If it's not there, it's not there. But if it is, we need to find it.'

'At least the others that we looked at appear to be in the clear,' Jane said. 'Nothing remarkable about any of them and they all had alibis for Friday night and each one for at least one of the other incidents we've been looking at.'

'Well, that's something, at least.' He picked up his desk phone and dialled.

'Fairweather.'

'Andy, it's Pete Gayle. Dave Miles was just telling me you've got some CCTV from around Sowton Industrial Estate the other night, in reference to the arson at the tow-truck firm.'

'Yeah, but we haven't identified anyone from it yet.'

'Have you got any decent stills from it?'

'Not yet.'

'What can you tell me about the perp?'

'Not much. Given that it's at night and he's wearing a dark baseball cap, there's no clear images of his face. He looks smallish, but it's a job to tell, between camera angles and the fact that he's riding one of those scooter things.'

The tingle of recognition ran down Pete's spine. 'And dark clothes, of course,' he said.

'Of course.'

'Is there a white flashing down the outside of his trousers?'

'How'd you know that?'

'It matches some footage we've got. Can I come and have a look?'

'Be my guest,' Fairweather said.

'Does that include tea and biscuits?'

'Ah, if you bring your own.'

'Some host you are. See you in a minute.'

'So, Price lit up the tow-trucks?' Dick demanded.

'It's looking possible,' Pete said. 'I'm going to find out.'

He stood up and, leaving his jacket where it was, headed out of the incident room, back towards the wide stairs behind the reception desk and up to the second floor, where the uniformed branch had their domain.

Andy Fairweather's bulk made his desk look small. His dark hair was cut down to little more than stubble, but his beard made up for it, bushing out in all directions as he looked up when Pete stepped into his small office off the parade room.

'You reckon you can identify this male?' he asked. 'If so, I'll get a team out and pick him up.'

'If I'm right, you won't need to,' Pete countered. 'We already picked him up. From that car fire up on Woodbury Common, Friday night.'

Fairweather gave a quick frown. 'The victim? That's a bit of a harsh revenge for a couple of tow-trucks, one of which will be back on the road in a week or two.'

Pete tipped his head in a shrug. 'We'll see, shall we?'

'Pull that chair round. I've keyed it up on one of the samples we've collected. Most places over there are just alarmed, but a few have got cameras instead, or as well. And Isca Recovery is one of them.'

'Instead or as well?' Pete asked, grabbing the back of the spare chair and dragging it towards the end of Fairweather's desk as the big man swung his computer screen around towards him.

'Instead.'

Pete nodded. It was perfectly reasonable. Sufficient for their insurance, no doubt, and a single expenditure rather than an on-going subscription. But at the same time, it allowed for comings and goings at odd hours to be unrecorded. Or at least, wiped from recordings made on the premises if the owners were up to anything they didn't want anyone to know about. Not that he had any evidence to support that suspicion at this stage.

He settled into the chair and leaned forward, elbows on the corner of the desk. The still image he was faced with on the screen was of a fenced yard outside an industrial unit, locked steel gates across the entrance and five recovery trucks parked side-by-side in front of the building the camera was looking across from the corner of. It was at night but there were streetlights on the road beyond the galvanised or grey-painted fence; one just out of shot beyond the corner of the screen, causing a faint glare across the lens, another behind the camera's viewpoint, but evidently a little closer, judging by the strength of the shadows. 'Go for it.'

Fairweather reached across and hit the Return key with a thick sausage-like finger.

The image on the screen jerked and after a second, a figure glided smoothly into the scene from up the road. Barely visible at first between the upright bars of the fence, merging with the dark background, just a hint of movement showed its presence until it reached the gates. Then it stopped, resolving into a human form, black on black, back-lit by the streetlight behind it.

Seeming unconcerned by the possibility of being seen, the figure reached into a pocket and then for the padlock on the gates. Fiddling with the lock for several seconds, then sliding it out, the figure opened one of the gates just enough to slip through, a strange, bulky, almost monstrous shape, dragging something behind it. Lowering the object, which Pete now recognised as a scooter, to the ground inside the gate that hadn't opened along with the padlock, they closed the gate behind them and turning towards the camera, straightened up. Now it was obvious, if it hadn't been before, that the figure, all in black, was a male with a rucksack on his back and, as Andy had said, a dark-looking baseball cap.

But in turning to lay down his scooter, he had revealed the pale flash of the white stripe down the sides of his tracksuit bottoms.

'Pause it,' Pete said.

Fairweather hit a key and the image froze, not quite sharp but with more than enough detail for what Pete wanted. 'There, you can see his size against the fence.'

Knowing that the fence would be a standard six-foot-ten in height, Pete guessed that the figure now stepping away from the gates was around five and a half feet tall. 'It fits,' he said. 'And so does the outfit.'

'All right.'

Pete wasn't sure if that was a question or just acceptance of what he'd said. He nodded.

Fairweather hit the button again and the footage played on. Moving along the fence line, the figure looked at each of the trucks lined up on the forecourt and moved deliberately towards the one second from the end. Swinging the rucksack off his back, he set it on the ground and leaned down to open it. They watched as he withdrew a petrol can, replaced the rucksack on his back and picked up the can. Removing the cap, he approached the recovery truck and splashed it liberally with the contents of the can, which he then set beneath the passenger door and reached into his pocket.

There was a flare of light in his hand. He tossed the tiny flaming object towards the truck and the fuel he'd spread over it flared.

'And there she goes,' Fairweather said and reached for the keyboard to pause the footage again. 'Looks like the second truck was caught up in it just because the yard isn't completely level. There was some run-off that went across to it. Pooled around one of its tyres.'

Pete nodded. 'Have you got anything from anywhere else of him coming or going?'

'Well, given the direction he approached the recovery yard from, and the mode of transport he was using, we went as far as the hotel off Honiton Road. He came from somewhere behind it, down the side and across towards the path leading into the industrial estate. But that's as far as we've had chance to get with it. Looks like your man, does it?'

'As far as you can tell from this, yes,' Pete confirmed. 'So, you won't be catching up with him anytime soon. Not in this lifetime, anyway.'

CHAPTER TWENTY-TWO

He made it back to what he thought of as the back end of Belmont Park with five minutes to spare. Parking on the road that led up towards the park's entrance, he could see no-one hanging around there. He climbed out of the car and locked it, strolling up the street and across to the park, passing between the stone pillars of the entrance and turning right on the path that led around the periphery. A few yards along was a bench facing out across the tree-dotted expanse of grass. He sat down to wait, taking out his phone and calling up the Internet. He might as well do something useful while he was here.

He'd told Jane to find out everything there was to know about Derek Tasker and his employer while the rest of the team headed out again to see what they could discover in the way of CCTV or other cameras that might provide evidence of how the scooter-riding arsonist had got to the hotel on his approach to the industrial estate, to set the fire. One line of that enquiry would be to find out where he'd got the fuel – presumably petrol – that he'd brought to the scene. Wherever that was would have been lit well enough to give them a decent chance of getting a clear image of him. Pete imagined he'd have used cash to purchase the fuel, but a picture of his face would be a huge help at this stage.

Pete wanted as much information as he could gather before interviewing anyone. The ability to catch them in a lie was as important as what they might or might not be willing to say. Often more so. Which was a major reason for the prevalence of "No comment" interviews, of course, but if he could persuade them to accept the futility of saying nothing, then the more he knew, the better he could perform his interrogation.

He was typing in his first search when a footstep sounded behind him and a male voice asked, 'Are you the copper?'

Pete looked up and around.

A male in his mid to late twenties, dressed in jeans and a blue polo shirt was standing six feet away, his dark hair covered with a red baseball cap and a slightly sour expression on his square features.

'Who's asking?' Pete countered, switching things around from the usual.

'Ian Reece.'

Pete stood up and turned to face him. 'In that case, yes, I am. Pete Gayle. Thanks for coming.' He didn't bother to extend a hand that he guessed would be ignored but shifted across to make room for both of them on the bench.

'What happened to Pricey? Really?' Reece asked as soon as they were seated.

'He was killed, put in a stolen car and the car was torched,' Pete said frankly. 'So, what I'm trying to find out is who he'd pissed off enough to do that to him. What can you tell me about what he'd been up to lately?'

Reece's expression had soured further, pulling into a grimace of disgust. 'I know he fell out with the guys he was working with last week. They'd shafted him somehow. He didn't go into details.'

'What sort of work was this?'

'Like I said – he didn't go into details. Shifting cars, something like that's all I know. I thought delivering. Set of trade plates and off you go, you know?'

'So you don't know who he was working for? How or where he found them? Where they're based? No names?'

Reece was shaking his head. 'He asked me for a lift home from over by the school once. Jimmy's. I suppose his scooter must have been busted or something. But I was at work, so I couldn't. He never asked again. But then he got himself another scooter so I suppose he didn't need to, did he?'

'When was this?'

He shrugged. 'I dunno. Couple of weeks ago, I suppose. Maybe three.'

'What, daytime?'

'No, it was at night. Just turned midnight.'

'I didn't know tyre places were open overnight.'

'They aren't. I was on another job. Breakdown recovery.'

Pete felt that familiar tingle. 'Really? Who with?'

'A mate. He's showing me the ropes, see if I fancy changing careers.'

'And do you?'

He grimaced. 'Hours ain't so good, but the pay's better. I ain't decided yet.'

'So, who's this mate with? Which firm?'

Reece frowned. 'It's above-board. Official. It's a recovery truck. They're allowed to carry passengers. Part of the job, isn't it?'

Pete shrugged. 'I was just interested, that's all. I was just visiting one earlier, as it happens.' *Albeit only on the computer through their CCTV,* he thought but didn't see the need to say.

Reece grunted.

'So…?' Pete nudged when nothing more was forthcoming.

'Richmond Motors.'

'Oh, that one down the back, off Richmond Road? I know it,' Pete said, nodding.

'Yeah, well. Like I said, it's all above-board. It ain't just my mate doing me a favour off the books or nothing.'

'That's fine,' Pete said, shaking his head. 'It's what Ewan Price has been getting up to that I'm interested in. Insofar as it might give me a nudge towards who killed him.'

'Well, I can't help you on that. Wish I could. He was a good mate.' His expression shifted as if he would have said more in different company. Something, perhaps, about revenge or retribution. Of the unofficial variety.

'Well, whoever it was, we'll find them,' Pete said. 'And they'll pay for what they've done. The right way.'

'What's that mean?' he demanded, frowning.

'That there'll be no need for anyone to get into any trouble by taking the law into their own hands. If they happen to know, or find out, anything that we don't already know.'

'Huh. Chance would be a fine thing. Pricey knew how to keep summat quiet when he wanted to.' His lip twitched. 'Is that it? I need to be getting back.'

Pete nodded. 'Just stay out of trouble, eh? Remember you've got a woman at home to look after. And be there for. And these people don't play nice. Ewan's is only one of a series of linked deaths we're looking into. We were hoping that he might be the key to them, that's why we're talking to you and his other friends.'

'A series?' Reece demanded. 'Who else have they done?'

Pete shook his head. They'd already eliminated Reece's workplace as a possible link between the victims. Both of his workplaces, in fact. 'You wouldn't know them.'

'How do you know?'

'Because we've checked. It's what we do.'

Another grunt. 'Well, I got to go.' He stood up.

'If you hear anything, let me know, yes?' Pete insisted, standing with him. 'Don't go following it up yourself, understood?'

Reece nodded once.

Now Pete extended a hand. Reece paused for an instant, then accepted it with a firm, dry grip that was as hard as Pete might have expected from a man who worked with his hands all day, every day – a determined and now deep-down angry man.

He hoped, as Reece turned away and headed for the gateless stone pillars, that he'd heed his advice and stay clear of Ewan Price's killers. For his own sake and that of the young woman he was now living with and calling "Mrs."

*

Pete used the entrance to a side-road to give him more room to turn the car around and was driving down past the Clifton Road carpark towards Heavitree Road when his phone rang.

He checked the number on the comms screen and tapped to answer. 'Jill. What can I do for you?'

'I've got him,' she said. 'There's a block of flats on Vaughan Road, in front of the Hill Lane school. Looks like something out of the 1920's or '30's. They've got cameras. He comes out the end of Hill Lane, around the end of the flats and across the road towards Whipton Barton Road. And you can work your way through from there to the hotel through that new-build section.'

Pete chuckled. 'That new-build's about three years old.'

'Yeah, but you know where I mean.'

'OK. Nothing between those two points, though? The hotel and Hill Lane?' He stopped at the junction onto Heavitree Road and waited for a handful of cars to pass right to left before pulling out behind them.

'It's all residential,' Jill said. 'There might be a doorbell camera or two but we haven't found them yet. Ben's working his way towards me from the hotel, though. Given where the offender popped out at that end, he had a look around and found a footpath leading through from the new estate into the hotel carpark. No doubt for the staff. Save them cluttering up the carpark.'

'Probably,' Pete agreed. 'And it'll certainly allow access to someone on a bike or a scooter. What's the image quality like of the footage you've got?'

'Sharp enough, but only a profile view. Looks like Price, though.'

'Good. Have you checked the school, if he went past it?'

'About to.' She paused. 'Boss?'

'Yes?' He could guess what was coming. And he wasn't disappointed when she spoke again.

'What are we doing this for? I mean, if it is who we think, we're not going to prosecute him, are we?'

'No. But all evidence is good evidence. Especially when it comes to prosecuting whoever killed him. If it was revenge for the arson, and we can nail that down as fact…'

'Yeah. OK.'

'I'm on the way back to the nick,' he said as he passed the old one – all boarded up and overgrown now – where they'd been based until the move out to Sidmouth Road during the Covid pandemic. 'Then I'll come out and join you.'

*

'I've found one little titbit of interest,' Jane said, looking up from her computer screen when he walked into the incident room a few minutes later. 'I don't know if it's relevant, but Derek Tasker's boss, John Miller, is mates with Ian Henderson of Storm Windows. I mean, not just because their businesses are just around the corner from each other: they're socially linked, too. Not just social media, either. They spend time together, go out together and all that. Actual, real links.'

'As you say,' Pete said, nodding. 'Interesting. We know Henderson's got an alibi for the night of the attack on the Lockwoods, but that doesn't mean he or one of his guys didn't case the joint for the car-thief. And if you can link Price to Tasker, to Miller…' He shrugged. 'You're forming a chain, if you can prove the links with something solid.'

'I haven't done that yet.'

'What about Miller? Is he clean?'

'As far as we're aware,' she admitted. 'But as you've said before, that might only mean he hasn't been caught yet. Having said that, though, there's nothing suspicious in his background. No previous work-related fires, for instance, or other big insurance claims.'

'OK,' he said with a nod. 'Does Henderson come up on any of the others' phone records? Price's, for instance?'

'No. Nor Tasker's. But are we sure Price didn't have a second phone just for his illegal activities?'

'Well, no, we're not. But we have got him contacting Tasker on the phone we've got, three days in a row.'

'Yeah, no texts, though, that would tell us what they were discussing, unfortunately.'

'True. I've got an idea, though. If he didn't have a second phone…' His mobile phone rang, interrupting him. He took it out and checked the screen. Touched the green icon as he raised it to his ear. 'Dave. What's going on?'

'We've got him,' Dave declared. 'The fuel purchase. I mean, you can't see his face and he used cash, but the silly sod swiped his points card, didn't he?' He gave a delighted chuckle. 'How daft can you get, eh?'

'Seriously?' Pete demanded.

'Yup.'

'And he's on camera doing it? And filling the can?'

'Two cans, actually.'

'Two? Hmm. He only used one at the recovery depot, but still.' There was still something in the rucksack when the arsonist left the place, he recalled. But, if it was another can of fuel, what was that intended for? He chuckled. 'It's amazing how much people are creatures of habit, eh? Get hold of Dick and see if, between you, you can track him back towards where he lived. I'll get Jill to try and track him back to where you are from Hill Road. You're on Prince Charles, right?'

'That's right.'

'He won't have taken the direct route from home, I don't suppose, but someone's got to have seen him or got a record on a doorbell camera or something.'

'We're on it.'

'Well done,' Pete concluded and hung up, then redialled immediately. 'Jill,' he said when she picked up. 'We've got confirmation of where he bought the petrol. Your next stop needs to be Pinhoe Road. He'll have come down Beacon Lane. I'd lay odds on it. The shops round the junction there should give us something.'

'Right. I've got the footage from the school. I haven't checked it, but I've got the file.'

'That's fine. We can check it later, as long as we've got it.' He hung up again. 'We're getting close,' he said to Jane.

'To convicting a dead man,' she said.

'Which is the first step towards finding out who he was working with,' he retorted. 'And who killed him. There's a link somewhere. And we will find it. Then we can close the whole operation down.'

CHAPTER TWENTY-THREE

'Shut that down for a while, you can come with me,' Pete said to Jane sometime later.

'Where to?'

Pete opened his mouth to answer but was cut off by the hiss of his radio and Bernadette Douglas's voice, muffled and tinny through the little speaker under the tail of his jacket. 'PC Douglas for DS Gayle.'

He unclipped the radio from his belt and keyed the mike. 'Gayle.'

'We've found the Jensen.'

'Great. Where?'

'Parked up on a side-street out towards Pinhoe. There's a triangle of streets with a central spine off the north side of Beacon Heath Road. Dead-end, goes nowhere so only residents would go up there.'

'Perfect for the purpose, then,' he observed. 'Great. Can you leave someone to keep an eye on it unobtrusively while I have a word with the Guvnor, see if we can set up something official?'

'No problem, Sarge.'

'Thanks.' He lowered the radio. 'OK, change of plan. At least briefly,' he said to Jane. 'Stay put, I'll be back in a bit.'

Clipping the radio back on his belt, he headed out and along towards the wide stairs that led up from behind the reception desk. A minute later, he was knocking on Colin Underhill's door.

'Come.'

He went in. Colin looked up from the twin mounds of paperwork on his desk and sat back, laying his pen down and looking at Pete expectantly.

'Bernie's team have found the Jensen,' Pete said, knowing he wouldn't be invited to speak.

'Are you getting it towed?'

'I thought it might give us an opportunity if we leave it in place with a watch on it,' Pete said. 'With your permission.'

'Can you spare the manpower?'

'While Bernie's crew are onboard. Not exclusively them, of course. That wouldn't be fair. I haven't put it to anyone else yet, mind. And we don't need to be too close. There's only one way out of where it is.'

'Unless they put it into a box van.'

Pete tipped his head. 'True. Which would double the workload.'

Colin nodded. 'And get you what?'

'Where it's taken, who by and potentially who to. In other words, the rest of the gang.'

'Sounds good. Do it. I'll clear it with the Chief.'

'Thanks, guv.'

'Anything else?'

'We're making headway,' Pete said and gave a concise summary of the progress they'd made that day.

Colin nodded again. 'On you go, then.'

Pete left him to his paperwork and went back down to the incident room to call Bernie Douglas and confirm the requirement for a double surveillance operation on the stolen car – one to observe it directly, the other to remain within sight of the entrance to the Christmas tree of streets in order to follow if it left.

It was a little after 3:20pm when, with Jane in tow, he headed out once more.

'A perfect time to get tangled up in all the school traffic,' Jane said as they stepped out into the brightness of the afternoon.

'Except there aren't any between here and where we're going.'

'You haven't told me where that is yet.'

'Isca Recovery.'

'Really? I thought they were suspects?'

'They're also victims though. It'd be unnatural for us not to go and have a polite word, wouldn't it?'

They reached his silver Ford saloon and he unlocked it, indicators flashing as it beeped in response to the remote.

'I suppose. If it's our case now, as opposed to Uniform's,' she said as they climbed in.

The doors clunked shut.

'The fact that it was started by someone matching Ewan Price's description makes it ours.' Pulling his seatbelt across, he clipped it in and started the engine. 'And there were only two trucks damaged out of the five that were there, so they'll still be open for business.'

'So, what's the plan?'

'General questions that they'd expect, plus show them Ewan's picture and ask if they recognise him. Admit he's a person of interest if they ask, obviously, but we haven't confirmed anything yet. Which is true, to a point. Also, with Tasker being a new guy, how is he getting on, what do they think of him, etc. And for him, does he know Ewan Price? See if he admits it and, if so, what he can tell us about him.'

'Sounds like a plan.'

They lapsed into silence for a few moments while Pete concentrated on driving until his phone broke the quiet. He glanced at the comms screen and accepted the call.

'Boss, we've got him passing St James',' Dave said. 'We're going to see if we can find any doorbell cameras down Mount Pleasant. Unlikely, any closer to where he lived, I should think.'

'You never know,' Pete countered. 'It's worth checking.'

'It's a shame the pharmacy one doesn't overlook the street, but what can you do, eh?'

'Not a lot,' Pete agreed, recalling the location Dave was talking about. The little pharmacy on Mount Pleasant was set back from the road, down a bank and behind a row of young trees. 'They've got them for their benefit, not ours, after all. We'll all meet back at the nick as close to half-past five as we can manage. Need a brief meeting before we knock off.'

'What about?' Dave asked, sounding intrigued.

'How to take the case forward from here,' Pete told him. 'I'll see you there.' He ended the call and glanced across at Jane. 'I'll tell everyone the good news at once.'

*

There were just two tow-trucks in the yard when Pete drove in through the gates, both towards the far end, away from the area of the fire, where the concrete was blackened and cracked. He parked near the fence at the front and the man busy scrubbing the wheels of one of the trucks straightened up, stopping what he was doing to watch wordlessly as they climbed out and headed for the small door with a Reception sign overhead that stood beside the currently closed roller shutter of what Pete guessed was the main garage area of the building.

Pete recognised him from his mugshot but didn't acknowledge him.

Inside there were four semi-comfy chairs and a large pot-plant on the public side of the counter that stretched across the width of the room, a desk behind it where a male in his forties was working at a computer.

He looked up as they stepped inside and left the desk to approach the counter. A couple of inches taller than Pete's six feet, his curly blond hair was cropped short around the sides and back but left longer on top. He was wearing blue overalls that matched his eyes with Isca Recovery embroidered on the breast pocket in red, matching the logo on the two trucks outside.

'How can I help?' he asked.

Pete produced his ID. 'I'm DS Gayle. This is DC Bennett,' he said. 'We're looking into what happened here the other night.'

The man's eyebrows rose. 'Detectives?'

'That's right,' Pete agreed. 'It's come to light that what happened here might tie into something we were already looking into. And you are…?'

'John Miller, the owner.'

Pete nodded and took out his phone. Scrolling through to an image from the petrol station CCTV that Dave had forwarded to him, he turned it so Miller could see. 'Do you recognise this male?'

Miller peered at the screen. 'Looks to be the same one who was on our cameras. The bastard who set the fire. But other than that, no, not really.'

Pete turned the phone back so he could see what he was doing and scrolled again. This time he found an image he'd obtained from Charlene Price of her son. 'How about this one?' he asked, watching Miller carefully as he showed it to him.

There was no reaction. 'No,' he said and looked up at Pete. 'Is that the same guy?'

'Yet to be confirmed,' Pete said. 'But we think so.'

'Who is he?' Miller demanded. He looked like he wanted to say more but didn't.

'Does the name Ewan Price mean anything to you?' Pete asked.

'No. Is that him?' he demanded, nodding towards the phone that was still in Pete's hand.

'The second picture was,' Pete admitted. 'So, he'd have no reason to have a grudge against you or the company?'

'No. Like I said, I don't know him.'

'And nothing like this has happened before?'

'No. Not even remotely like it.'

'You've had no significant problems recently? Disgruntled customers? Or drivers who you've let go? Rivalries with other firms? Hostile takeover bids? Demands for protection money?'

His lip curled in a sneer at the last suggestion. 'No. None of that.'

'And you've taken on no new employees recently?'

'Well, yeah, one, but… You don't think this was… Actually, it was his truck that was torched, but…'

'Who's he?' Pete asked, keeping up the pretence of ignorance.

'Derek Tasker. He's out the front there, cleaning the other trucks that aren't out on the road.'

Pete nodded. 'We saw a guy out there. When did you take him on?'

'End of last year. Early December. But this can't have been related. I mean, that's a few months ago. Why now?'

Pete shrugged. 'How's he getting on here?'

'Fine. He's a good worker. Gets on OK with the clients.'

'And where did he come from? Where did he work before?'

Miller's lips tightened. 'He'd been inside. But he'd got previous experience of the job, from before all that, so... I thought I'd give him a chance. And I haven't regretted it,' he finished firmly.

'Fair enough,' Pete shrugged. 'We'll have a word, while he's here, but as you said, there's no reason to suspect a connection. We'll have to talk to all your staff.'

They heard the shutters roll up on the garage space at the other side of the dividing wall.

'That's probably him coming in. I'll fetch him.'

'That's all right,' Pete said. 'You carry on with what you were doing. We'll go around. In fact, *I'll* go around. Jane...' Turning his gaze to her, he tipped his head towards the man across the counter.

'Right.'

As he headed for the door, he heard her asking, 'So, you run this place on your own, do you, Mr Miller?'

He stepped outside and around into the big, open garage area of the building.

Tasker was just inside, winding up the bright yellow hose he'd been using. He looked up as Pete's bulk moved into the gap under the roller.

'Wondered how long you'd take.'

Pete tipped his head. 'I'm DS Gayle,' he said. 'And you're Derek Tasker. I'm aware of your record, obviously, but I'm not here to cause you any problems. Just to find out what went on here. Or more particularly, why it happened. Which means interviewing everyone involved with the business.'

Tasker's lip twitched in what could have been a shrug or a sneer.

Pete took out his phone and brought up the picture of the arsonist. 'Do you recognise him?' he asked, showing Tasker the image.

'The guy who did it.'

'Yes. But other than that. Does he look familiar?'

'Maybe a bit, but not enough to be sure.'

Pete scrolled through to the picture of Ewan Price. 'How about him?'

Tasker glanced up at him then back to the phone. 'He's a mate of mine. What about him?'

'How do you know him?' Pete asked.

Tasker shrugged. 'Met him a few months ago. In the Job Centre.'

'Got chatting in the queue?' Pete suggested.

'Yeah. Then we run into each other in town. Hung around a bit. Not much else to do at the time. Both out of work.'

'When did you last see him? Or talk to him?'

Tasker's brow twitched in a brief frown. 'I don't know. A few days ago. Last week sometime?'

'And you were OK? No problems between you?'

'No, why should there be?'

It was Pete's turn to shrug. 'I don't know,' he said. 'Things happen. People fall out. Especially when money's tight.'

'It ain't anymore,' Miller said, raising his hands to indicate their surroundings. 'I got this.'

'And a move on from the halfway house,' Pete added for him.

'Yeah, well, you only get to stay there short-term, don't you? A few weeks to get yourself sorted.'

'And you're renting a place in Whipton, right?'

His eyes narrowed. 'That's right.'

'So, you've no idea why Ewan might have a problem with this place?'

'No.'

Pete nodded. 'OK. And you don't know anyone else who might have done it? Or why someone might?'

'No.'

'All right, then. I'll let you get on.'

Tasker grunted and reached for the hose again to finish what he was doing.

'Oh, one last thing,' Pete said. 'Do you know any of Ewan Price's other friends?'

Tasker frowned. 'What's the interest in him, anyway? He ain't got a record, as I know of.'

'No, but he is dead,' Pete retorted, dead-pan.

Tasker blinked. 'Dead?'

'Killed. In a vehicle fire, as it happens.'

Tasker's gaze flicked this way and that. 'And you think…? Nah. John wouldn't do anything like that. And I certainly didn't.'

'Where were you last Friday evening?'

'I worked 'til 7:00. Went home, got some tea. Had an hour or so in the pub with a mate. Not Ewan. Then home to bed. I was on-call Saturday.' He spread his hands – one of them holding the hosepipe – to indicate their surroundings.

'So, if not Ewan, who was the mate? And which pub?'

'Mark Grey. And the Queen's Head.'

Pete's eyebrows rose at the name of the pub across the road from Polsloe Bridge railway station. Jane and Dave had been in there only the day before while Pete himself was just across the road. 'And who's Mark Grey?' He wasn't familiar with the name.

Tasker shrugged. 'Just a mate. Got a transport company.'

'And he didn't offer you a job when you came out?'

'Hadn't got a spare truck at the time, had he? And they ain't cheap.'

'Fair enough. What about after the pub? You've got no-one who can verify where you were the rest of the night?'

'Like I said – I went to bed. Alone. Mark dropped me home and that was it.'

Pete's lips quirked. He held Tasker's gaze for a moment but it didn't falter. 'I'll need his number to verify this, obviously.'

Tasker took out his phone, brought up his contacts list and held it out to show him.

Pete lifted his own phone, took a picture of Tasker's screen, checked it had worked and nodded. 'Thanks.'

He ducked under the shutter and returned to the office next-door.

Jane was seated in one of the customer chairs, Miller back at his computer.

'All done?' she asked, looking up as he entered.

'Yep. We've got another quick stop to make, though.'

Miller looked up and Pete nodded to him. 'Thank you, Mr Miller. We'll liaise with our uniform colleagues and come back to you if we need to. Or when we find something relevant.'

Miller nodded and Pete led the way outside.

He waited until they were in the car with the doors closed before saying, 'We need to pop back to Polsloe Bridge. Check Derek Tasker's alibi for Friday night.' He switched on the engine and turned the car around. 'And while we're at it, get onto the PNC, will you? Look for a Mark Grey. He's who Tasker claims to have been there with.'

'What, in the pub?'

Pete nodded.

Moments later, as he drove through the industrial estate, she looked up from her phone. 'Nothing on Mark Grey. Have we got his details?'

'Phone number,' Pete said. 'In the photos on mine there.'

Minutes later, he was driving north on a wide, fairly new-looking road with mature hedges up either side making it seem almost rural when she looked up again. 'Well, that gives us his address and the fact that he's a company director. Blackhorse Transport. Blackhorse being one word like the village. I suppose to avoid problems with Lloyds.'

'And where are they based?'

She raised an eyebrow. 'I'll let you guess.'

'Honiton Road?'

She tipped her head in a shrug. 'Close. Sowton Lane.'

'The one that goes off opposite the pub?'

'Yes.'

'I didn't know there was anything down there. The odd farm, maybe, but nothing else.'

'Maybe he bought one of the farms,' she suggested. 'Or inherited it and diversified.'

'We can look him up later and find out, if needs be,' Pete said. 'For now, he's just a possible alibi for Derek Tasker.'

*

Pete had to make an effort to keep a straight face when they stepped into the large bar area a short time later. The woman behind the bar was the comedy-sketch archetype of the busty barmaid, although she was trying hard to fight back the advancing years with an over-abundance of makeup. She had to be well into her fifties, he guessed, her black blouse stretched almost to bursting across her chest and opened far enough at the neckline to try and ease the pressure from within.

She glanced across as they entered and raised an eyebrow at Jane.

'Another of my colleagues,' Jane said by way of introduction. 'This one's my boss. DS Gayle.'

The woman nodded. 'What can I do for you today?'

'We need your CCTV footage from Friday evening,' Pete said. 'And to know if you recognise this male.' He held up his phone with a copy of Derek Tasker's mugshot open on the screen.

'Yeah, he comes in here now and then. Was in Friday, in fact, if I recall.'

Pete nodded. 'OK. Good. Can we see that footage?'

'We only got cameras outside,' she said cautiously.

'That's OK. I gather he was with someone. Did you notice him? Or do you know him?'

'Know him? No, I hadn't seen him before. Smart-looking feller, though. I'd recognise him if he came in again. Well-mannered, too.'

Pete nodded. 'I see.'

She paused. Then glanced around the bar, checking if she was needed elsewhere. 'OK, if you want to follow me…'

She led the way along the central bar towards the rear of the building. Stepping through a doorway at the end, she came around an intervening stub of wall and through a door. 'This way.'

She took them through the kitchen and into a corridor, where she opened a door into an office space. 'It's on there,' she said, pointing to the computer. 'But you know that,' she added, speaking to Jane. 'You all right with it? I'm on my own, this time of day.'

'Yes, no problem,' Pete assured her.

'It's on,' she said, speaking to Jane again. 'Just give it a waggle.'

She left them to it and Jane sat down, woke up the computer while Pete stood at her shoulder, and opened the program that ran the CCTV. Typing in the date and time they were interested in, she hit Return and the screen was filled with an image centred in a black background with a set of playing controls along the bottom. She hit Play and Fast Forward. It didn't take long before they saw Derek Tasker walking towards the front door with another male.

'Go back,' Pete said.

Jane complied. A dark coloured Range Rover appeared to reverse out of the carpark.

'There,' he said.

She paused it. Zoomed in. 'And there we have it,' she said. 'Nice and clear.'

Taking out his phone, Pete took a photo of the screen with the Range Rover's number plate clearly visible beneath and between the dipped headlights. 'Perfect,' he said, checking the result. 'Now, what time did they leave and was it together? Tasker suggested about an hour.'

Jane hit Fast Forward and they sat back to wait.

After several minutes, she hit Pause, rewound the footage and paused again. 'There it is. Closer to an hour and a half, but we'll let him off, I suppose.' She hit Rewind again and seconds later, paused when the two men emerged from the front entrance of the building. 'Yep. Looks like they're together to me.' She hit Play and let it run. The two figures crossed towards the parked SUV and climbed in. She hit Pause. 'Have you got a thumb drive to put it on?'

Pete reached into his jacket pocket and handed one over, peering at the screen. 'Well, that confirms his story, but it's not an alibi for Ewan Price's death. 9:23. That gives him plenty of time to get out there, meet him, kill him, set the fire and get away. Or whatever order it was done in.'

'It'd be a long walk home with a decent chance of being seen along the way,' Jane argued.

'Not if he got a lift in a nice, fancy Range Rover. Or some other vehicle.'

Jane looked up at him wide-eyed. 'What, so you're accusing this Mark Grey of being involved now?'

Pete shrugged. 'Not necessarily. It could have been anyone. Tasker could have just used him as a partial alibi. But as you say, he's not likely to have walked home from Woodbury Common so someone else was involved, at least to a degree.'

'If Derek Tasker himself was.' She pulled the drive out of the port on the computer and handed it to him. 'Here.'

'We've got Tasker's address. Let's see what we can find between here and there and see if he was dropped off as he said.'

'OK. I'm just saying we can't afford to get too single-minded on it, that's all,' she said, closing the program on the computer. 'We need to keep our options open until we've got something solid.'

'I know,' he said. 'But we need some sort of theory to work off, to find that solid basis. Or not, in which case we move on.'

She held his gaze for a moment, seeming to check if he was genuine or was trying to fob her off with what she wanted to hear. Then, appearing satisfied, she nodded once and got up. 'Off we pops, then. We've got a meeting to get to, back at the nick, haven't we?'

CHAPTER TWENTY-FOUR

Pete and Jane were last into the incident room, making up the full complement of his team, along with the Ops Support team.

He dropped the thumb drive from his pocket on his desk and shrugged out of his jacket to leave it hanging on the back of his chair while he approached the whiteboard in shirtsleeves and tie.

He clapped his hands to gain their attention. 'OK, has anyone got any case-cracking revelations before we start?' He let his gaze flicker around the assembled team. 'No? Didn't think you would, unfortunately. So, Jane and I have just come from the pub at Polsloe Bridge. Their cameras – and the barmaid – confirm Derek Tasker's story about the first part of Friday evening. Although that still leaves him free to have committed the murder of Ewan Price. He says he went home to bed because he was working the next day.'

'Home alone?' Dave checked.

Pete nodded.

'But he's still on parole, right?'

'Yes. For another two years.'

'Then we don't need permission to check his mobile data.'

Pete tipped his head. 'And we have got his number. Get onto that, would you, Ben?'

'Boss.' The spiky-haired PC nodded.

'In the meantime, some of you will be aware that one of us isn't here. I take it Diane's keeping an eye on the Jensen?' he asked, directing the question at Bernie Douglas.

'Yes, Sarge.'

'OK, I've had a word with the guvnor and he's agreed that we should make that an official surveillance. Which means shifts, including members of both teams here. Two people at a time – one to observe from wherever Diane is now while the other stays plotted up on Beacon Heath, within sight of the entrance to Central Avenue without being obvious.'

'There's a side turning on the other side, just along from there that someone could park in and be able to observe the junction,' Bernie reported. 'There's nowhere to park on Beacon Heath itself without being obvious.'

'OK. And where is Diane, exactly?'

'The target vehicle's parked at the roadside on Fox Road. She's in her car, further up, beyond it. There's parking down both sides, so it's easy enough to blend in comfortably from a distance.'

'Good.'

'I know that area,' Jill said. 'I went to school with a girl who lived up there. You can go straight up Central Avenue and around the top to come down Fox Road instead of having to go past the Jensen.'

'Good,' Pete said with a nod. 'We know Price didn't take it, so not knowing who did, we don't know where they live. Might be within sight of where they parked it.'

'We'll have Derek Tasker's mobile data in the morning,' Ben reported, putting his phone down.

'Thanks, Ben.'

'What's our interest in him, in particular, anyway?' Dave asked.

'The fact that he's a known associate of Ewan Price's. The fact that he's got a record for car theft. And the further fact that he's now got a job driving a recovery vehicle,' Pete told him. 'You put a car on the back of one of them – no-one's going to take any notice of you doing it – strap a cover over it and you can take it anywhere you like with no-one, including us, being any the wiser.'

'Except whoever owns the recovery vehicle,' Jill argued. 'I got picked up in one a couple of years ago, with my previous car. That's why I changed it. Once that happened, I couldn't trust it anymore. But chatting with the driver on the way back here, he was telling me how they're tracked every which way but loose. The tacho's only the start of it. Then they've got Satnavs, plus GPS tracking so customers can track them to the breakdown location – all of it hardwired in, so you can't just switch it off or unplug it without that being recorded and the owner eventually knowing about it. So, if he's involved in the car thefts, then so's his boss.'

'Who hasn't got a record,' Jane pointed out. 'And he seemed like a straightforward type of guy to me.'

'Well, Tasker was hiding something,' Pete argued. 'I don't know what yet, but he certainly wasn't telling me everything he knows.'

'The Jensen should tell us what we need,' Dave said. 'We follow that when they move it, and it'll lead us to them, whoever they are.'

'*If* they move it,' Dick argued. 'If they haven't been scared off by all this trouble over Price's death and the fire at the recovery depot.'

'It was taken after both of those,' Pete pointed out. 'The only reason to leave it alone now would be if they're onto the fact that we've spotted it.'

'We were just cruising at that stage,' Bernie said. 'In unmarked cars. I was down that road I mentioned off the other side of Beacon Heath. Diane and Trevor went up Central Avenue, then she went round Fox Road and he did Brookside. She spotted it, carried on past and called it in as she came back around the bottom. So I can't see that she'd have been spotted by anyone.'

'We should be OK, then,' Pete said. 'It's just a question of how long they'll leave it there.'

'It was taken Saturday night. It's Tuesday now,' Jill said. 'They won't leave it much longer, surely? I suppose it depends on what they're doing with it, where they're taking it and how, but...' She shrugged.

Pete nodded once more. 'You're right. Hopefully, they'll move it tonight or tomorrow night. So what we're here for is to arrange the watch detail.'

'Diane's OK for another hour if needs be,' Bernie said.

'I can take over from then,' said the young male member of her team who, the previous morning, had found the footage of the car they were discussing.

'All right, you do six 'til midnight,' Pete said. 'Who's up for the Beacon Heath watch?'

'I can go and grab some chips and a coke, get there for six if someone lends me a car,' Dave offered.

'You can have mine if you pick it up from my place and bring it back after,' Dick said.

Pete nodded and let his gaze wander around the team. 'I'll take over from then. Who's on with me?'

One of Bernie's team, a tall, willowy redhead, raised a hand. 'I can do it.'

'I'll take the graveyard shift on Fox Road,' offered another uniformed officer.

'I'll have Beacon Heath, then,' said another.

'OK, that takes us through to dawn,' Pete said. 'Jane, do you want to take six 'til noon on Fox Road, and Bernie, put someone on Beacon Heath and we'll arrange things from there in the morning if necessary?'

Jane nodded. 'Can do.'

'Trace, how about you?' Bernie asked. 'You're a morning person.'

'OK.'

'That's settled then,' Pete concluded. 'Let's all get off home for now. The rest of us meet up here in the morning.'

*

He'd parked on the left side of the side-road, just far enough down from the junction to not stand out while still being able to see across to where Central Avenue emerged onto the main road, diagonally across to his right. The footpath along this side of Beacon Heath Road was backed by grass, but on the corner to his right was a tall, mature horse-chestnut tree, now in full leaf and liberally dotted with spires of white blossom that gave him just enough shelter. To his left, the grass was backed by a high, dense hedge belonging to the 1980's brick-built house that was the first of a long, narrow fill-in estate running down the hill behind him.

With the passenger window lowered a couple of inches to allow fresh air in while not being visible from the target's potential viewpoint, he was also using his mp3 player and earphones to keep himself awake and alert with music when his radio hissed and a female voice came through.

'Target moving,' she said. 'Target moving. Single male occupant. Moving downhill.'

Pete switched off the music and tucked the earbuds away in the inside pocket of the black leather jacket he was wearing with a khaki green T-shirt and jeans, his attention focussed completely on the junction across from him as he wound the side-window up and sank lower in his seat.

Picking the radio up from the passenger seat, he keyed the mike. 'All received.'

'Target going out of sight,' the redheaded officer, who Pete had learned was PC Chloe Sutton, reported.

Which meant he was going around the turn at the bottom of the straight stretch of road she was parked on, coming towards the exit from the little Christmas-tree shaped estate of 1950s houses and bungalows.

'Roger,' Pete responded into the radio and glanced around before hunkering down even further.

There was no-one in sight on the main road or the street behind him – either on foot or in vehicles. That was something to be thankful for, he thought. It never ceased to amaze him how much traffic was around at these times of the night. It was approaching ten-to-one in the morning.

The glow of headlights on the tarmac in the junction across from him was followed by his first sighting of the lights themselves: Jaguar-like double rounds at either end of a wide grille fronting the big bonnet of the distinctively shaped old touring car with its sloping rear.

Its indicator started to flicker as it neared the junction.

'Shit,' Pete muttered, grimacing as he sank down so he couldn't be seen at all and picked up his radio again. 'Target indicating right, right, right onto Beacon Heath.'

The target was turning towards him, towards the city centre, instead of the expected direction, away towards Pinhoe and out of the city.

'Received,' Sutton responded.

Lying across the central console, his head just high enough to be able to peer out with one eye, he watched the car cruise past him, the driver taking his time, not rushing; not wanting to draw attention, Pete guessed. He waited for it to get twenty yards along from the junction he was sitting in before straightening up and reaching for the ignition. Starting the car, he switched on the side-lights, then his indicator, and eased up to the junction, waiting for the last moment before switching to low-beam headlights.

By the time he made the turn, the Jensen was gone from sight.

With the road stretching away straight in front of him, it was not there at all.

'Dammit,' Pete cursed.

Thirty or forty yards along, there was another almost-crossroads, the left turn just before the right this time. It had taken one or the other.

He fought the urge to put his foot down, instead picking up the radio again and keying the mike. 'Temporary loss,' he reported. 'Temporary loss.'

Then he was at the left-hand junction, which ran down the hill between partially-leaved trees, looking more like a rural road than an urban one with the estate he'd been parked in the entrance of concealed behind trees and a thick hedgerow. He caught the glow of taillights and made the decision to go after them. Swung into the road with just one flick of his indicator.

A few yards further and he got a clear view of the vehicle ahead.

Rectangular taillights with a chrome bumper beneath and the unique wrap-around rear window.

He breathed a sigh of relief.

'Target heading south on Summer Lane,' he reported. 'Repeat, south on Summer Lane. Normal speeds. OV One, join pursuit but hang back for now.'

'Received. Joining,' Sutton responded.

Trees overhung the road, the streetlights flickering through the branches, some of which were beginning to come into leaf. The houses on his left got closer to the road, the hedge in front of them lower so that they were more visible, but still unobtrusive. Then the school entrance showed on his right. As he passed the school with it's low, clipped hedge, the vegetation on his left got higher and denser, the road still stretching away long and straight ahead, the Jensen at least fifty yards in front.

Pete made no effort to close the gap between them.

A glance in the mirror showed headlights. He lifted the radio. 'Is that you behind me, OV One?'

'Yes, yes.'

'Speed currently 27 miles per hour. Put your foot down and come past us like you're in a hurry,' he said. 'Then you can plot up again further down, on Summer Way, to make sure he carries on past towards Whipton. I'll pull off a bit further down and let you take point from there.'

'All received.'

The car ahead rocked over a speed-bump and Pete pursed his lips. That wasn't helpful in these circumstances. It would make his presence behind the target all the more obvious as it pushed his headlights upward, albeit briefly. But there was nothing he could do about it.

Then the car behind him surged forward as Sutton put her foot down, coming hard on the clear road. She passed him doing at least fifty and kept going, passing the Jensen too and fading off into the distance.

The driver of the Jensen didn't react, hopefully thinking she was just another mad driver, having fun while the road was clear and there was no-one around to witness it.

Pete passed another pedestrian entrance to the school, then a couple of vehicle entrances before a side-road showed on the left that he knew was for the carpark of Exeter Arena, the green glow of traffic lights just beyond at a pedestrian crossing. They wouldn't be going in there at this time of night: it was gated.

He watched the target drive on past and down towards where the road narrowed under an old brick arched railway bridge.

By the time he'd followed suit, the Jensen had gone from sight again. They were back into residential streets now, curving this way and that between a mix of pre- and post-war houses, set back on either side of the road behind gardens that were raised up behind solid walls, making it feel like a sunken lane.

A few more gentle twists left and right and the radio hissed again.

'Subject just passed me,' Sutton reported. 'Took the left, left, left into Summerway.' Moments later, Pete reached the junction. Turning in, he saw Sutton's dark hatchback parked facing him on the right, the headlights just flicking on.

What were they playing at now? This was a residential street, albeit a fairly long one with side-streets off it. Were they trying to throw or detect anyone following? Or just staying off the main roads as much as possible to avoid detection by a random patrol car or traffic cameras?

If the latter, they had a couple of options of where to emerge. Three, in fact, when he thought about it. And there were only himself and Sutton to cover them.

He stopped the car, reversed quickly, his window buzzing down, to stop alongside her. 'Go left out of here, down to the village and left again onto Pinhoe Road,' he said quickly. 'And move yourself in case they come out at Thackeray Road. Go.'

As she sped off, he reversed quickly out of the junction and followed her, keying the radio as he went.

'DS Gayle to Control. Eyes needed at top of Hill Barton Road, like now. Subject driving dark red Jensen Interceptor. Observation only: this is a follow and trace operation.'

'Received.'

Pete concentrated on driving, following Sutton's Golf at a rapid pace down through the random mix of shops, houses and bungalows that led into the centre of Whipton village. They turned left at a crossroads and, a few yards later, filtered out onto Pinhoe Road where mid-century semis were accessed up sloping drives while, on the far side, larger houses stood back behind a strip of grass with mature trees and shrubbery.

A junction showed on the left and Sutton pulled over, letting Pete pass. He flicked on his blue lights but resisted the temptation of the siren, just in case, and hit the accelerator, coming up fast behind a black-roofed white hatchback. Overtaking it, he surged onward, leaving Sutton to figure out for herself where best to plot up on the junction she was covering.

'Where's that observation on Hill Barton?' he demanded into the radio as he rapidly approached the junction with the road that led southward, towards the Middlemoor police HQ and the station beside it.

He now had tall hedges on his side of the road, opposite a row of red-brick semis.

'On way, Sarge.'

He passed the first sign for the junction.

'How soon?'

The road curved gently left. Another car showed in front of him. A dark-coloured saloon. It was time to commit or back off.

'Car Echo three-seven responding. One minute, coming up from Sidmouth Road.'

'Roger.'

He went for it. Passing the other car almost on the second possible point of emergence from the estate on his left, he kept his foot down, thankful for the extra lanes in the road here as he cut back in, heading for the final option.

The traffic lights in front of him flicked from green to amber but, with blue lights still flashing, he ignored them. Then he was there. He braked hard, swinging the car into a junction on the left, immediately before a small supermarket. Where could he park up? Just past the entrance to the supermarket's carpark, he found his answer. Five or six parking spaces were empty in front of a pale green building with the weird mixture of signage on the front for a bed shop and a karate club. He pulled over and reversed into the end space so that he was partially protected from view to his left by a brick wall that was half the height of the car.

With a sigh, he killed the headlights and was reaching to switch off the engine when his radio hissed.

'Observation in place, top of Hill Barton Lane, opposite Sainsbury's carpark.'

'Received,' he responded. 'Do not engage target if spotted, we want to know where he's going.'

'Roger.'

Pete relaxed into his seat. Now to wait.

CHAPTER TWENTY-FIVE

He felt like he'd barely had chance to catch his breath when the glow of headlights swept into view from his left, a car turning into the tree-lined road beyond the row of small businesses, one of which he was parked in front of.

Was this his man?

Automatically, he straightened in his seat, then instantly realised his mistake and slid down so that he could just peer out over the bottom edge of the windscreen.

Sure enough, he saw twin circular headlights coming towards him.

Could be.

The car came past at a steady pace, not rushing. He saw the distinctive sloping shape of the rear.

Yes!

Reaching for his radio as he slid down further in his seat, he keyed the mike. 'Target spotted; target spotted. Exhibition Way, heading for Pinhoe Road. About to follow.'

He gave it a count of two, then pushed himself up in his seat far enough to see out.

The Jensen had passed the supermarket carpark entrance and was indicating left.

Now they were heading out of the city. Maybe.

He keyed the radio mike again. 'Target left, left, left on Pinhoe Road.'

Starting his engine, he waited for the Jensen to make the turn, then flicked on his headlights and eased out after them.

Thankfully, the traffic lights stayed green long enough for him to emerge onto the main road and he accelerated after the Jensen just enough to keep it in sight as, beyond the supermarket and a handful of small industrial units, the road began its sweeping curve to the right.

The Jensen stayed on the main road rather than taking the left fork that would have taken it around behind the car hire site that had once been a filling station – a site that Pete recalled visiting on a previous case. Knowing the road – and that there was another turning a little further around the curve – he closed the gap a little more. Then he keyed the radio once more. 'Subject committed. South on Cumberland Way.'

He was thinking fast as he eased off the accelerator, surprised as always by the amount of traffic that was on the roads at this time of night as he allowed the Jensen to gain a little more distance on him. It made his job of following without being noticed easier.

The road was taking them directly down towards Sowton Industrial Estate, where both Storm Windows and Isca Recovery were based. But also towards Honiton Road, which led out directly to Blackhorse, where only hours ago, Jane had informed him that a known associate of Derek Tasker's, Mark Grey, had a haulage company.

He picked up his radio once more. 'Three-seven, use your lights and sirens. Get down onto Honiton Road as fast as you can and out to Moor Lane Roundabout. Officer Sutton, do the same.'

'Roger,' came the patrol officer's response.

'I've got no lights and sirens, sarge,' Sutton came back.

'I know but do your best. Just stay safe.'

'Received.'

Trees and bushes were lining both sides of the road in front of him as Pete continued south. Then, as more new-build housing showed on the left, the road curving away to the right, he saw the Jensen's indicator begin to flicker.

'Damn,' he muttered. Now what were they playing at?

But then, he realised. The road they were signalling into swept away through this new-build housing estate, over the motorway and through another new estate to ultimately emerge onto the Honiton Road, almost directly across from Mark Grey's business, if not home address.

Of course, there were a lot of places in between there, but…

He lifted the radio again.

'Subject left, left, left onto Tithebarn Way. Sutton, get yourself out to the bottom end of there, ASAP and come up it at normal driving speed to try and intercept. As before, do not engage. Just observe, report and continue.'

'Received.'

'Three-seven, lead Sutton out there and plot up at the bottom end of Tithebarn.'

'Roger.'

Now he could hang back, letting the Jensen get out of sight, knowing that, if it carried on at normal speeds through to the far end of the road it was on, it would be picked up from the other end. And if not, they'd have a restricted area to search with no way it could emerge without being seen.

Although, if the driver had spotted them and now abandoned it somewhere in the streets off this road, escaping into one of the hundreds of houses or in another vehicle, that could still leave them back at square one in the investigation.

He grimaced as he drove up the long, curving hill beneath streetlights that glowed yellow in the night, illuminating the new-build houses crowded on either side of the clean, new tarmac, the road ahead clear. Hoping the Jensen driver was continuing straight on.

He held his nerve, though he glanced into each of the sideroads he passed along the way. Kept going. A few more bends and he reached the end of the built-up area and the bridge over the motorway. Beyond that a tall hedge sheltered the left side, the road curving away beyond it onto a long stretch that was clearly visible under the half-moon. Taillights showed in the distance ahead. Quickly, he pulled over into a gateway and reached for his glovebox. Took out the tiny binoculars he kept in there and put them up to his eyes.

He was just in time to catch the briefest glimpse of the taillights through them before they vanished around another bend in the road. Breathed a sigh of relief as he was sure he recognised the vehicle.

Leaving the binoculars on the seat beside him, he set off again.

His radio hissed.

'PC Sutton for DS Gayle. Target spotted continuing south.'

'Received. Don't react to it, Sutton,' he responded. 'Just keep coming towards me until you can't see it in your mirrors then use the next junction to turn around.'

Reaching the bend where the car in front of him had gone from sight, he entered another area of new-build housing, the road continuing around in a long, sweeping curve that seemed to carry on forever until finally the road straightened, but now it was rising up towards a low crest so he could still not see the stolen car ahead of him.

To his right, the houses – all weird shapes and a mix of white render and buff brick – ended abrupt with what looked like either a low-rise block of flats or a wilfully weird short terrace, a side-road going up the far end of it. Parked nose-out in the side-road was a dark hatchback.

'Is that you, Sutton?' he asked into his radio.

'Sarge.'

She flashed her lights.

'Come on, then,' he said as he passed her. Saw her car begin to ease forward.

She pulled out behind him.

Pete keyed the radio once more. 'Three-seven, where are you?'

'Entrance to the science park, just up from the southern end of Tithebarn, sarge.'

'Target must be almost with you.'

'Yes, yes. Target sighted. Approaching at normal speed.'

'Can you see which way he turns at the end?' Pete asked.

'Yes, yes.'

'Stay put and report, then.'

'Will do.' Immediately, they were back on. 'Signalling left, left. Turning with signal.'

Then Pete was close enough to see the patrol car parked up beyond a low post and rail fence. 'I see you,' he said. 'Sutton's behind me. Come out in position three.'

'Will do.'

Pete passed the junction where they'd sat and, in front of him, the road curved right then reached the junction with the dual-carriageway section of the old Honiton Road, replaced now for most purposes by a newer through-road that bypassed the villages of Blackhorse and Clyst Honiton to carry on past the southern edge of the airport.

He made the junction and put his foot down hard. Now he needed to have the stolen car in sight again. He could see the faint glow of taillights some distance ahead, but he needed to be sure it was his quarry. The houses of Blackhorse village appeared on his left and, far ahead, he saw the car he was following, but it was too far to make out details, especially at night. He kept going, checking briefly in the mirror that the other two cars were still with him.

They were.

The road here was long and straight. He gained ground quickly on the Jensen, which was still moving at a steady, unremarkable pace. Soon, he could make out the shape of its lights and the gleam of its distinctive back window under the streetlights. Then its right indicator flickered on, blinking orange in the night.

It was turning into Sowton Lane, towards the location of Mark Grey's transport company.

Here we go, he thought, easing off the accelerator. *That's it, take us to Daddy.*

The lights went from sight, but then…

Is that the same car? Is he turning round? He was sure he could see the distinctive gleam of the back window as a vehicle came up the side-turn into view. Was it the same one? How many of that model were still on the roads after half a century, never mind around the city of Exeter?

As the distance closed, he could see it was definitely the same model and dark in colour. It had to be.

Then it was coming back towards him.

'Shit,' he muttered. They must have spotted – or at least suspected – him. Or been suspicious of the patrol car that was now behind him.

Whatever the case... Pete reached for his radio and keyed the mike. 'Target coming back at us. Blue lights and block the road. Don't let him through. I'll pass and close his back door.'

'Roger.'

'Will do,' Sutton added.

The Jensen passed him and he saw the pale glow of the driver's face staring across at him. Then blue lights began to flash behind him. He yanked the wheel hard across, swinging the Ford side-on across the road, tight behind the Jensen as the patrol car swung across, blocking its forward path and Sutton's lights angled across, too, closing the side-exit from the box formation.

Pete was reaching for his seatbelt release when he heard the roar of an engine and the Jensen bumped up onto the grass verge. It scraped the high, ragged hedge, surging past the patrol car, then lurching back down onto the tarmac to speed away.

'Shit.' He hit his accelerator, following its path.

Clear of the marooned patrol car, he flicked on his lights and sirens, then grabbed the radio again. 'Subject failing to stop,' he barked. 'West-bound on old Honiton Road, Blackhorse. Any available units to intercept.'

A glance in his mirror showed the patrol car reversing to make the turn while Sutton waited to follow it.

The Jensen driver could go anywhere from here: back the way he'd come or down onto the main A30 trunk road and left, heading east towards Clyst Honiton, right, into the city or onto the M5 motorway in either direction. Pete didn't know what speeds the

Jensen Interceptor could achieve but he did know that there were more than enough options open to its driver to lose him if it took to the smaller roads around here.

He guessed that, despite its age, with the size of its engine, it could probably give his Ford a run for its money. The patrol car would probably have to take over, once it caught up, if the stolen car took to the motorway.

But they had to get there yet. Not that that would take long, at the speed they were doing. Pete's foot was down to the floor as he fought to stay with the older vehicle, which was no more than a hundred yards ahead of him and going hard.

In moments, the road split for the grassed central reservation approaching the junction on their right. They were going way too fast to make that.

'Subject straight on past Tithebarn Way,' he reported into the radio.

They powered on past the junction, the road in front of them curving left then right. The streetlights became closer as they passed the science park on their right, nearing the junction with the main east-west trunk road. A junction flashed past on their left, then one on their right, leading into the science park. The low rising gradient they were on crested and began to dip away as they entered the sweeping left curve that led down to the T-junction at the end, the Jensen still pushing hard.

He'd have to slow down anytime now or he wouldn't make the junction, whichever direction he chose, Pete thought, easing off his own accelerator.

Finally, the Jensen's brake lights flared. The heavy car began to fishtail as if the driver couldn't make up his mind which way to go. Then it happened. Pete's car juddered as the ABS kicked in, but the Jensen didn't have that advantage. The driver pulled it around into the left fork of the junction, tyres squealing their protest with smoke rising from them. there was a bang and sparks flew as the offside wheels hit the kerb of a low traffic island and the car lurched over to the left. Another bang as it hit the verge on that side and again bounced off, lurching across two lanes as it approached the traffic lights at the end, which were on red, though no traffic was crossing them on the road they were approaching.

Pete heard the roar of the Jensen's big V8 engine as the driver dropped down a gear in an effort to slow it further, but it was clearly too late. Committed by momentum, if nothing else, he shot the red light and pulled it around to the right, despite being in the left lane. Again, the tyres squealed, smoke billowing up from them as the car lost grip and went into a sideways slide.

Pete kept his foot on the brake, the ABS taking control now and slowing the Ford quickly as he watched the car thief struggle with the older vehicle as it leaned away from his attempt to change direction. Pulling further, harder around, the heavy car slowing all the time, its right-hand tyres lifted off the tarmac. The front one hit the kerb of the central reservation, kicking it up further. Then the far side hit the verge on the south side of the road, first the front wheel, then the back and, with the suspension soft with age, it was too much. Pete saw the dark underside as it lifted high, it's speed and momentum pushing it on in the direction it had been taking and wanted to maintain despite what the driver was attempting.

Pete shot past it and stopped a few yards ahead, allowing the two cars behind him room to react as the Jensen crashed back down onto four wheels, the roar of the engine reducing as the tyres bit tarmac again and it spurted forward. But it had been too much for the rear suspension. The leaf spring on the driver's side collapsed on impact, tugging the car around sharply to the right as the tyre bit into the lining of the rear wheel-well. The near-side front tyre hit the kerb again and the car bucked and stopped.

Pete shed his seatbelt and was out of the Ford, ignoring the wail of sirens from his own and the patrol car as he ran the few steps to the stricken Jensen and snatched at the driver's door.

'Out,' he snapped at the man inside. 'Now.'

CHAPTER TWENTY-SIX

'Morning, all,' Pete said as he stepped into the incident room and approached his desk at just after 9:30am.

Several faces looked up at him.

'Didn't expect you in yet awhile,' Jane said. 'You want a coffee?'

'Hmm. I'll get it. I'm on my feet already. Anyone else?'

Heads were shaken around the table except for Ben. 'Please, boss.'

Pete dropped his jacket over the back of his chair, grabbed Ben's mug and headed across to the coffee maker. Returning, he handed Ben his drink and sat down. 'Have you heard back from Derek Tasker's phone provider yet?' he asked the spiky-haired PC.

'Not yet. I could chase them.'

'Give it an hour,' Pete conceded. 'Any other fun facts I should know about?' He looked around the cluster of desks, widening the question out to the whole team, apart from Dave who was still absent, having been on watch-duty until midnight.

'We've got an address on Tasker's buddy, Mark Grey,' Jane said. 'He's not living at the farm on Sowton Lane. The house there's unoccupied. He lives in Blackhorse, on Blackhorse Lane. Seems like he's renting a place up there while they make the place at Sowton liveable. He bought it as a bit of a do-er upper,' she added with a grin.

'You mean a wreck?' Dick asked from beside Pete.

'It had been lived in for fifty-odd years by the same old boy who'd inherited it from his parents,' she said. 'Which probably means he was born there. Grey bought it at auction nineteen months ago. Probably as a base for his haulage company, which he'd set up six months before that, based at that industrial estate out at Hill Barton. I suppose he thought it'd be cheaper to run in the end, with the added bonus of a house on-site.' She looked at Pete. 'I'm just getting into the company history. Financials and so on.'

He nodded. 'OK. I need to make a phone call while I think of it.' He picked up his desk phone and dialled an internal number.

'Fairweather.'

'Andy, it's Pete Gayle. Have you got the arson report on the Isca Recovery fire?'

'No, still waiting for it.'

'OK, I'll chase it.'

He hung up and redialled, this time to the fire service, which had its Exeter base next-door to where he sat in the police station.

'Fire and Rescue, how can we help?'

'Hi, this is DS Gayle, Exeter CID. I'm looking for a report on an arson attack last Thursday night.'

'Which one?'

'Isca Recovery. What do you mean, which one?' he added quickly.

'There were two that night,' the telephonist said. 'What are the odds, eh? We get maybe one a month, on average – if that. Then two in one night. And it's not like they were close together, either.'

'Really? Where was the other one?'

'Out towards Clyst Honiton. Blackhorse.'

'Really?' Pete repeated, his tone heavier. 'Where exactly?'

'Why? You reckon they could be linked?'

'I don't know. Yet.'

'OK, well… Give me a sec. Here it is: Blackhorse Lane. A private residence. Accelerant poured through the letterbox and over and around the back door. Two people inside. They'd got out through a window before we got there, so no injuries.'

'Interesting. What number?'

'Seven.'

'OK, thanks for that. What about the report on my one?'

'It'll be out tomorrow. Like I said, we normally only get one every four or five weeks. Two in one night slows things down a bit on the admin side.'

'OK. Sooner the better, though. And the case is mine now, rather than Sergeant Fairweather's.'

'I'll make a note, send it on to the investigator.'

'Thanks.'

He hung up and lifted his head to look across the desks at Jane. 'Blackhorse Lane. Mark Grey. What number is he living in?'

'Seven.'

His eyes widened. 'Well, that's not a coincidence.'

'What?' she demanded with a frown.

Pete explained what he'd just discovered.

'Hmm. You're right. Derek Tasker's employer – and his specific truck – plus his buddy's home address. We need to know exactly what they've got in common, don't we?'

Pete nodded. '*Everything* they've got in common, I'd say.'

'I can get onto that. I suppose you're going to interview the lad you nicked last night?'

'That's what I came in for. Dick, do you want to sit in? Play the father-figure?'

'Grandad, you mean,' Jill said with a grin.

'Oi, Titch!'

'That suggests a kindly face, not an old sourpuss,' Jane cut in.

'Don't you start,' Dick grumbled. 'What's this? Pick on me 'cause Dapper's not here?'

'Look at what Ben's going to suffer if you go off to the interview rooms, then,' Jill said.

'Hey, what have I done?' Ben demanded.

'Been born male,' Dick told him.

'That's a sexist remark if ever I heard one,' Jill declared.

'Not a remark at all,' Dick retorted. 'An observation. Are we going, before this turns into a battle of the sexes?' he asked Pete.

'Might be wise,' Pete agreed. 'You know we'll never win one of those.'

*

A few minutes later, Pete and Dick were settled on one side of the table in Interview Room 2 of the custody suite, opposite the youth Pete had arrested the night before on the A30, just a few hundred yards from where they sat now.

'You're sure you don't want a solicitor present?' Pete checked.

The young man shrugged. 'What for? Not much point, is there? And a site quicker to do without.'

Pete tipped his head. The lad seemed to think this was a formality and he'd be bailed in no time flat. He'd learn the truth of that soon enough, he thought. 'It's up to you. As you were told when you came in last night, one can be provided. Otherwise, we'll get on.'

The lad shrugged. 'Go for it.'

He was small for his age, Pete thought. Not that that made him unique. He thought of his own son, Tommy. Of Ewan Price. Of Jill Evans, come to that. Dark haired, baby-faced and slight of build, the lad could have made an ideal jockey. 'All right,' he said and reached across to switch on the digital audio and video recorder. 'Harry Brooks – it is Harry, rather than Harold, is it? Officially?'

His nose wrinkled. 'Yeah.'

'I'll remind you that you're under caution. You don't have to say anything but anything you do say can be given in evidence. This is a formal interview being conducted at Sidmouth Road police station by DC Richard Feeney and myself, DS Peter Gayle with said Harry Brooks.' He quoted the date and time. 'So, where were you off to when we stopped you, then, Harry? It seemed like we interrupted your plans a bit.'

'No comment.'

'You were going down Sowton Lane until you spotted us behind you, is that correct?'

'No comment.'

Pete allowed himself a small, brief smile. 'We looked you up before we came in here, obviously. We're aware this isn't your first visit here. Your record goes back to before we moved here from Heavitree Road, in fact. Since you were sixteen. Thefts. Car-thefts. Burglaries.'

'So?'

'So, it seemed like you'd gone quiet, turned your life around, until last night. Or maybe until Saturday night. What changed? What caused the reversion?'

Brooks' eyes narrowed. 'No comment,' he said.

'You won't be getting off with a slap on the wrist again this time, you know,' Pete told him. 'B&E, TWOC – taking without consent, driving without a licence or insurance.' He shook his head. 'That, I don't get. I mean, given your record of car thefts, I'd have thought you'd at least get a licence.'

Brooks sneered but said nothing.

'And added to all that, there's handling stolen goods, as the car had been left up on Fox Road for a couple of days before you picked it up last night.'

'Eh?' Brooks interrupted with a frown. 'You can't have it both ways. Either I nicked it or I handled it afterwards.'

'Well, you tell me, then,' Pete said with a shrug. 'Which is it?'

Brooks started to respond but stopped himself. 'Uh-uh. I ain't that daft. No comment.'

'OK, then we've got arson. Times two.'

'Arson? What fucking arson? Don't come that. I never done no arson.'

'You fit the description of the person who did, and both cases are related to a spate of recent aggravated burglaries and vehicle thefts. And murders.'

'Whoa! Hold on, hold on. No way, mate. You ain't fitting me up with that lot. Not a chance. If that's your game, I will have a bloody lawyer.'

Dick leaned forward. 'We're just laying out the situation for you, Harry,' he said. 'The facts we've got that we're trying to figure a way through to the truth behind them. That's all.'

'Well, you're way off course, then,' he sneered. ''Cause there's no way I'm tied into that lot. Murders. Aggravated wot-nots. Fuckin' arson. You've seen my record. None of that fits me, so what's the game here? What evidence have you got that any of it's anything to do with me?'

'You're on camera, matey,' Pete told him. 'CCTV. At the depot. On the way to it. At the petrol station. Other places.'

'No, I bloody ain't. And what depot?'

'If you're demanding a solicitor, we can't discuss it any further,' Pete said. 'You go back to your cell and we go back to our office and call the CPS to place the charge.'

'No, you bloody don't. I want to know. What evidence have you got against me? I want to see it.'

'So, now you're saying you don't want a solicitor present?' Pete checked.

'That's right.'

'OK.' He took out his phone and brought up the photos folder. Found a still of their suspect at the petrol station, paying for the two cans of fuel and turned the phone to show Brooks through the protective clear screen between them.

'That ain't me,' he said instantly. 'I ain't got no trousers like that.'

Pete stared at him for a stretched second. 'We will check on that, obviously. But if not, where were you?'

'When?'

'Last Thursday night into Friday morning.'

'Well, that's easy enough. I was at home. In bed.'

'Can anyone vouch for that?' Pete asked.

'Yeah. My mum. She was in the next room. If I'd gone out, she'd know about it.'

Pete raised a sceptical eyebrow.

'If that's true, you're in the clear then,' Dick said. 'Of that, at least. But what about the Jensen? And why the relapse?'

'I'm saying nothing about that.'

Pete leaned forward in his chair again. 'Were you wearing gloves when you did the break-in for its keys?'

Brooks grinned. 'No comment.'

'Why take them off?' he asked with a confused frown. It was a ploy. There were no fingerprints at the scene, but Brooks didn't know that. 'What a mistake-a to make-a. Leaving us a nice clean set of dabs there that come right back to you.'

Brooks sneered. 'Why didn't you come straight round and pick me up, then?'

Pete shrugged. 'We've had more important – more urgent – things to deal with. The murders I mentioned before. The aggravated burglaries. Arson. Your case – if those aren't – was a bit further down the pecking order. Only so many bodies to cover the workload, you know?'

'Well, no, them others ain't mine. Like I said.'

'So what about what DC Feeney asked? Why did you do it? Why now, after all this time? What is it – two years since you were last involved with us?'

'About that,' he said with a shrug.

'So, why now?'

He stared at Pete for a beat, assessing his attitude, which had shifted from firm, bordering on aggressive, to sympathetic, wanting to understand. Shrugged again. 'A favour for a mate.'

'What mate?'

'Hah! What, and drop him in it? What do you take me for? An idiot?'

Pete was tempted to say, 'Yes, exactly that,' but he resisted. 'No,' he said instead. 'But I'd question why a friend – I mean, a real friend – would ask you to commit a crime. So, if not who, why? And why would you agree to it?'

He pursed his lips. 'It's complicated, innit?'

'How so?'

'It wasn't the mate who asked me. Not himself. He was... It was another mate of his.'

'A friend of a friend, then,' Pete said. Which removed him by one step, hopefully making it easier for the lad to talk about. 'So, what? Your mate would have done it, but couldn't, so they wanted you to step in, as a favour?'

'Yeah.'

'OK,' Pete said, nodding acceptance of that. 'So, what about this second guy? I take it you know him. Enough to recognise him, at least?'

'Yeah.' His tone said *'Duh.'*

'How?'

'Met him in the pub with... My mate a couple of times.'

'Recently or over the years?'

'Recent.'

'So, you know his name.'

'No.'

'No? How can you spend time with a bloke in a pub more than once and not know his name?'

'Nicknames.'

'And his is…?'

He shrugged. 'Del. Like in Fools'n'orses, but without the Boy.'

'Del.' Pete shared a glance with Dick. *Del as in short for Derek,* he thought and, from his nod, Dick was thinking the same.

'Do you know what Del does for a living?'

Brooks shook his head. 'Didn't come up, did it?'

'OK. So, your mate, who was middle-man in all this – who's he?'

'No, he weren't. Del called me direct. Said Ew… My mate was going to do a job, but couldn't, so could I help him out? Just the once. And get paid a pony for my trouble.'

'And you jumped at it?'

He shrugged. 'A pony's a pony, innit? And just the once, what's the harm? Not like he was a stranger, was it?'

'Did he say why your mate couldn't do it? Or suggest you ask him yourself?'

'Said he was out of town on a job.'

Pete gave a quick grimace. 'And your mate was Ewan Price, correct?'

Brooks' eyes widened. 'How…? I ain't answering that.'

Pete nodded. 'Fair enough. But I can tell you, he *was* out of town. At least that's where he was found.'

'What d'you mean, found?'

'I mean found in a burning car,' Pete said. 'Murdered.'

'Huh?' Shock and grief merged on Brooks' face as his mouth dropped open as if gulping for air. 'You're…'

Pete shook his head. 'Sorry, Harry, but no, I'm not joking. I'm deadly serious. Ewan's dead. Killed in one of the cars he nicked. That's why he couldn't steal that Jensen for Del and whoever else he's working with.'

'Shit, man.'

'I'd show you pictures, but that would be cruel and unusual. They're not pretty.'

Brooks was shaking his head.

'Do you need a minute?' Dick asked him, maintaining his role.

Brooks sucked in a breath and blinked. 'No. Let's get this over with.'

'So, given how Ewan died, I need to know everything you can tell me about this Del.'

'What, you reckon it was him that done for Pricey? What am I, then, next on his list?'

Pete shrugged. 'It looks to me like he uses and abuses. Leaves no witnesses. What does that suggest to you?'

He sneered. 'It suggests bullshit, that's what it suggests.'

Pete shook his head. 'There's no bullshit going on here, Harry. I was at the site. And the post-mortem.' He grimaced, nose wrinkling at the memory.

'It's true,' Dick added. 'I wasn't there, but DS Gayle was and I've seen the reports.' He grimaced for effect. 'Nasty business. Very nasty. The only saving grace, I suppose, was that he was already dead when the fire was started. But even that…' He turned to Pete. 'Isn't there a picture of the necklace he was wearing?'

Pete nodded. 'Good thought. Yes.' He took out his phone again and found it. Showed it to Brooks. 'Do you recognise it, Harry?'

He stared, eyes narrowing, then nodded once and looked up at Pete. 'I recognise it. He said it was made special. His mum got it done for him.'

Pete nodded. 'That's what she told me, too.' He let the silence stretch for a few seconds. 'So, that's what we're dealing with here. B&E, traffic offences – they can go by the wayside, if you can help us get justice for Ewan. For his mum.'

Brooks held his silence.

'How long had you known Ewan?' Pete asked.

Brooks blinked at the change in direction. 'Since we was kids. Twelve.'

'And you know his mum?'

He nodded.

Pete matched the gesture. 'I met her the other day. Seemed like a nice lady. Doing her best in difficult circumstances. One of the down-sides of our job: we often have to meet people at the worst moments of their lives. Sometimes giving them the worst news they've ever received. So, what turned Ewan bad?'

He straightened in his chair. 'He were…' He stopped. 'He got picked on at school a fair bit. His size, for one thing. And he was shy with it. That didn't help.'

'So, he didn't have many friends?'

Harry shrugged.

'Other than you?'

Another shrug.

'So, why cars? What got him into nicking them?'

Brooks shrugged a third time. Then blinked. 'He didn't start off with 'em.'

'So, where did he start? At school?'

'Yeah.'

'What, revenge for getting picked on?'

'Yeah. His way of getting back at 'em. Then, after... Well, there was... He did a bit of shop-lifting. Bag-snatching, that sort of thing. Next thing I knew, he told me about nicking one of them scooters. Electric ones.'

Pete frowned. 'How?'

'Just shoved the guy off it and buggered off quick.'

'What...? What gave him that idea?'

'He said the guy was an arsehole. Riding it up the pavement like he owned the place. Pricey thought he'd teach him a lesson. And they're illegal to ride on the pavements, ain't they? Or the roads. So, what was he going to do about it? Admit to the police he'd been breaking the law to report it being nicked? And they're worth a bit, so... Win-win, right?' He spread his hands. 'He sold it a few days later. Got a couple of hundred for it. Then, after a bit, he did it again. And again. And I was... Well, at that time... You know my record.'

Pete nodded. 'So, it was you that put him onto the idea of cars? A step up?'

He grimaced. 'He was already into them from working at the garage. I showed him how to drive in one I'd nicked. An old banger. Vauxhall Nova. We'd have a scort round the lanes at night. He took to it like a natural.'

'What happened to the car?' Pete asked.

'We burned it in the end. Rode home on one of his scooters.'

'So, you worked together? Stealing cars?'

His mouth tightened. 'We done a few. Not many. He was… That chip on his shoulder: it pushed him too far. Made him too wild. Unpredictable. I got caught one time and I used that as an excuse. Carried on, on my own, but... He'd started doing his own thing while I was away, so I stayed clear, in that sense.'

'But you stayed friends?'

'Yeah.'

'So, you'd want his killer put away for it. Punished.'

'Of course.'

'Then help us do that, Harry.'

He frowned. 'How?'

Pete tipped his head. 'Last night. Your sudden change of direction.'

'What's that…?' He paused. Took a breath. 'They told me not to go there if there was any other vehicle in sight. To turn round and go and park up in a side-turn opposite the science park until the coast was clear, then try again.'

Pete recalled the side-turn he was talking about – a dead-end like a lay-by that was also the entrance to a house and a couple of fields caught between the old Honiton Road and the newer A30 trunk road, just short of the junction between the two. 'Why there?'

He shrugged. 'It's handy. Good views all around.'

'OK,' Pete accepted. 'But before that – before you spotted us – you were going where, bearing in mind it's a dead-end road you turned around in?'

'Some farm. Del was going to meet me there. Pay me. Give me a lift home after...' His voice tailed off as his gaze turned inward.

'Just Del?' Pete asked, wondering if he was thinking about what had happened to Ewan Price. He hoped so.

'Far as I know,' Brooks said with a shrug.

'And this farm – where exactly is it?'

'A little way down there on the right. There's a gateway on a left-hand bend. There'd be a couple of trucks in there. Artics.'

Pete was nodding. 'Artics belonging to…?'

'MGI Transport.'

'MGI?'

'That's what he said.'

'What, and Del works for them, does he?'

Brooks shrugged. 'I suppose. Why else go there?'

'And you're sure that's all you know about him? You don't know who he is? Where he lives? Who else he hangs around with?'

'No.'

'So, this one deal – this one theft – that's all you've had to do with him apart from meeting him a couple of times in the pub with Ewan Price?'

'Yeah.'

Pete took out his phone once more, scrolled through more pictures until he found a mugshot and held it out for Brooks to see. 'Is that him?'

Brooks' eyes widened in shock as he stared first at the picture on the phone, then at Pete. 'How…? Yeah, that's him. How'd you know that?'

'Our tech guys are going through his phone data as well as yours as we speak, Harry. How many calls and texts are they going to find between you and him?'

'Three, four. Him asking me to do it. Then last night, arranging the pick-up and delivery.'

Pete withdrew the phone and put it away. 'And that's all?'

'Yeah.'

'Whatever's on those phones... Whatever *has been* on them, our guys will find it, Harry. You understand that, don't you? Just because you deleted it doesn't mean it's gone.'

He swallowed hard. Nodded. 'Yeah.'

'So, there's nothing else you want to tell us about?'

'No.'

'Bearing in mind that, if we find that you've lied to us here – about anything at all – then all deals are off. You'll be looking at hard time.'

'I ain't lied.'

There was a knock at the door behind Pete and it opened just far enough for Ben Myers to stick his head in. 'Boss?' He jerked his head back in a beckoning gesture.

'What is it, Ben?'

'We've just heard something that might be relevant.'

'OK.' He pushed his chair back. 'Excuse me a minute, Harry.'

'DS Gayle is leaving the room,' Dick said for the recorder as Pete stepped out, closing the door behind him.

'What is it?'

'Derek Tasker, boss. He's in the RDE. In a bad way. They thought he was an attempt suicide. He was found on the motorway, under the bridge. Tithebarn Way. But then, when they started treating him, they found a stab wound. No ID on him, which is why it took so long to figure out who he was.'

Pete's mind flashed back briefly to the previous night, when he'd followed Harry Brooks along there – over that very bridge – in the stolen Jensen. 'And there's no knife lying about in the area?'

'What, suicide by two means, to make sure of it?'

Pete shrugged. 'You never know.'

'This was a stab-wound, not a cut. Or cuts,' Ben said. 'And to the kidney.'

Pete grimaced. 'Not likely to be self-inflicted, then.'

'No.'

'His boss, cleaning house? After the Ewan Price murder and the bungled delivery last night with the Jensen?'

'Could be. It looks that way, doesn't it?'

'But he's alive? Tasker?'

'Yes. For now, at least. He's in a bad way, though, they said. The stab wound's the least of it.'

Pete grimaced. He could imagine. A fall of eighteen or twenty feet onto tarmac wouldn't have done the guy any favours, with the added possibility of being hit by a vehicle that would have been doing seventy miles an hour or more… He was very lucky to be alive. 'OK. Thanks, Ben. Does the guvnor know about this?'

'Not yet, boss. We thought about you first.'

'Best tell him, then. He won't be happy. If Tasker dies, that could be our link to whoever he was working with gone for good. Unless we can link them digitally or forensically.' He drew a breath.

'I'll go and let him know,' Ben said.

'OK. We're winding things up in here so we won't be long.'

'Right.' Ben nodded and set off along the corridor as Pete turned back to the interview room.

'DS Gayle re-entering the room,' Dick said for the recorder.

Pete shut the door and sat down. 'A bit more bad news, I'm afraid, Harry,' he said. 'Del's in the RDE. Critical, but alive. He was attacked and left for dead. First Ewan, then Derek. Del. Seems like someone's seriously cleaning up: getting rid of any possible links or witnesses.'

CHAPTER TWENTY-SEVEN

It was mid-afternoon on a Friday when Pete walked in through the big stone portal of the Devon and Cornwall Police HQ, next-door to the station, and followed the familiar route through the corridors past the big control room with its spread of desks, each filled with a twin-screened computer, to the next door along.

He and his team had spent the last two and a half days collating and checking evidence while Derek Tasker lay unconscious in his hospital bed under constant guard. They'd gone through phone records and accumulated CCTV footage as well as interviewing potential witnesses and interrogating on-line sources of information from Companies House, the Police National Computer system, electoral registers and more. Only a couple more links in the chain of evidence remained to be added before they'd be ready to interview the man they suspected of being at the top of this criminal tree and Pete was hoping to find one of them here.

He opened the door without knocking.

'Afternoon,' he said into the semi-darkness of the windowless room with its array of screens covering one wall and subdued ceiling lights that were set to avoid affecting the contrast on the CCTV monitoring screens.

'Bugger, that's your easy Friday afternoon done for,' the big-bellied but short-statured camera operator said to the woman seated beside him.

Pete had not met her before. She was at least as tall as her companion, though they were both seated so she may have been taller. A quick glance gave a pleasant first impression. Probably in her late thirties, her collar-length dark hair had a soft wave to it and her grey eyes held a twinkle of humour.

'Graham,' Pete said. 'At least introduce me before you start throwing the usual insults about.'

Graham gave a mock-bow. 'Apologies, I'm sure. Miriam, this is DS Gayle from next-door. Meaning the nick, rather than the Control room. Pete, this is Miriam. She's Peggy's replacement. If you don't manage to put her off the idea in the next few minutes.'

'Miriam.' Pete extended a hand, which she took.

Her hand was small, but her grip was firm and dry.

'Nice to meet you.'

'So, what are you after?' Graham demanded. 'This isn't going to be a social call.'

'It could be,' Pete argued, wide-eyed.

'But it isn't.'

Pete tipped his head. 'Not this time.'

'So, what are you looking for?'

'Honiton Road motorway junction, last Thursday night into Friday, early hours, for a start.'

'For a start?' Graham retorted and turned to Miriam. 'See what I mean? What else?' he asked Pete.

'Are there any cameras covering the Tithebarn Way bridge over the motorway?'

Graham shook his head. 'You're out of luck there, mate.'

'OK. Back to Honiton Road, then, this Tuesday night into Wednesday morning.'

'The M5 junction?'

He nodded.

'What are we looking for?'

'The first occasion, a male on an electric scooter, heading outbound between 10:30 and 11:00pm. And possibly returning a little while later, although he may have gone around Tithebarn Way on the way back. Then, on the second occasion, I'm looking for a Range Rover. This one will be later. Between midnight and 3:00am. I've got the registration here.' He took his notebook from his pocket and flipped it open.

'On a scooter?' Graham checked? What's he wanted for?'

'Arson,' Pete cut in before Graham could add something facetious like, "Speeding?" 'Except, we won't be arresting him because he's already dead.'

'Eh? What are we wasting time tracking him down for, then?'

'To make sure it was him, to get a step closer to who killed him.'

'Oh, right. OK. So, we've got...' He stopped as Pete's phone began to ring in his pocket.

He took it out and checked the screen. 'Excuse me, but hold that thought. Or even act on it while I take this.' Accepting the call, he raised the phone and said, 'Hold on a sec.'

He stepped out of the room and closed the door behind him before raising the phone to his ear again. 'OK, I'm with you.'

'It's Diane Collins, Ops Support. Derek Tasker's awake.'

'Excellent. I'm on the way.' He ended the call and stuck his head back into the CCTV room. 'You'll have to carry on without me. Sorry. Got to go.'

'Your scooter rider's woken up, has he?' Graham demanded with a quick grin.

'No, but one of his buddies has. The one who got chucked off the motorway bridge a couple of nights ago.'

Graham's eyebrows shot up. 'Oh, right. OK, we'll see what we can find for you.'

'Thanks.' Pete ducked out, closed the door and hurried away.

As he walked quickly away from the complex of buildings that housed the force headquarters and always reminded him of a World War Two military base, he took out his phone again and let Jane know what was happening so that she could pass it on to the rest of the team. Then he broke into a jog out to the road and down to the station, next-door. Picking up his car from there, he headed straight for the hospital and, once inside, to the Intensive Care Unit.

Derek Tasker was in one of the half-dozen side-rooms. Pete nodded to the ward sister at the central desk and crossed directly towards the closed door. Knocking gently with a knuckle, he stepped in to find the dark-haired constable in a comfy chair in one corner, facing him, while Tasker was propped up on a stack of pillows in the bed to his right in the windowless room, an array of monitoring equipment around him, displaying numbers and moving graphs in multiple colours, one of them beeping steadily in reaction to his heartbeat.

His eyes were open, staring at Pete as he stepped in. They blinked – his only reaction to the newcomer.

Fighting to keep any reaction to the injured man's appearance off his face, Pete gave him a nod and turned to Diane. 'How's it going?'

'All quiet and peaceful, so far,' she reported. 'He woke a couple of minutes before I called you. Doc said he'll be in and out for a while, but he should be OK.'

Pete nodded and turned to Tasker. He looked a mess. His head was bandaged, his face scratched and scabbed. His right arm was in plaster and the extra bulging of the bedsheets suggested his leg was too. 'Derek. Sounds like you're a very lucky man. I'm Pete Gayle with Exeter CID. I'm looking after your case.'

'Hmm,' was his only response.

'Do you remember much about what happened?'

'No.' His voice was a hoarse murmur.

'You sound dry. Do you want a sip of water?'

'Please.'

The over-bed trolley had been pushed to one side while he was unconscious, so didn't need it, but on there were a jug of water, a plastic cup and a straw in a paper wrapper. Pete stepped across, poured some water and unwrapped the straw, put it into the cup and brought it to him.

Tasker sipped and blinked then winced in pain as he relaxed back on the bed.

'Better?' Pete asked, moving the cup away a few inches.

'Yes.' His voice was still weak, but smoother, less scratchy.

'Let me know if you want more. I won't stay long. You'll be tired. But do you know where you were found, or when?'

His head twitched from side to side.

'You were on the motorway, under the bridge that carries Tithebarn Way over it. You're lucky to be alive. From your injuries and position, it seems like you'd been stabbed and tipped off there. Luckily, a truck driver stopped in the live lane to protect you, put his hazards on and called an ambulance. It's a good thing it was stupid o'clock in the morning. During the day, there's no way you'd have survived with the amount of traffic on there.'

As he spoke, he watched Tasker carefully. His expression, though weak, went through shock, fear, horror, gratitude, anger and pain. It settled on anger.

That was good, Pete thought. It would encourage him to remember and to help them find out who had done this to him and hopefully bring them to justice, though even without his phone, which hadn't been found on Tithebarn Way or on the motorway when the ambulance picked him up, they had the records from it and had already found that he'd been called by an unregistered burner phone only twenty minutes before he'd been found, the phone's location at that point placing him at home, as might be expected at that time of night.

They'd yet to identify the burner phone in question, but it had been in fairly regular contact with him.

Pete called up the number in the notes on his own phone and held it out for Tasker to see. 'Do you recognise that number?'

The injured man's eyes narrowed.

'Who does it belong to?'

'Grey.'

Pete nodded and withdrew the phone, putting it away. 'You went to meet him that night.' He made it a statement rather than a question.

A dip of his eyelids indicated the affirmative.

'Was it just him who was there?'

A tiny shake of the head. 'Don't remember.'

'You might want to give that some thought. Evidently, he stabbed you. Tried to kill you.'

Tasker blinked.

'Why? What had you done to piss him off that much?'

His lips narrowed and his eyes closed. Pete wasn't sure if he was tiring or just avoiding the question.

'What about the car fire on Woodbury Common? Were you there?'

His eyes opened, his expression suddenly fearful.

'I'm not accusing you of setting it,' Pete told him. *Not at this point, anyway,* he added silently in his mind. 'But whoever did had to get away from there somehow. And we've got your phone records, obviously. That's where I got that number from that I just showed you. It called you that night, too. *He* called you. Grey. A while before the fire was reported. What did he want?'

'To follow him. Keep watch while he torched it.' His voice was fading. He was getting weaker by the second.

'All right, Derek. I can see you're getting tired. We'll leave it there for now. Speak again later, OK?'

Tasker blinked, then let his eyes close and stay that way.

Pete turned to Diane. 'You're all right here, are you? Don't need anything?'

She shook her head. 'I'm fine. He knew the bloke, then. The one who tried to kill him?'

Pete nodded. 'And we know a man called Grey who's attached to this case, albeit loosely, don't we?'

She tipped her head. 'Good luck proving what he's done, though. And I mean that sincerely.'

Pete pursed his lips. 'We're going to give it a damn good go,' he said. But if Mark Grey was as clever as he seemed to be, it was going to be far from easy.

CHAPTER TWENTY-EIGHT

The call came almost six hours later.

'Gayle,' Pete said, picking up the phone in the hallway of his home.

'It's Di. He's awake again.'

Pete's eyes widened in surprise. 'Di? What shifts are you working?'

'Ten 'til ten. Keeps the changeover well away from the nurses', plus it means the night person's a bit fresher in the wee hours.'

He grunted. 'OK. How's the patient?'

'Seems a little bit stronger. But that might be because they changed his pain meds while we were waiting for you this afternoon. Because he'd come out of the coma, they said. He's angry. Wants to see you.'

Good, Pete thought. But gently does it, for now. 'All right. I'm only a few minutes away. See if you can calm him down a bit. Anger can be tiring. The more time I can spend talking with him, the better.'

He hung up and stepped back into the sitting room.

'You're going in,' Louise said as Annie looked up from her seat with a disappointed expression.

'The patient's awake again and wanting to talk,' he said.

'You'd best go and listen, then.'

He flashed her a smile and leaned down to kiss her. Turning to Annie, he reached out to ruffle her hair, but slow enough that she could duck away. Instead, he settled a hand on her shoulder. 'I'll see you in the morning.'

He headed out and, in less than ten minutes, he was parking his car at the hospital.

Little had changed in the ICU. There were a different batch of nurses, but the same subdued lighting and gentle beeping from monitoring machines. He showed his badge to the ward sister and crossed directly to Derek Tasker's room.

Diane Collins was still in her chair in the corner, Tasker still propped up in the bed across from her, though this time he looked brighter.

'Diane,' Pete said, nodding. 'Derek. You remember me?'

'Yes. Not your name, though. Sorry.' His voice was still soft and whispery, Pete noticed, but he did seem stronger than last time.

He tipped his head. 'I'll let you off, given the circumstances,' he said with a grin. 'Pete Gayle.' He pulled up the spare chair and settled beside the bed. 'Can I get you anything before we talk?'

'No.'

'OK.' He took out his phone, set the voice recorder going and set it on the trolley that was now in position over the bed. 'Rather than scribbling illegible notes, I thought it'd be easier to record what we say and type it up so you can read it and sign it later, if you agree with what I've typed. Is that OK?'

'Yes.'

'All right, then. This is a witness interview. You're not under arrest. Not that you'll be running off anywhere, eh?' he added with a grin. 'But I will remind you of your rights. I have to. It's the rules.' He shrugged. 'So, you do not have to say anything. But it may harm your defence if you do not mention when questioned something which you later rely on in Court. Anything you do say may be given in evidence. You understand?'

'Yes.'

'OK, let's make a start, then. You remember what I told you earlier. Diane said you were angry. So you'll want to help us as much as you can, right?'

A slight nod and a gleam in his eyes was Tasker's response this time.

'Good. So, taking things in order, tell me about Ewan Price. How'd you meet, for a start?'

'Job centre. He was on the dole. Been sacked from that garage on Pinhoe Road. Not happy about that, he weren't.' He shook his head slightly, remembering. 'I was on probation. It ain't easy getting work when you come out of prison.'

'OK. So you met, got talking. Got to know each other. Was it you that recruited him into the car thefts?'

His eyes narrowed, lips pressing tighter.

'I'm not trying to stitch you up here, Derek. Just asking questions, getting a feel for what went on,' Pete said and paused to let that sink in. 'OK, if you don't want to answer that, let's move on. He got involved. But then something went wrong, obviously. He turned round and torched your truck. And Mark Grey's house. What brought that on?'

He blinked. 'He was out of control. Grey didn't want that kind of attention. So, he told me to tell him we weren't going to deal with him anymore.'

'You had to tell him because you'd brought him in?'

He nodded.

'So, how'd you know Grey?'

'Friend of a friend. Guy I was inside with. Styles.'

Pete's eyes widened at that. 'Adrian Styles?'

'Yes.'

'And things go round and round,' he said. 'My team put Styles away. Must be three years, now? For a seven-year stretch. So, what – Grey took the idea of the car thefts from Styles and decided to pick up where he'd left off?'

'With a tweak or two. He switched the exports from Bristol to Southampton. It's further away, but it's a bigger port. Easier to slip the odd container through without it being noticed. And he can sell anything to anyone,' he added with a sneer.

'Ewan wasn't the only one out there, taking the cars for you? Or for Mark Grey,' he corrected himself.

Tasker's eyes closed, his head twitching from side-to-side.

'We've got Harry Brooks in custody. Who else was there?'

His lips pressed briefly together. 'Only other one was Paul Jacobs, but he's gone.'

'Gone?' *Another of Grey's victims?*

'Abroad. Went with the Jag.'

'How?' Pete asked, frowning.

'He took it to the pickup. Had a bag with him. Food, water and a drill to make some air holes in the container.'

'I see.' Pete recalled the footage of Jacobs from Blackboy Road, walking away with his rucksack on his shoulder. He couldn't see a battery-powered hand drill being powerful enough to put sufficient holes in the side of a shipping container to provide enough fresh air for Jacobs to survive an extended journey, but... 'Where was the Jag going to?'

'Spain.'

Pete nodded. Jacobs might expect to survive that far, though it would take a few days to get there. It would be worth checking with the local police. 'Do you know which port?'

'South's all I know.'

'OK.' That was something he could look into, either on the Internet or through the Transport Police. 'So, now we're up to date. I can see why both you and Mark Grey were pissed off at Price, but how did that go down with the MG?'

Tasker pressed his lips together once more. 'Grey asked me to call him. Get him to snatch one and bring it direct to the drop-off on Honiton Road, not park it up for a couple of days as usual. Urgent job 'cause there was a truck due. He met him there instead of me. Next I knew was a call at half-nine that night. He was coming to pick me up to follow him and fetch him back. Turned out I had to keep an eye out while he set the fire, too.'

'What vehicle did you use?' Pete asked.

'His pick-up.'

'I didn't know he'd got one.'

Tasker shrugged with his mouth. 'It might be his wife's. Old Toyota. He uses it for knocking about. Rough work. Saves the Range Rover for posing.' His lip curled in a brief sneer.

'So, he was driving the Toyota the night he attacked you?'

He blinked. 'Yeah.'

'What I don't get is why he'd do that,' Pete admitted. 'I mean, if Ewan had got out of hand and couldn't be trusted anymore, OK. Especially if he'd lost the plot enough to go out there and torch the guy's house. But you… What had you done?'

'I introduced him to Pricey so it was my fault, I suppose. And I'm a witness.'

Just a witness? Pete wondered. *Or were you more hands-on than you've admitted to, Derek?* But now wasn't the time for those questions. 'True,' he said. 'But that makes him one ruthless SOB, if we hadn't already decided that from Ewan Price's death. I mean, I don't know how much detail the doctors have gone into for you, but I gather a quarter of an inch higher and he'd have punctured your kidney. You'd have bled out before you ever got here, even though you survived the fall.'

'S'why I'm talking to you.'

Pete flashed him a grim smile. 'I gathered. And I appreciate it, Derek. But from what you've said, it might be fairly urgent that I'm elsewhere with an armed response team. If Grey was cleaning up after himself, that leaves two choices. He's either planning to shut down the operation and distance himself from it or do a quick flit. In which case, we might already be too late, but we need to get there and find out ASAP. So you rest and we'll talk again, another time, OK?'

He reached for his phone as Tasker nodded.

'Get him,' he said.

Pete placed a hand gently on his shoulder. 'I plan to.'

He called Colin Underhill while he was walking out through the corridors of the hospital towards his car.

'Yes?' Colin's answer was as brusque as usual.

'Guv, it's Pete. I've just been talking to Derek Tasker. Seems like we might have a situation. He confirmed it was Mark Grey that attacked him. Which makes me wonder if he was cleaning up before doing a flit. So we could do with getting him into custody before he does that, if we're not already too late. I'm on the way out there now, but I could do with Armed Response backup, given what he's shown himself to be capable of.'

'I'll get them in motion. Blackhorse?'

'Yes.'

'Take Dave with you as backup. He's closest.'

'OK, will do. Thanks.'

The line clicked dead. Pete pressed the red icon then used speed dial to call Dave Miles.

'Hello? Boss?'

'Yes. Get yourself togged up; we're going to arrest someone if he hasn't already done a runner. The male who killed Ewan Price and tried to do the same to Derek Tasker. I'll pick you up in a few minutes.'

'Grey?'

'Yes.'

'OK. Or I could meet you at Moor Lane and follow you out there.'

'All right, do that,' Pete said as the outside doors slid open before him.

'Right.'

He was barely out of the hospital grounds, driving along a street lined with the scrappy-looking hedge of the hospital grounds on his left, opposite a row of low bungalows, when his phone rang with an unlisted number.

He used the car's comms system to answer it. 'Gayle.'

'It's Graham. Much as I hate to admit it, you were right.'

'What about?'

'We've got confirmation of your male on a scooter going out towards Blackhorse on the night you were asking about. The bad news is, he didn't come back that way.'

'Shame. Did you get a decent view of his face?'

'Yes. Running it through the system, it comes back as Ewan Price.'

'Excellent. Thanks, buddy. I owe you one for that.'

'Yes, not as much as you're about to. Miriam's sister moved a few months ago, out to Hutchinson Road. It's off Tithebarn Way, in amongst all that new building that's been going on over there. Apparently, there's still what they lovingly call a marketing suite just across from there, belonging to one of the building companies. And it's got cameras on the front. We haven't got the footage. They're closed, this time of night. But it's a possibility.'

'You beauty. If I wasn't busy elsewhere I'd come in there and kiss you.'

'You bloody wouldn't. You could send Jill Evans to do it instead, mind.'

Pete chuckled. 'In your dreams.'

'How do you know about them?' Graham demanded with mock horror.

'I know you.' Pete reached a mini-roundabout and took the right fork, heading north away from the hospital. 'I'll come and see you in the morning. You going to have Miriam with you again?'

'Yes. All week. She's training.'

'Right. I'll bring her a donut, too, then. Anyway, what are you still doing there at this time of night? Long past your bedtime, isn't it?'

'It's called doing you a favour.'

'Well, thank you, kind sir. I appreciate it.'

'And that sounds so genuine.'

'It is,' Pete protested. 'There was no need for you to stay and do it tonight.'

'Except there's bugger all on the box tonight.'

'Ah, now we get to it,' Pete said as his phone pinged with an incoming text. 'Well, off you go to bed and don't spare the cocoa. I'll see you tomorrow.'

'Yes, Mum.'

Pete hung up, chuckling. Pulling over outside one of a row of mid-century semis, he checked the phone for text messages and found one from Colin Underhill.

ARU will meet you at target address.

'OK, then. On we go,' he muttered, putting the phone back down in the central console and setting off again up the hill.

A few minutes later, as he approached the big roundabout on the edge of the city, at the northern end of Sowton Industrial Estate, he spotted Dave on the paved verge, sitting astride his big, black motorbike. Crossing the roundabout, he flashed his headlights to the leather-clad figure and pulled over beside him, winding down his passenger side window.

'Armed Response are meeting us out there,' he called.

'OK.' Dave dropped his visor into place and kicked the bike into rumbling life.

Checking his mirrors, Pete flicked on his indicator and led the way off the verge and away towards the motorway junction and the target address beyond it.

*

The Armed Response Unit's vehicle was a big German SUV, all done out in the Battenburg design on its sides with yellow and orange chevrons on the back. It was parked up on the wide pavement just inside the narrow road that cut back at a sharp angle into the village off the north side of the old Honiton Road. Pete pulled up alongside and the black-clad male officer in the passenger seat rolled his window down, matching Pete's move.

'DS Gayle,' Pete said and jerked his thumb back over his shoulder. 'That's DC Miles on the bike. You're with us?'

The man nodded. 'As per DI Underhill's request.'

'That's right. The target address is along here. Number seven. Believed two occupants – husband and wife. The male is suspected of one murder and one attempted. Unknown access to weapons.'

'Understood. You want to knock and we'll remain as back-up or do you think we should go in hard or call in a negotiator?'

'The first option sounds best to me,' Pete said. 'We'll give them a knock and see what happens from there. If he turns nasty, then it's your shout.'

The man nodded.

'OK, let's do it,' Pete said and slipped the car back into gear, easing it forward along the lane, which was only just wide enough for one vehicle. Buildings along both sides gave way on the right to a hedgerow, then a side-junction. Beyond that were fields on his right and a row of good-sized detached bungalows, set back in substantial gardens on his left, some of them displaying numbers or names on signs by their gates. He found the one he was looking for, its number displayed on the brick wall that extended up one side of its driveway, separating off the lawned garden. It was brick-built with two bay windows either side of a front door under an arched porch. There was no vehicle on the drive, though either or both could have been in the double garage that the tarmacked drive led to past the side of the home. No lights showed at the windows, though for all he knew, the sitting room could be at the back, overlooking the rear garden.

He pulled in, leaving plenty of room for the patrol car and Dave's bike behind him, and killed the engine. Climbing out, he stepped up to the front door, Dave at his elbow, now without his helmet while the two officers from the patrol car hung back for now.

His hand was raised, about to knock on the door when a voice came clearly from behind him. 'They're not there.'

Pete turned, looking around. Spotted an older male in a dark dressing gown over pale pyjamas peering at him from the front door of the neighbouring property, over the low brick wall that separated them. He lowered his arm and turned to approach the boundary. 'Since when?' he asked.

'Yesterday afternoon.'

'And they've not been back?' Pete asked, standing at the hip-height wall.

From a little closer, the man looked to be in his sixties, iron-grey hair unkempt, his skin deeply lined over heavy features. He shook his head. 'Nope. Looked like they'd packed plenty.'

'What vehicle did they go off in?'

'The truck. Old Toyota.'

Pete nodded. 'Do you happen to know the registration of that?'

He quoted it easily from memory and Pete tipped his head, impressed.

'Most people have a job to remember their own.'

'I haven't got one and I see it often enough.'

'Right.' Pete nodded again and raised his warrant card. 'I'm DS Gayle, by the way. Exeter CID. Do you happen to have a spare key for this place? You know – in case of emergencies.'

He hesitated.

'It'd save us busting the door. If they're not here, we're going to have to search the place anyway. See if we can find out where they've gone. Unless they told you?' he added with a raised eyebrow.

'They didn't. But, yes, I've got a key. For the landlord.'

'I'm sure he'd appreciate us using it rather than breaking the door, Mr...?'

'Tomlin. Frank.' He nodded and turned to go back inside. In moments, he emerged again and crossed towards where Pete waited. Handed him a pair of keys on a metal fob. 'Front one's the silver one.'

'Thank you. I'll bring it back when we're done.'

'What's he done? To warrant all this? Or is it about the fire?'

Pete grimaced. 'I can't say, at this stage. Suffice to say, it's serious. And violent.'

He grunted. 'Always thought there was something about him. He was never nasty around here, but... Well, you know. You get a feeling about someone, don't you?'

'I know what you mean. Thanks again for these,' Pete said, raising the keys. 'We'll get on, let you get back indoors.'

He turned back towards the target address, surprised that the door showed no signs of fire damage. It had already been replaced. He wondered who by. Was it Storm Windows, perhaps? He shook his head, dismissing the thought, opened the door and stepped cautiously in. 'Police,' he called into the dark and silent interior.

Here, he could see signs of the arson attack. The parquet flooring was charred and pitted in places, the wall to his right blackened and smoke-damaged. His nose picked up traces of both the smoke and the petrol used to start the blaze.

There was no response to his call. He beckoned the others in behind him.

'Police. We're coming in. Show yourselves now and you'll come to no harm.'

CHAPTER TWENTY-NINE

They quickly made sure there was no-one in the two-bedroom bungalow, including in the expansive loft, then Pete lifted his radio from its clip on his belt and keyed the mike. 'DS Gayle to Control.'

'Control.'

'I need a full alert put out on Mark and Andrea Grey, including all ports, and their Toyota Hilux.' He quoted the registration number. 'Also, an ANPR trace on that vehicle ASAP.'

'All received.'

'Mark Grey is wanted on suspicion of murder and attempt murder,' he told the woman in the control room.

'Understood. Alert going out now.'

'Thanks.'

Standing in the central hallway, he looked around at the several doors opening off it. 'We need to search this place thoroughly,' he said. 'And we need to find out everything we can about Andrea Grey. Who she is, where she's from, who she might go to if she's in trouble.'

'I don't suppose Ben's gone to bed yet. I could give him a call, get him onto that,' Dave suggested.

Pete nodded. 'Do it. And while we're here...' He lifted the radio again. 'DS Gayle to Control.'

'Control.'

'Is there a unit available to attend an address on Sowton Lane and check for occupants? Same owner as my location, so double crewed would be safest. He's known for violence.'

'Received. I'll see what we've got, Sarge.'

'Thank you.' He lowered the radio. 'Right, let's make a start. Dave, you take the sitting room. I've got the main bedroom. Danvers, you start with the kitchen. Brooks, the second bedroom and we move on from there, ending with the garage and loft.'

*

Pete had finished in the bedroom, finding nothing useful in there apart from the fact that, as the old guy next-door had said, they seemed to have packed generously for a trip, and he was now in what should have been the second bedroom, but Mark Grey had it set up as an office. He'd gone through the desk and was opening the filing cabinets when his radio hissed and a female voice came through, 'Control for DS Gayle.'

He quickly lifted it off its clip and keyed the mike. 'Gayle.'

'They've found the Toyota you were talking about at the farm on Sowton Lane. Along with a very distressed Andrea Grey. She was bound and gagged, dumped in a built-in cupboard in the kitchen. They heard her trying to shout as they were coming back from finding the truck behind a wooden shed towards the rear of the property.'

He frowned. 'No sign of Mark Grey?'

'No, Sarge. They're still searching.'

'All right. I'll go down there.'

'Received. I'll let them know.'

He returned the radio to his belt. 'Dave,' he called.

'Boss?'

Getting the direction from Dave's reply, he headed towards the rear of the bungalow and found Dave emerging from the dining room, next to the kitchen.

'They've got the wife and her truck at the farm,' he told the leather-clad DC. 'I'm going over there. Can you carry on in the office when you've finished in there? I've checked the desk already.'

'Will do.'

Pete headed quickly out the front. There was enough room for him to be able to manoeuvre his car out past the patrol car and Dave's bike so, in moments, he was driving away.

It didn't take long to get to the old farm, part-way down the lane towards the little hamlet of Sowton. He pulled in through the wide entrance – new gates looking incongruous between unkempt hedges – and stopped beside a patrol car in front of the old red-brick double-fronted house, giving his sirens a quick blast before he turned off the engine to announce his presence.

He was less than halfway to the house when a uniformed officer stepped around the side of the building into view.

'DS Gayle?'

'That's me,' Pete agreed, and showed the man his ID to confirm it. 'Where is she?'

'Inside. There's an ambulance on the way to check her over, but she seems to be OK, for the most part.' He was a man in his forties, Pete saw when he got closer, meeting him at the front door of the house. A couple of inches shorter than Pete, but heavier set and with his dark hair a little on the long side. 'A day or so tied up in a cupboard in a cold, abandoned house won't have helped her peace of mind,' he said. 'But physically, she's not too bad. Says an assailant Tasered both of them from behind. Bound them. Left her here and she doesn't know what he did with her husband but she heard him drive away after a while, so he must have had his own vehicle here, tucked away out of sight somewhere.'

'Somewhere in earshot of where he put her,' Pete pointed out.

'Yes, so round the back. But we're limited to torches out here. There's no electric.'

'And they were Tasered?

The officer shrugged. 'That's what she said. And, although they're not legal, you can get them – or something very similar, anyway – on the black market.'

'I know. You haven't found her husband yet?'

'No. Still looking, but it's not easy by torchlight, while trying not to destroy any evidence of the assailant's presence.'

'Still, if he's here, just somewhere separate from her, we can't leave him until morning.'

The officer nodded towards the door in front of them. 'It's all unlocked. We found the keys in the pickup. She's in the first room on the right: the old sitting room.'

'OK, thanks.'

The officer turned away to go back the way he'd come as Pete reached for the door handle and stepped inside.

The place was dusty and unloved. Cobwebs hung from the ceiling and between the banisters of the stairs which led up in front of him against the left wall of the wide hallway. A door opened off at their base, another directly across from it and more beyond. He stepped directly across to the right, where the door stood open. Between the moonlight from the window and the torch he'd brought from his glovebox, he could see old, dusty furniture in there and a big old TV in the far corner that had to be a foot deep to allow for the cathode ray tube, so was at least twenty years old.

'Hello?' The female voice sounded weak and nervous.

Stepping in, Pete's torchlight quickly found her on a sofa that faced the window from the back of the high-ceilinged room. She was small – almost childlike – sitting there in a denim skirt and white blouse, dark hair tied back in a ponytail, a silver foil blanket wrapped around her, eyes wide and scared as she stared back at him.

'Hi,' he said. 'I'm DS Gayle. Pete. With Exeter police. How are you doing?'

'I'm… I'm OK. Where's Mark? My husband?'

'We haven't found him yet. But they're out there, looking. And there's an ambulance on the way to check you over. Make sure you're all right. What happened?' He stepped in closer and took a seat in one of the dusty old green velour armchairs that matched the sofa and sat at an angle to either side of it.

'We were… Mark had come in and told me to pack a case, we were going on holiday. A long one. Well, that's the first I'd heard of the idea, so I was… Well, anyway, we did it. He said he just had a quick job to do here, first. And we took the pickup because of parking it long-term. Less likely to have a problem than the Range Rover. So, anyway, we got here. He'd got a bin-bag in the back of the pickup. He fetched it and we went around the back. It was a load of shredded paper that he wanted to burn. There's an old oil drum out there that we've been using as an incinerator, so…' She paused again. 'We just came around the corner at the back of the house and all of a sudden I felt this terrible, intense pain all through me. I just collapsed there on the ground. I was faintly aware that the same thing was happening to Mark. Then someone was zip-tying my hands and Marks, and our feet, and… He brought me inside, put me in the cupboard and told me someone would find me.' She stopped with a shuddering sob. 'I didn't believe him. I mean, no-one comes here, other than us, and no-one was due to until… What day is it?'

'It's Friday night.'

She shuddered again. 'No-one was going to be coming here until Monday, when the electrician was due to reconnect the power. I'd have been… God! I'd have been dead by then!'

'So…' *What the hell did they want with Mark? Why tie him up and take him with them?* 'You said a man tied you up and brought you inside. Did you see his face? Recognise him, maybe?'

She shook her head. 'No. He was wearing a mask. Ski-mask kind of thing, but in black. Like they do in the movies. Criminals and so on. You know the sort of thing.'

Pete nodded. 'But you'd have seen something of his skin. Was he white, black, Asian…?'

'White.'

'And his eyes. What colour were they?'

'I don't know. I tried to avoid looking at them.'

'OK, don't worry about it now. Anything else that struck you about him? His size, his smell, his clothes. Anything at all.'

She shook her head. 'I just remember being lifted as if I were nothing and carried over his shoulder. He was wearing jeans and boots. Like work boots. And a coat. Like a waxed jacket, but it wasn't.'

'So, military, maybe?' Pete suggested, half to himself.

'Maybe.'

And strong, even though she was small. 'All right. Well, that's all I'm going to ask you for now. We'll just wait for the ambulance crew. They shouldn't be long. Except one thing. Did Mark tell you where you were off to?'

'No. He wouldn't. Said it would ruin the surprise.'

Pete pursed his lips briefly, but it wasn't important at this point. 'OK.'

*

The two officers spent another hour searching the closed barn, sheds, open-sided Dutch barn and the overgrown and weed-choked land and hedges all around them while Pete saw Andrea off in the ambulance for a proper check-over at the hospital then checked the rest of the house.

They didn't find Mark Grey.

He accepted the house keys from the uniformed constable, locked it up and followed them out of the property, heading back to Blackhorse and the Grey's bungalow there, where he found Dave and the two armed-response officers had completed their search and come up similarly empty-handed. The patrol car was gone, but Dave was waiting for him on the drive.

'Any joy over there?' he asked as Pete wound down his window.

Pete shook his head. 'She's OK. As much as you can expect, at least. But there's no sign of Mark Grey. And nothing incriminating over there. She did say he'd burned a load of papers, though, after shredding them.'

'Sounds thorough. Almost as if he'd got something to hide.'

'What about here?' Pete asked. 'Anything?'

'Bugger all,' Dave said with a shake of the head. 'Clean as a whistle. I mean, there's prints, DNA, whatever you want like that, but nothing relating to our case.'

'And no sign of where he was taking her?'

Another shake of the head. 'No digital devices left behind. Not even any receipts or boxes from them. Or from a travel agent or anything else like that,' he added.

'OK, well, their travel plans are irrelevant, to a point, now. The question is, who snatched him and where did they take him?'

'And why?' Dave added. 'I mean, why not just off him there, on the spot, if that was the plan. Or them, come to that.'

Pete tipped his head. 'That thought had occurred to me. Something to think about further tomorrow, in daylight.'

'Home time?' Dave asked.

'Yep. Let's get out of here.'

Dave kicked his bike into life and this time, Pete followed him along the lane towards Honiton Road. Turning right out of the sharply angled junction, Dave raised a hand and roared off, Pete following at a more sedate pace. He was well on his way towards home, though, when his phone rang abruptly, jarring through the quiet hum of the engine in the street-lit night.

He glanced down at the comms screen. An unlisted number. Touched the green icon.

'Gayle.'

'Boss, it's Ben. Where are you?'

'Lower Hill Barton, on the way home. Do you want me to turn around?' Doing so would point the car south, towards the station on Sidmouth Road.

'No, but you'll want to pull over.'

'Why?'

'I've been looking into Andrea Grey, like you asked, and you'll never guess who she really is.'

'I didn't ask you to keep at it to bloody near midnight,' Pete protested, slowing and stopping the car outside one of the row of mid-century semis that lined the left side of the residential street.

'Well, there was nothing on telly and I don't go to bed that early anyway, so...'

'What have you found?' he broke in.

'Well, Andrea Grey, formerly Andrea Shannon – her husband died in an accident six years ago and she kept the surname until she remarried to Mark Grey, three years ago – her maiden name was Styles.'

Pete blinked. 'You mean the same as Adrian Styles?'

He recalled the small, wiry ex-marine with a swallow tattoo on his cheek who he'd finally arrested after a convoluted investigation four years earlier. And who had been in prison with Derek Tasker.

'Yep,' Ben said. 'They're brother and sister.'

'And here's her new husband running almost exactly the same deal as Adrian was,' Pete said. 'Isn't that a coincidence?'

Ben chuckled. 'I didn't think you believed in them, boss.'

'I don't.'

CHAPTER THIRTY

Having told Ben to go home and get some rest, Pete hung up and made another call, grimacing even as he tapped the numbers at the need to wake the man he was calling.

It was answered on the third ring. 'Yes?'

'Guv, it's Pete. Sorry to call at this hour, but we've had a busy evening and I need your input.'

'Tell me.'

'Well, the Grey's had left before we got to Blackhorse. He was planning a flit, but...' Pete updated him on the latest developments in a few terse sentences. 'So, I'm thinking we need to keep a close eye on her. A twenty-four-hour eye.'

Colin grunted. 'Agreed. Where are you?'

'I was on the way home, until I learned that about Andrea. Now I'm on the way to the RDE, to talk to her. As a witness, at this stage. Offer sympathy and reassurance. That kind of thing.'

'Can you hang on there until I get someone organised to take over, then?'

'Yes, sure.'

The line went abruptly dead. Pete touched the red icon, checked his mirrors and swung the car into a three-point turn.

In a few minutes, he was at the front desk of A&E at the city's main hospital.

'How can I help?' asked the thirty-something female behind the protective glass screen.

Pete showed her his warrant card. 'I'm looking for Andrea Grey. She was brought in by ambulance a little while ago.'

'Hold on. I'll check.' She typed into her keyboard, eyes on the screen in front of her. 'Ah, yes. She's already been transferred to the medical ward for observation. You know where to find it?'

'Yes. Thanks.'

He headed back outside, around to the main entrance and through to the ward. The three nurses at the central desk directed him to a six-bed bay where he found the curtains drawn around Andrea's bed. He took a seat near the window and waited for those working on her to emerge. First out was a young male doctor. Pete got up and followed him out of the bay.

'Doctor,' he said, keeping his voice low in respect for the late hour. 'DS Gayle. How's Mrs Grey doing? Can I talk to her briefly?'

The white-coated young man turned, glanced at Pete's ID and met his gaze. 'She's weak, dehydrated, she hasn't eaten or drunk for over twenty-four hours and she needed cleaning up. We'll keep her in overnight and, no doubt, tomorrow, at least. She's awake for now, though, so when the nurses have finished with her, you can have a brief word, if you need to.'

Pete nodded. 'I won't take any longer than necessary. I don't know if you're aware; her husband's missing, presumed abducted.'

The young man's eyes widened in shock. 'No, I didn't know that. I'm sorry. Um… Yes, of course, take as much time as you need, Detective, as long as she's willing and strong enough. But do keep your voices down, won't you? The other patients need to sleep.'

'Of course.'

The doctor nodded and moved away towards the nurses' station.

Pete turned back towards the bay, where one of the nurses was already emerging. The other pulled the curtains back from around Andrea Grey's bed and stepped away, looking at Pete with a frown as he approached. He raised his warrant card wordlessly and she carried on out of the bay.

With Andrea watching, he carefully drew the chair he'd been using over towards her bedside.

'I'll keep it brief,' he said. 'You'll need to rest.'

'Have you found him? Mark?'

He shook his head. 'He's not at the farm, nor at your bungalow. And we didn't find any signs of a struggle or blood, either, so as you said, they must have taken him away somewhere. You haven't got your phone with you?'

'It was in the truck.'

'We didn't find it there. Neither yours, nor your husband's. It could be that whoever took your husband took them with him for some reason. I don't know why, but you never know,' he added with a shrug.

She blinked. 'They can be tracked, can't they? So, if he's got them…'

Pete nodded. 'Yes. As I said earlier, we will find him. But in the meantime, we'll put a police guard on you.'

Her eyes widened. 'Whatever for?'

'For your safety, Mrs Grey.'

'But… If he'd wanted to kill me, he could have, easily, when he attacked us.'

Pete pursed his lips. 'He could. But did he need to? I mean, you said yourself, that place doesn't get many visitors. Not to give you nightmares, but you could have been there for God-knows how long. And that takes no effort on his part. So someone's on the way and they or other officers will stay with you for as long as it takes.' His voice was soft, but his tone brooked no argument.

Still, she tried to resist. 'Yes, but…'

'This wasn't his first try, was it?' Pete insisted. 'There was the fire at the bungalow.'

She frowned. 'And you think…?' Her eyes got wide and haunted.

Pete tipped his head. 'Don't you? Two attacks in a few days? What does Mark do, that he'd generate that much hostility?'

She sighed. 'Nothing that I know of. He just runs a trucking company.'

'So, you can't think of anything that might have caused all this? Or anyone? Has Mark told you about any problems, recently?'

'No.' She shook her head. 'He just does his job and works on the farm – sorting it out so we can move in sooner rather than later.'

'So, what does he ship with the company?'

She blinked and gave a deep yawn. 'I don't know. All sorts of things, I expect. He doesn't really say. All he ever talks about to me, as far as that's concerned, are the lorries, the drivers, the routes. The price of fuel and insurance. I mean, they pick up loads and take them places. It doesn't matter what's in them, really, does it? As long as it's not people or something, I suppose,' she added with a little smile.

'So, where does he keep all his paperwork?' He already knew the answer to that, but if she was going to play the innocent, it would do no harm to let her think he was falling for it, at least for now.

'At the bungalow. He's got a room set up as an office. Until we move down to the farm. He already uses it for the trucks.' She let her eyelids dip.

'Down that skinny little lane?' Pete countered with a frown.

'It's not that far down, though, is it? Not far enough to disturb the people in the village.'

Pete tipped his head. 'I suppose. I was just thinking, big trucks, little lane… Not an ideal mix.'

She drew a breath. 'Yeah, but a place on an industrial estate's so bloody expensive, isn't it? You've got to save where you can to make the job pay, with the price of fuel and all that, and wages for the drivers having to go up because of inflation.'

He nodded. 'All right, I'll let you rest. Probably speak again tomorrow.'

She closed her eyes.

Quietly, Pete replaced his chair where he'd found it beneath the window and stepped out of the bay.

He didn't have long to wait for the doors at the far end to open and a uniformed constable to raise a hand in greeting and walk down the length of the ward towards him. A few quick words and he was on his way out of the hospital, heading for his own bed at last.

*

'I can't see how she can have been living with the guy and not known what he was up to,' Jill declared. 'Especially if he was taking her off on impromptu long holidays and burning shredded papers before they went. I mean, who the hell does that without having something to hide?'

They were in the incident room, the whole team in one place again, having deployed a specialist search crew to the farm on Sowton Lane soon after daybreak.

'I don't know,' Dave said and turned to Jane, at his other side. 'Do you know everything about what Roger does while you're at work?'

'I know enough,' she declared. 'But I would start to query things if he suddenly came home and told me to pack a suitcase and, on the way, we were going to stop off and have a bonfire of a load of paperwork I'd never seen.'

'Yeah, but suspicion's not proof, is it?' Dick countered.

'So, let's find some proof,' Pete added. 'Because you're right, Jill. She's playing the innocent little woman card – and as far as we can tell, she was genuinely in that cupboard for nearly forty-eight hours – but I don't trust her. That could just have been a ploy that went wrong. A mistake. Or not.' He shrugged. 'Just because her brother was behind the last set-up like this doesn't mean he's involved, this time.'

'I still want to prove whether he is or not, though,' Dave declared.

'Me, too,' Pete agreed. 'If only because, if he is, there's a serious problem with security at Long Lartin prison that needs dealing with as soon as possible. But the main thing here is that there's at least one person out there – and more likely two – who're involved in the murder of Ewan Price and the attempted murder of Derek Tasker, as well as now, the disappearance of Mark Grey. And regardless of who their victims are or were, they need taking off the streets. So, what have we got? Tasker's phone data, for one. We need to identify every one of his contacts. He's admitted being up on Woodbury Common the night the MG and Ewan Price's body was burned up there. The phone may or may not confirm that. Let's make sure. But also, they needed to get there and back. He says he drove Mark Grey's – or more accurately, Andrea Grey's Toyota. Would that have GPS built in, that we could download and trace?'

'What year is it?' Ben asked.

'2010.'

'It should, then.'

'And it's at the farm,' Pete said and picked up his radio. 'DS Gayle to Control.'

'Control.'

'Can you contact the search team at Sowton Lane and ask them to download the GPS data from the Toyota Hilux that's out there and get it to us in Incident Room One ASAP?'

'Will do, Sarge.'

'Thanks.' He set the radio back on his desk. 'Right, that's that. What else?'

'We could do with the Greys' phones,' Jane said. 'Neither have been found, though, right?'

'Right.'

'And no paperwork for them?'

'No.'

'So, presumably, that was amongst the stuff he shredded and burned. Which is suggestive.'

'But, as Dick said, suggestion isn't proof.'

'No, but if we can find out those numbers…'

'Yeah.' Pete's desk phone rang and he picked it up. 'DS Gayle.'

'Detective Sergeant,' said a heavily accented voice. 'This is Corporal Aguilar with the Guardia Civil in Cadiz, eSpain.'

Pete's eyes widened in surprise. 'Corporal. What can I do for you?'

'You made an enquiry regarding a shipping container that was destined for the port here.'

'Uh… Yes, I did. Well, a port in southern Spain, anyway. We weren't sure which one.'

'It is here. It arrived yesterday and was awaiting release from Border Control. We opened it this morning and found, along with three cars, a body. A male.'

'A body?' Pete checked. 'How did he die?'

'Asfixia. How you say…? Suffocation. He had drilled three small holes in the wall of the container. He had a drill. He may have intended to drill more, but his drill… The broca… Piece? It was broken. And the three holes, they were high up in the side of the container. You may be aware, Sergeant, that carbon dioxide is heavier than air. If he had drilled them low down, they may have been enough, but high up… No.'

Pete grimaced. 'A nasty way to go.'

'Nasty. Is true. Not just that, but at sea, he had been… Mareado. Sickness of the sea.'

Pete's grimace intensified into a cringe. 'God, I bet that stunk after a few days in a confined space. I'm sorry you had to find that, Corporal. Did he have any identification with him?'

'No. Plenty of cash, but no documents.'

'A phone?'

'Si. A phone.'

'Well, that's something. The data from it, along with a photo if you can get one, should allow us to identify him.'

'He has been dead two or three days, Sergeant. The photo will not be pretty.'

'No, but we suspect we know who he is anyway. We just need confirmation.'

'I will send them.'

'Thank you. You've got my email?'

'Si. It was on the notice.'

'OK, good. Thanks for the call.'

'Buenos dias, Sergeant.'

'You too, Corporal.' Pete hung up.

'Corporal?' Jane asked.

'Spanish Guardia. They have a military structure,' he told her. 'This one was from Cadiz. That notice that you sent out about the container Grey shipped out from Southampton, Dick...' He glanced at the man beside him. 'They found it. With three cars and a body inside. He evidently didn't have a pleasant final few hours.'

'But it sounded like he had his phone with him,' Dave said. 'Not that we were ear-wigging.'

'Oh, of course not,' Pete said with a wry grin. 'Yes, he did. The corporal's sending me the data. At least, what he can as an email, I suppose. Which will be enough to enable us to get the rest from the provider.'

'Tasker's phone was off at the time of the car fire on Woodbury Common, boss,' Ben said.

Pete looked across at him, one eyebrow raised.

'But the last call received by it before it was switched off was from an unregistered phone.'

'What time was that?'

'21:33.'

'Grey,' Pete said, recalling what Tasker had told him the previous evening. 'That's one of the numbers we're looking for.'

Ben grimaced. 'It's Saturday, boss. We're not going to get the data on it before Monday, even with a warrant.'

Pete's computer gave a soft ping. 'Email,' he said and checked the screen. Sure enough, it was an email from Spain. He opened it and found a message in remarkably good English from Corporal Javier Aguilar of the Guardia Civil. At the bottom were two attachments: a jpeg picture and a zipped file.

Pete downloaded both and opened the jpeg.

'Yuk,' he muttered. 'You were right, Corporal.'

The picture was not a pleasant one. It was a close-up of the victim's face, which had taken on a greenish tinge beneath the vomit smeared across its chin. But a glance up at the whiteboard confirmed the victim's identity.

'It's Jacobs in the container,' he told Jane and Dave, who were both looking across at him expectantly. 'And I've got a zip file from his phone. I'll share it to everyone here, then unzip and print it. I take it we've got plenty of paper in the printer?' he asked, leaning forward, to direct the question towards Ben.

'I reloaded it this morning,' he confirmed.

'OK, then, let's see what we've got.'

A few clicks, a short wait while the zip file creator unlocked the information, and Pete paused to stare at the screen.

He released a low whistle. 'This is going to take a while.'

CHAPTER THIRTY-ONE

'What gets me is, why did whoever it was snatch Mark Grey and take him away somewhere, and leave his Mrs behind?' Dave said as the printer on the end of the cluster of desks began pushing paper through, slowly stacking it on the output tray.

'Well, they obviously wanted something from him, didn't they?' Jill retorted.

'Yes, but again, why leave the wife behind? I mean she'd be a bargaining chip, at least, wouldn't she? "Give me what I want or I'll hurt her and you'll watch."'

'Unless they were under orders not to hurt her,' Jane suggested.

'Or it was her that set it up in the first place,' Dick added. 'And it went wrong somehow.'

'Or him,' Jill countered.

'In which case, was he running from us or from someone else?' Dave asked. 'Like his partners in crime, for instance.'

'All valid points,' Pete said. 'But how do we answer any of them?'

'We need to find him. Or whoever took him,' Ben said. 'But how? There's no cameras out there. We can't get hold of his phone records for forty-eight hours, at least. And what forensic opportunities are there? Not that they'll be working over the weekend, either.'

'She wasn't sexually assaulted,' Dave said. 'Just bound and gagged.'

'What about the bindings?' Jane asked. 'Any chance of DNA from them? Or the pickup?'

'They were already out of the pickup before they were attacked,' Pete reminded her.

'All right, the house, then. Door handles.'

'Doubtful. We had to find her and get her out of there, remember. And everyone was wearing gloves, of course, but you've still got to use the handles to open the doors, same as the assailant. So anything they left would be smeared, at best, and potentially contaminated.'

'The bindings, then. Zip ties, right? And the gag.'

'Her socks, tied together so the knot could go in her mouth,' Pete said.

'Improvised, then,' Dave said as Jill grimaced in disgust. 'As opposed to the zip ties, which were pre-planned and prepared. A bit odd.'

'Unless it suggests a change of plan on the fly,' Dick said. 'They were expecting just him.'

'Possible,' Pete allowed. 'The DNA and the change of plan. But the question remains, where've they taken him?'

'Somewhere quiet,' Ben said. 'If they're going to question him. I mean, they're not going to be polite about it, are they? So, somewhere isolated, where no-one will hear them. Or him.'

'Like the farm itself,' Dave pointed out. 'In which case, why take him anywhere?'

'Familiar territory,' Jane suggested. 'A controlled environment. The farm might be ideal, but they don't know who might come around there or when.'

'Another farm?' Jill asked.

'To figure that out, we need to know who we're dealing with,' Pete pointed out. 'And the only way to find that out, right now, is ask people who know him. We've got Derek Tasker safely tucked up in the hospital. Who else is there? His drivers, of course. His wife, but as we've already said, she might be involved. He's got no police record. What about family, other than Andrea?'

'No kids,' Ben said. 'One sibling: an older sister. Parents are in Salisbury. He's a solicitor. She doesn't work.'

'Where's the sister?' Pete asked.

'Salisbury, too. Married with two kids. She's a solicitor, too. In her dad's firm.'

'All very nice and middle class,' Pete said. 'So, how did Mark end up down here, running a freight company?'

Ben shrugged. 'We'd need to talk to the family, or the wife, to find that out.'

'We should inform them of the situation,' Pete said.

'That's a couple of hours' drive from here,' Dave pointed out.

'Probably. But it needs doing. The other thing that needs doing is talking to his drivers. They might know something, have seen or overheard something.'

'They've got to be suspects, though,' Jill pointed out. 'I mean, they took the cars overseas, knowingly or otherwise.'

'Then we use that against them, to encourage them to talk,' Pete said. 'Complicity in a crime like that could lose them their HGV licence, at a minimum. If not involve prison time.'

The phone on his desk began to ring and he picked it up. 'DS Gayle.'

'Sarge, it's Gareth Newton. Search team. We've gone over the place on Sowton Lane with a fine-tooth comb. There's nothing to indicate who the assailant was or where they took the second victim. All we've got is a screwed-up wad of paper which was tossed away between the house and the gate. It was about eighteen feet from the actual driveway, in amongst the grass and such.'

'And why did you pick on that?'

'It looked fresh, so we recovered it, unfolded it carefully over a cut open evidence bag, and found it to be two pieces of paper, actually: a pair of e-tickets.'

'To what, or where?'

'Ferry from Poole to Guernsey, this morning. Two foot-passengers. Mark and Andrea Grey.'

'To Guernsey? That's interesting. Thanks, Gareth.'

'No problem, Sarge. I'll drop it into Forensics, shall I?'

'Please.'

Pete hung up. 'So, their flit was going to be to the Channel Islands.'

'Not exactly Barbados or Brazil,' Dave said. 'But it could be just a stepping-stone. From there to France – or anywhere else, by plane, I suppose.'

'True. Not that it helps us in the immediate sense. Let's get talking to folk while they're potentially not at work. He's got three drivers, right? Dave, you and Jill take one. Dick, you and Ben take a second. Whoever finishes first gets the third one. Jane and I'll go to Salisbury, talk to the family, see what background we can get. You never know; they might know where he'd fancy going if he was fleeing beyond the Channel Islands, too.'

'What about all this?' Ben asked, indicating the printer on the back of his desk, which had finished spitting out pages while they were talking and had a thick bundle now sitting on its out-tray.

'It'll wait for after we've talked to actual people,' Pete said. 'I'd best call the guvnor and get permission to cross borders into Wiltshire, before we go, but you lot don't need to wait for us. You've got their addresses from his company records, I take it?'

'Yes, boss.'

'Off you go, then. Knock them up and, if they're not in, check with the neighbours and move on. Calling them is a last resort as we don't know who's involved and who isn't.'

*

Pete sat forward on the modern leather sofa, facing the dark-haired woman, dressed in jeans and a striped blouse who was seated in the armchair across from him, her husband in the matching chair beside her.

She was in her late forties, wavy hair cut to collar length in a style that didn't really suit the width of her face, he thought, but that could have been exacerbated by the situation and her fraught expression.

'So, what can you tell us?' she demanded before he could speak.

'Not much at the moment,' he admitted. 'Which is why we're here, Mrs Clarke. I was hoping you could tell us a little about your brother – things, possibly, that your parents wouldn't know. Who his friends are. His work associates. Anything he might have been into that caused this situation.'

She pursed her lips.

Pete was glad that he'd visited the parents first. It had given them a chance to call her with the news, as he'd guessed they would as soon as he and Jane left them, and her a chance to get over the worst of the shock while he and Jane stopped off for a bite of lunch before coming here. 'I know you're a solicitor as well as his sister,' he said. 'And I can tell you that we're not here to dig dirt or create trouble for him. We're not interested in any minor legal irregularities that he might have been involved in. We just want to find him and bring him home safe and sound. And to do that, we need to find out where he's gone and who with.'

She frowned. 'You make it sound like he's gone voluntarily.'

Pete shook his head. 'Sorry. We don't believe that, no. He clearly was planning to leave, at least for a while, but the tickets were found, screwed up and thrown away on the property. Why buy them, then ditch them? And his wife was left, bound and gagged, in a house that's clearly unoccupied, so there'd be no telling if or when she'd be found and rescued. Which suggests he went under duress, at least. And I gather he's not a small man, or a weak one, so I'm sure he'd have resisted if he was able.'

The house they were in was a modern detached one, in an estate on the western edge of the city. Large and double-fronted, it spoke of a degree of wealth that Pete was never going to match. The interior was immaculately decorated and spotlessly clean. The tools left out in the front garden suggested they'd been gardening when her parents called to say that Pete and Jane were on their way over from the northern side of the city.

'Of course he would,' she declared. 'Andrea's the best thing that's ever happened to him. But, as for...' Her husband reached across to take her hand and she stopped, cut off in mid-flow. Drawing a breath, she went on, filling the silence that Pete had left. 'Well, I have to admit, he was always one for the easy route in life. He'd never work harder than he had to or pass up an opportunity for easy money. I was surprised when he started the haulage firm. But I don't see what any of that could have to do with what's happened.'

'Do you know of any friends of his that we could talk to?' he asked.

She shook her head sharply. 'Not since he moved down to Exeter, no. We don't get down that way. Too busy. He comes up occasionally – he and Andrea – but… No, I can't help you with that. I'm sorry.'

'That's OK. Thinking of those abandoned tickets, can you tell me where he liked to go on holiday?'

Another frown. 'You're talking as if you can't ask Andrea these questions. I thought you said she was all right.'

'She is. Or she will be. But it's best to get multiple perspectives on these things. You and she might know different sides of him, different aspects of his life, his interests.'

'Hmm. Well, I know he likes southern Spain. He spent some time down there, a few years ago.'

'Yes, we've found links to that area for him, business-wise.'

'He likes Morocco, too. It wasn't to my taste. We went there with him once. He wanted to show it to us. Very enthusiastic. But…' Her nose wrinkled in distaste. 'I didn't understand the attraction. I suppose the cost of living's a lot less down there. He's always been into the high life, or as near to it as he could afford. But anyway, they're the only places, other than the Caribbean, that he's ever expressed any significant liking for.'

'The Caribbean?' Pete asked. 'Where, specifically?'

'Barbados and St Lucia.'

Pete nodded. 'Both known for luxury holidays.'

'As I said, Detective, he likes a bit of luxury. Always has. Never one to scrimp on the finer things.'

'And what about his friends? What sort of people does he mix with, away from work?'

'People who can advance his work or his social standing.'

Pete raised an eyebrow. 'You sound like you don't necessarily approve.'

She pursed her lips. 'I just understand him, Detective. He was spoiled pretty much from birth. And I suppose I'm as guilty of that as anyone. Big sister.' She shrugged. 'But he took it all onboard and grew to expect it of life in general. I'm afraid people are there to be used, as far as he's concerned. Friends. Colleagues. Family. We're all steps on his ladder to wealth and contentment. Although, I wonder what contentment will ever look like for him. And now…'

'Yes,' Pete said. 'This. But we're doing our best to find him, I can assure you. Talking of which, I need to ask you what mobile number you've got for him.'

She frowned. 'Again, why ask me?'

He shrugged. 'Sometimes, people have more than one. One for work or whatever. If we can't trace one, the other might offer a clue.'

She was a property specialist. She wouldn't necessarily be all that familiar with criminal proceedings, he thought. And if she was…

'I'll have to get the book.'

Getting up, she left the room. Returned in a few moments with a small address book, which she flipped open. 'We don't use it very often. Here it is.' She read it out and Pete started to write it down but stopped when he realised it was the same one they'd already found.

'That's the one we've got,' he said. 'Thank you, though. We'll let you know when there's any significant news.'

'Is that it?' she asked with a frown.

'Unless you can think of anything else that might help point us in the right direction?'

Her lips pressed together once more. 'Not really, no. Which is sad, when you consider he's my brother, but it's true, nevertheless.'

'All right. We'll be on our way, then.' He stood up and extended a hand. 'Thank you for your time.'

*

Pete called Dave as they left the city. 'How've you got on?'

'We've spoken to one of the guys, Dick spoke to another. They've both got alibis and clean records. Number three, we're still trying to track down, but he's not making it easy. Not answering his phone, and he's nowhere that we've been told to look for him, so far.'

'And who's he?'

'Eddie Chapman.'

'Background?'

'Lives alone. Done some time. Eighteen months for TWOC, back in 2018/19. Nothing since. Not that he's been charged with, anyway. He's off probation, as of three years ago.'

'Hmm.' Pete's mind was whirring. 'Was he ever linked to the Styles and Shehu mob?'

'Not that we could prove, no.'

'But the timing matches.'

'That's right.'

'It'd bear looking into deeper. Along with his full history, not just last known. Any other links to Styles, Tasker or anyone else tied up in this?'

'Not that we've found as yet.'

'And where's his truck?'

'Eh?'

'His truck. It's not at the farm, so where is it? They're trackable, these days. Not just with tachographs, but built-in satnavs, plus fleet tracking systems like Apex and Garage Manager.'

'So, each vehicle can be tracked?'

'Yes. Helps fleet managers do their job, among other things. Get into the computer system that it's run from, at the bungalow in Blackhorse, plug in the registration, and it'll give you a dot on the map in real time,' Pete told him. 'Go to Andrea Grey, ask her for the password for the computer. If you tell her it'll help find Mark, she can't refuse without looking guilty, can she?'

'Right. No. OK, we're on it.'

'All right. We're on the way back now. We'll see you in a couple of hours or so.'

Pete hung up as he drove northward up a long, straight shallow incline with fields of bright green pasture stretching away on either side, some of them dotted with the pristine white blobs of distant sheep and lambs, new life contrasting vividly with the images swirling in his mind of death, destruction and darkness.

CHAPTER THIRTY-TWO

It was a little under an hour later and they were driving along a section of A-road with the far side bordered by large concrete blocks placed there to protect the work teams who were in the process of constructing a second carriageway alongside the one they were on when Pete's phone rang again. He glanced down at the comms screen and tapped it to answer. 'Gayle.'

'Boss, it's Dave again. Where are you?'

'Just west of Wincanton. Why?'

'We've tracked down Eddie Chapman's lorry. It's currently stationary. In Dorset. On the A35, near a little village called Askerswell, between Bridport and Dorchester. A quick search on the maps site on the web suggests it might be in a lay-by along there.'

'OK.' They passed under a bright yellow speed camera pole and Pete automatically glanced down to check his speed. It read 48mph, just under the 50-limit set within the construction zone. 'That'd be over an hour away from where you are. It's barely thirty miles from here. Get the guvnor to liaise with the Dorset force and send the location details to Jane. They can contact us direct and we'll meet up with them and approach it in a team effort. We've got to assume he's armed, at least with a couple of stun guns of some sort, from what Andrea told us. Which side of Askerswell is it?'

'West. Between there and Loder's Cross. Looks like it's on a dual carriageway section.'

'OK. Get Colin onto it and we'll head south.'

'Will do.'

Pete reached for the comms screen to end the call as Jane's phone pinged with an incoming message. It was already in her hand, following his instruction to Dave. She opened the message and read it then switched to a maps app. Zooming in, she paused. 'Ah.'

'What?' he asked, not liking her tone, as red and white cones began to divide the road ahead as it merged into the existing dualled section.

'There's two lay-bys along there, a mile or so apart.'

'Both on the dual carriageway?'

'Oh, right. No. One of them's on the single carriageway section.'

'That's all right, then.'

He turned off the main east-west trunk road and headed south down a long, straight stretch that he guessed must have had its origins as a Roman road. He hadn't got far down there when his phone rang again.

'DS Gayle,' he said, answering it through the comms system.

'This is Sergeant Cutler with Dorset Tactical Firearms Unit. I was asked to contact you regarding a lorry on the A35.'

'That's right. The driver is a suspect in a dual abduction. One of the abductees was recovered at the scene. We're guessing he still has the second – the husband of the one we recovered – but there's been no communication that we're aware of. The first victim said he was armed, though, with a pair of stun guns.'

'Understood.'

'One of my DC's is with me. We're on the way to the lorry's location, currently a few miles north of Yeovil, on the way back from another job, so we'd like to meet up with your team and be there for the apprehension, if that's possible.'

'Are you trained for an armed situation, DS Gayle?'

'No. Nor's my DC so, obviously, we'll stay back out of your way for the actual arrest.'

'Right. We're about ten miles closer than you, the other side of Dorchester from the target location, so we can meet you at Dorchester and go from there if you like.'

'Perfect.'

They arranged a meeting location and Pete ended the call.

'Probably only about five miles difference now, then,' Jane said.

'Yes, but we've got to get through Yeovil. Or around it, if there's a ring-road.'

She took to her phone again and, in moments, looked up. 'Looks like you could be in luck,' she said. 'There's a turn-off on the left as you come into Yeovil that leads around to the Dorchester road, keeping you out of the town centre.'

'Good. Point it out when we get there, will you?'

'OK.'

*

As the lay-by they were heading for was on the east-bound side of the dual carriageway, they went on past it, unable to see if the lorry was still there because of the dense growth of trees protecting the parking area from the roadway, and swung around into the second lay-by, also separated from the road by a stretch of grass and trees, a few hundred yards further along. They stopped here and Pete and Jane got out to approach the blue and yellow Battenburg-painted SUV of the local force. The driver wound down his window.

'We've just had our colleagues check the lorry's tracking status and they tell us it hasn't moved,' Pete told the four uniformed men.

'We'll approach on the quiet, then: pull in as if we're stopping for a tea-break, get out and have a stroll to start with,' the man in the front passenger seat said. 'You pull up a few yards behind us. We'll get the lay of the land and proceed from there.'

Pete nodded. 'Sounds like a plan. Are we ready?'

'Yep.'

'OK, then. Lead the way.'

He and Jane returned to his Ford to follow the big German car through and out of the lay-by and back the way they'd come.

The dual carriageway started as they climbed a long tree- and hedge-lined hill and the second lay-by, with a farm entrance at the start, opened off just beyond the crest. Pete checked his mirrors as the police vehicle in front of him signalled in and, with no traffic close behind, copied the signal, easing over into what appeared to be more of a narrow track than a lay-by, with a strip of grass up the middle and overgrown hedges pressing close along either side. A few yards in, he could see the articulated lorry blocking the track, its dark red shipping container filling the space between the encroaching greenery.

The patrol car stopped, brake lights flaring in the shade of the hedgerows, and Pete pulled up behind it. They watched as two of the four Dorset officers climbed out, stretched lazily and wandered forward as if they'd got all the time in the world, although the one on the left had to push through the new growth of hazel stems to get past the container on its trailer.

They quickly went from Pete's sight and he and Jane sat waiting, as did the other two uniforms in the car in front of them.

It didn't take long for them to return, the one on Pete's side of the big trailer shaking his head, mouth pushed up in a shrug. Pete waited for him to pass the patrol car and approach, buzzing his window down.

'No sign of him. Cab's locked up,' he said.

'What about the back? The container?' Pete asked.

The man nodded. 'That's locked, too.'

'Best check it, hadn't we?' Pete suggested.

The local man turned and waved a silent signal to the bigger, older officer on the far side of the patrol car to do just that.

It took just seconds for the officer to retrieve a set of bolt croppers from the back of the car and approach the container.

'Stay put,' the man outside Pete's window said and stepped forward to rejoin his colleague. The other two emerged behind him and closed the doors quietly, taking a defensive stance with Tasers drawn at either side of the big car's bonnet as he approached the back of the container, exchanged a word with his companion, and drew his Taser. The other man swung the bolt croppers up into position. One hefty squeeze was all it took. He lowered the tool to the ground and removed the broken padlock, checked with his companion and reached for the handle of the locking bar.

Swinging it all the way back, he pulled the big metal door open just far enough for his companion to step into the gap, Taser aimed and ready.

And, after a beat, step back again.

Words were exchanged and Pete and Jane were beckoned forward.

They climbed out and stepped past the big SUV.

'What have we got?' Pete asked.

'See for yourself,' said the older man. 'But be warned. It ain't pretty.'

'Not an empty container, then.'

'Not quite.'

'OK.' Pete took out his phone and switched it to torch mode, already smelling what he was going to find inside. He stepped forward, his torso slipping between the open door and the edge of the truck bed, aiming the light into the cavernous darkness.

The container was almost empty. But not quite.

It had been lined with Celotex, he saw, the four-inch-thick, silver-coated insulation boards covering the floor, ceiling, walls and even the insides of the doors. And at the far end, he could see the reason for all that effort and expense.

It wasn't to control the temperature inside, but to muffle sound – to prevent it from emerging to the outside world. The sound in question being the screams of the man whose blood had pooled beneath where he was strung up, X-fashion from hooks that emerged through the insulation where the sides met the roof and floor, no doubt attached securely to the metal walls of the container.

Pete glanced sideways at the watching officers. 'I see what you mean. Give me a hand up, would you?'

The older of the two frowned. 'Do you think you should?'

'We need to ID him.'

'Yeah, but…'

'He's probably one of two males, both of which I've got photos of.' He lifted his phone slightly while keeping it aimed into the container.

'OK.' He stepped forward, crouching slightly and cupped his hands, fingers interlaced, for Pete to put a foot into.

In a moment, Pete was inside and, keeping close to one side of the space – the far side from the heap of clothes he'd seen in the corner near the still-closed door – advanced along it towards the suspended figure.

As he drew closer, he could tell more clearly what had been done to the man. The signs of torture were extensive. Mostly small, fine cuts, there were nevertheless dozens of them spread over his fingertips, hands and feet, along his arms and across his torso as well as around his genitals, where more severe damage had been done.

He had been crudely circumcised and castrated, the results now lying amid the mess of blood beneath him.

The pain from all those little cuts would have been excruciating, Pete imagined. Like paper cuts, only harsher, and no doubt inflicted one at a time until he finally told his tormentor what they wanted to know. If that's what it was about, rather than purely for the sake of cruelty. And then, the final cut, from which he'd probably bled out, Pete guessed, though that in itself wouldn't have been quick.

Pete sucked in a breath through his teeth and crouched to better see the victim's face.

He didn't need to bring up the comparison shot on his phone to know who this was. And he didn't need to reach out to check the victim's wrist or neck for a pulse. Beneath the ferrous tang of the now mostly dried blood that had spilled across the floor was a heavier, denser smell – one that Pete would never mistake for anything else, no matter how faint it was against other, stronger scents.

The smell of death.

He straightened up. Checked the pulse anyway, but was not surprised when he didn't find one, and returned to the open doorway. Jumped down.

'Best get Forensics here.'

'They're on the way,' the senior uniformed man said.

'Who is it?' Jane asked.

'Mark Grey.'

CHAPTER THIRTY-THREE

'Shit! So, where the hell does that leave us?' Dave exclaimed when Pete rang him from the car while they waited for the Forensics team to arrive.

'Looking for Eddie Chapman,' Pete said. 'What can you tell me about him, in terms of where he might have gone, if he was travelling under his own steam and by his own volition?'

'In terms of holiday destinations or favourite spots, nothing at this stage. As far as family – he comes from Torquay, originally. Moved up to Exeter when he came out of prison. Deliberate decision, on his part, to get away from known drug connections. Stay clean.'

'OK, we need to talk to colleagues and friends as well as family members. He's alone now, but is there an ex-partner? Get warrants for his address and his banking activity, with up to the minute tracking on the latter, on the basis that he's missing from a crime scene. We don't know if he's an offender or another victim. And he doesn't take this truck home from work, so how does he get to and from Sowton? Do a vehicle check and, if it's a car or motorbike, get an alert out on it. Nationwide and all ports. On him, too, while you're at it. And check his phones and socials as well as getting back to Grey's other two drivers. Any contact might be the one we need to talk to, to track him down.'

'Right, we're on it.'

Pete ended the call. 'While we wait for Forensics, let's go and have a word at the farm, over there. See if anyone saw anything useful,' he said to Jane.

He stepped out of the car and went to tell the local officers what they were doing. 'Could you guys check the place I noticed at the other end of the lay-by?' he asked.

'Baz and Jerry,' the oldest member of the team delegated. 'Off you go. We'll wait for the white-coat brigade.'

Pete returned to the car, climbed in and reversed it back to turn into the gated farm entrance that led off the start of the lay-by.

Beyond a thick clump of tall evergreens, the drive led into a wide area of hard-standing, a barn directly in front of them while a big house stood over to the left, behind a gardened area split by a path that led to the porched front door. Pete parked at the opening of the garden path and they stepped out, heading for the house.

A large, dark-haired woman in her fifties, dressed in a check shirt and jeans opened the door to their strike of the big black iron knocker. 'Hello?'

Pete held up his warrant card. 'Hi. I'm DS Gayle. This is DC Bennett. We just wanted to ask you about the lorry in the lay-by out there. Do you know when it arrived, or if there was another vehicle with it when it did?'

She shook her head. 'I never saw it arrive, but my husband's been moaning about it. He was going to report it as abandoned if it hadn't moved by tea-time, but seeing as you're here…'

'When did it arrive, as far as you know?' Pete asked again.

'Not sure exactly. Wednesday night, Thursday morning.'

'Where is your husband? Could we have a word with him?'

'You're going to be getting rid of it, are you?'

'We'll be recovering it at some point, yes.'

'Good,' she said with a firm nod. 'Bloody nuisance, it is, cluttering up the place like that. Selfish sod. George is in the shed, over there.' She nodded to the big timber-clad building behind them. The sound of a power-tool broke the silence from that direction. 'There you go. Working on something.'

'Thank you.' Pete nodded to her and turned away, letting Jane lead the way out through the flower-filled garden to the expanse of tarmac beyond which, no doubt, had been a farmyard at one time, but now reminded Pete more of a carpark for a farm shop. Crossing it, they saw that the man-sized entrance cut into the big double doors in the long side of the old building stood open. Pete stepped inside and saw that it was set up as a workshop. A bench stretched the full width across the left-hand end. A bale sledge took up a large portion of the floorspace, it's framework a complicated maze of pale green steel and wires. A man stood with his back to them at the workbench, sparks flying in a dense arc from the angle grinder he was using. Large, like his wife, he was broad and powerful-looking in dark blue overalls and heavy boots, dark hair sprouting wildly from beneath a tattered-looking cap.

Pete used a break in his use of the angle grinder to call out. 'Hello.'

The man turned, setting the grinder on the bench.

Pete held up his warrant card. 'Police. Could we have a word? It won't take long.'

The man stepped forward, approaching them.

'You're George, are you?' Pete asked.

He nodded, joining them a couple of paces in from the doorway.

'DS Gayle and DC Bennett,' Pete introduced. 'We're here about the truck in the lay-by out there.'

'Good,' he said, speaking for the first time, his voice deep and dry-sounding. 'I was going to call your lot about it later on, if it were still there. Been dumped, has it?'

Pete tipped his head in a non-committal gesture. 'When did it turn up?'

'Thursday morning, sometime before ten.'

'You didn't see it arrive?'

He shook his head, lifting the cap with one meaty hand to scratch at his forehead. His hair sprang out in all directions until he replaced the cap, restricting it again. 'Already making a damn nuisance of itself, though. A 4x4 was having to back out from behind it.'

'What kind of 4x4?' Pete asked.

'One of them weird-named ones. Begins with H. Not a big one. Bronzy colour.'

Did you see the registration? Or the driver?'

He nodded. 'Woman. Glamorous-looking blonde, she were. Had a bloke in with her that didn't match at all. Fat and scruffy against her smart and stylish, you know?'

Pete nodded encouragingly.

'And the registration?'

'It were a Devon one. WA ten summat. Why? You reckon they might have witnessed summat?'

Pete shrugged. 'It's something to explore. What about this scruffy male? Can you describe him?'

'Fat. Stubble. Dark top. Polo shirt. Blue, I think. And a tatty old cap. Baseball type. Faded red and frayed around the edge of the peak.'

'That's very precise,' Pete said.

He shrugged. 'Contrast, weren't it? Incongruous, like. So, what's going on with the truck, then? Abandoned, were it? Or nicked? I seen there's a lock on the back.'

'Yes, we've got a forensics team on the way to check it over, then it'll be recovered.'

'Forensics? What, like CSI, you mean? So, it's a crime scene?'

'It is,' Pete confirmed. 'But we can't say much more than that, at this stage. Thank you for your help, though.'

George grunted. 'S'all right.'

'Oh… One other thing,' Pete said. 'Would it be OK for us to leave our car out here for a little while, to let the Forensics guys get in and do their job? It won't be for that long and we'll be on our way.'

He nodded. 'It ain't overcrowded out here.'

'Thanks.' Pete reached out to shake his hand and was met by a large, powerful paw that was dry, dusty and firm. He shook it and they stepped back outside, leaving the man to his work.

'So, whiskey alpha ten on a bronze Hyundai, possibly a Kona,' Jane said as they walked away towards the gate, which was hidden from here by the big conifers. 'The passenger sounds like it could have been Eddie Chapman, but who's the driver?'

'Or they could have been innocently caught behind it, like he said,' Pete countered. 'It wasn't a quick job, what was done to Mark Grey. And it would have been messy.'

'Maybe they wore overalls, like George. Took them off and put them in a bin-bag.'

'Hmm. They'd have had to do something like that or make a mess in the vehicle afterwards. Gloves, too, I should think, and at least wipe down their shoes.'

'That bad, was it?'

'Have you heard of the old Chinese torture, death by a thousand cuts?' he asked.

Jane grimaced. 'OK. That's nasty.'

'Very,' he agreed.

By the time they got back to the lay-by, the Forensics team had arrived and began working and the two uniformed officers were back from the other farm.

'They didn't see anything,' they reported when Pete asked. 'They don't use the lay-by. Their gateway's a few yards up the road from it. And it's pretty well sheltered.' The officer raised a hand to indicate their surroundings.

'Hence why it was chosen, I suppose,' Pete admitted. 'Though that suggests prior knowledge.'

'Well, the driver might well have come this way on a regular run,' the younger man suggested.

'True. Still, we've got one lead. Can you run a partial registration for us, while we're here?'

'Course.'

Pete quoted what they'd got and one of the team relayed it to their dispatch office.

'Three possibles,' the reply came back. 'All sold from a dealership in Exeter.'

'As we'd expect,' Jane muttered.

The female dispatcher read out the full registrations and their owners, with addresses, which Pete wrote down in his notebook, none of them striking a chord in his memory.

'All received,' he said when she finished. 'Thank you.'

A white-overalled male was approaching them along the side of the lorry. 'DS Gayle?' he asked.

'That's me,' Pete told him.

He nodded, suddenly self-conscious. In his early twenties, Pete guessed, he looked younger, was tall and skinny with acne-marked skin and rimless glasses.

'The cab was wiped down,' he reported. 'No fingerprints at all in there. Plenty of DNA, but no prints. Except one partial set on the outside of the driver's door.'

Pete grinned. 'And do we have a match on them?'

The young scientist nodded. 'They come back to a known person. Edward Colin Chapman.'

'Just the one set, you say?'

'Yes.'

'So, put there after the cab had been wiped down.'

'It would appear so, yes.'

'Excellent. Thanks for that.' He turned to Jane. 'We'll have to re-visit George, over there, with a proper photo line-up at some point, but that makes him complicit, at least.'

'But why wipe the cab down, if he'd been driving it?' she demanded. 'It was his truck. His prints are supposed to be all over it.'

'Unless he wanted to make it look like it'd been nicked,' suggested the eldest of the uniformed officers in the patrol car. 'Whoever did that might wipe it down.'

'Exactly,' Pete agreed. 'So, we need to get our hands on this latest version of Fast Eddie, as fast as we can.'

He heard a footstep from behind him and turned to see another white-overalled figure approaching along the side of the Forensics van, a small, clear evidence bag in his hand.

'A slight complicating factor, Detective,' he said.

This was an older man, Pete noted. Shorter than his companion and more confident in his manner.

'Which is?' Pete asked.

'This.' He held up the evidence bag. 'It appears to be the victim's wallet. Found amongst the clothing pile in the corner, which we presume belonged to him, though not in a pocket – apparently just discarded amongst them.'

'And what's complicating about that?'

'We found a fingerprint on it that doesn't belong to the victim. And nor does it belong to your driver, Edward Chapman. In fact, it appears to be female, from the size. Assuming, of course, that we're not dealing with children here. The complicating factor being, it overlays all the other prints on the wallet, which do belong to the victim.'

'And the person it belongs to?'

'Is not on record.'

CHAPTER THIRTY-FOUR

Pete stepped into the dimly lit individual room that Andrea Grey had been transferred into from the bay on the other side of the ward and nodded briefly to the uniformed officer seated beside the window with its half-closed blinds before focussing on the woman in the bed.

'Andrea. How are you doing?'

She was frowning. 'I know where I've seen you before. You were at my brother's trial. At the sentencing.'

He nodded. 'I was.'

'Why?'

He cringed inwardly. This was not a subject he wanted to be discussing with her, especially now. Death notifications were never easy – he was glad, at least, that the local Wiltshire force had been willing to send someone round to Grey's parents and sister in Salisbury, to tell them of his loss – but they were harder than ever when the surviving loved one had reason to be antagonistic. And he needed this woman's help, at the end of the day – one way or another. 'I was the arresting officer. He was behind some serious stuff. A lot of people got hurt.'

She grimaced. 'What are you here for?'

'To check on you. And I'm afraid I've got some bad news.'

'What?' she demanded, her eyes narrowing.

'We found Mark. He didn't make it.'

Her chest seemed to stop moving as her mouth dropped open, eyes widening in shock. 'He's…?'

'Dead,' Pete confirmed. 'I'm sorry.'

A high-pitched keening whine broke from her throat. 'He's dead?'

Pete nodded and reached for her hand which lay on top of the bed clothes.

She snatched it away before he could touch her. 'You...' She blinked and her eyes were suddenly swimming with tears that broke free and ran down her cheeks almost in slow-motion. 'You...' Her face twisted. 'You were too busy accusing him of all sorts to look for him properly. You let him die.'

Pete shook his head. 'He died the night he was taken. Or early the following morning.'

'You let him die!' she wailed, ignoring his words. 'You bastard!' she beat the covers at either side of her legs and began to cry properly, sobbing and wailing.

Pete stood back and exchanged a glance with the officer set to guard her.

And her reaction showed that it was guarding that she needed, not supervising. She hadn't been involved in her husband's abduction and death. Those tears were real. She'd genuinely loved him.

The uniformed woman's lips pushed up and together. She could try to comfort the grieving woman, but that would only alienate her from both of them, at this stage. There was little they could do but let her cry it out.

Pete tipped his head and she stood up to follow him out.

'How's she been?' he asked with the door closed behind them and a nurse approaching quickly.

'What's happened?' the white-uniformed nurse demanded.

'She's had some bad news,' the constable told her. 'We're just letting her cry it out for a minute.'

The nurse went past them into the room.

'She's been fine,' the constable told him. 'Quiet. Calm. Seemed to be getting stronger, slowly. Asked about going home.'

'And what did you tell her?'

'That it wasn't safe until we caught the person who attacked her and her husband. That you were doing all you could.'

'And she accepted that?'

'At the time, yes.'

'No visitors, or people trying to visit?'

She shook her head. 'All quiet.'

'Well, that's something, at least. They don't know she's alive, and more importantly, here.'

'Any idea who they are yet?'

He pursed his lips. 'We think one of his drivers is involved. Who he's working with, we don't know yet. But we've got some leads.'

From here, he'd be going to meet up with Jane again at the station and go out to interview the three Hyundai owners on the list in his notebook, only one of whom was female.

They'd start with her, he thought.

'Good. She seems genuinely distraught in there.'

Andrea Grey's sobs had eased slightly, but they could still hear her crying.

Then the nurse stepped out. She looked accusingly at Pete. 'She could have done without that news, at this stage,' she said. 'She's still weak.'

'I know,' he said. 'But she had a right to know. It was her husband.'

'A right, yes. But did it have to be now?'

'There's never a good time for news like that,' he said. And he'd given it enough times to know that much.

She humphed and moved off to go about her business.

'Are we going back in?' the constable asked.

'Give her a minute alone.'

They waited in companionable silence for more than a minute before going back in and closing the door gently behind them.

Andrea was quieter now, though still weeping, wiping her eyes with a tissue that was balled up in her hand.

'I'm sorry for hitting you with that kind of news,' Pete said. 'But you had a right to know. And yes, Mark was involved in some criminal activity, but that made it more urgent, not less, that we find him. The truth is, we weren't going to find him alive, however urgently we treated the case. But you can help us find his killer.'

Her hand thumped down on the covers again. 'How?' she demanded. 'I don't know who took him.'

'Did you meet his drivers?'

'Yes, once or twice. Why? You're saying it was one of them?' She swiped quickly at her eyes and fixed him with a fiery gaze.

'Not necessarily,' Pete said. 'But it was one of his trucks that was used to transport him to where he was found, so we have to eliminate them. What did you think of them?'

She shrugged. 'They seemed all right, I suppose. I didn't get to know them.'

'What about any of his other business associates? Did you know any of them?'

'No. That was work. We had a home life. Kept the two separate, mostly. Like most people do, I expect. I mean, we'd exchange how our days had gone and stuff, as you do, but it wasn't the be all and end all. Just a way to make a living.'

Pete wondered how much of that living was made legally, but now wasn't the time to bring that up. 'So, there wasn't a problem with any of the drivers?' he persisted instead. 'You didn't get a bad vibe off any of them? Mark didn't sack one recently or anything?'

'No.' She frowned. 'Why all these questions about the drivers? What are you driving at?'

He gave her a quick flash of a grin at the unintended pun. 'As I said, one of his trucks was used.'

'Well, they could have nicked it. Just because they're able to drive a lorry doesn't mean they worked for Mark.'

'True, but we have to confirm or eliminate these things as they come up.'

'Well, just find them. Whoever did this. And put them in prison. Preferably, the same one our Adrian's in.'

Pete's cheeks twitched in a quick grimace. 'That's something else I need to ask you about,' he said.

'What?'

'Did Mark have much to do with Adrian?'

'No. Nor did I, come to that. That's why I was only at his sentencing, not the rest of his trial. We was never close. I don't reckon he's ever been close to anyone. It's not the way he's made.'

'He wasn't cruel? To you? Abusive?'

'No!' she protested. 'What is this? No, he was just… Distant. A bit cold, I suppose you might say.'

Pete nodded. 'OK. And back to Mark. He never associated with any of Adrian's friends or co-defendants?'

'What friends?' she shot back. 'Like I said, he's a bit of a cold fish. Never had many friends, that I know of.'

Pete's lips pushed together. 'All right. I'll let you rest and recover.'

*

Pete stopped his car at the kerb on a residential side-street north of the hospital. Mid-century red-brick semis lined both sides, leading his eye towards the looming stone spire of a church opposite the end of the street he was on. He glanced at Jane in the passenger seat beside him. There was no bronze-coloured SUV on the street – Hyundai or otherwise.

'She could be at work,' she offered.

These houses had no garages, or even drives. They'd been built for Council tenants, who would not have had cars at that time.

'Or on the run, after what we saw over at Askerswell.'

Jane shrugged. 'Best go and find out, eh?'

'We'll give her a knock first, then ask the neighbours if we need to.'

They stepped out of the car and went to do just that. Ringing the doorbell, they waited. There was no reaction. No sound from within. Pete pressed the bell again. Still nothing. He shrugged. 'You go left, I'll go right?'

'OK,' she agreed.

They stepped out to the pavement. He went to the attached property, Jane to the nearest of the next pairing, separated from the target address by a low brick wall and a gap of four or five feet.

Approaching the door which, like the neighbours', was in a small inset porch, he rang the bell.

The door was answered by a male Pete guessed to be in his sixties with short grey hair, thinning on top, and a lean build under his white T-shirt and jeans.

'Hello.' His tone and expression were cautiously neutral.

Pete held up his warrant card. 'Hi. DS Gayle, Exeter CID. I'm trying to track your neighbour down. Seems like she's not in. Do you know where I might find her? Where she works or whatever?'

He grimaced. 'Haven't seen much of her, the last day or two. I don't know where she works. Keeps herself to herself. Way it is, round here.'

Pete nodded, recalling a visit he'd made some time ago to an address in the next street down the hill from where he stood now: that of a known drug dealer and his divorced father. He'd been trying, at the time, to track down what turned out to be a witness rather than a suspect in another case. 'OK. When did you last see her, or her vehicle? Hyundai, isn't it?'

'I think so, yes. Must have been... I was going to say yesterday, but I don't know as it was. Maybe the day before. Thursday. Yes, there was a bit of banging about. Doors slamming and such.'

'What sort of time was that?' Pete asked.

'Afternoon. Two-ish, maybe. I don't know. I wasn't taking that much notice, really.'

'All right. Thanks for your help.' He nodded to the man and stepped away.

Jane was emerging onto the pavement two doors down. He went to meet her.

'Anything?'

She shook her head. 'They don't know her that well. She's been here two or three years. Got a daughter, aged seven. Evie. Goes to Woodwater school, rather than Burnthouse Lane, which is closer. Mum takes her in the car and brings her home. She's played with their grandkids a few times, in the back garden.'

Pete repeated what he'd been told at the other side. 'We'll try a few across the road, then go to the school.'

*

Woodwater school was a modern, angular, white-rendered building behind a high brick wall, the playing field that extended down the road from it, protected by heavy-duty grey steel fencing.

Pete pulled into the small carpark area and they headed for the glass doors in the angle where two sections of the building met. He pushed the buzzer beside the doors and identified himself. In moments, a stocky, fifty-ish brunette in a flower-print dress emerged from one of the doors he could see through the glass and approached. She pressed the release to open the doors. 'DS Gayle?'

'That's right,' he agreed, and showed her his warrant card. 'And this is DC Bennett.'

She examined it, then looked up to meet his gaze. 'Thank you. I'm Barbara Minter, the head here. Come through.' She led the way across towards the door she'd emerged from. There was no reception desk, as such, but several labelled doors opened off the entrance hall, he noticed as they crossed it, and corridors extended from the rear in both directions behind safety glass screens.

'Come in,' she said as she reached the door, which he saw had her name on a brass plaque just below his eye level.

He hung back, allowing Jane to precede him.

The woman stepped around her desk and sat down. 'How can I help?'

'As I said on the phone, we're here to ask about one of your pupils. Evie Parr.'

The woman frowned. 'We don't have an Evie Parr here, Detective.'

Pete raised an eyebrow. 'We're actually looking for her mother, Katrina Parr. We assumed Evie would have the same surname, but... She's a single mother, so it's possible we're wrong in that. The address is Kingsway.'

She nodded and reached for her computer mouse. 'Let me check.'

Tapping into the instrument, she clicked and scrolled for a moment. Then: 'Ah. You mean Evelyn Shehu.'

Pete felt his eyes snap wide. He exchanged a glance with Jane. 'Shehu?' he checked. 'That's right. Evelyn Shehu.'

'OK. That's helpful. Is she in school today?'

'No, she's absent. Last attended on Thursday of last week. We have tried to contact her mother, but to no avail.' Her tone was increasingly disapproving.

Pete pursed his lips. 'I wouldn't be surprised if that continues to be the case. Have you got any details on the mother, other than her address?'

'Only the application she submitted for Evelyn to join us.'

'And that would have been three years or so ago?'

'That's right.'

Pete nodded. 'OK. Thank you. That's been very helpful.'

'Can I ask, what do you mean when you say we won't be able to reach Ms Parr?'

'I suspect she may have moved on. In something of a hurry.'

CHAPTER THIRTY-FIVE

He loomed over the end of the bed, sucking air in through flared nostrils as his hands gripped the iron footer to either side of the medical clipboard, Andrea staring back at him, wide-eyed.

'What do you know about Katrina Parr? Or Shehu?' he demanded.

Her eyes widened further. 'She's not…?'

He allowed his head to twitch sideways. 'Not that we know of. Tell me about her. Everything.'

She blinked. 'She was a dancer. Of a sort. Stripper, really. One of those big, expensive men's clubs up London. Alex met her in there. They got tight. She wasn't Katrina then. Kat. And instead of Parr, she used Perfect. Anyway, he took her out of there. Away from that world. And less than a year later, he married her. They come down this way for his work and, in another year or so, she had little Evie. Why the interest in her?'

'She's missing.' Pete had dropped Jane back at the station then come straight back here, radioing the guard who was now standing behind him as he strode into the hospital without using any names other than his own, to let her know he was on the way.

'Missing?'

'How well do you know her?'

A frown tightened her brow. 'Fairly. As well as anyone, I should think. Down here, anyway. She was… We helped her out after Alex – Alexander – after you lot killed him and the court took her house and pretty much everything else as proceeds of crime, despite her husband having just died, leaving her with a kid to raise on her own. They stayed with us for a bit, while the council were sorting a place for them.'

'You say down here. Was she still in touch with people back in London? Family? Old friends?'

'Family, yes. Parents. That was all, as far as I know. She'd left the rest behind, and gladly so.'

'What about Mark? How did she get on with him?'

Her eyes narrowed. 'You make it sound like I ought to be suspicious. There was nothing like that between them. They were friends. Same as me and her. That's all.'

'Friends? Not business partners?'

'Eh? How was she supposed to go into business? She'd just lost everything but a few sticks of furniture.'

'It's not always about the cash,' he said. 'Sometimes, it's the plan. You get others to invest and you run it. Own it, if only in name.'

'What are you on about?' she demanded.

'Did she ever meet Eddie Chapman?'

She shook her head quickly. 'I don't know. You were... What's he got to do with anything?'

Pete stayed silent, waiting while her brain processed what little he'd given her, joining dots, making connections.

Then her eyes went wide again. 'No. You ain't saying...'

'His lorry was left in the next county. He didn't walk away from it.'

'And... No. No way. She's a friend. We stood by her when she needed it. Took her in, even. Why would she...? No.' She shook her head firmly. 'What are you trying to do here, drive a wedge between me and everyone I know? It's not enough, you've got my husband killed, now you want me completely alone? What for? What's all this in aid of? What did I ever do to you?'

Pete was shaking his head. 'I'm not trying to isolate you, Andrea. I'm just looking for who killed Mark. And Eddie was seen leaving the scene where his lorry was left. In a car that matched Katrina's, driven by a woman who matched her description.'

'You're lying!' she declared, starting up in the bed. 'You're a fucking liar!'

Pete shook his head. 'Why do you think I'm asking about her? We got her name from the partial registration that a witness provided. Followed it up and found that she's not at home and hasn't been for days. And her kid hasn't been in school for just as long. What am I supposed to think?'

'Well, not that! No way. She's… She's a friend!' She slumped back, wet-eyed.

'I'm sorry, Andrea, but I have to follow the evidence, wherever it leads,' he said. 'And right now, it's leading me towards Katrina Parr. Which club was it that Alexander met her in?'

'I dunno. Just an expensive one, that's all she said.'

'And she was from there? London?'

'Yeah. That's where she said her family were.'

'OK. One last thing for now. We recovered Mark's wallet. The cash was all left in it, and most of the cards. There just seems to be one card missing. At least, the way the leather's worn, it looks like there was one in the space that's now empty. If I showed you a picture, do you think you'd be able to tell me what card it was?'

She grimaced. 'I don't know.'

'Will you have a look?'

She shrugged.

Pete took out his phone and brought up a shot he'd taken of the wallet in its evidence bag, held up by the forensic technician to show the space that had been left empty. He turned it to face her.

She paused, staring. 'That's a company account. I never had anything to do with it. I don't know what bank it was. Just a black card. That's all I can tell you.'

'You're sure you don't know what bank it was? There wasn't a logo on it that you remember?'

She shook her head. 'I only saw it once or twice. He never used it when I was with him and I don't make... Didn't make a habit of rummaging in his wallet.' She frowned a challenge at him.

Pete nodded. He could understand that. He wouldn't go into Louise's purse or she into his wallet without asking. 'OK. Thank you. That'll do for now. I'm sorry to have had to bring you more bad news, but I had to find out all I could, and you were the obvious source.'

She sneered at him wordlessly as he stood back from the bed.

Pete nodded to the guard and left the room. As he walked away up the length of the ward, he lifted his radio from his belt. 'DS Gayle for guard on male victim.'

'Yes, Sarge?'

'I'm on the way to you.'

'Received.'

He pushed through the doors at the end of the ward and turned left along the sunny corridor with its full height glass wall on his left. It wasn't far along to the next ward, where he turned in and headed along to another private room, right next to the nurses' station. He knocked and went in.

'Derek,' he said and exchanged a nod with the guard who was standing just inside the door.

Tasker looked up at him from the bed. 'Detective.'

'How are you doing?' Pete asked.

'I hurt in places I didn't even know I'd got but the staff here tell me I'm lucky to be able to feel anything, so I suppose I ought to be thankful for the pain, in a way. And I expect it'd be a lot worse if they hadn't got me on the meds. Although I did tell them not to use opioids on account of me being an addict. Former, at least.'

Pete was nodding. 'Sounds like you're on the mend. That's good.'

'So, what do we owe the pleasure to?'

'I wanted to ask you about Eddie Chapman.'

Tasker's eyebrow rose. 'What about him?'

'Whatever you can tell me.'

'We was inside together. Same wing, at least, for a while. I didn't know he was working for Grey until I met him, driving one of his trucks. He's part of the car thing. Shipping them abroad. Delivered some of them direct to the clients. He's proud of that.'

'What about away from work, if you want to call it that? Down-time. Family. Social life?'

'I know he's originally from Torquay. But he never talked about his family. Not to me. He's got a flat down near the park and ride, off Rydon Lane. What he does for a social life, I ain't got a clue.'

'What does he drive?' Pete asked. 'Or does he, other than the lorries?'

'Yeah, he's got a battered old Skoda. Works on it himself to save garage fees.'

'That'll lower the tone round where he lives,' Pete said with a grin, thinking of the relatively new-build area Tasker had described him living in. 'I bet the neighbours love him.'

Tasker shrugged. 'He don't care. Tells anyone that comments to mind their own and, if they push it, he pushes back. He's got the weight for it and he ain't afraid to throw it around.'

'I see.' Pete nodded. He was building a picture of the man, and it wasn't a pleasant one. 'How'd he get on with Mark Grey? Any problems there?'

Tasker shook his head. 'Not that I'm aware of. Although, I wouldn't be, necessarily. Unless one of them decided to do something about it. I never seen Eddie kick up against him. Why? What's the interest in Eddie?'

Pete gave him a quick hint of a smile. 'We were aware that Eddie drove for Grey. And not just legitimate loads.'

'Yeah, but… Hang on. "Drove?" As in past tense? I mean, I know you'll be delving in, breaking it all up and that now, but has something happened that I don't know about?'

Pete tipped his head. 'Mark Grey's dead.'

Tasker's eyes shot wide. 'Dead? How? When?'

'Killed. Wednesday night, Thursday morning.'

'Jeez. That's a turn-up.'

'Isn't it,' Pete said. He knew Tasker hadn't had any visitors since he'd been in the hospital. If he had, they'd have been logged and he'd have been informed immediately, so there was no way Grey's death was a result of a revenge attack on Tasker's behalf. 'Saves you the trouble of going after him when you get out of here, though, eh? Or testifying against him. Although, there's still the matter of Ewan Price and that MG he was found in.'

'Hey, I told you about that. You can…' He stopped abruptly.

'I can what?'

Tasker pursed his lips. 'I was going to say, "track my phone," but I switched it off, didn't I? Grey told me to, so I expect he did the same.'

'And now I can't ask him for his version of events,' Pete said.

Tasker grunted. 'And you ain't going to accept my word. So, where's that leave me?'

Pete shrugged. 'It depends,' he said. 'I mean, technically, we could charge you for Ewan's death anyway. Joint enterprise. But whether we would or not...' He spread his hands. 'You were about to tell me what Eddie Chapman gets up to, other than tinkering on his car, when he's not driving trucks. And where he might be inclined to go off to if he knows that gig's up.'

Tasker frowned. 'I don't know him that well. We was on the same block, not in the same cell. And it was only for a few months. And back here, well... Like I said, I didn't know he was tied up with Grey until I met him one night, by chance, a few months ago. Only thing he said to me in that sense was one night, he was all pleased with himself that he'd got a trip to the Canaries booked up. Sun and sand and naked girls all over the place, he said.'

'When was this?'

'Couple of months ago. February. He was going the next week.'

'Just for a week?'

'Yeah.'

'Was it somewhere he'd been before?'

'I don't know. It sounded like it, but...' He shrugged.

'All right. And the Skoda. Did you ever see it?'

'Yeah, 'course.'

'Tell me about it.'

'Pale blue. Older type, like I said. I don't know the model, but it was a boxy, old-fashioned sort of thing.'

'Registration?'

He grimaced. 'Christ knows. I weren't looking that close.'

Pete's lips pressed briefly together. 'All right. I'll accept that, for now.'

Tasker's head pulled back. 'What do you mean, for now? Have I ever lied to you? No.'

Pete tipped his head. 'Basic police training,' he said. 'ABC. Accept nothing, Believe no-one, Challenge everything.'

Tasker shook his head. 'That's a sad way to live, isn't it?'

Pete drew a breath. 'But necessary, if we're going to solve crimes. If we believed everyone who said, "It wasn't me, guvnor," we wouldn't get anywhere, would we?'

*

He found his whole team in the incident room, working.

Dave looked up from his computer at the opening door. 'Hey, we thought we'd said something wrong and you'd fallen out with us.'

'No more than usual, in your case,' Pete told him. 'What's been happening?'

Ben looked up and around as he dropped his jacket over the back of his chair and pulled it out to sit. 'Good job you called about Eddie Chapman when you did, boss,' he said. 'We got the warrants in place and, between ANPR and his bank card usage, we've tracked him to Birmingham airport. His car's in the long-term parking there and he's booked on a flight out to Alicante, tomorrow morning. We don't know where he's staying overnight, but West Mids will pick him up when he turns up for the flight.'

'Well, that's good news,' Pete said. 'A bit of luck and we'll get to have a chat with him tomorrow.'

'So, what's the latest with you?' Jane asked.

'Well, it seems like we've duplicated some work. I also found out what Eddie Chapman drives, though I hadn't got as far as the VRN. The missing card from Mark Grey's wallet is a "black one…"' He used his fingers to form air quotes. 'And Katrina Parr, formerly Shehu unless the reversion is unofficial, is from London.'

'Yes, Jane told us about Katrina Parr and a few other bits and pieces,' Dave replied. 'It sounds like they rebuilt the setup Adrian Styles and Alexander Shehu had, four years ago. But who's they? Was it Styles again, from inside? Or Mark Grey? His wife? Or Katrina, trying to rebuild what she lost?'

That's what we've got to figure out,' Pete said. 'And prove, if we can.'

'I still wonder if Andrea being left like that was a set-up to make her look like an innocent party, for our benefit,' Jill said. 'It could easily have gone wrong. Or not, from the point of view of whoever left her there.'

Pete shook his head. 'I know what you mean, but I don't think so. Her reaction to her husband's death, when I told her, was real. If that was pre-planned, it wasn't by her.'

'Who, then?'

'As Dave said, there's several choices until we can eliminate them.'

Dick chuckled. 'There's already been plenty of that, on this case. The gang eliminating each other, for one reason or another.'

'We'll need to get an all-ports alert out on Katrina Parr, then,' Dave said.

'If we're not already too late,' Dick added.

'Yes, you do that, Dave. Ben, get us an address for her parents. Dick, find out if the Hyundai dealer's still open and, if so, what it'll take to get the tracking data from her 4x4. Even if she got it second-hand, it will have been bought there originally. I'll get onto the Met and get them looking for her and the car.'

CHAPTER THIRTY-SIX

Jane had already left for the night, Dick was on his way to the door of the incident room and Pete was putting his jacket on, ready to leave when Ben's computer pinged and he clicked into his messages.

'Oh. Here's a turn-up,' he said.

'What's that?' Pete asked.

'Eddie Chapman. Either there's more than one of them, or he's not in Birmingham anymore.'

'Why?'

'He's just booked a flight from Manchester to Tenerife, leaving at 10:20 tomorrow morning. From a travel agent in the city centre there.'

'Really?'

'The all-ports bulletin we put out flagged it,' Ben explained.

'OK. Nice one.' Pete pulled his chair out and sat down again. Firing his computer back up, a quick search gave him the phone number he needed and he placed a call on his desk phone.

'Greater Manchester Police. How can I help?'

'Hi. This is DS Pete Gayle with Devon and Cornwall Police.' He gave his badge number. 'We've got an all-ports out for a fugitive from down here and it's just flagged him up as being in your area. Would you be able to check on that for us and confirm or deny it's the same person?'

'What have you got?'

Pete gave her the details.

'The travel agent's will be closed by now, I expect. But we have officers permanently at the airport. We can flag his name at the check-ins and pick him up from there.'

'It ought to be flagged anyway on an all-ports, but it can't hurt to make doubly sure. We don't want a suspect in a murder fleeing the country, do we?'

'We certainly don't. OK, I'll pass it on. Thanks for your call.'

'Thank you.' Pete put the phone down. 'Good catch, Ben, but they won't pick him up until tomorrow, at the airport. Travel agent's shut by now.'

'He probably left it to the last minute to make the booking with that in mind,' Jill said.

'Probably,' Pete agreed. 'Thought he was being clever again.'

She chuckled. 'Little does he know, eh?'

'As long as they do pick him up in the morning,' Dave said.

'We've still got no evidence that he actually did anything illegal,' Ben pointed out.

'No, but he's a suspect,' Dave argued. 'That's enough for now.'

'To arrest him, yes, but to hold him? I mean, until we get his phone records and that, what have we actually got? His truck was used. Even with a witness saying he was there, that doesn't mean he knew what was in the container or what happened in there. And no DNA, fingerprints or blood evidence.' He shrugged. 'I'm just saying. That gives us 24 hours from tomorrow morning, when they pick him up. And we won't get the phone records in that time, never mind prove anything with them.'

'Hey, just because Dick's left the building doesn't mean you've got to take over from him,' Jill said.

Ben sighed. 'I'm not. I suppose I'm just tired, that's all.'

'Well, there's nothing we can do about it now,' Pete said. 'So let's get home and get some rest. Get back to it tomorrow. If you're all up for it, bearing in mind the overtime budget.'

Dave's eyebrows shot up. 'There's an overtime budget now?'

'No.'

*

The call came in at 9:45 the next morning. Pete had been in the incident room for just over an hour. He was going through printouts of the data from Paul Jacobs' phone with a set of highlighters, building a picture of the phone's usage and connections to see what that might add to their knowledge of the gang's activities and membership.

He capped the orange highlighter that was currently in his hand and set it down.

The call was an external one, he could tell by the ring mode as he picked it up. 'DS Gayle, Exeter CID.'

'Hello. This is PC Cruthers, Greater Manchester. You've got an alert out on an Edward Chapman?'

'That's right.'

'Just to let you know, we've got him in custody. He was apprehended five minutes ago at Manchester airport, attempting to board a flight to Tenerife.'

'Excellent news. Thank you. I'll let my DI know and we'll arrange for him to be transported back down here.' He put the phone down and picked it straight up again to dial Colin's number. 'One in the bag, one to go,' he announced to the team.

It was picked up on the first ring. 'Yes?'

'Guv, it's Pete. Manchester have got Eddie Chapman in custody. We need to get him back down here and interviewed ASAP but we're all tied up building the evidence to be able to hold and charge him and Katrina Parr, if we can find her, so could you arrange a prisoner transport?'

'OK,' Colin said and hung up.

'What time does that Hyundai dealership open?' Pete demanded of no-one in particular.

'About ten minutes,' Dick said. 'Or they're supposed to.'

'Get down there. Speak to them in person. We need that tracking data ASAP,' Pete told him.

'All right.' Dick shut down his computer and stood up to leave.

'The Hilux confirms what Derek Tasker said,' Jill said from across the desks. 'It left Blackhorse on the night of Ewan Price's death, came into the city, was just around the corner from Tasker's address at the time he said he was picked up, then went out to Woodbury Common, came back into the city and back to Blackhorse. And then, the night of his attack, it was on that bridge around the time he went off it.'

'Good. Nice work,' Pete said. But it didn't help with what they'd got left to do – catching Katrina Parr and convicting her and Chapman. And, realistically, he thought, they weren't going to convict Chapman of anything unless they could somehow show that he was involved in collecting the stolen cars into the containers for transport. Transporting containers without having seen the contents was standard practice, after all.

He needed to talk to Tasker again.

*

His injuries were going to take time to heal, but Tasker looked stronger, Pete thought when he got to the hospital and stepped into his room.

'Morning. How are you feeling?' he asked.

'A bit better every day,' the man admitted.

'Good. We've arrested Eddie Chapman. Caught him trying to flee the country.'

Tasker's eyes widened in surprise. 'He does that regularly. What's so different about this time?'

Pete gave him a brief smile. 'He hadn't got his truck. We have. Or at least, Dorset Constabulary have. I told you yesterday that Mark Grey was killed. Well, he was found in the back of Chapman's truck. And we know Chapman was there. He was seen. And now he's caught trying to do a runner. So, I need to ask you some more questions. And these are going to get a bit harder, Derek,' he added, his tone getting heavier.

Tasker frowned. 'What questions? I never had nothing to do with that.'

Pete shook his head. 'I know that. You were in here. But would Eddie have done it in revenge for what Grey did to you, do you think? You were old buddies, after all.'

'No! And I certainly didn't put him up to it.'

'I didn't say you did, did I?' Another shake of the head. 'No, Derek. I need you to tell me exactly what Chapman's role in the car thefts was.'

'He didn't have one. Apart from picking them up after and taking them wherever Grey had arranged for.'

'He picked them up? From where? And how, exactly?'

'There's a bit of a dead-end road off the old Honiton Road. It was cut off by the new road going through. It's not far from the farm. He'd pull up in there, open the doors at the back of his container and drop a pair of ramps out of it.'

'OK.' Pete frowned. 'So… And here's probably the hardest part, from your point of view, but it makes everything else you've said credible and we can make a deal with the CPS on that basis… Where do you fit into this scenario?'

He stared at Pete for a long moment, assessing, judging, thinking through his options. Then finally pursed his lips. 'I was the man in the middle,' he said. 'I connected Grey to the lifters. Then, when the jobs were done and the cars had sat and cooled for a couple of days, they brought them to a fixed location, I picked them up and delivered them to the lorry. It kept him one step removed. Two steps, with Eddie, not him, collecting them.'

'But he met at least some of the "lifters," as you call them. Ewan Price, for one.'

'Yeah, reluctantly, when there was no other way. Pricey was getting obstreperous. Grey wanted to drop him. He didn't like the idea. Didn't see why.'

'So, why was it?' Pete asked although they'd covered this ground before. That was often the way with interviews like this. You went over and over something. And one thing led to another.

'The violence,' Tasker said. 'There was no need for it and it was going to draw attention we didn't want. I tried telling him, but… I reckon he enjoyed it. It was almost like, for him, it was the main purpose, rather than the cars.' He shook his head. 'I couldn't make him see sense and nor could Grey, when they met. And then…' He stopped.

'Then what?' Pete asked.

His mouth twitched in a resigned grimace. 'Well, you know what, don't you? The fires at the recovery place and Grey's house.

There was no way they was coincidence and no way Grey was going to let them go. Pricey put a target on his own back, doing that, stupid sod.' His arms lifted in a shrug. 'And then…'

'This,' Pete said. 'To keep you quiet? Or revenge for introducing Ewan to the mix in the first place?'

'Does it matter? Especially if Grey's dead.'

Pete shook his head with a grimace. 'Not really. But you're willing to testify that Eddie Chapman loaded those cars up? That he knew they were stolen?'

'I ought to say, "No." If Eddie done for Grey, or helped, he did me a favour, didn't he? Deliberately or not. But then, why would he do that? I mean, he was onto a nice little earner there, between the legit loads and the cars. A good wage.'

'Unless Mark Grey was winding it all up, after all that's gone on in the last few weeks, and Eddie saw his income stream drying up and wanted to get rid of any witnesses. I mean, you're in here. As far as Mark Grey was concerned, you're dead. If Eddie thought the same…'

His shoulder twitched in a shrug. 'I suppose.' Then he frowned. 'But why would Eddie think the same? Who'd have told him about what happened? Grey wouldn't. Defeat the object, wouldn't it?'

'So, was Eddie there? Involved, directly or otherwise?'

Tasker pursed his lips. 'I don't… I don't remember,' he admitted. 'I know Grey was, but…'

'So, how did you get there?' Pete asked. 'And why? What did he tell you you were going there for?'

He shook his head. 'I don't remember. I'd have gone on my bike, I expect. You haven't got it?'

'No. It hasn't been found. What does it look like?'

'Ordinary. Green and white frame. Raleigh. Not new by a long way, but it does the job. Gets me to work and back, into town, stuff like that.'

Pete nodded. 'I don't remember seeing it anywhere, but we'll look out for it.' And they would, he thought. As well as asking Tasker's neighbours to confirm its existence. 'But getting back to Eddie Chapman…'

'I don't know. It don't make sense. I mean, how would he know what happened to me? But then, why would he doubt that I'd keep quiet, if it came to it? We was inside together. That forms a bond of sorts. And by implicating him, I'd be implicating myself. Not like Grey. He was never directly involved at our end of things. He could plead ignorance. Say it was all down to Eddie.'

Pete shook his head. 'Not realistically. Someone had to sell those cars. Or, if they were stolen to order, someone had to receive the orders. That would have been Mark Grey, I imagine. Though we've still yet to find the evidence on his computer. Or anywhere else.'

Tasker grunted.

Pete could tell he was starting to tire, but he had just one more question, for now. 'So, you don't know anyone else who was involved in Grey's end of things? The planning. The set-up. The orders and so on.'

He shook his head. 'It was all compartmented. One dealt with one thing, another dealt with another. What you didn't need to know, you weren't told about. Safer that way, isn't it? You lot break the chain somewhere, it's harder to find the other links or, if you do find them, to make anything of it.'

Which all made sense, but… 'You're sure about that?' he pushed. 'You never met anyone, however briefly? Never heard Grey or Chapman mention anyone?'

'No. I just did my bit and minded my own business.'

Pete stared at him for a stretched second. 'We haven't got your phone, but we have got it's records,' he said. 'And we are going through them. If we find you've not told me everything, all deals are off. You realise that, don't you?'

His lips twitched in irritation as his phone buzzed into the quiet between them. He took it out and checked the screen. It was work. He lifted it to his ear. 'Gayle.'

'Boss, it's Jill. We've got a bite.'

'What sort of bite?'

'The Hyundai. It's popped up on ANPR. Well, it's probably hers. On false plates. The real one showed up in Sidmouth.'

'All right. Where?'

'Essex. East-bound on the A12 at Brentwood.'

'Get onto the locals and get it stopped.'

'They're already aware. Searching for it as we speak.'

'OK. Let me know when they find and stop it if I'm not back by then.' He hung up and returned his attention to Derek Tasker. 'Sorry about that. Now, where were we?'

Tasker gave him a sour look. 'I've told you everything I know.'

Pete looked at him, maintaining his silence but Tasker didn't flinch.

'All right,' he said finally. 'Thank you. Again.'

CHAPTER THIRTY-SEVEN

'Eddie. It's good to meet you at last.'

Pete pulled up his chair in the interview room of Exeter police station's custody suite, opposite the man who had arrived from Manchester just twenty minutes ago. Beside him, Dick sat silently waiting just as, beside Chapman, his grey-suited solicitor sat at an angle from the table, clipboard on his knee with a legal pad and pen poised, ready to take notes.

Chapman himself looked exhausted. His curly blond hair was greasy, his chin stubbled, his blue eyes had bags under them and his hands were stuffed into the pockets of the grey tracksuit bottoms he'd been given at Manchester's Longsight Police Station, when his own clothes were taken from him for forensic examination. They were now in the laboratories at Middlemoor, having been sent south with him.

He was trying hard to keep his expression neutral, Pete saw, but it wasn't quite working.

'You don't mind me calling you Eddie, do you? Everyone seems to, as far as I can tell.'

Chapman's lips pushed briefly upward.

'OK,' Pete continued. 'You know why you're here, of course. They'll have told you that up in Manchester. But just to reiterate...' He nodded for Dick to start the recorder. 'Edward Colin Chapman... Was that deliberate, on your parents' part? The link to Colin Chapman, the Lotus boss?'

He grunted. 'Me dad was a fan.'

Pete nodded. 'Right. So, anyway, back to officialdom. Edward Colin Chapman, you're here under arrest on suspicion of involvement in the theft of multiple motor vehicles… No need to go into the full list at the minute… and of handling stolen goods as well as of involvement in the murder of Mark Grey, of whom you're a known associate.'

The murder accusation made him blink. 'Murder? Based on what?' he demanded, frowning.

'This interview is being recorded for evidential purposes,' Pete continued, deliberately ignoring his outburst. 'And, being under arrest, you remain under caution. Do you understand?'

'I don't understand how you can dump a bloody murder charge on me,' he protested. 'I never bloody touched him.'

Pete gave a brief hint of a smile. 'You were there, Eddie. You took him there. We have the evidence to prove that. Mr Palmer here can confirm that. He got here long enough before you did to be able to do his due diligence, seeing as you asked for a solicitor before you left Manchester. Isn't that right, Mr Palmer?'

The solicitor nodded.

'So, let's get on, shall we?' Pete said. 'This is an interview being conducted by myself, being Detective Sergeant Peter Gayle of Devon and Cornwall Police, and my colleague, Detective Constable Richard Feeney with Edward Colin Chapman, in the presence of his appointed solicitor, Mr Palmer, at the Sidmouth Road Police Station in Exeter, Devon.' He gave the date and time. 'Now, we all know you're not a stupid man, Eddie. Quite clever, in fact. Going all the way to Birmingham for a flight. Leaving the car there, so it would be found, confirming you were in the area while, all the time, you were off up to Manchester on public transport for an entirely different flight to an entirely different location. And using what we could easily find out was a favourite destination of yours.' He tipped his head. 'If we hadn't got that all-ports alert out on you when we did, you'd have been free and clear and we'd have had no idea where you were.'

Chapman's nose twitched. 'Didn't work though, did it?'

'Not quite, but it was a damn good try. My question is, why? Why go to all that effort?'

He frowned. 'What do you mean, why? You know why. To get away from you lot.'

'Yes, but an elaborate plan like that took some putting together, didn't it? Some effort. There had to be more than fear of us behind that, surely?'

'Like what?' he demanded with a trace of belligerence.

'I don't know,' Pete said with a shrug. 'Fear of someone else, maybe? The idea that what could happen to one man could happen to another. You.'

'Eh?' His head jerked back with a quick frown. 'What the hell's that mean?'

'I think you know the answer to that, Eddie,' Pete said. 'Anyway, before we start with the questions, here's something else for you to think about. We don't arrest people for no reason. We need reasonable cause. Evidence. Now, most solicitors, no doubt including Mr Palmer here, will advise their clients to go, "No comment," throughout any police interview, on the basis that it's our job to prove you guilty, not yours to prove yourself innocent, so why help us?' He shrugged. 'A perfectly sensible approach in some circumstances. In this case, though, we've already got enough evidence to charge you. So a no comment interview will do you more harm than good when it comes to court. I mean, this interview will be played back for the jury. You sit there and show no recognition of your crimes, no contrition, no apparent conscience… Well, how would you feel, if you were one of them? And from the judge's point of view, the same applies. So your sentence will be that much harsher. That much longer. I know you've been inside before, Eddie. You know what it's like. I dare say, the shorter you can make it, the better you'll like it, eh? So, my advice to you is to talk to us, openly and honestly. Help us make the best of this situation, both for the victim's family and for yourself. Do you understand?'

He pursed his lips and glanced at his solicitor, who was writing furiously. Then, looking back at Pete, he nodded once.

'For the tape?' Pete prompted.

'I understand,' Chapman said.

'Good. So, let's start at the beginning. How did you meet Mark Grey?'

'A job interview,' he said with a shrug. 'He was looking for a lorry driver. I'd got an HGV licence, so I applied.'

'So, for a legitimate job?'

'Yeah.'

'OK. And you got the job. Started working for him. Transporting containers, yes?'

'Yes.'

'And how long had you been doing that when the other part of the job came up? The illegal part.'

He pursed his lips, thinking about whether or not to answer.

'You heard what I said before, Eddie. About evidence. We've got phone records – both yours and Mark Grey's. Plus witness testimony.'

Chapman's lip twitched in what might have been a sneer. Then he sighed. 'A year or so,' he said finally. 'He come to me when I got back from Southampton one night. Said he'd got a side-line in the making. Did I want in?'

'And he explained what the side-line was?'

He nodded. 'It's outline, at least.'

'So, as far as you were concerned, this was Mark Grey's set-up.'

'Yes.'

'No-one else's?'

He shook his head. 'Just Grey.'

'And you agreed to get involved.'

'The money was good. And I needed it, to get a decent place. Get out of the rat-hole I was in. Plus, he didn't give me a lot of choice.'

'What does that mean?'

He shrugged. 'He was on his uppers, he said. Things had stayed tight since after Covid so, if we didn't do this, the firm would go under. I'd be out on my arse. And who else was going to take on an ex-con with no references? Because he said, if I didn't, that's where I'd be.'

Pete's mouth quirked. 'There was a rising demand for drivers after the slump following Brexit and Covid,' he argued. 'Someone would have.'

'A risk, though, weren't it? A risk I didn't need at the time.'

'So you agreed to it. And it was all going well. What happened? What went wrong?'

Another shrug. 'All he said to me was you lot were getting too close, so he was winding it down for a bit.'

'And then what? How did he end up in that container, on his way to Dorset?'

'How would I know? All I knew was there was a container needed shifting. It was on the trailer, ready to go, so…' He shrugged. 'I hooked it up and off I went.'

'So, how did you know about it? Who told you? And how did you know where to take it?' Pete asked patiently.

His brows tightened. 'There was a docket waiting in the cab. I got a text. "Urgent load for transfer. All ready at yard. Will pick you up."'

'Will pick you up? Was that usual? Given that you'd got your own car.'

'No, but I wasn't going to complain, was I? Saves my petrol.'

Pete shrugged. Now he was getting to the nitty-gritty of the case. 'So, who picked you up?'

Chapman's lips pressed together. 'No comment.'

Pete's eyes widened in surprise. 'Really? After all the progress we've made, up to now?'

'My client is quite within his rights to offer no comment,' Palmer said, speaking for the first time during the interview.

Pete ignored him. 'Come on, Eddie. You were doing so well. To throw it all away now, at this stage… Why?'

His eyes narrowed. 'You might be offering me a deal, but I'm still going to do time, ain't I? And I've heard about the Swallows. I don't even have to be in the same clink as Grey's brother-in-law, he can still get to me.'

Pete knew he was referring to the swallow tattoo worn by Adrian Styles and many of his former Royal Marines colleagues. Men who were trained to maim and kill. Men who, in many cases, were in prison because they'd failed to successfully reintegrate into civilian society, for whatever reason. 'So, you weren't as ignorant as you tried to make out,' Pete observed. 'You knew about the history of the whole set-up. That Styles set it up originally and we dismantled it.'

A reaction flickered across his face and was gone. 'After. Later.'

'If you're so worried about Adrian Styles, why talk to us at all?' Pete asked. 'It can't be any better for you, having killed his brother-in-law than it would be telling us about his partner's wife.'

Chapman blinked but said nothing.

'Better, I'd have thought,' Pete continued. 'I mean, if she killed Grey, then helping us prove it would go down nicely with him. A positive move on your part, from his point of view, surely?'

Chapman's lips pressed together. 'No comment.'

Pete drew a deep breath and let it out. 'All right, Eddie. If that's what you want to do. You *will* be charged with Mark Grey's murder. You understand that, don't you?'

He blinked but said nothing.

'We can place you there. In her car, leaving the scene.'

'No comment.'

'And you may have made a neat job of wiping down the cab to make it look like someone else might have nicked the truck, but you missed a bit.'

He gave a quick frown.

Pete tipped his head. 'On the outside of the driver's door,' he said. 'You wiped it down, yes. But *then* you shut it. Remember?' He gave a brief smile. 'So, we've got physical as well as witness evidence. Now, let's revisit, shall we? Who picked you up to take you out to the farm at Sowton?'

His lips tightened. He took a breath. 'No comment.'

Pete sighed. 'OK. Were you aware, when you left there, of where you were going to stop? The lay-by in Dorset.'

'No comment.'

'Were you aware that she was following you in that Hyundai? Was that pre-arranged, to bring you home, having left the truck where you did?'

'No comment.'

'Was he killed there, in the lay-by, or before you arrived at Sowton to pick up the lorry?'

His top lip twitched. 'No comment.'

'If it was the latter, Eddie – if you didn't know he was in there – then you're not guilty of murder. Why would you offer no comment on something that would get you off a murder charge?' Pete demanded.

Chapman waited, maintaining his silence.

'OK. So, logic suggests from that that you were complicit in the killing. And torture. Is that what you were afraid of? That the same might happen to you? Hence the elaborate escape plan?'

The slight sneer that twitched Chapman's lip showed the lie in that.

'No? So, what was it?'

'I told you. I didn't want you lot catching up with me. I didn't want to go back inside.'

Pete tipped his head. 'And yet, here we sit with your clothes in a forensics lab, waiting to be tested for DNA, and your phone already having given us plenty to place you at the crime scene, along with the other evidence I've already mentioned.'

And your question is, detective?' Palmer demanded.

Pete turned to speak to him at last. 'You know as well as I do, Mr Palmer, this is a conversation, not an interrogation. It's an opportunity for your client to help himself. To explain himself. To put his side of the story on record. I'm just trying to help him do that.' He turned back to the fat man. 'So, what's it to be, Eddie?'

Chapman's jaw clenched and released. 'No comment.'

Pete's lips pursed. 'On your head be it, then. We'll just have to see what Katrina Parr – or do you know her as Shehu? – has to say when she gets here from Essex. Shouldn't be long. She's well on the way by now.' He paused for a beat, to see if that would draw a reaction, but it didn't. 'Interview concluded, then,' he said and quoted the time before nodding for Dick to switch off the recorder.

*

'What do you reckon?' Pete asked Dick once they were out of the interview room with the door closed firmly behind them.

'I don't know. Fear of Styles makes no sense, like you said in there. Nor fear of her.'

'And yet, let's be real here. It can't seriously be about him having a crush on her. I mean, what the hell would she see in him?'

Dick shrugged. 'The heart wants what it wants, regardless of logic sometimes. You know that as well as I do.'

'Yeah, in a twelve-year-old. What's he? Forty-two?'

'Some people never grow up. At least not in that sense. We deal with them all the time, one way or another.'

'I know, but...' Pete shook his head. 'It still doesn't compute. Sorry, but... Where is Katrina Parr by now?'

Dick checked his watch. 'She was due to leave Woodham Ferrers at 10:00. It's a good four and a half hours from here, given decent traffic, so...'

'Another hour or so.'

Dick nodded as they reached the custody desk. With no-one waiting to be booked in, Pete stepped straight up to the high counter.

'Can you put Mr Chambers back in his box for a bit, Mandy?' he asked the female desk sergeant. 'And give us a bell in the incident room when our other candidate turns up, will you?'

'Will do.'

As they stepped away from the desk, Pete heard her ask one of her colleagues to see Eddie Chapman back to his cell.

CHAPTER THIRTY-EIGHT

Pete felt his eyes widen as he stepped into the interview room and saw Katrina Parr for the first time. He forced himself not to react further and moved towards his chair, allowing Jane room to come in behind him and close the door.

Katrina was stunning. Even in police issue grey T-shirt and tracksuit bottoms, with no make-up, she looked like a model on the cover of a magazine with her long, artfully waved blonde hair swept clear of a high brow above large brown eyes, a narrow nose and bow-shaped lips.

Pete blinked and sat down across from her, Jane settling beside him.

'Miss Parr,' he said. 'Or can I call you Katrina? I'm DS Gayle. Pete. This is DC Jane Bennett. You must be tired. You've covered a lot of miles in the last few days.'

Her top lip twitched dismissively.

'Are you OK? You don't need a drink – a coffee or anything?'

'No.' And that one word shattered the illusion. Her voice was coarse and scratchy, her accent like something out of an East-end soap opera.

Pete smiled. 'Good. We'll make a start, then.' He nodded to Jane to start the recorder. 'For the sake of formalities, this is an interview being conducted at Sidmouth Road police station in Exeter, Devon, of Katrina Parr by myself, DS Peter Gayle, in the presence of DC Jane Bennett and Miss Parr's solicitor, Martin Driscoll.' He quoted the date and time. 'I'll start by reminding you, Miss Parr, that you're under caution and anything you say can be used in evidence against you. Conversely, I think I should point out that anything you refuse to say can be used in the same way.'

'That's not the way it works, and you know it, Detective,' Driscoll said, his plummy voice in sharp contrast to his client's. 'My client is innocent until proven guilty.'

'And circumstantial evidence is enough to sway the jury, Mr Driscoll, as you also know,' Pete countered. 'I was just making that clear for your client's benefit. A refusal to deny, for example, can be seen as a tacit admission.' He shrugged. 'I'm just saying…'

'Well, please don't, Detective. I must insist that you confine yourself to asking the questions you have and leave it to my client to decide whether and how to answer them.'

Pete turned back to Katrina Parr, rather than pursuing a pointless argument with her well-paid solicitor, who's tactic was obvious. 'So, Katrina, where were you off to with a ticket to Holland and a pair of false number plates, eh? And your daughter left behind with your parents when she should have been at school.'

She let her head tip slightly. 'Holland,' she said with a sarcastic sneer. 'For work.'

'For work? What kind of work would that be, then?' he let his accent deepen, sounding more like a country bumpkin than a city-based detective.

'I'm a dancer.'

His eyebrows rose. 'Really? What sort of dancer?'

'Exotic.'

'Ah. So, you were off to Holland to work as a… Dancer. And that was more important than your little girl's education? Or even being with her?'

Her eyes narrowed. 'No. I was planning to get myself established – settled – then bring her over there. Start a new life. What's wrong with that? People do it all the time.'

'Especially people with something to run away from,' he said.

Her mouth tightened in anger but she didn't respond.

Pete shrugged. 'Why else use false plates on the car and get your parents to book the ferry ticket for you?'

'I told the other lot – I didn't know about the plates on the motor. Somebody must have put 'em on there for a laugh or summat. And my dad booked the ferry 'cause I was busy.'

'Packing?' Pete suggested.

'Yeah.'

'In that much of a hurry, were you? What were you running from? Or who?'

Again, her eyes narrowed. 'I was…' She sighed. 'I was scared. There was stuff going on, stuff I'd got in the middle of, that I wanted out of. Away from.'

'What stuff?'

Her head shook quickly. 'I'd been having a fling. His Mrs found out. She can be a vicious bitch when she wants to be, just like her brother. He's in clink for murder. She was threatening me with the same and I believed her.'

Pete pictured Andrea in her hospital bed. Then in that dark, filthy cupboard. *Really?* he thought. 'So, rather than apologise, try to talk her down or just stay away from them, you packed up and ran? All the way to a foreign country?'

'Where I come from, people say stuff like that, they mean it. And she told me about that kid. In that car, up on the moor. That fire. Said the same would happen to me. And…' her face began to screw up in the first sign he'd seen of actual emotion from her. 'And to Evie,' she finished in a choked voice. Then she fixed him with those big, brown eyes again. 'I weren't going to let that happen. So, yeah, I ran for the hills.'

Pete let a grin flash across his mouth. 'Not the best destination for hills,' he said. 'Holland.'

Her eyes flashed with annoyance.

'Sorry,' he said. 'So, this male that you were… involved with… how did you meet?'

'He was a mate of my husband's. My *late* husband,' she added with a sneer. 'But you'd know all about that, wouldn't you? Being as you lot killed him.'

Pete blinked. 'I wasn't there when Alexander Shehu died, Katrina, but I do know we didn't kill him. Not willingly, at least. We wanted to talk to him, but he gave us no choice. Came out of the house firing a weapon. There was no other way for our officers to respond.'

'Yeah, right,' she sneered.

'I know the man who was in charge of that operation,' Pete told her. 'He wouldn't allow his men to fire without good, solid reason. But you were telling us about Mark Grey. He was a friend of Alexander's?'

'Yeah. So, when Alex was killed, him and his Mrs, Andrea, they stepped up. Helped me out. Especially when you took the house and everything else off me, as well as Alex,' she added bitterly. 'Fucking proceeds of crime, they said. As if me and Evie knew anything about that. Bastards.'

Pete rocked his head. 'Some people are all about the technicalities, not the realities,' he said. 'I know there was never any evidence you were involved in what Alex and Adrian Styles were up to.'

'Too fucking right, there weren't.' Her eyes flashed with anger. 'Didn't stop 'em, though, did it? Chucked us out on our ears. Uprooted little Evie. An innocent little kid. Had to start again from scratch, we did.'

'But you managed,' he said. 'Between getting a council house – you were lucky there, I can tell you – Mark Grey's help, as you said, and your own strength and resourcefulness, you made it.'

Her lip twitched in what might have been a sneer.

'But… Are you saying you had to pay for his help in kind?' Jane asked.

Her eyes flashed. 'I'm not a fucking slag.'

Jane shook her head. 'I didn't mean willingly.'

Katrina grunted.

'You said Mark and Andrea helped you,' Pete said. 'In what ways?'

She shrugged. 'Friendship. Moral support,' she said, flashing a glare at Jane. 'I spent time with them. *We* did. They even took us in for a while. Took a real shine to Evie. She was a sweet little kid. Still is.'

'And the thing with Mark grew out of that?' he suggested.

She shrugged.

'And what about the cars? How did that come about?'

A frown snatched her well-sculpted brows together.

'Was it a purely financial thing?' he persisted. 'You needed the money? We know Mark's business was struggling at the time. We've got his financial records. So, who's plan was it? His or yours?'

'Dunno what you're on about.'

Pete drew back in his chair. 'Oh, come on, Katrina. You've already said you knew about the MG. About Ewan Price.'

'I said they told me what happened to him.'

'And Mark helping you out was more than just with a moral type of support, wasn't it? He was transferring money into your account on a regular basis, this last couple of years. As I said, we've got his records.'

'Don't mean I knew where it came from, does it?'

'What, you thought it was just a good-will gesture, did you? That amount?' He shook his head. 'I don't believe that any more than you do, Katrina. Any more than a jury will.'

'You can't predict what a jury will think, any more than the rest of us, Detective,' the solicitor broke in. 'They're notorious for being unpredictable.'

'But most of them have at least some common sense, Mr Driscoll. So, what about it, Katrina? Whose idea was it to resurrect the car theft ring? Yours or Mark's? Or was it a joint enterprise?'

'I didn't know nothing about it. Not until near the end, when it started falling apart. He told me what he'd been doing. That you lot were onto it. Getting close so he was having to close it down for a bit, let it cool off, so the money would have to stop.'

'So, you did know where it was coming from,' Jane said.

'I knew who; not where or what from.'

'What, you didn't ask?'

She blinked. 'I asked if he was sure he could afford it. He said yes.'

'So, if you knew about it, why didn't you report it?'

Her expression tightened. 'I just said – he told me you already knew. And he could be a scary sod when he wanted to be. I was scared of him, all right?'

'So, when the time came – or the opportunity – you took it,' Pete said. 'Got in first. Hit him before he could hit you. Is that right?'

'What?' she demanded with a frown.

Pete spread his hands. 'The money was drying up. Your safety was at risk. You saw a chance and you took it.'

'What are you on about?'

He sat forward, arms on the table between them, his gaze trapping hers, locking onto it. 'What I'm on about is what happened to Mark Grey, Katrina. Your cut of the proceeds was about to dry up, so you decided to snatch the whole cake, instead of just your slice of it, and to hell with Mark and Andrea Grey – literally, in his case, before you'd finished with him, eh?'

She was frowning deeply by now. 'What the fuck are you trying to stitch me up with here?'

'We're not trying to stitch you up with anything, Katrina. We've got witnesses as well as evidence. The fingerprint you left on his wallet, for instance.' He sat back in his chair.

'Whose wallet?' she demanded.

'Of course, we've got Eddie, too,' he said instead of answering. 'He's in a cell here. I spoke to him earlier. Poor, soppy sod. Recent conquest, was he?'

'Eddie? Eddie who?'

Pete drew his head back at that. 'Eddie who? Eddie Chapman, Katrina. The man you were seen with, leaving the scene where Mark Grey's body was found. That Eddie.'

'What the fuck? Marks…' She stopped.

'The good news is, Andrea's still alive,' Pete told her.

She shook her head. 'Hold on. Wait a minute. You said Mark's body. He's dead?'

Pete pressed his lips together, saying nothing.

'Mark's dead?' she repeated. 'How? When?'

He tipped his head. 'Really? That's the way you want to play this, is it? Didn't I mention, we've got witnesses?' He turned to Jane. 'I said that, didn't I?'

'You did,' she confirmed. 'Including Eddie Chapman.'

He nodded. 'I thought so.' He turned back to Katrina. 'So, in this case, ignorance is not bliss, and the pretence of it can't work.'

'Look, I never had nothing to do with that. How could I? When did he die?'

'Early hours of Thursday morning, according to the post-mortem report,' he said. 'In the container you were seen leaving in that lay-by in Dorset. And now we've got your vehicle and its contents, it's only a matter of time before we find that card you took from him. From his wallet which, as I said before, has a nice clear fingerprint on it. A female one,' he emphasised.

'Well, it ain't mine,' she declared. 'No way. I weren't there.'

Pete shook his head sadly. 'You're not listening, Katrina.'

'And neither are you, Detective,' the solicitor broke in. 'My client has said she wasn't there.'

Pete ignored him, focussing on the woman in front of him. 'You were seen. With Eddie. In your Hyundai. At the scene. We've got the car. We will extract the tracking data from it.'

'Well, that'll prove it then, won't it?'

'Exactly.'

'That I weren't there.'

Again, Pete shook his head, this time exasperated. 'How much evidence to you imagine we need, Katrina? Modern cars have satnav capability, GPS tracking. They're more exact than phones. And there's only one place that bank card can have come from when we find it. Plus your fingerprint.'

'It ain't my print. It weren't my car. I ain't got no bank card.' She frowned quickly. 'What the fuck would I want with a bank card when I was trying to disappear? Cash, that's what I was going to be using for the next few weeks, until I could get set up right.'

'Few weeks?' Pete demanded. 'How were you hoping to pull that off, in a foreign country?'

'I still got some of Alex's connections. Family and that. They'd have helped.'

'So, you were running.'

'Yes, I was running. But not from you lot, *Detective*.' She put a heavy, sarcastic emphasis on the title. 'I was running from the person who was behind all this. The person who set it all up. Who benefited from the whole thing. And I was right, weren't I? If it's true that Mark's dead, that proves it.'

'So, who is this mystery person?' Pete asked, not believing a word of it.

'Who do you think? Whose brother set the whole thing up last time, with my husband as the front-man? Andrea bloody Grey, that's who.'

He frowned, head shaking in disbelief. 'Andrea Grey is another victim in all this,' he said. 'We found her. As I said, fortunately alive.'

'Well, she's fooled you, then, ain't she?'

Jane leaned forward. 'Have you got any evidence of this?' she asked. 'Can you prove it?'

'No, but you can. If you bother to look.'

'How?'

'What, you want me to do your job for you now? You're bloody joking, ain't you?'

'If what you say is true, then it's to your benefit,' Jane argued.

'Yeah, if I want to be on the run for the rest of me life,' she sneered. 'I ain't that stupid.'

'You were willing to do just that a few hours ago,' Pete said. 'In fact, that's exactly what you were doing.'

She grunted. 'Well, I ain't saying no more. Do your jobs. If you're able. If you can be bothered.'

She sat back, folding her arms resolutely.

*

'Do you believe her?' Jane asked when they were out of the room, heading for the custody desk.

Pete felt a flash of déjà vu, except last time it had been Dick Feeney asking the question. He drew a breath. 'We can't dismiss it out of hand. We need to find out, one way or the other.'

'How?'

'The data from the car. Forensics. That fingerprint. She was willing to provide hers, to prove the point, which says a lot.'

'Yeah. Assuming she knows what they mean.'

He smiled briefly. 'She's a lot of things, but I don't think stupid is one of them. Not *that* stupid, anyway.'

'So...'

'We run the print. We check the car. Those false plates it was wearing: the tape on the back of them would have DNA, I'd have thought.'

Essex police had sent the overlay plates, still attached to the real ones, along with the Hyundai to the forensics section at Middlemoor.

They'd found that they were not false plates as such, but laminated overlays that had been fixed over the real plates with double-sided tape, holes cut in them to allow the screws fixing the real plates to the car to show through as normal.

A careful job that would have taken some time and care.

'Yes, but all that takes time,' Jane said. 'And how long have we got her in custody for?'

Pete blinked. 'She's a proven flight risk, arrested in connection with a murder. They can't bail her.'

'And we can't charge her until we get those results back,' she countered.

'Or other evidence. It looks like it's time for another chat with Andrea, doesn't it?'

CHAPTER THIRTY-NINE

Pete went alone to the Royal Devon and Exeter Hospital, leaving Jane to go and speak to DI Colin Underhill about what they'd discovered from Katrina Parr. He called ahead and made sure that the guard – who turned out to be Diane Collins again – would turn on her body-worn camera when he arrived and, on the way down the ward towards Andrea's room, he took out his phone, set it to voice recording mode and held it to his ear as he knocked and entered the private room.

Lowering the phone, he kept it in his hand as he shut the door and nodded to Diane. 'PC Collins,' he said. 'Your turn again?' He reached up with his free hand to touch his lapel, in the place where her camera was clipped to her uniform, an eyebrow raised in query.

She nodded. 'Sarge.'

He turned to Andrea, the physical contrast between her and Katrina Parr more striking than ever. She was several inches shorter. Where Katrina was curvy, she was slender. Her hair was dark, almost straight, and much shorter than the other woman's flowing locks and her face, though pretty in its own way, was pale against Katrina's tan. 'How are you feeling today, Andrea? Getting stronger?'

She tipped her head. 'A bit better each day.'

'Good,' he said, nodding as he drew up a chair and set his phone on the combined wardrobe and cupboard at her bedside. 'Good. I thought I'd come and see you this afternoon because we've got some news.'

'Yes?' she shifted in the bed, sitting up a little straighter.

'We've got Eddie Chapman and Katrina Parr in custody. They were both caught fleeing the country.'

'Wow.' Her eyes widened. 'Both of them?'

He nodded. 'Yes, so I wanted to let you know that and see if you've remembered any more about what happened to you.'

She shook her head. 'No. Sorry. I wish I could, but it's all…' She grimaced. 'It's like a dream. Like it happened, but distantly somehow, you know?'

'Yes, I think I know what you mean.' He gave her a brief smile. 'I've been in a scrape or two myself. The trouble is, there's some things in what they're saying and some things in what you've said that don't add up. Don't make sense. With what you've gone through, you'd be confused, of course. That's only to be expected. But… I need to understand everything clearly to be able to charge them with what they've done, you see? The Crown Prosecution Service want certainty before they'll move forward and we don't want them getting away with anything, do we?'

'No.' Her eyes widened as she said it. 'Definitely not.'

'So, with that in mind, I need to go over everything again with you, but officially. And for that, I've got to remind you before we start of the police caution. Which is that you don't have to say anything, but it may harm your defence if you do not mention, when questioned, something which you later rely on in Court. Anything you do say may be given in evidence. OK?'

'What, so I'm under arrest now? What for?'

He smiled and shook his head. 'I don't see a need to arrest you. It's not like you're going to run off anywhere, is it? No, as I said, it's just a matter of keeping things above-board. To obtain evidence by way of questioning is the official quote, isn't it, Diane?'

'That's right, Sarge.'

'So, now that's out of the way,' he said, turning back to Andrea. 'There's a few things to go over.'

'Like what?' she asked with a frown.

'Well, firstly, the Hyundai.'

'What, Kat's?'

He shook his head. 'No, the one that looks like it – same model and colour – that you hired for three days last week.'

She blinked, the rest of her face – her whole body – remaining stock-still.

'What was that in aid of?' he asked.

She still didn't respond.

'It seems like the aim was to deliberately set up Katrina for Mark's death. We checked the mileage on it. And the number plates. Filthy with all the dirt that's stuck to the residue of that tape that you stuck laminated copies of Katrina's plates over them with. We'll get the GPS data from it tomorrow, to confirm what we know from the mileage and witness testimony. Katrina said you'd found out about their affair. That you'd threatened her and her daughter. You really did a job on them, didn't you? Her and Mark. Tortured him to death and set her up as a patsy for it. And poor old Eddie Chapman, trailing along like a love-sick puppy. Did he know what you were up to in that trailer?'

Her expression had been growing steadily more bitter, rage-filled and hateful as he spoke. 'Course not,' she said with a sneer. 'He never went in there. Just hooked it up and drove off like always.'

'So, Mark was already dead? And you just followed Eddie to bring him home, so he could collect his stuff and run?'

Her top lip twitched in affirmation.

'OK,' he said. 'And the card from his wallet. Clearly, Katrina hadn't got it, so why even admit to its existence when I asked about it?'

'Well, it was obvious, wasn't it? There had to have been something there. And he might have given her a card of some sort, for all I knew.'

'So, what was it? And where is it?'

Her head twitched. 'No comment, officer. That's what they say, isn't it?'

Pete tipped his head. 'No doubt we'll find it, eventually. Like we've found a lot of other things. The memory on the printer you used to make the false number plate overlays, for instance.'

She frowned.

'What, you didn't know they had a memory of their own? Yes,' he nodded. 'Not all of them but a lot do. And the missing phones. Mark's. Yours. Derek Tasker's. All neatly disassembled, of course, but with fingerprints on the batteries and SIMs. All in a nice, neat package in the bin outside Eddie Chapman's place, where he dumped them before he hit the road north.' He flashed her a smile. 'In too much of a hurry to get away, I suppose, eh? Of course, we haven't had time to check the prints yet, but they're small. Feminine. Are they yours, Andrea?'

'I'm saying nothing.'

This time, his smile was more pronounced. 'That's OK. The evidence will speak for you. The thing is, why now, all of a sudden? I mean, you'd known about Mark and Katrina for a while, hadn't you?'

'I told you: I'm saying nothing.'

'Was it the fact that we were closing in on Mark's operation? You needed to cash in while you could? Before it was too late? Take the money and run?'

She stared at him, her eyes narrowed. 'I earned it,' she said at last. 'It was mine to take, after what they done to me. And the scheme was Ade's in the first place, not theirs. They nicked that, just like they nicked them motors.'

'What, Katrina was in on it, was she?'

'Course she was. Him and her set it up together. Her idea. Thought she was owed after your lot took everything from her, didn't she? And he went along with it. He had the connections to offload 'em. Sell 'em. And the lorries to take them overseas in. The drivers to do it. Well, one, anyway.'

'Eddie.'

She nodded.

'Who you'd met. And who took a shine to you.'

'Yeah,' she said with a sneer. 'I asked him to do something once: he couldn't do it quick enough. So, I knew, when the time come, I could use him.'

Pete nodded. Did this woman's manipulative heartlessness know no bounds? 'So, did he help you when you got back from Dorset? Tie you up because you asked him to?'

'No,' she said with a sneer. 'Less he knew about what I was doing, the better. I did that myself.'

'How?' he asked, genuinely wanting the answer.

'There was a plunger under the sink. I wrapped the tape around it, sticky side out. Knelt down with it between my ankles and...' She lifted her hands, clasped together, and waved them in circles.

'Then put the plunger back where we found it, taped your feet and hopped into the cupboard?' he demanded incredulously.

She nodded. 'Shut it with my mouth on the latch.'

Pete shook his head.

'I been in worse places in my life,' she said. 'And for just as long, or longer. Me an' Ade, we didn't have a nurturing childhood.'

Pete grimaced, not wanting to think about what she was suggesting. 'Your parents are both dead now, though, right?'

She gave a slow nod.

Again, he didn't want to think about what that might mean. 'But... How long would you have waited in there?'

She shrugged. 'Not much longer, I expect, but... I'd have busted out of there and made like I'd escaped somehow. There was knives and such, I could have cut the tape if it come to it. Left it there as evidence.'

'And all to get revenge on your husband and his girlfriend.'

Her face twisted. 'Who'd come into our house as a poor, pathetic victim and lured him away like the whore she is.'

Pete tipped his head. 'Still... Harsh is an understatement here, isn't it? Eighty-six cuts, in total.' He shook his head. 'OK, a few of them no doubt when you were cutting his clothes off, but... What was the circumcision about?'

Her mouth pushed up. 'I wanted to chop it off completely, but he'd have bled out, wouldn't he? Too easy for him. And too messy. I had overalls on, and bags over my shoes, but still...'

'Yes, the pathologist found the killing wound amongst all the others. Well-hidden, but it was obvious at the post-mortem. Not that I was able to attend that. Too busy elsewhere. But the doctor was impressed. Using the sternum as a fulcrum to lever the blade across inside him. Took the top off his heart like a boiled egg, he said. And very little blood loss externally because of the depth and the downward angle of the wound, going in between the second and third ribs. Where'd you learn a thing like that?'

'From Ade. He told me about it years ago, when he was in the Marines.'

'But you just said you didn't want him to bleed out. Not quick, anyway.'

Her lips twitched in a sneer. 'Yeah, but he'd passed out by then, hadn't he? After I neutered him. No point carrying on when he couldn't feel anything. And I had to make sure, didn't I?'

Pete pursed his lips. 'So, what happened to the overalls and the bags on your shoes?'

'Burned 'em.'

Pete remembered the incinerator at the farm, blackened and almost burned through in places from long and sustained use, though there had been nothing of evidential value in it. 'And the knife? Must have been a carving knife, from what the pathologist said.'

She gave a tiny nod. 'Back where it belongs, isn't it? With the rest of the set.'

'What – in your kitchen?'

She shrugged. 'Look odd for it to be missing, wouldn't it?'

'And what about the blonde wig and the number-plate covers from the hire car? What did you do with those?'

'Binned 'em in town before I took the car back. Hotel on Queen Street.' She gave a hint of a smile. 'They'll be long gone by now.'

He nodded and paused for a moment to let his brain absorb all he'd heard. Then he locked his gaze onto hers again, still amazed at how she'd fooled him when he'd spoken to her before. How real her tears had been for the loss of the husband who she'd not just murdered, but tortured to death. 'What about poor little Evie? What happens to her after all this?'

She frowned. 'What about her? I was never going to do her any harm.'

'Except to put her mother in jail for twenty years, for something she hadn't done.'

'For something she *had* done,' she declared, brown eyes flashing. 'Theft. Of the worst kind. Of my husband.'

Pete paused again, lips tight. 'I think we'd best leave it there for now,' he said. 'And on the strength of what you've said, I am now arresting you on suspicion of the murder of Mark Grey. There will be other charges added to that, but…'

She grinned. 'Good luck proving any of it.'

Pete shook his head and picked up his phone. 'You were under caution, Andrea. What we've said has all been recorded on here and on PC Collins' body-worn camera.'

She jerked up in the bed, a snarl twisting her features. 'Fuck you, bastard!' She fell back, too weak to maintain the posture. 'That'll never stand up in court. Never *get* to court. It'll be thrown out. You're not allowed to record somebody without their knowledge or consent.'

Pete shook his head. 'You were under caution, remember. And police body-worn cameras are common knowledge. Well-publicised. Plus, there's all the forensic evidence to support your freely-given statement. Rest easy, Andrea. You won't be going anywhere for a while. For a long while. Except prison, of course. And the court.'

CHAPTER FORTY

It was two days later and they were waiting for the last of the forensic results to come through when Pete's radio, on the desk beside his computer monitor, hissed and a familiar voice came through.

'SG-one for DS Gayle.'

He reached for the radio and keyed the mike. SG-one was the police guard with Derek Tasker. And at this moment, that role was evidently being fulfilled by Bernie Douglas. 'Go ahead, SG-one.'

'Subject has further info for you, Sarge.'

'On the way.'

'Has he remembered something or is his conscience pricking him hard enough to admit something he hadn't before?' Dave posed as Pete stood up, hooked his jacket off the back of his chair and shrugged into it.

'Patience is a virtue,' Pete reminded him as he picked up his radio and mobile phone.

Jill chuckled. 'Yeah, but not one of Dave's.'

'What's that mean?' Dave demanded.

'Wait and you'll find out,' Pete said before a long discussion could get started, distracting them from the work that was still on-going to string together the locations and time-line of contacts from the phone data they'd accumulated from the suspects in the case.

It took him no more than a few minutes to get to the hospital and the ward where Derek Tasker was still recovering from his injuries. He nodded to the dark-uniformed sister at the nurses' station and knocked on the door of Tasker's room before stepping inside.

'Bernie,' he said, nodding to the tall, rangy, black-uniformed blonde. 'Derek. How are you doing?'

'Still sore, but the tablets are helping more than they were,' Tasker said. 'I remembered something. We were watching a bit of telly... Well, I was. And it triggered it. Like a flash in my brain. An image, clear as day. Well, night, with street-lights.'

'Yes?'

'I was up on that bridge. I asked Grey why we were meeting there. He said it was half-way. Which it is, pretty much, I suppose,' he added with a shrug that caused him to wince. He let the air hiss out of his lungs and drew in a breath. 'Anyway, he said something about having some bad news and then the passenger door of his truck opened... We was both stood outside it, by the railing... And out steps the woman.' He blinked. 'I'd never seen her before. "Who's this?" I says. "My better half," he says. "She knows about what we've been doing. The cars." Well, I went to shake her hand, say hello, and next thing I know, there's this pain – agony, really – in the side of my head and a punch to my back and everything's all spinning and tipping and it seemed like there's hands all over me and... I blacked out.'

'Well... What did she look like, this woman?' Pete asked.

'Smallish. Dark hair. Slim. No glamour-puss, but pretty, I suppose.'

Pete nodded and took out his phone. Opened up the picture folder and scrolled through. 'Is this her?' he asked, presenting the phone for Tasker to see.

His eyes flashed. 'Yes, that's her. Is she his wife?'

Pete nodded. 'She is. Was.'

'Have you found out who killed him yet?'

He nodded again. 'We're just putting the final pieces into the puzzle now. Then we'll be laying charges. About the only thing still outstanding is your bike.'

His mouth twitched in a grimace. 'That's long gone, isn't it? University town. It'll have been resprayed and sold, won't it? Or just parked up amongst a load of others if it wasn't dumped in a hedge somewhere.'

Pete nodded. 'I expect you're right. We have put a description out there, with a photo that we found on your phone.'

'You've got my phone?'

'Yes. It's one of several we're going through for evidence on the car-theft ring.'

His lips pursed. 'Yeah, well… That is what it is, ain't it? At least you've got it. And all the photos on it. They won't be lost.'

'True. But you know you're probably going to do time for involvement in the car thefts, if nothing else, don't you?'

He tipped his head in a shrug. 'But that's just time. That phone's memories.'

'Then I'd suggest you download them and keep them safe somewhere,' Pete said. 'When you get the chance.'

*

Two hours later, with all the DNA and fingerprint evidence in hand, he went round to the custody suite. He started with Katrina Parr. Opening her cell, he stepped inside as she looked up from the bunk across the far end of the small space.

'Katrina. I'm here to tell you, you're being released. Andrea maintains you were involved in the car theft ring. That it was your idea, in fact. But we can't prove that. Whether she's lying, which wouldn't surprise me, or whether you were just very clever about how you handled it, which wouldn't surprise me either, I can't prove. So, you will be charged with the driving offences you committed on your way from here towards Harwich and then you'll be bailed. Without your passport and under strict conditions. Do you understand?'

'What conditions?' she demanded, swinging her feet to the floor.

'The custody sergeant will go through all that with you.' He extended a hand towards the door. 'Come on. Let's go.'

'Let's go? Is that it?' she demanded, frowning. 'No apology for false arrest? For keeping me here for days, away from my kid, without any evidence?'

'I wouldn't push my luck in your circumstances, Katrina,' he said. 'There is also the opportunity for child neglect charges, if we chose to pursue them. Or if the Met did, as that's where you left her.'

'Yeah, safe with my parents,' she retorted with a sneer.

'Not the point,' Pete told her. 'Are you coming or do you want to stay?'

She stood up and flounced towards him. 'No, I bloody don't. And screw you, Mr bloody Copper.'

Once she was processed out and had left the building, he went to Eddie Chapman's cell. Once again, he stepped inside. 'Eddie,' he said. 'We've collected all the evidence in this case and the CPS have decided on the charges to be laid against you. Come with me to the custody desk and we'll get you processed.'

Chapman blinked dully up at him from the bunk at the far end of the cell. 'I'm going to prison?' he asked.

Pete tipped his head in a beckoning gesture. 'Come on.'

He led the fat man to the custody desk and stood beside him. 'Eddie Chapman, Terry,' he said to the duty sergeant. 'Ready for his charges.'

'Right.' He tapped a few keys on his computer and looked up past the screen at the blond man facing him at the window. 'Edward Colin Chapman, you're charged with the offences of conspiracy to take a vehicle without the owner's consent, being the Volvo V90 belonging to Mr Samuel Lockwood of Whitehorn Lane, Pennsylvania, Exeter, and conspiracy to take a vehicle without the owner's consent, being the Jaguar S-Type belonging to Mr Alan Jackson of Dunrich Close, Exeter. You are further charged with handling stolen goods, being those same vehicles, and transporting them across an international boundary with the intent to illegally dispose of them. Have you got anything you want to say to those charges?'

Chapman shook his head.

The sergeant waited a beat, then continued. 'In that case, you will be bailed to appear before the court at its convenience, under the conditions that you will surrender your passport with immediate effect – I see it's amongst your possessions that we're holding here – and that you will not leave the city of Exeter and also that you will attend this police station twice a week until the date set by the court for your hearing. Do you understand those conditions?'

He nodded.

'Good. Right.' He turned to his colleague. 'Dan, get Mr Chapman his belongings, will you? Without the passport.'

*

Chapman had been gone no more than an hour when Pete's desk phone rang – an internal call. He picked it up. 'DS Gayle.'

'Pete, it's Terry in Custody. We've got your latest flame down here, fresh from the RDE.'

'Excellent. I'm on the way.' On the basis of the forensic discoveries that had been reported earlier, he'd been onto the CPS for a charging decision on Andrea Grey.

He put the phone down and stood up.

'At least you're keeping fit,' Jane said. 'What is it now?'

'Andrea's arrived.'

'Ooh. Can I come?'

He smiled. 'Have you got nothing better to do?'

'Else, yes. Better…' She shook her head. 'There's few things in life better than seeing an evil individual like her banged up solidly in a cell.'

'True,' he admitted. 'But we shouldn't crowd the place. Unless she puts up a fight. Then I'll give you a shout.'

She sighed. 'OK. I'll be ready and waiting.'

He grinned and headed around to the custody suite, where he found Andrea Grey standing at the desk, flanked by a male and a female uniformed officer from Bernie Douglas' team. 'Doctors released her, then?' he said.

The young male officer nodded. 'Yes, Sarge.'

'Excellent. Good to see you've recovered from your ordeal, Andrea,' he said. 'So, now you're here, we'll make things official. Sergeant Phelps, you've got the charges.'

Terry nodded. 'I have indeed. Andrea Grey, you are charged with the premeditated murder of your husband, Mark Grey.'

'On a trumped-up confession that won't last ten seconds with a judge,' she snapped. 'You've got no other evidence.'

'We've got more than enough other evidence,' Pete told her. 'Including this.' He took a clear plastic evidence bag from his jacket pocket and held it up. 'The cash card that you took from your husband's wallet in that container where you killed him. With your DNA as well as his on it. We found it tucked into the slit in the underside of the driver's seat in the Range Rover, where you hid it. And, again, DNA confirms that you put it there, not Mark. So the forty-five thousand pounds that's on it will be confiscated as proceeds of crime.'

Her teeth were bared in a snarl as she struggled against the two officers holding her upper arms in an attempt to get at him. When she couldn't, she spat at him. 'Bastard! I'll fucking have you for this. And if I don't, Ade will, when he gets out. Or before that, if he sends someone else. You better keep one eye open twenty-four-seven from now on, I'm telling you. You're marked, you are. Marked for death. You and your family.' She fought free of the officers pushing her head downward so that she couldn't spit at him again and did exactly that, but missed, as far as Pete could tell.

'You're not the first to threaten me by a long way, Andrea,' he said. 'Worse than you have been there before. And they're dead, not me.'

As the female constable drew a spit hood over Andrea Grey's head, Pete took out his handkerchief and wiped the spittle from his suit jacket where it had landed on her first attempt.

Terry waited until she was under control, the female officer gripping both her upper arms firmly from behind. When she was still and seemingly calm again, he continued. 'You are further charged with grievous bodily harm with intent and conspiracy to commit grievous bodily harm with intent, in relation to the attempted murder of Derek Tasker on the Tithebarn Way bridge over the M5 motorway. Do you wish to respond to these charges?'

She shook her head. 'What?'

'Didn't we tell you?' Pete said. 'Derek survived. He will be able and very willing to testify to what happened to him.'

Her lip curled in a snarl within the semi-transparent hood. 'Fuck you.'

Pete shook his head. 'No, thanks, Andrea. We're way past that.'

She sneered. 'It wasn't an offer.'

'I'll take that as a no, then,' Terry said. 'Take her to her cell, please.'

The two officers manoeuvred her away from the desk.

'You all right?' Terry asked as she was led away to the cells.

'Yeah,' Pete said, though in truth, her words were less water off a duck's back than he'd pretended. The thought of unknown people hunting him – and more particularly, endangering his family – was the stuff of nightmares. Truly, viscerally, horrifying. And Andrea Grey was the type who would hold the grudge and pursue it.

He headed back around to the other wing of the station and opened the incident room door just far enough to stick his head through the gap. 'Jane,' he called.

She looked up.

He tipped his head in a beckoning gesture. 'You were so keen, you can come with me.'

Her eyebrow shot up even as she reached for the off-switch on her computer screen. 'Where to?' she asked as she rose from her seat but he ducked back out and waited for her in the corridor.

'Not to see Andrea Grey,' he said when she emerged.

'Oh? Who, then?'

'Time we visited Ewan Price's mum. And after that, the other victims' families.'

She grimaced. 'Yeah, I suppose. At least, this end of the case – telling them we've made an arrest – is better than giving death notifications.'

'Although, in this case, it's not the arrests that'll interest them, seeing that the actual killers, apart from Mark Grey's, are dead themselves.'

She shrugged. 'Natural justice?'

He allowed himself a brief smile as they reached the back door and stepped out into the sunshine. 'Cheaper than our version, I suppose. And, in this case, a damn site quicker.'

'Yeah, but is it as satisfying?'

This time his smile was fuller. 'For the victims' families, or for us?'

'Hmm. Not always the same, is it?' she admitted.

'No,' he said. 'But that's probably because we don't usually know the victims. So, for us, it's a puzzle solved. A victory gained. But for them, it's still a loved one lost and our victory can't ever change that. Any more than natural justice can.'

'True,' she said as he took out his remote and pressed it, the Mondeo's indicators blinking in response. 'But at least we make the world a bit safer in the process.'

THE END

ACKNOWLEDGEMENTS

My thanks are due to Miriam Covill for showing me some of the locations featured in this story and for her unwavering encouragement. I would also like to thank Andrew Taylor of Powerpark Recovery, Jason Hawkes of Drayton School, Christine and Richard Ell, and Russell Feltham and others on the Exeter Past and Present Facebook page for their contributions to the research. And, as ever, my eternal gratitude and appreciation go to my partner in crime (fiction) and all else, without whom I simply couldn't do it; Pru.

AUTHOR'S NOTE

I hope you enjoyed this book. If so, please do go to whichever platform you purchased it through and leave a review to help other readers make an informed buying decision.

https://www.amazon.co.uk/JackSlater/e/B003X8IMEC/ref=dp_byline_cont_ebooks_1

https://www.kobo.com/gb/en/search?query=jack%20slater&fcsearchfield=Author

https://www.barnesandnoble.com/s/jack%20slater/_/N-8qa

If you have any other comments or observations on the books, you can contact the author on jackslaterauthor@mail.com or see the website https://jackslaterauthor.site123.me He can also be found on Facebook: https://www.facebook.com/crimewriter2016 where you will find the latest updates on his writing and lots of other relevant content.

Pete and the team will be back soon with another case to solve in Book 16 of the series.

ABOUT THE AUTHOR

Raised in a farming family in Northamptonshire, England, Jack Slater had a varied career before settling in biomedical science. He has worked in farming, forestry, factories and shops as well as spending five years as a service engineer.
Widowed by cancer at 33, he remarried in 2013, in the Channel Islands, where he worked for several months through the summer of 2012.
He has been writing since childhood, in both fiction and non-fiction. *No Limit To Evil* is the fifteenth crime novel in the chart-topping DS Peter Gayle mystery series.

Other books by the same author:

Nowhere to Run (DS Peter Gayle crime thrillers, Book 1)

A missing child. A dead body. A killer on the loose.
Returning to Exeter CID after his son's unsolved disappearance
Detective Sergeant Peter Gayle's first day back was supposed to be
gentle. Until a young girl is reported missing and the clock begins to
tick.

Rosie Whitlock has been abducted from outside her school that
morning. There are no clues, but Peter isn't letting another child
disappear.

When the body of another young victim appears, the hunt escalates.
Someone is abducting young girls and now they have a murderer on
their hands. Time is running out for Rosie, but when evidence in the
case relating to his own son's disappearance is discovered the stakes
are even higher…

No Place to Hide (DS Peter Gayle crime thrillers, Book 2)

A house fire. A suspicious death. A serial killer to catch.
When a body is found in a house fire DS Peter Gayle is called to the
scene. It looks like an accidental death, but the evidence just doesn't
add up.

With only one murder victim they can't make any calls, but it looks
like a serial killer is operating in Exeter and it's up to Pete to track
him down.

But with his wife still desperate for news on their missing son and
his boss watching his every move, the pressure is on for Pete to bring
the murderer to justice before it is too late.

No Way Home (DS Peter Gayle crime thrillers, Book 3)

A dead body. A mysterious murder. A serial killer on the loose.

A taxi driver is found murdered in a remote part of Exeter. He is a family man, no enemies to be found. There is no physical evidence, except for dozens of fingerprints inside the cab. How will DS Peter Gayle ever track down his killer?

Then another cab driver is found dead. Now this isn't just a case of one murder but a serial killer on the loose, once again…

No Going Back (DS Peter Gayle crime thrillers, Book 4)

A gruesome find on a woodland walk. A body posed and naked, the killing savage and frenzied. Was the victim known to her attacker? Or is a serial killer emerging in South Devon? With no clues at the scene, DS Pete Gayle and his team must identify the victim before they can even start looking for a suspect.

No Middle Ground (DS Peter Gayle crime thrillers, Book 5)

A missing father. A desperate daughter. A terrible discovery.
A new case is the last thing DS Pete Gayle needs right now, but when it falls right into his lap, he has no choice. Justice is crying out to be served. With a career-making trial about to begin and his son in imminent danger from a pair of psychopathic brothers, Pete goes on the hunt in what could turn out to be the biggest case of his life.

No Safe Place (DS Peter Gayle crime thrillers, Book 6)

His young son is recently dead, his traumatised daughter is going through hell and his station chief is out for his blood – or at least his career – when DS Pete Gayle is called to a murder scene on a residential street in Exeter.
A body has been found, horrifically tortured and left outside a women's refuge. She is quickly identified as a resident, the victim of domestic abuse.
But the obvious suspect was three hundred miles away, so who did this? And why?
Haven't these women been through enough?
Touched by the plight and the resilience of the shelter's residents,

Pete must track down a vicious and sadistic killer before more can fall prey.

No Compromise (DS Peter Gayle crime thrillers, Book 7)

A brutal murder. A man jailed. A new witness who claims he couldn't have been there.

Already in the middle of a violent and complex case, DS Pete Gayle gets entangled in a tangled web of lies and intrigue. With a man in jail for a murder he may not have committed, the reputation of the station and the whole force is on the line. Pete has to face one of the hardest choices of his life. To break ranks and go against another officer risks losing friends, colleagues and career, but if he ignores the case, will he be able to live with himself?

No Compassion (DS Peter Gayle crime thrillers, Book 8)

A vicious rape, a woman left traumatised. A previous victim is quickly identified. Then more come forward.
A serial rapist is attacking the women of Exeter in their beds at night.
There are fingerprints and DNA but no matches, CCTV but no identification.
With the press clamouring for answers DS Pete Gayle and his team must work through a maze of conflicting evidence to identify and arrest the offender before he can commit another brutal attack.

No Stone Unturned (DS Peter Gayle crime thrillers, Book 9)

A murder in mysterious circumstances.

A woman is brutally slaughtered just feet from her sleeping family. But no-one hears a thing and none of them belong in this grand and expensive home. Who are they? Why are they here? And why was this woman killed?

DS Pete Gayle must draw on all his skills as an investigator to figure out what went on here and why.

No Good Deed (DS Peter Gayle crime thrillers, Book 10)

A young woman sits quietly compliant at a sea-front bus-stop as a police officer takes a bloody knife from her hand. 'I'm safe now,' she says.

But safe from whom? Who is she, where has she come from and whose blood is on that blade? These are just a few of the questions

DS Pete Gayle must answer in the latest book in this top-selling series.

No Fair Hearing (DS Peter Gayle crime thrillers, Book 11)

A young man with special needs is beaten to death by a vicious mob on an estate where the residents live in constant fear. When DS Pete Gayle begins to investigate all he finds is a rumour about the victim that is quickly proved false and a wall of silence more solid than the stones around the city's old prison. Was this just pointless spite that went too far or is there more behind the horrific death? Pete must battle a mini-crime wave designed to keep him in the dark as he seeks justice for an innocent victim and his distraught family.

No Fear of Consequences (DS Peter Gayle crime thrillers, Book 12)

A student disappears in broad daylight just yards from the university. With potential witnesses beginning to disperse across the country for the Christmas break, DS Pete Gayle is under extra pressure to figure out what happened as quickly as possible. Did she leave of her own accord, unable to cope with the pressures of university? Was she snatched by an ex-boyfriend, a stalker or a random attacker? Or was she targeted because of the way she'd chosen to supplement her student loan?

One disturbing discovery after another draws Pete and his team through a minefield of sensitive information, much of which he is all too aware, as a father himself, would be horrifying to the victim's parents. But he has to follow the evidence, wherever it may lead.

No More Than Bones (DS Peter Gayle crime thrillers, Book 13)

Exeter-based DS Pete Gayle is already busy with a child-snatching case when pathologist Dr Tony Chambers calls CID to report that a body has been found in Exwick cemetery. And this burial, in a shallow grave among the trees bordering the graveyard, is not an official one. With nothing but the skeletal remains to go on, Pete must find out who the dead man is, how he got there and, most importantly – who put him there?

No Second Chance (DS Peter Gayle crime thrillers, Book 14)

A rumour on the streets. A courier caught in the act. Somewhere in or close to Exeter, someone is making guns and selling them on the black market. Someone secretive enough to cover his tracks by any means necessary and ruthless enough to kill without compunction.

DS Pete Gayle and his team must work with the National Crime Agency to catch him before he can spread any more death and destruction across the streets of the UK's major cities as well as closer to home. But how can they track down a ghost who works in the shadows and leaves no witnesses when all they have to go on is a cryptic nickname?

Nowhere to Run: The Dark Side

The other side of the mirror from DS Pete Gayle's investigation in
Book One of the series, Nowhere to Run – this is The Dark Side.
A young girl is snatched from right outside her school.
While she fights to survive in the clutches of her abductors, her
family is ripped apart by guilt and recriminations. And, with no
demand or even a message to go on, they are forced to rely on the
police to find her. But not even the officer in charge of the case is
aware until it's too late of just how close he is to the kidnappers.

The Venus Flaw

Murder and corruption in the Maltese government combine with the
concealment of a horrific secret in a minefield of intrigue and
violence.
When Dan and Wendy Griffin find a cave full of prehistoric artwork
on the coast of Malta they are plunged into a living nightmare.
Someone is trying to keep something hidden, but who? And what?
Unable to trust the police or the British Embassy and with no clues
other than the cave itself and the fact that one of the men trying to
keep them from it works for the National Security Service, they must
try to figure out what is going on before one or both of them are
killed.

Made in United States
Troutdale, OR
06/14/2025

32126141R00244